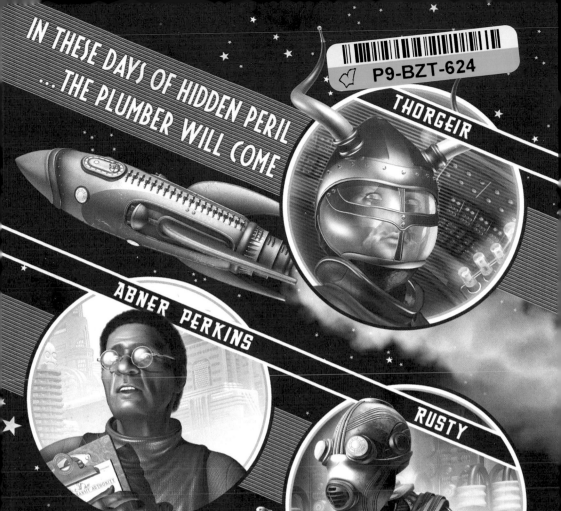

IN THESE DAYS OF HIDDEN PERIL
...THE PLUMBER WILL COME

THORGEIR

ABNER PERKINS

RUSTY

DR. KRAJNIK

21 ILLUSTRATED CHAPTERS OF ADVENTURE
COMPLETE IN THIS ISSUE

SLAVES *of the* SWITCHBOARD *of* DOOM

SLAVES *of the* SWITCHBOARD *of* DOOM

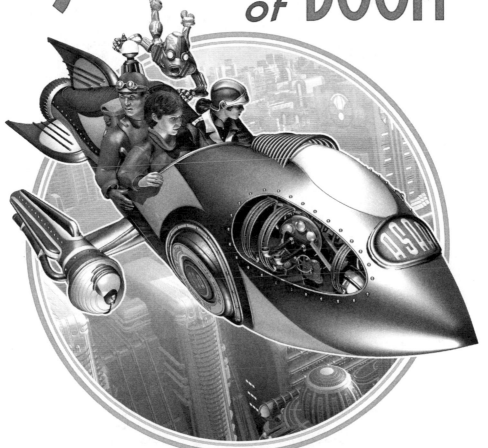

A NOVEL OF RETROPOLIS
WRITTEN AND ILLUSTRATED
BY BRADLEY W. SCHENCK

A TOM DOHERTY ASSOCIATES BOOK
NEW YORK

TOR

SF
Schenck,
B.

SLAVES OF THE SWITCHBOARD OF DOOM

Copyright © 2017 by Bradley W. Schenck

A Tor Book
Published by Tom Doherty Associates
175 Fifth Avenue
New York, NY 10010

www.tor-forge.com

Tor® is a registered trademark of Macmillan Publishing Group, LLC.

The Library of Congress Cataloging-in-Publication Data
is available upon request.

ISBN 978-0-7653-8329-7 (hardcover)
ISBN 978-1-4668-9122-7 (ebook)

Our books may be purchased in bulk for promotional, educational, or business use. Please contact your local bookseller or the Macmillan Corporate and Premium Sales Department at 1-800-221-7945, extension 5442, or by email at MacmillanSpecialMarkets@macmillan.com.

First Edition: June 2017

Printed in the United States of America

0 9 8 7 6 5 4 3 2 1

SLAVES *of the* SWITCHBOARD *of* DOOM

1

The Temple of the Spider God

The Scarlet Robots of Lemuria had begun to climb the walls of the citadel by the time Dash remembered to check the time. He frowned: he really should have picked a shorter story.

He folded the magazine carefully, stowed it in his back pack, and pulled out his ray pistol.

You have to be cautious when you're sneaking around on the Moon. Dash had perfected a kind of belly-hop, all toe tips and stomach muscles, that propelled him up to the edge of the ridge in a series of tiny hops, his chest gliding about an inch above the powdered stone. He kept his helmet low. From the ridge he could see right down into the depression in the crater where two priests stood, guarding the Temple of the Spider God.

From Dash's vantage the entrance was nothing more than a rough square in the gray stone. All the action was inside. Dash stayed low behind the ridge. He'd moored the Actaeon about a quarter mile away, in a new spot—he never used the same one twice—and from here not even the tip of its nose cone could be seen. The priests of the Spider God paced back and forth before the entrance to their Temple with no idea just how much was about to change.

Dash checked the time again.

Right on schedule a powdery plume erupted in the hillside above the Temple. There was no noise, of course, but the two priests felt the rumble underfoot and turned their glassy faceplates toward the explosion. Dash had his ray gun out and was already on the move before they'd finished their turn.

The first priest went down from Dash's ray blast before he even knew that Dash was there, but the second was smarter: with one hand he swept his spear behind him while drawing his own pistol with the other—all while leaping ten feet straight up—and spotted Dash, who was still twenty feet away. The priest came down with the grace of long practice.

The priest fired off a single beam before the spear came out again to slice an arc of vacuum just in front of Dash's feet.

Dash hated those spears. You had to either close in and grapple, or dance back out of range; and once he'd gotten out of range of the spear the pistol would start up again, every time. So as soon as the spear swept past, Dash lunged forward, head first. The dome of his space helmet slammed into the priest's belly and knocked the big man over. Dash landed on top of him, only to find himself staring down the barrel of the priest's ray gun.

The priest made Dash drop his ray gun and motioned him toward the temple door. As they passed the other guard, the priest toed his midsection. The fallen priest stirred a little. They left him out there, and passed through the open doorway into the Temple's airlock. As they entered, a hatch descended silently from the lunar rock, sealing them in.

Dash tensed when he felt his captor's hand heavy on his shoulder, but he waited until the chamber had filled with atmosphere. He didn't flip the switch on his belt until the inner door rolled open.

The electromagnet in Dash's back pack came alive silently and charged the thousands of hidden threads in his clothing: Dash became a magnet that yanked him down onto the airlock's grated floor. He braced his feet and let himself fall backward. The priest, still gripping his shoulder, went down beneath him, exactly as planned.

The priest's spear clattered loose on its lanyard and his ray gun scraped across the floor. From here on out it was purely hand to hand.

Head shots were impossible—neither one of them had removed his helmet. They traded body blows and rolled across the grating, wrestling through the doorway and into the interior of the Temple. Dash got one arm around the priest's throat. But when he tried to roll on top of the other man he found his magnetized legs had stuck to the grating. Well. *That* was unexpected.

The big priest knocked him back, smashing Dash's helmet against the airlock wall. A hairline crack crawled out across the dome right in front of Dash's eyes. The priest pulled Dash's head back and slammed it into the wall again, and this time a couple of glass slivers rang on the helmet's rim.

Dash saw the priest's face crinkle into a grin and he grinned right back as his fingers curled around the man's fallen ray gun, on the floor under Dash's back. His grin stayed where it was: but the priest had a change of heart when Dash brought the gun's barrel around and pointed it at the man's face.

From then on, it was back to the plan.

After binding the priest's wrists and ankles with a couple of ties from his back pack, Dash retrieved his ray gun and tossed the priest's weapons into a little room off the Temple's main hallway. The walls were bare and gray with some kind of coating spread over the ancient lava tube to seal it against the vacuum outside. But as plain as the tunnels were, the rooms were furnished comfortably with wooden furniture, as well as plenty of tapestries and pillows. Dash figured that one of these little rooms ought to be the one where they were holding Princess Fedora.

But he was wrong. When he reached the hallway's end he hadn't seen a trace of her.

A gong sounded from somewhere farther inside the Temple. He

wasn't sure whether that meant their rituals were ending, or if they were rolling right along—he didn't even know what went on in there. But he'd rather not be standing there when the priests filed out. Where was the Princess?

Dash walked back past the last few doorways. Hadn't he seen . . . ?

In the middle of one room's floor was a circular hatch. It stood conveniently open, with the top of a ladder peeking over the edge. It was like a well . . . but a well on the Moon? He stepped into the room and gave the hatch a long look. *You don't really want to be down there with an open door behind you, do you?* But since the room's door was made of steel, with a doorframe to match, it didn't take him long to rig his electromagnet up to the thing. The door snapped shut with a muted ring. He tried it. It didn't budge.

Dash opened his back pack and shuffled through its contents; but after a moment he realized he was only stalling. He steeled himself and went down the ladder.

Dash unfastened his helmet's seal and pulled it off his head. "Princess Fedora?"

The ladder had ended just above the floor of another, smaller hall. He looked left and right. A narrow groove ran down each side of the tunnel. The grooves looked a little like the tracks for the traveling heat ray the priests had surprised him with last month. Not much of a challenge, really; he located the emitters and wedged them in place. Then he found the pressure plates and deactivated them before he started to explore the hall.

He almost missed the lava pit. *Getting careless,* he thought.

At the hall's far end he found a single locked hatch. He rummaged in his back pack for his lockpicks, and after a few minutes' painstaking work, the door swung open to reveal a small but luxurious stone chamber, draped with tapestries and strewn with carpets and cushions. Dash grinned. Princess Fedora lay draped across the pillows and looked up, bored, to see him standing in the doorway. Like this happened every day.

"Princess Fedora!" He reached out toward her. She spat at him, scratched his arms, darted between his boots, and ran out of the room.

"*Mraaow!*" she complained. Dash caught her before she got too far. He put one of the pillows in his helmet and after much effort, and a few more scratches, he got her curled up safely inside.

A few minutes later he'd made his way back to the airlock just in time to catch the first priest, now recovered and untying the second. Dash stunned him with another blast from his pistol and helped himself to the priest's helmet. The second priest glared at him while Dash arranged Princess Fedora in that new, airtight carrier. She seemed sleepy, but he knew better than to think she was finished with him. He pulled the helmet's seal extra tight.

He looked down at the second priest. "It's Thorgeir, isn't it? I'm afraid I'm gonna have to ask you for your helmet, too, seeing as you broke mine."

Dash knelt to unseal the helmet's collar. The bound priest endured the removal of his helmet with a fearsome scowl. "We'll meet again, Dash Kent."

Dash nodded toward Princess Fedora. "You could always just stop taking them, you know."

But Thorgeir seemed to be out of conversation, so after donning the priest's helmet Dash took his leave. For now he was happy to get the Princess back to his rocket, and the two of them back to Earth. He had some chores to take care of.

TUESDAY, 9:46 PM

Except for the constant, hushed rhythm of cables unplugged and replugged, the switchboard was always as quiet as a library, especially during the night shift. That persistent sound was one that Nola heard even in her dreams. She was operating for seven Info-Slate owners this evening and that took a great deal of skill, as she hoped the others had noticed.

Three of her clients were Air Safety and Astronautics officers. Nola unplugged the cable for one client's main pane and switched it, in one swift, fluid motion, to the feed for pilot registrations. Her hand hovered over the connection. She was sure she'd missed something.

Her eyes stayed on that plug even as she swapped the connections for two of her other clients. The ASAA officer had requested a registration search for a vehicle. The type of vehicle in the search was a commercial transport, yet she'd asked for the Private Registry. Nola completed another switch and with deft practice linked the first officer's sidebar connection to the Commercial Registry. Somewhere over the streets of Retropolis she knew that the officer's Info-Slate had rung a soft chime.

That should take care of that, Nola thought. Then she forgot all about it while she kept up with the new requests from all seven of the distant Info-Slates.

Between their main panes, sidebars, and message lists Nola's hands were doing a constant dance when—and this was practically unheard of—her *headset buzzed.* One of her clients was requesting a voice connection!

Nola slammed the button immediately. Maybe none of the other operators had heard. What had she done wrong?

"Officer da Cunha?" she whispered. "How can I help you?"

A finger tapped her shoulder. Nola blushed. It was Mrs. Broadvine, her supervisor, and she wasn't alone. Nola breathed into her microphone, "Excuse me, Officer. I'll be right with you."

Mrs. Broadvine took the headset and microphone and looked at them with the pinched expression she reserved for things that were not up to her standards. She turned to her companion. "The voice system," she explained, "is intended for emergency use in cases where the Info-Slate operator has confused a request." She looked down at Nola. "It is seldom used."

"May I?" asked the bald man in the hat. Mrs. Broadvine handed him the headset and microphone. He spoke softly for a moment, and then he listened. The constant clicks and pops that rustled up and down the bank of operators seemed full of meaning: dire, hidden meaning. Nola felt sure that every operator on the line was straining to hear the conversation. She could have just *died*.

The bald man in the hat handed the gear back to Nola. "Quite the opposite, this time," he informed Mrs. Broadvine. "An officer has just called to thank your operator for correcting *her own* mistake by providing the correct information, in addition to the information that was requested."

Mrs. Broadvine, wincing, was wrestling with Nola's cables; her eyes kept darting to each of the seven clients' panels. It must have been years since she'd worked as an operator herself. The operators on either side sat impeccably straight, eyes fixed on the switchboard, and yet somehow gave all of their attention to the drama that was playing out at Nola's station.

The man in the hat looked down at Nola from what seemed to be a very great height. "Do you make that kind of correction often?" he asked.

Nola turned away from Mrs. Broadvine's ordeal to offer the bald man a slight smile. "Oh, sometimes I do," she said. "It all depends on how familiar I am with that kind of request. I mean, I know the registration indices pretty well; if it was a zoning inquiry, though, one of the other girls would probably know better than me."

He was writing in a little notebook. "So . . . it comes down to your individual experience, then." He frowned. "I don't suppose there's a . . . a clearing house, a repository, of all that information?"

Nola shook her head. "There are just so many possible inquiries. . . ."

The bald man snapped his notebook shut. "I see. No one operator is like another, and each one has her own strengths and weaknesses. So for every advantage it's likely that there's an equal disadvantage."

Nola wasn't quite sure what answer she could make to that, but it seemed like none was needed: the bald man's attention had already gone elsewhere. Nola rescued her clients and Mrs. Broadvine from one another, and by the time she'd gotten caught up she was alone again. She had completely forgotten the officer on the line.

"Miss Gardner?" came the voice over the headset. "I didn't mean to get you in trouble. I just wanted to say thanks."

Nola checked Officer da Cunha's panel and read the Registry connections she'd made. "I don't think that *was* trouble, really, but I'm not quite sure what it was. Or even who."

"He said he was Howard Pitt, that engineer from the Transit Authority. You know, the Tube Man."

The name sounded familiar. "Are you all set with your inquiry? I couldn't help but notice it was one of those old Actaeon rockets—the interplanetary ones. So of course it wouldn't be a private citizen."

"That's the odd thing," said Officer da Cunha. "It *is* a commercial registration, but the owner seems to be an individual named Kent. Kelvin Kent. He describes his business as 'Freelance Adventurer.' But his registration's current, anyway. I was sure surprised to see that big old rocket touching down in the city."

Nola glanced at the panel while her fingers swapped cables and flipped switches for her other clients. "Oh, yes, I see. That's unusual."

Officer da Cunha thanked her again and hung up. Nola's hands had never slowed in their dance over the switchboard. *Freelance Adventurer,* she thought. *That sounds like an interesting line of work.*

TUESDAY, 10:09 PM

The work wasn't without its challenges, Pitt was the first to admit; but it was still just a sideshow. The main event, now, that was what really required his attention. He strode down the steps of the Info-Slate Switching Station with the kind of concentrated purpose that came to him by nature. A tall man made even taller by his signature hat, Howard Pitt somehow projected the idea that he'd just returned from, say, the Grand Canyon, after having bridged it, or from the Serengeti after installing an aqueduct that would change its history forever. Howard Pitt radiated purpose and accomplishment.

It was a quality that wasn't shared by many of his colleagues. Although the engineers of Retropolis were undoubtedly accomplished and didn't lack for purpose, they were typically a bit myopic, and either rather thin or prodigiously stout, and they usually began their conversations with an "Ermm . . . ," a "Hmmm . . . ," or sometimes, an—

"Ahh, excuse me, sir."

Pitt paused and, by habit, looked down at the spectacled, rather thin person who'd spoken. Pitt shifted to rest his hand on the holstered slide rule at his hip. "It's Perkins, isn't it."

It wasn't a question; more like an assertion that happily for Perkins was true, since otherwise he might have had to offer a correction.

The contrast between the two men was remarkable. Abner Perkins was an experienced engineer with the Retropolis Transit Authority, typical of the breed described above and, in fact, although he did not know it, practically its archetype: from the ink stains on his breast pocket to the socks that he would discover, later that evening, *didn't* match after all. A world that could create two such different engineers might be capable of anything.

"Yes, sir. It's Perkins. I had some questions about the specifications for the Tube system."

"You will understand," said Pitt, "that I've resigned from the Transit Authority as of yesterday. From now on I have to be considered a consultant." His hand idly stroked his holstered slide rule. "You can request a meeting with me during business hours, under the terms of my contract."

"Well, yes, sir, of course I can. But I knew you'd be making another visit to the Slate Switchboard, and, erm, I happened to be near here, and . . . well, I . . . didn't think there'd be any difficulty."

Pitt stared down at Perkins impassively while the smaller man stared in a completely different way at the pavement. "No harm done," Pitt said at last.

"Oh, good." Perkins pulled out a sheaf of papers and held them in front of him. "I've been trying to understand the overage in the air pressures you've required in the Transport Tubes. They, ah, they seem to be roughly five hundred percent of the air pressure that the system, well, that it actually needs. It's such a significant difference that, well, I just . . ."

"Safety precaution," said Pitt. "If there should be any failure of the system there must be sufficient air pressure remaining to deliver those passengers still in the system to its nearest exit. If you calculate the greatest distance between exits and the air pressure that's necessary, I think you'll find that everything is in order."

"Yes!" Perkins seemed to be on familiar ground. "I did that, of course, but I noticed that far less pressure would be required if we, ah, if we were to add two more exits on that route. It's, uhm, it's just so much *longer* than any of the others. . . ."

Pitt began to take long, emphatic steps down the street. "Naturally," he called back, "you could add those additional stations later on, and then reduce the required air pressure. At your *convenience*."

Perkins pulled another sheet from his stack and waved it. "Sir? Mister Pitt, sir? There's also the question of the inertrium overage. . . ."

It was too late, though. Abner Perkins stood alone, waving his sheets of specifications, and felt somehow . . . insignificant.

Perkins scanned the manifests again. The Tube system had just required so *very much* inertrium, and he couldn't imagine where it had all gone. Maybe if he understood the design better. . . .

A robot, laden with packages, bumped into Perkins and apologized. Abner turned to see the entire city that he had (not unusually, for Abner) been ignoring while he considered his own thoughts.

The city of Retropolis extended for many miles in every direction, including the vertical one. For that reason no one could really take it *all* in. But Abner knew it all so well that his mind filled in the gaps behind the many-storied towers, the lit glass domes, the lively monorail terminals, and the canopies of the trees that, huddling in the streets, cast their cool shadows along pedestrian walkways.

Buildings like machines and machines like buildings crowded the bases of the towers. The great skyscrapers themselves receded, level by level, so that sunlight could reach the parkways between them, and they always made Abner think of elongated ziggurats with glass-paneled sides. Pedestrian skyways bristled from the sides of the towers to bridge the streets.

Utility robots moved smoothly along the walkways, cleaning litter and sweeping leaves out of the way of the people—both human and mechanical—who were rushing about their errands. There was the occasional collision, like the one Abner had just suffered, but overall there was more than enough room for everybody. And in the higher reaches—where the skyscrapers did indeed scrape the sky or, anyway, its clouds—personal rockets with open cockpits swept along in their own unimpeded arcs under the watchful supervision of Air Safety and Astronautics officers. The ASAA rockets passed overhead in a regular grid that gave them a good view of all those pedestrians and rocket pilots below; and, above even the ASAA rockets, buoyant inertrium airships floated along their stately routes, giving tourists and the more unhurried citizens of Retropolis the best possible view of the city.

Abner took a deep, contented breath. He loved the city, every time he remembered that it was there.

But just now his own business worried him. He squinted at the papers in his hands. He was sure these things would all make perfect sense once he'd had the chance to think about them properly.

TUESDAY, 10:51 PM

Rusty exited the Tube Pod with more equilibrium than most people; but then most people were not mechanical, and so they had a tendency to be unsteady. The new system was seeing a lot of use despite the fact that people on the way out of a Transport Pod would often need a moment or two to wait for the world to stop spinning.

Rusty felt this might explain why some human people *enjoyed* the Tube Pods. He hadn't made up his mind just yet.

One advantage to the Tubes, in Rusty's opinion, was that only a single Pod could arrive at any one station at a time. A minute or two would always separate them; this was convenient if you knew you were being followed. Rusty set a brisk pace down the street in order to get as far as possible from the Pod Station in the next one to two minutes.

His pursuers didn't worry Rusty. He knew who they were; he knew what they wanted; he knew they weren't going to learn what they wanted to know; and, when it came right down to it, he was used to them. But if he was going to be followed then he knew that he was expected to be evasive and in this, as in most things, Rusty did his best to oblige.

He turned into an alley.

Not a dark, dirty, and uncomfortable alley, full of garbage and persons of questionable intent: this was Retropolis, after all. This alley was more or less what an alley *ought* to be: broad and clean, leading decisively between the buildings on either side with plenty of room for two vehicles to pass each other, even though ground vehicles were practically extinct. It was, normally, well lit.

Tonight it was surprisingly dark.

Several lights that should have illuminated the alley had been broken. Right around the middle of its length the alley actually looked a bit threatening, which is to say that you couldn't tell *what* it looked like.

Rusty paused.

Most people, whether they were human or mechanical, would have known this was unusual. But one of the many jobs Rusty had tried through the years was in the Light Maintenance Division of the Public Works Department. So *unlike* most people Rusty knew that these lights had been checked, cleaned, and polished earlier that day, just as they were on every day; Rusty knew that this damage was very recent. He also knew that actual damage to the lights was so rare that a single broken street light could become a kind of legend, a story that Light Maintenance workers would gather to tell on dark, stormy nights when all the lamps had been polished, but they still weren't ready to go home; a story that would begin: "It was on a night much like this one, a night when the golden streetlights pulsed bravely against the eternal darkness that brooded around them, their polished caps and bezels glinting brightly in the gloom; a night when no one who could help it was to be seen abroad, and strange things roamed in the empty streets. . . ."

Rusty had always enjoyed those stories.

As he stood quietly at the edge of the lighted end of the alley, Rusty felt—just a little bit—that he had become a part of that ancient legend of The Night The Lamp Went Out. He looked behind him at the well-lit, empty end of the alley, and then he turned with precision to walk right into the darkness, where a moment later he stumbled over something on the ground.

He bent over it, the lamps of his eyes glowing, and he saw something horrible.

Two minutes later, several men came along the street and looked down the darkened alley. No one was there.

2

The Secret of the Robot in the Attic

The switchboard operators' lunch room was a wide, pleasant space with its own Auto-Mat and twelve tables. It offered just a little more seating than a single shift of operators needed. This was sensible: the designers knew that the operators would form cliques and countercliques whose defections, reversals, and sudden changes of loyalty would make the lunchroom a lively and ever-changing environment.

It was well lit and cheerful, as though the room was in happy denial of all these baroque interpersonal relationships, their secret alliances, and their bitter feuds. It was, in spite of office politics, a place that a single shift of operators could think of as their own comfortable kitchen.

It was not a place that could host *all three* shifts of operators without dispelling that illusion completely.

Nola and her fellow operators found themselves crowded into a confining, gleaming space whose pristine surfaces and too few chairs now looked strange and unsettling. In the middle of all that hygienic brightness all three shifts of switchboard operators crowded close together like a herd of wild operators out on the primeval prairie.

The only predator in sight—if she was one—was Mrs. Broadvine. Their supervisor stood primly at the end of the room while the herd of operators settled down into what chairs there were. Nola saw Freda Detwiler offer her own seat to Rhonda Bancroft, who was feeling poorly, and this was remarkable given their long-standing disagreement about Rhonda's shoes. Countless other little kindnesses between the traditional rivals in the herd seemed to promise a new era of understanding all up and down the switchboard. But this was not to be.

Mrs. Broadvine was holding a large stack of slips of paper. Every one of the slips was pink.

When she finally spoke, her voice was weighted with so much tenderness that few among the herd would have recognized it if she hadn't been standing right there in front of them.

"Ladies," she began, "no matter what inherent talent you each have, and no matter what little problems we may have overcome together, you all have developed into operators who perform their duties in the proper . . . no, I mean to say in the *highest* tradition of switchboard artistry. I want you to know that I am proud of every one of you."

Each pair of eyes dropped to the pink slips in her hands.

Mrs. Broadvine swallowed. "So it is with great sadness that I have to tell you that our entire department has been judged unnecessary."

She took a pink slip off the top of the pile; she looked at it; she nodded. Then she put it in her pocket. The entire herd of operators gasped.

"You may have noticed Mr. Howard Pitt's observation of the switchboard department over the past weeks. Mr. Pitt is a well-respected civil engineer who formerly served the Retropolis Transit Authority, but who now acts as a roaming consultant for any agency who, who, who . . ."

Mrs. Broadvine collected herself. "For any agency that needs to be made *more efficient*. Mr. Pitt has re-engineered our own operation. We are hereby notified that our services are no longer required."

The operators exploded into protest and denial. "Who's going to mind the switchboard, then?" called one. "Who's minding the switchboard *now*?" demanded another. "What are we all supposed to *do*?"

Mrs. Broadvine called for order, which she got, and asked the three shifts to gather together into columns. She passed out their pink slips row by row. Each switchboard operator stared at her own slip, and then at her neighbors'. It was so complete a calamity that they felt more united at that moment than they'd ever felt before, cliques and countercliques notwithstanding. Mrs. Broadvine herself looked like she was about ready to break down, and—incredibly—the operators each tried to comfort her as they walked past.

Nola looked at her own slip. It was neat, short, and to the point.

> *The Info-Slate Company (a division of Volto-Vac Industries) thanks you for your excellent service, which is no longer required.*
>
> *A final paycheck and a generous parting bonus is available at the Business Office.*

She turned the slip over. The back side was completely blank.

She had a thought. She dug her own operator's Info-Slate from its bag and offered it to Mrs. Broadvine, who shook her head just once. "I haven't been given any instructions for collecting your Info-Slates," she told them, "and so as far as I'm concerned, ladies, they are yours to keep."

The operators looked thoughtfully at their Slates. The Slates were expensive; in addition, there was a sizable market for them.

"Though of course this might be an oversight on the part of the company."

The operators frowned.

"So I suggest you hold on to them until the books are closed for the quarter. After that their existence won't be very obvious to anybody, and I expect you can do as you like with them."

The operators smiled. Mrs. Broadvine was showing a side of herself that they hadn't noticed before and—in spite of the traditions of their herd—they were beginning to like her.

Nola wasn't sure she wanted to sell her Slate. The Slates had been such a large part of her working life that she thought it would be a little bit like selling her left leg; although on reflection she realized that she didn't know her left leg anywhere near as well as she knew the Info-Slate system. She thumbed the sleek tablet on and looked over an array of information. The shift schedules were now blank. Her message pane had a new, pink-highlighted entry that she suspected had something to do with the slip in her hand. She looked intently at the screen and then, deliberately, she tapped the button for a voice connection to her operator. The Slate chimed; nothing else happened.

Freda Detwiler had been watching her. "It's like there's *nobody there*," Freda said.

A knot of operators formed around Nola. They each pressed the same button on their Slates, and each of them got the same result.

Nola selected the Commercial Vehicle Registry and scrolled over its contents. The Info-Slate had put her at her last location in that list, on *Kelvin "Dash" Kent, Freelance Adventurer: Investigations, Retrievals, Lost Entities; No Job Too Small or Large.*

"Who's that?" asked Freda.

"Somebody who solves problems. I think."

Nola selected the Zoning Ordinances Registry. It popped up in her main pane so quickly that she knew her operator—whoever that was—really knew her business. She'd rather hoped there'd be a delay.

There at the top was the customary flashing notice about the Experimental Research District, that zone of the city where all scientific research was supposed to be located. Nola scrolled past it. She knew about a violation of that one, all right, but it would *stay* unreported if *she* had anything to say about it.

Nola switched (again, quite rapidly) to a news feed that was full of praise for the new Tube Transport System. Hmmm. She paused.

Once again, she pressed the button that should have given her voice access to her operator. There was still no answer.

"They're doing a good job," she admitted to the crowd. "I sure wonder who they are. I wonder *where* they are."

"No one at the televideo phone switchboard knows anything about this," Mrs. Broadvine told her former staff. "Whoever Pitt's operators are, they're brand new. It *is* surprising how well they're doing."

Nola nodded unhappily. "Is that what you're going to do, Mrs. Broadvine?" she asked. Yesterday, such a question would have been unthinkable. ". . . go back to the televideo switchboard?"

As soon as she'd asked Nola remembered that there were already plenty of shift supervisors over there. Mrs. Broadvine shook her head.

"No, Miss Gardner. There's no place there for me. But you ladies," she added in a louder voice, "you ought all of you to go to the televideo switchboard in the morning. They may have some places available."

She turned back to Nola and, in a much lower voice, she said, "Though those of you who get there *this afternoon* may have the best chance at a position."

Nola liked this new Mrs. Broadvine. It seemed like a terrible waste that she hadn't met this version of her before.

The new and improved Mrs. Broadvine moved off to comfort the rest of the herd. Nola thumbed across her controls, feeling strange to be on *this* end of the Slate system, and found herself back where she'd started.

Investigations, Retrievals, Lost Entities; No Job Too Small or Large.

"Girls," she said. "You know those parting bonuses? I've got an idea, if you're all willing to pool your resources."

In the end even Mrs. Broadvine made a contribution.

It had taken Rusty most of the morning to reassemble the other robot's left arm; now both were working normally. But he had no idea what to do about her legs because the problem with her legs was that they weren't there.

At first Rusty assumed her legs had been discarded (and that was horrible enough) but once he'd carried her up to his attic apartment and given her a thorough examination he'd found that there weren't even hip joints of any kind. The strange robot had been built *without any legs at all.*

Below her waist she had a simple flange, somewhat scarred from the bolts that used to be there. This robot had been fastened in place and *forced* to work.

Rusty wasn't accustomed to anger: it was completely at odds with his nature. That somehow made his anger more intense because in

25

addition to his outrage Rusty felt a sharp and very personal anger at the thing that had *made him* feel angry.

He reserved that anger for later use.

The legless robot was sitting on a stool in the sunlight next to Rusty's big window. That was the best place for his houseplants, too, and from there the light diffused across the attic, picking out highlights on the aquarium and the terrarium, illuminating his collection of interesting mosses, and casting a homely light across his bookshelves.

Rusty was usually very happy in his attic.

The transom over the window was open. A couple of ornithopters fluttered in and settled on the strange robot's shoulders. She took no more notice of them than she had of Rusty or, in fact, of anything else.

That she couldn't speak was perfectly all right, in Rusty's view. But neither could she read or write—as far as he could tell—and that made communicating with her a challenge.

Now that she was put back together he'd concentrate on finding a way to talk to her.

Down in the street below, the men who were watching only knew that Rusty had been at home for a long time now. That was a break in his routine, and so it would be reported.

THURSDAY, 12:11 PM

Dash Kent, also known as Kelvin, was on hold again. The televideo screen was blank but he could hear its tinny performance of "Gotta Get Up and Go To Work" from across the room. He was keeping one ear on that, but his eyes were on the shattered globe of his space helmet. The helmet was the whole reason he'd spent most of the morning on hold, first with O'Malley's Adventure Outfitters and then with

Aero-Vac Accessories Ltd. (the manufacturer); now he was back on hold with O'Malley's again.

"Gotta Get Up and Go To Work" concluded, to be replaced by "If I Ever Get a Job Again." Dash felt an urge to get off the phone and go . . . do something. Something else. He started to wonder how they picked those songs.

His copy of the catalog was on the table next to the two much more sinister helmets he'd taken from the priests of the Spider God. He knew those helmets were perfectly usable, but he didn't want to be seen in public wearing one: there could be misunderstandings on a grand scale. He could probably cut off the horns, and that would help; but he frowned at his own helmet with its shattered dome.

It was right there on the catalog page:

Aero-Vac Certified Space Helmet, With Self-Cleaning Airways and Indestructible* Dome

The asterisk bothered him. He'd looked for that footnote for the longest time, but it just wasn't there.

The hold music sputtered out and Dash dove across the room at the televideo before they could hang up on him again.

"O'Malley's Adventure Outfitters, where we make your dreams of adventure a reality! This is Margaret. How can I help you?"

Dash made it just in time. "This is Dash Kent, that is, this is Kelvin Kent even though everybody calls me Dash, and I'm calling back about order number A06-LLJK89-04/A, which was for an Aero-Vac helmet that's supposed to be indestructible, and which isn't. This one, anyway."

He was holding the helmet out for inspection. Margaret of O'Malley's smiled at him.

"I'm so sorry that you experienced a problem with your order, Mr. Dashkent. Unfortunately these helmets are certified by their manufacturer, which is . . ." She looked down at the same catalog Dash had been reading, "Yes! That would be Aero-Vac Accessories, Ltd. I'll just transfer you."

"NO!" Dash yelled. "That is, no, please, no, thank you, I've already talked to them and they transferred me back to you, on account that I made the purchase from you and you have to handle any returns or exchanges."

He breathed, finally.

"I see!" said Margaret of O'Malley's, slightly less brightly than before. "May I have your order number?"

Dash was working his way through the order number again when his doorbell rang. "That's . . . *L* like in lion, followed by another *L* like in lion, and excuse me for just a moment, please."

He leaped for the door. Margaret of O'Malley's said, "What was that after *L* like in lion, Mr. Dashkent?"

She looked up to see a complete absence of Mr. Dashkent, and said, "Well then, we're happy to have been of service, and we look forward to your continuing business."

Behind him Dash heard the *snap* as she disconnected, and it was for this reason that he was making an unusual face when he opened the door to meet Nola Gardner.

He saw immediately that she may have been expecting something quite different and—a little too late—he rearranged his face. She looked down. "My name is Nola Gardner," she said. "I think your helmet is broken." She looked back up. "Are you Dash Kent?"

Dash could tell she was hoping he'd answer, "No, he's my uncle, let me introduce you."

He nodded. "That's me." It was about then that Dash understood this might be a client, so he swung open the door and gestured inside. "Please, come in!"

"I was sort of wondering about your advertisement," she told him once they were seated at the table. "The part that says *Lost Entities*. What kind of *entities* do you bring back . . . ?"

Dash nodded. "That's the standard language, it's kind of traditional, for finding and recovering just about anybody who's lost, you know, like a missing person, say, or a . . ." He coughed into his hand. ". . . cat."

"A . . . ?" Miss Gardner repeated. "I didn't quite . . ."

Dash faced her squarely. "Or, say, a cat."

"A cat."

"Yep, especially in this neighborhood, especially lately, because they seem to come here pretty often to take 'em."

"They . . ."

"The priests of the Spider God."

"The priests of the . . ."

"Spider God."

"Oh." She seemed to be thinking about this pretty hard.

"So, you know, since they seem to be coming here so often, to take the . . ."

". . . the cats . . ."

"Yep, the cats; I go up there pretty frequently. . . ."

"Up there?"

"To the Moon, you know, where they take the cats, and then I bring 'em back."

"The . . ."

"The cats. I bring back the cats."

"From the Moon. From the Spider priests of the Moon God, on the Moon."

"No, Miss, sorry, but it's the priests of the Spider God. Which are on the Moon. At the, or should I say under, the Marius Crater."

Miss Gardner pulled something out of her purse. Dash saw that it was a tablet, about the size of a magazine, with a glowing screen just like a televideo's and a couple of rows of buttons and dials. "Excuse me for a moment," she said.

Dash watched her turn the dials and push the buttons while she brought up one screen of information after another. She looked surprised, at first, and then she seemed upset by something she saw, and then she raced through several items very quickly, and then she set the tablet down.

Dash waited.

"They really do, don't they?"

"Miss?"

"The priests of the Spider God. The cats. Whatever do they do with them?"

Dash shook his head. "I don't know, and I'm pretty sure I don't want to know. I just bring 'em back."

Miss Gardner looked at him in an entirely new way; a way, in fact, that Dash had always hoped someone would use to look at him.

"Well, that's a very good thing for you to do."

Dash thanked her. "But I can't say I get them all, you know. I certainly do go after all the cats I hear about, and at very reasonable rates, which are negotiable, with the possibility of a payment plan. Do you know where *your* cat is, Miss Gardner?"

"Do you . . . your advertisement, though, it wasn't *all* about cats, was it? I mean, I don't have a cat."

Dash regrouped. "No, Miss, I am not restricted to cat-related ventures. Was it a person, maybe a . . ." Dash was distracted, apparently, by something under the table. ". . . a boyfriend, say? Or a girlfriend?"

Miss Gardner shook her head and told him about the Info-Slate switchboard, the way it had closed, and how no one seemed to know who was operating it anymore.

Dash indicated the Info-Slate. "That's one of them there, is it?"

Miss Gardner showed him how the Slate worked. She explained about the bank of operators behind the scenes who pulled, re-routed, and connected all the cables that switched the various windows on the Slate from one display to another.

"So it's just like a televideo," she explained, "or a whole *set* of videophones, except that mostly what you're looking at is *information*. About just about anything. That's why the ASAA officers and other civic departments use them so much. They're a little expensive for people like you or me."

Dash nodded. "That's really something. Thanks for showing me."
He settled back in his chair. "But nobody's operating it anymore."

Miss Gardner disagreed. "Somebody *must* be operating it. But it's no one who's ever done the job before. It's nobody from the televideo switchboard, either. And whoever it is, they won't talk to you when you press the button for a voice connection.

"And all our jobs, well, they're just *gone*," she finished.

Dash took all of this in.

"Well, that's sure an interesting puzzle," he agreed.

Miss Gardner dug deeper into her purse. "So I remembered about you from a Slate inquiry a couple of nights ago and I looked you up, and we—that is, the switchboard operators, and Mrs. Broadvine, she's my supervisor, we'd all like you to find out what's going on. We took up a collection . . ."

She showed Dash a slip of paper. ". . . and if you're willing we'd like to hire you to find out why we were all fired, and who's operating the switchboard now."

Things had been a little lean of late and so Dash was very interested in the number she had shown him. More than that, though, he had been looking for a way to expand out of the cat business. It was all well and good for a beginning, and he was glad to help out the cats, but he'd always hoped to work his way up to, say, space pirates, or thwarting interplanetary tyrants, or . . . Dash looked at a stack of magazines on the sideboard. Something more in line with the old family business. With maybe not so many claws.

He turned back to Miss Gardner. "I would be very happy to look into this for you," he said. "I have just a little thing or two to take care of upstairs, first."

THURSDAY, 12:43 PM

He's sure not what I expected, Nola thought. Truth to tell, when he'd opened the door with that peculiar expression, holding a broken space helmet like it was some kind of sacred artifact, she'd really hoped that this was Dash Kent's *nephew*. And then there was all that confusion about the cats and the Moon, though that had turned out to be . . . well, surprising.

He couldn't be much more than twenty; he might be a year or two younger than she was herself. But he did seem awfully *sincere*.

And retrieving those cats had to be pretty dangerous work. She had read the Info-Slate's entries about the priests of the Spider God with genuine dismay. Those poor cats!

She trailed after Dash on the stairs of his apartment building. It was far from being a *new* building, but what she could see was very clean and well maintained. Some kids on the third floor landing looked knowingly at Nola for reasons that were not obvious. One called out "Hello, Kelvin," but was shushed by the other. "He's being *Dash* now," the girl said, with an impressive amount of disdain.

That would go far on the switchboard, Nola knew. Disdain was a useful quality.

Dash, or Kelvin, nodded to the children but moved on quickly.

On the fourth floor he paused. "I'll just be a minute," he told her.

He knocked on number 4C and greeted its occupant. "It's just me, Mrs. Nakamura."

Once he went inside Nola found that the walls, clean as they were, were rather thin. "Let's just see that old sink, then," he was saying. She moved away from the door and looked down the stairs. The two children were grinning up at her.

One boy, one girl, and so alike that Nola was sure they were related.

"Get him to show you his *rocket,*" the boy advised her. "It's on the *roof.*"

Nola considered that. "Oh, I don't know," she said. "Lots of men keep their rockets on the roof. Nothing special about that."

The boy looked disappointed. The girl, on the other hand, approved.

"Now," Nola went on, "say it was something like, oh, I don't know, maybe an Actaeon Model Fourteen? The one with the extra cabin and the optional viewports? That would be *amazing* to see on a rooftop. I'd *love* to see that."

"Oh! Oh! Oh!" the little boy cried, his hand shooting up like he was in class where, come to think of it, he probably should be. "You've *got* to go up there! That's *exactly* what he's got!"

The little girl's brows drew down into a bar of disapproval. She glared at Nola. Nola smiled.

"He's not coming back," the little girl said. "That sink's a goner. Believe me. He's gonna have to go get a whole *new* one at the *store.*"

Nola tried to imagine a half-size switchboard staffed by evil-minded, half-size switchboard operators, each one too filled with disdain to answer a voice call from an Info-Slate. Who knew? It could be as simple as that.

Dash-or-Kelvin came back out of Apartment 4C. He was not carrying an old sink. "So just go a little easy on it, please, till Saturday," he said through the door. "It oughtta hold up just fine if you don't put any more popcorn down there."

He saw Nola and stopped. "I," he said.

She waited, but there didn't seem to be anything more.

"Can we go up to the roof?" she asked. "It's just, I understand you keep an Actaeon Model Fourteen up there and I'd just *love* to see it."

She didn't look back. But she knew she'd made an enemy for life.

"Nice kids," she said, and Dash nodded carefully.

"The Campbells," he told her. "Evan and Evvie."

"Shouldn't they be in school, though?"

He nodded again but he left it there, so Nola did, too.

They stopped on the sixth floor, where Dash investigated a suspicious stain on the ceiling; and then on the seventh, where he discovered its source and made a note in a little notebook; and then on the ninth, where they had tea with Miss Roth and where Nola met Princess Fedora, who was now, for the time being, an *indoor* cat.

"Until Kelvin does something about those terrible Spider God people," Miss Roth whispered.

"They do sound just awful," Nola whispered back. "What do they do with . . ."

Miss Roth stopped her. "Don't even ask," she said. Nola understood from this that she didn't know, either.

After Miss Roth, it was a clear run straight up to the roof, where Nola saw the Actaeon Model Fourteen. It was just as huge and interplanetary as it was supposed to be, and it truly was unusual to see it on the roof of an apartment building. She marveled.

Besides the rocket, there was a sort of a shooting range up on the roof, along with an area ringed by sand bags and scorched with the memories of old explosions, and a shack with one large door and dozens of small, open windows.

"That'll be the ornithopter cote," Dash explained. "Mind your head."

The view up here was just wonderful. Nola looked along the monorail tracks high overhead, where they hung between their massive pylons; she could just make out the much smaller Transport Tubes that piggybacked along the line. The monorail's Red Line rumbled. The train swept up into view, thundering mightily, and then was gone at once as it flew along its single rail toward destinations unknown, at least to anyone without a train schedule.

Nola could have looked it up on her Info-Slate if it really mattered. She preferred not to know.

Several airships floated, here or there, across the skyline. Nola watched a gridlike pattern of ASAA rockets make their patrols above the city. She wondered how many of them had been clients on her own panel, back at the switchboard, and it wasn't until that moment that she felt the full, painful loss that she'd suffered that morning. *Never again.*

But all she said was, "It's beautiful up here."

She got no argument from Dash. "Here's the shooting range, of course; there's where I test explosives. I've got a laboratory down in the basement"—Nola looked alarmed—"no, no, nothing like what they do in the Experimental Research District. It's just for, you know, analyzing chemicals and all. It's safe."

Nola hoped so. A lot of people lived in this building, and the zoning laws were there for a reason. *Well, for most people, anyway.* She felt a certain familiar guilt.

"So I guess this must be your building, then, Mr. Kent?"

"Ha! No, not mine, not exactly. It all belongs to the Trust. Fact is, I just work for them."

His smile evaporated.

"I mean, I pitch in here, as a kind of a temporary sideline while the adventuring business takes off. It was all my father's, you see, until he . . ."

Nola nodded. "I guess he was in the adventuring business, too?"

Dash laughed again. "No, not him," he said. "Dad was a *magazine publisher.*"

SATURDAY, 5:04 PM

Doctor Lillian Krajnik stepped up to the Constellation Boulevard office of the Retropolis Travel Bureau, opened the door, and after a swift examination of the outer rooms she plunged past the agents and into the inner offices. One by one, she opened the doors off the hallway and poked her head inside. She didn't seem pleased with anything she saw.

In each office she held out the picture and she asked the question.

Her bearing was so determined that no one, in any one of those offices, had even thought to protest before she'd shut the door and moved on. At the end of the hall she shook her head at the potted plant she found there and whipped around.

The agents at the front desks watched her return with anxious faces. Lillian sniffed. They were no help, either.

She shoved the doors open and stepped outside again, turned left, and approached the office next door. *Maybe in here,* she thought. It would all work, provided she was thorough.

35

3

EYRIE OF THE HAIRLESS ENGINEER

Well, Abner," Herbert said, "you know I'd be glad to help if it was possible. Or even probable. But the way things are, I couldn't even fill an order for a couple of cubic feet of inertrium. You can see how bad it is."

Abner could see: the evidence was all around him, though mainly it was above him.

An inertrium warehouse, like an inertrium foundry, is exactly like any other kind of warehouse or foundry provided that you look at one of them upside down. Inertrium warehouses have all of the same bins, pallets, and cranes as a warehouse that stores steel, for example, except that the inventory in an inertrium warehouse is bumping up against the ceiling. The cranes are also arranged very differently since they're positioned to pick up a gravity-resistant block of inertrium and drag it down to the floor. Otherwise, though, the whole business was just like any other, just inverted.

You do find some pretty well-engineered ceilings in the inertrium trade. The risk of a whole warehouse tearing loose from its foundations and floating away into space is something the insurance companies take pretty seriously.

36

Abner could see that this warehouse—the largest of its kind in the city—was almost completely empty. A few small inertrium blocks of the kind that are sold to hobbyists were available in little numbered bins overhead. There were some bags of powdered inertrium hanging upward like balloons next to Herbert's desk. But the great cranes, winches, and gantries were still. The warehouse was as quiet as a museum.

Herbert and Abner were old friends. Usually their business could be transacted by televideo, but since this was an unofficial inquiry Abner had come down in person.

"I've sent most of my workers home on leave until we can get more stock in," Herbert told him. "I've never seen anything like it."

"So," Abner said, "if I were to place an order for about fifty cubic feet of processed inertrium, how long would I have to wait?"

"Fifty cubic feet! Fifty? What are you building, an airship?" Herbert didn't even need to look at his ledger. "I couldn't fill an order like that for *at least* three weeks. We've had such a spike in demand this month that the foundries have depleted their stocks of ore, and you know that means we have to wait till the new ore's dragged in from the asteroid belt." He shook his head. "It's just the kind of thing you dread, Abner, a temporary burst of demand. You can't increase your production to match it because in another month or so you'd be overproducing."

Abner nodded. He'd had a pretty good idea how things stood.

"And this is all due to the orders from the Transit Authority? For the Tube Transport system?"

"No, no, it's not just that." Herbert paged through his ledger. "See, there's also this large order from Monday, a really large one, for renovations to the Info-Slate system; and here . . ." He flipped back another page. ". . . yes, there it is: another order, a few days earlier, from Ray-O-Zap, for some kind of new corporate headquarters."

They looked down at the orders.

"That sure is a lot of inertrium," Abner concluded.

Herbert snapped shut his ledger. "Enough to build a city, is my guess. And you've got to to ask why, don't you? Is Ray-O-Zap building some kind of floating headquarters like, like the Palace of Paramagnetism? And what the blazes does Info-Slate need with inertrium, for that matter?"

Abner had been asking himself the same thing. These three projects, all on their own, had exhausted the city's supply of the lighter-than-air metal.

"What about overseas?" he asked.

"Same thing. No one, and I do mean no one, has enough inertrium on hand to fill your order. Believe me, I've been calling, and not just for you, Abner. Everybody's in the same boat."

"Could I have a look at that order book?"

Herbert handed it over. Abner scanned the orders for the past two months. There was a normal amount of traffic until just a few weeks back; then these three projects had suddenly started to make very large purchases until the supply was exhausted. He looked more closely at the relevant orders. He looked again.

"It seems like all these purchase orders were signed by Howard Pitt," he said.

Herbert took back his book and ran his eye over the columns. "Criminy, Abner, I do think you're right."

Abner looked one more time around the empty warehouse. "Of course, Herbert, since your warehouse is practically empty this would be the perfect time to build out that extension you used to talk about."

They considered what it would take to make the addition to the warehouse. Abner recommended a young engineer he knew who might do the work at a reasonable rate, and Herbert seemed determined to give it a try.

But Abner's mind was on other things as he left the inertrium warehouse.

I do wonder what he's up to, he thought, *that Howard Pitt. I sure do wonder.*

Howard Pitt's new office was way up at the top of the same tower that housed the Morological Museum, which Dash had always meant to visit but somehow hadn't got to yet; and between the ground floor and Pitt's eyrie, Dash learned, was a whole network of doormen, security desks, and surveillance devices that might have rivaled the security at the Temple of the Spider God. Purely out of professional curiosity Dash tried to compare the two. He devised three plans that *might* have defeated the tower's defenses if he wasn't trying to be civil on this job.

He eventually got about two-thirds of the way up the tower using nothing but charm, friendliness, and a certain kind of helpless good-will that he knew would get you almost anyplace. But on the sixtieth floor he came to a sudden stop.

The guards up there showed a whole new level of immovability. Dash very nearly got escorted all the way back to the sidewalk; but he managed to limit his losses to one floor. On the fifty-ninth floor he reviewed what he'd learned and examined his options.

If he was a flow of hot water trying to make it from the basement's boiler to the top floor, the guards on sixty would be a plug in a rusty old pipe. It would take all kinds of pressure to get them out of his way, and in the end that pipe would probably burst before he got past them. Dash took off his back pack and hefted it.

He'd brought his gun, of course, even though this wasn't that kind of job. But it was impossible to use it here unless he had a swift get-away in mind. The guards would call in the ASAA officers and the job—like Dash's career—wasn't likely to survive *that* encounter.

He turned his attention to the windows.

The whole building was a modern, sealed environment. He hefted his pack again. No problem there. Just briefly Dash wished that he'd been able to afford one of those rocket packs the window washers used. He'd sure wanted one. But they came pretty dear, those packs, and he'd had other priorities—the Actaeon, mostly—to worry about. Maybe if things picked up some, and he managed to save a bit . . .

He realized his mind was wandering and put a stop to that with the kind of discipline that he was still working on. So: the windows were no problem, and that meant he'd need to scale the building.

Dash dug his glass cutter out of the pack and set to work.

THURSDAY, 2:58 PM

"His father was a *magazine publisher?*"

Nola nodded. The herd of operators (and Mrs. Broadvine, who was now a sort of honorary member of the herd) had gathered at the Astro for lunch. If a few had been late—possibly due to explorations at the televideo switchboard's employment office—no one mentioned it.

Mrs. Broadvine was unconvinced. "He sounds so young," she said, but this sentence, as dubious as it seemed to her, had a completely different effect on most of the operators. They nodded with a lot of enthusiasm.

"His father owned about sixteen different, you know, *popular* magazines, like *Astonishing Future Stories,* and *Six-Gun Frontier Stories,* and, ah, *Tales of Breathless Romance.*"

There was a respectful pause, followed by a reflective silence. Mrs. Broadvine seemed quite moved.

Freda's brow developed a wrinkle. "And they'd, what, they'd act out the stories . . . ?"

Nola could see she was still stuck at *Breathless Romance.*

"Well, some of the writers were sort of, fanciful, I guess is the word, and so their heroes did things that weren't really possible. Things in the *adventure* line."

Freda seemed relieved; oddly, though, Rhonda looked a little disappointed. *It takes all kinds of flowers to make a garden,* Nola reminded herself.

"Mr. Kent *hated* things in his stories that couldn't really happen.

So if he was suspicious about something in a story he'd take Kelvin, which is Dash, of course, up to the roof or down to the basement, and they'd *test* the story. At the shooting range, or the bomb . . . thing . . . or in the lab downstairs, and if they couldn't reproduce what the writer had written, then there'd be . . . you know, there'd be heck to pay. Rewrites. Rejections. Ghost writers.

"So even though Dash didn't get a lot of *formal* education he knows just about everything there is to know about ballistics, and about, well, physics, and chemistry, and so on, as they relate to adventuring. It's how he got his *expertise*."

With the exceptions of Mrs. Broadvine (who remained skeptical) and Rhonda (who was still thinking about something else) everyone at the table seemed impressed.

Freda stared into her coffee. "And he fixes things around the house, too?"

This wasn't really going the way Nola had planned.

"The important thing," she said, "is that he's agreed to help us. He's trying to get the truth out of that Mr. Pitt *right now*."

THURSDAY, 3:03 PM

Getting *out* of the building hadn't been a problem. Even getting *up* the building had been pretty simple, thanks to the suction pads that Dash had mounted on his shoes and gloves. But getting back *in*, now, that might be another thing altogether.

The tower's architect had been pretty helpful. There were deep pilasters and nice, wide ledges that Dash appreciated, especially at this height; and just now Dash had perched on the shoulders of a conveniently placed statue. This was his kind of architecture.

But the top floor of the building was something else again.

All around *that* ledge there were decorative railings that were surprisingly sharp and pointed, for example, and all those points seemed to be pointing *down*.

The ledge itself—unlike all seventy-nine ledges below—slanted outward in a shallow, acute angle that managed to make it nearly impossible to climb. Dash measured it with his practiced eye: there was about ten feet of outward slope, which was, without being *boastful* about it, exactly enough to prevent you from stretching out to grab the edge.

Any more surprises beyond the ledge were well hidden because Dash couldn't see past the ledge at all.

The top floor inspired a whole different kind of appreciation for its architecture. It managed to be as well defended as an ancient castle in a sort of quiet and self-possessed way that you wouldn't really notice unless you were clinging to a statue seventy-nine floors up, and looking at it with considerable interest, the way Dash was doing now.

Dash had a feeling that Howard Pitt's floor had been a special order item.

He shrugged out of his back pack and hung it around the statue's neck, then opened the pack to take an inventory of its contents, which he already knew pretty much by rote.

His climbing gear was all in order. A series of pitons . . . he looked up again. Yep, about eight pitons, forced into place with their explosive charges, and probably a second line, just to be on the safe side. That left the spiky railing; but he knew he could melt that with his ray gun. It was all pretty simple, really.

But he had no idea what he'd find when he got over the ledge, or whether anyone was watching up there.

So he pushed the button on his ornithopter call and relaxed in the statue's shadow with *Astonishing Future Stories* number 117. That was the issue with *The Cypher of the Robot of Atlantis.*

THURSDAY, 3:14 PM

"That little robot's just a mystery, through and through, Mr. Roy," Harry's technician told him. "He must have got in on Tuesday night—

right after we lost him in the Transport Tubes; my apologies again, sir—'cause his lights have been going on and off at sunset and sunrise, and we can see movement through his window. But he hasn't come out for anything."

Harry Roy shuffled through the earlier reports. "But it says in here that on Wednesdays he always puts in a day's work with the Civilian Conservation Corps, and on Thursdays he's usually over at the League Hall."

The League of Robotic Persons, over on Rue du Rur, was an organization that Harry Roy knew pretty well. Though not, of course, from the inside.

He sat back in his chair and had a look out over the assembly floor. The Ferriss Moto-Man Company employed its own, for the most part, which meant that about ninety Big Lugs were tromping their deliberate way down the assembly line with all of the parts, lubricants, and raw materials that kept the line pumping out more Big Lugs just like themselves. Everything down there was looking just fine.

". . . ever since we started following him," the technician was saying. "He might miss a day or a half day from time to time, but two days in a row? It's just unheard-of."

Harry nodded.

"Well, something's up, then. But we've got no way of knowing whether we should be interested unless we get a look inside."

"Well . . ."

Harry glared at him. "There has to be a way to get in there. There's got to be some pretext you can use."

The technician ticked off all of his previous pretexts. "There's tele-video maintenance, but the building super there, that Kelvin fellow, he handles all those repairs. Ditto plumbing, heating, and electricity, also sewer connections and so on. Packages get delivered to the lobby or the super's office. Somebody has to buzz you in. The roof, well, you'd just have to see it, sir. I wouldn't want to set down on that roof without a squad from the Space Patrol, sir."

Harry looked it up in the reports and raised an eyebrow. "Lot of gunfire there," he observed.

"Yes, sir, and also the explosions. We think there's these little surveillance machines flying around, too."

"Any trouble with the authorities about the business on the roof?"

"Apparently not, Mr. Roy. Some kind of *special license*."

Harry thought it all over. "I wonder if Rusty picked this building because it's so hard to get at."

"Well, he was already living there when you told us to follow him. So I guess I don't know."

Harry got up and walked over to the window where he could see the Big Lugs at work.

"We've got no reason to think he's dangerous, or even suspicious, except that we can't tell where he was built. I've got to say it seems like that's the way he wants it."

There was no argument there.

"But who *did* build him?" Harry turned. "It's nice work; in fact, it's excellent work. But you know what kind of regulation we deal with here. Every one of the Lugs that comes off that line comes with its indenture certificate and a schedule of payment. Just the way it should be."

They watched the assembly line—a line that never stopped—delivering Lugs-in-progress to one station after another where they were progressively fitted, riveted, turned, adjusted and readjusted until, at the end of the line, they emerged as mechanical people.

Harry had always thought there was something beautiful about the line in spite of its clamor and grime.

He turned back to his employee. "If somebody's making robots on the sly, making robots like this Rusty fellow, we've got no way of knowing whether they're being made up to standard. We've got no way of knowing if they're getting their indenture papers. We can't know what happens to them."

The technician smiled and nodded eagerly. "Yep, if they're not giving out those indentures they could be selling something we can't sell. Not *legally*. You could buy a robot *forever*. What a business!"

Harry looked at him for a very long time.

"Send Davies in," he said, "and on the way out, tell Miss Baker that you've been fired."

Some people just didn't belong in robotics. That's all there was to it. Harry watched the assembly line while he waited for Davies. *It's just like a big, long maternity ward,* he thought, *except for all the noise.*

If he ever found himself in an actual maternity ward, Harry would be in for a surprise. But the sentiment was still worth having.

THURSDAY, 3:32 PM

As soon as he heard the sound of the ornithopter's rapid wingbeats Dash stowed his magazine in the back pack and shrugged the pack over his shoulders. The ornithopter—about the size of a pigeon, though its wingspan was wider—settled comfortably on the head of the statue. It preened and then looked up at Dash with what looked like curiosity, and probably was. You just couldn't be sure.

"Hey, buddy," Dash said, "could you pop over that ledge and get me some pictures? I need to see what's up there."

The ornithopter cocked its head and swiveled it, taking in the ledge. It gathered its legs under itself and pushed off, wings beating with a bright, mechanical *ping ping ping,* and spiraled out, around, and over the ledge. Dash listened to the *pings* as they beat down the face of the wall; in a moment, they *pinged* back past him and down to the other end of the ledge. With an anxious expression, Dash listened while it hovered there for a bit; but to his relief nothing distracted it before it came back down to alight on the statue.

Dash bent over the tiny televideo screen on its back and pressed REPLAY.

The ornithopter's cameras had as brief a memory as the little creatures had themselves. But since it hadn't gotten sidetracked up there Dash was able to watch a nearly complete replay of its travels up and down the top floor of the tower. He whistled. You really had to admire this kind of preparation.

He recognized the motion sensors: they were top-of-the-line Kilroys, perched solidly along the wall, and they were spaced with great care so that their view fields overlapped; each one was flanked by a pair of rotating cameras with night vision filters ready to swing down, come nightfall.

Dash sped through the recording. Yep, there were the alarm lines—clearly visible but unreachable in their transparent tubes. He knew that the tubes themselves would be rigged with sensors. Then there was a set of devices that he didn't recognize. These were long cylinders that you might have overlooked, since they blended so well with the coping along the ledge's cornice. They were placed right about where you'd expect to find a handhold if you were climbing up.

Dash stroked the ornithopter's head. It looked like climbing over that ledge would have been a really bad idea. "Good job, fella."

The little mechanical bird bobbed its head and continued to watch him. "Yeah, hang on there. I need to work this one out," Dash said.

Pitt's top floor office was completely prepared for his ascent from below. Dash was pretty sure that coming down from the roof would be at least as much of a problem. "That's some solid craftsmanship up there," he told the ornithopter, which concurred—Dash guessed—with a tinny chirp. It hopped up onto his shoulder.

So if there was no way to get up there on the outside of the building, it seemed like he'd have to go back in. Dash couldn't expect to find any less of a defense indoors, either. He just hated getting captured. It seemed like sloppy work. Even when you did it on purpose.

He looked to the ornithopter for a little reassurance, but it wasn't built for that sort of thing. Then he realized that there might be *another* way to get in there.

Dash took a sheet of paper and a pencil out of his pack. He wrote carefully, using the statue's head for his desk.

> *Am on side of building on floor below. Would Like to Talk.*
> *Sincerely, D. Kent.*

He took a wad of putty out of its waterproof pocket on the back pack and pressed it in a tacky glob to the front of the note. "Could you stick this to the window upstairs?" he asked the ornithopter.

It chirped and flapped away over the ledge and returned a moment later. When Dash pulled out his magazine the ornithopter settled onto his shoulder and hid its head under one wing. Its little solar collectors extended with a sigh. Nap time.

About twenty minutes later Dash heard a window slide open down below. *I guess they're not all sealed after all,* he thought.

A voice came up from somewhere below the statue's feet.

"Are you up there, Mr. Kent? He wants to see you."

Dash woke the ornithopter and sent it back to its cote. He clambered down with a smile for the security guard. The guard seemed a little less pleased to see *him*.

They took the stairs.

Howard Pitt's office was about the biggest office Dash had ever seen, and even though his experience wasn't all that wide it was still a very big office. It was nearly as big as the whole top floor of the building. The big severe rectangular windows let in a great deal of natural light: so much that you didn't need a lot in the way of artificial lighting to help it along, not in daytime, anyhow. There were drafting tables all around the edges of the room, some of them bigger than doors, and one of them nearly as large as those big, bright windows were. Half-height bookshelves marked off the working areas. These

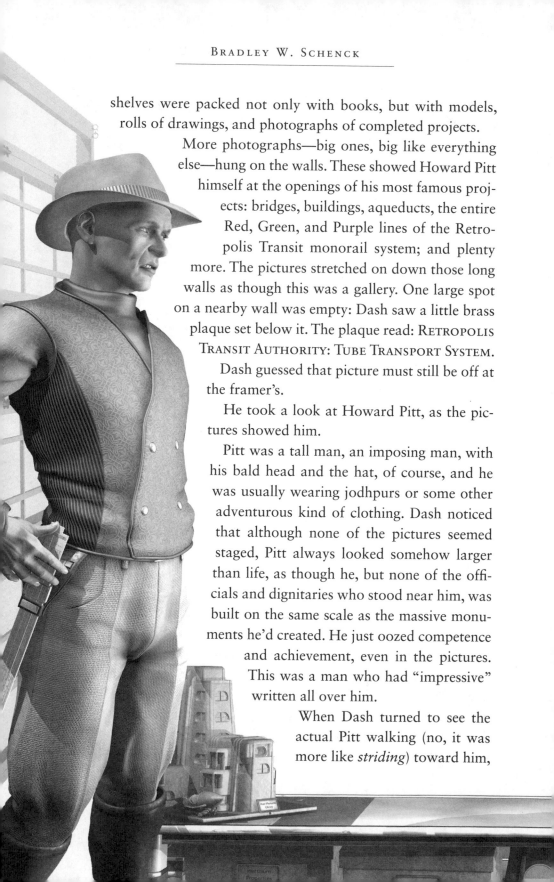

shelves were packed not only with books, but with models, rolls of drawings, and photographs of completed projects.

More photographs—big ones, big like everything else—hung on the walls. These showed Howard Pitt himself at the openings of his most famous projects: bridges, buildings, aqueducts, the entire Red, Green, and Purple lines of the Retropolis Transit monorail system; and plenty more. The pictures stretched on down those long walls as though this was a gallery. One large spot on a nearby wall was empty: Dash saw a little brass plaque set below it. The plaque read: RETROPOLIS TRANSIT AUTHORITY: TUBE TRANSPORT SYSTEM.

Dash guessed that picture must still be off at the framer's.

He took a look at Howard Pitt, as the pictures showed him.

Pitt was a tall man, an imposing man, with his bald head and the hat, of course, and he was usually wearing jodhpurs or some other adventurous kind of clothing. Dash noticed that although none of the pictures seemed staged, Pitt always looked somehow larger than life, as though he, but none of the officials and dignitaries who stood near him, was built on the same scale as the massive monuments he'd created. He just oozed competence and achievement, even in the pictures. This was a man who had "impressive" written all over him.

When Dash turned to see the actual Pitt walking (no, it was more like *striding*) toward him,

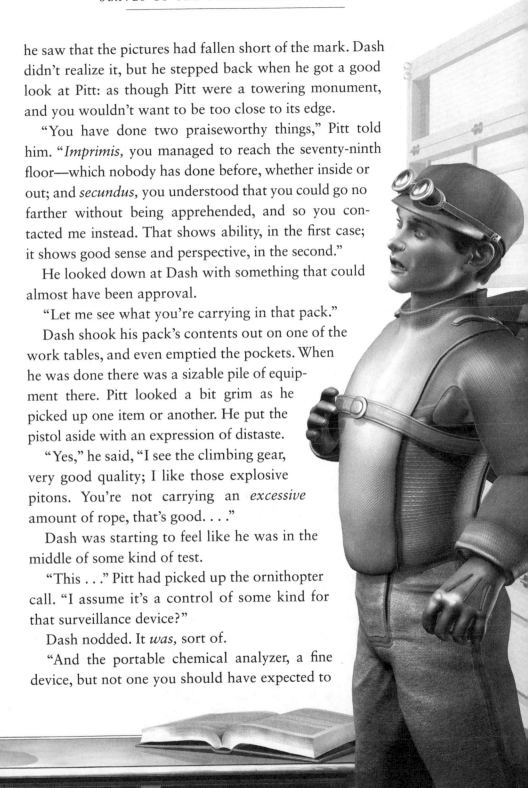

he saw that the pictures had fallen short of the mark. Dash didn't realize it, but he stepped back when he got a good look at Pitt: as though Pitt were a towering monument, and you wouldn't want to be too close to its edge.

"You have done two praiseworthy things," Pitt told him. "*Imprimis,* you managed to reach the seventy-ninth floor—which nobody has done before, whether inside or out; and *secundus,* you understood that you could go no farther without being apprehended, and so you contacted me instead. That shows ability, in the first case; it shows good sense and perspective, in the second."

He looked down at Dash with something that could almost have been approval.

"Let me see what you're carrying in that pack."

Dash shook his pack's contents out on one of the work tables, and even emptied the pockets. When he was done there was a sizable pile of equipment there. Pitt looked a bit grim as he picked up one item or another. He put the pistol aside with an expression of distaste.

"Yes," he said, "I see the climbing gear, very good quality; I like those explosive pitons. You're not carrying an *excessive* amount of rope, that's good. . . ."

Dash was starting to feel like he was in the middle of some kind of test.

"This . . ." Pitt had picked up the ornithopter call. "I assume it's a control of some kind for that surveillance device?"

Dash nodded. It *was,* sort of.

"And the portable chemical analyzer, a fine device, but not one you should have expected to need today, I think; the same goes for the Enigmascope, which is at best unreliable. . . ."

"You, you just have to keep it really *clean* . . . ," tried Dash.

Pitt actually said "Hogwash," a word that Dash had never before encountered in the wild.

"The various magnifiers and sound devices could have been useful. But altogether," Pitt said with an air of finality, "altogether, young man, you are carrying a great deal of equipment that you couldn't have expected to need."

Pitt indicated the ray gun. "That, of course, is an item that I *hope* you didn't expect to use."

Dash assured him that this was the case.

"And these?" Pitt pointed at the magazines. "I can't imagine what use you thought *they* would be."

Pitt seemed to have lost interest in the back pack, and maybe even in Dash.

"You will find, as I have, that it is best to use only those things that are necessary. *Only what is necessary.* To encumber oneself with . . . more . . . confuses the issue, not to say the mind, and only makes simple solutions needlessly complex."

He gave Dash a look. "*Nothing* must be needlessly complex," he said. "The simplest solution is always the correct one."

He paused. Dash sensed that maybe—just maybe—he was being given a second chance. He felt like he really wanted one.

Pitt visibly forced himself to be patient. "Do you know what equipment I carry at all times? The equipment that is in almost all cases *necessary* . . . and sufficient?"

He pulled his slide rule from its hip holster. "This. *Just* this. As opposed to . . . that."

Dash's eyes followed Pitt's down to all the gear that somehow looked . . . childish, *unnecessary,* in its sprawl across the table. Then he looked back at the slide rule and a small, besieged part of his brain tried to think of a way he could have fought his way into the Temple of the Spider God armed only with a slide rule.

The rest of his brain decided that he simply wasn't *smart enough* to think of the way to do it.

Dash looked at his feet. He made a couple of tentative motions with his hands, and then he scooped all the gear into his back pack, even though it was far too late to hide it from Pitt, as he wished he could.

"You didn't have a plan, did you?" Pitt demanded. "You came here with every scrap of equipment you had, and you . . . you *improvised*."

Dash couldn't meet Pitt's eyes. "Yes, sir, I guess I did."

Pitt seemed disturbed. "It's a betrayal of the ability you *do* have," he told Dash. "I wonder if that could be salvaged." Then he seemed to lose interest.

"Your note," Pitt remembered. "You said you wanted to speak with me."

Dash stared blankly. Why *had* he come here? Then he remembered Miss Gardner and the switchboard.

"It's the switchboard, Mr. Pitt. The switchboard for the Info-Slates. You've fired all the operators and closed their office down, and there's nobody operating it, but it's still working and you can't get through to an operator, but the Info-Slates still work. And it's, ah, it seems sort of strange, is all, and I wanted to find out why. Uh, what, that is, I wanted to find out *what* was going on, and so I tried to come up here and that wasn't very easy, and then I wrote you that note."

Pitt seemed surprised. "The switchboard," he said. "Really?"

He walked over to one of the windows, Dash trailing behind him.

"The switchboard was *inefficient*. It was complicated, cumbersome, and prone to operator error. Its strengths all lay in individual talents that were inconsistent, where they existed, and difficult to replicate. The operators were a jumble of parts, each one a different size and shape, that were expected to work smoothly in a single, flawless machine.

"It could take months to train an operator up to standard. If a significant number of operators had left or been lost, well! The entire system would have collapsed."

Pitt gestured out at the skies over Retropolis: alive with individual rockets and hovercars that were all watched over by a few ASAA officers, swooping and patrolling around them.

"The Air Safety and Astronautics Association depends on the timely response of their Info-Slates. So do a number of other organizations. It is too important a service to be entrusted to such an antiquated and unreliable system."

Dash and Pitt looked out over the city.

"Well . . ." Dash said. "What did they do wrong?"

Pitt slapped the window. "Wrong? They did the same things that people always do wrong. Look at them!"

Dash was nearly sure that he wasn't supposed to be looking at the switchboard operators. *Nearly* sure. Pitt seemed to be pointing down at one of the skyways, where pedestrians milled through a suspended tube between two buildings. There was quite a crowd in there. The crowd was moving in uncertain knots and clumps.

"They start and stop; they pause, they collide; they try to go fast, and then they have to slow down again when they catch up to whoever's right ahead of them. They behave erratically, *inefficiently.*

"If only they moved naturally, as particles do, they'd slide right along at an even pace; if they followed the laws of fluid dynamics they'd make their way effortlessly from one place to another. If they had the grace to act like waveforms they'd propagate their precise and predictable way through the universe. But do they? *Do they?*

"No. They do not.

"They spend their days doing only that which is *not* necessary. They prevent civil engineering systems from working the way they should do. The way they are *supposed* to do. I try to enhance their lives and their excursions and I try to make their lives more *efficient,* and they respond with this. *This.* It isn't enough."

Pitt's eyes rose from the city and rested—comfortably, at ease now—on the sky above.

"It isn't enough. Not yet."

"So I guess that's why you built the Transport Tubes, then?" Dash asked. "So folks would . . . move like particles?"

Pitt's eyes remained on the sky.

"I built the Transport Tube system to solve the problem. Yes, that's just what I did."

Dash had made it all the way back to the street before he realized that he'd never been told who was minding the switchboard now. The whole interview was a kind of a painful lesson that hadn't really taught him much except that he didn't measure up, somehow. His back pack hung off its straps like so much dead weight.

He looked up at the city—beautiful, he was sure, if maybe not as *orderly* as it might be—and he noticed that the big full Moon had risen in the afternoon sky to hang over it all, like it was watching over them. He was so distracted by the sight of the Moon that he walked right into a small man in spectacles.

"Gosh, Mister, I'm really sorry. My fault, my fault completely. Are you okay?"

When they'd established that he *was* okay, Dash walked uncertainly back toward home.

Abner collected himself. The young man who'd collided with him had been very polite, but Abner knew that he himself been lost in thought while he stared up at Pitt's office. *That man is up to something,* he thought, *and I don't believe it's any good.*

It seemed like he might have to find out what that was.

4

Journey to the Alley of Abomination

SATURDAY, 5:12 PM

K rajnik, Lillian, Doctor . . . ," mused the doorman, paging through his list. "No, ma'am, I do apologize. You're not listed."

Lillian nodded. There was something about Lillian's nod that told you she wasn't really agreeing with you; it's just that humoring you was probably more practical than any of the alternatives. An astute person would start wondering, right about then, what the alternatives *were;* but the doorman just flipped the cover back onto his notebook and smiled, job done.

"Your shoes," said Lillian.

The doorman, confused, looked at her and then—in that reflex that dates back to the dawn of the age of shoelaces—he looked down. "Yes?"

"You ought to take them off."

He grinned. "Much as I might like to, ma'am, that's against our dress code." This, his friendly, expectant, but *inflexible* expression told her, was about as far as he was going to go. He looked right and left, eyes bright, obviously on the lookout for somebody who was still there.

Lillian shrugged; you could only do so much. Her eyes dropped to his feet and she turned a dial on the earpiece of her glasses. Nothing much happened at first except that the doorman's eyes started to twitch. He pursed his lips with the slightest possible discomfort. He looked down at his shoes. "That's odd, isn't it?" he murmured.

By the time he reached for his shoelaces it was already too late. His feet had swollen to about one and one-quarter times their usual size, and although he didn't know it yet, this was only the beginning.

The doorman found a shoehorn lying on the pavement, right where she'd been standing. Behind him the door was swinging closed.

THURSDAY, 7:42 PM

Harry Roy had decided that his employees just weren't up to the job: not this job, anyway. He cruised his hovercar slowly above the streets as though he wasn't sure where he was going, gradually wandering closer and closer to the top floor of Rusty's apartment building. Whatever that little robot was up to in there, Harry felt certain he could puzzle it out.

He reached a point opposite the attic window and paused the car. He pulled out a street directory and paged through it like the most perplexed tourist in history.

Over the top of the pages he could see that Rusty's curtains were drawn. But they were lightweight curtains, and they let in a lot of light. Harry could make out the faintest flicker of movement through them.

Since the street directory was incomprehensible, Harry-the-Tourist pulled out a pair of magnifying goggles that were a big help to Harry-the-Spy's view of the window. Rusty was watering some plants on the sill. It looked as though somebody else was sitting near the window. Rusty bent and did something there, and then came back to the windowsill without his water can.

Rusty looked up. He waved at Harry, then pointed at himself, and then upward. The robot disappeared from the window and emerged, a moment later, up on the roof.

Harry put the street directory away. He shrugged, and then let the car drift up so he could see what was going on up on the roof.

He was beginning to see why his men had run into some difficulty with this assignment.

As she stepped out of the dimness of the stairway, fresh air came rushing past Nola as though it had an appointment downstairs and it didn't want to be late. The Campbell twins had shadowed her all the way up, after they'd let her in and directed her to the roof; she could still hear their hushed voices arguing on the landing below until the door swung shut behind her.

After that stairwell the sky seemed unusually wide and clear. The sun was taking its time going down, and it had already been joined by a large full Moon that hung over the city. Nola took a deep, contented breath, and she looked around for Dash.

She found him over by the ornithopter cote. He was looking at nothing in particular and he didn't seem to notice Nola when she approached him.

"Hello, Dash," she said. "I told the other operators what you're doing, and they're all very grateful."

Dash could have looked a little more pleased by the news. "I don't think I did much, as it turned out."

He gave her a very short version of his interview with Pitt.

"I didn't learn a thing, not really."

For some reason his eyes kept wandering over to his back pack.

Nola figured she could understand, at least a little. "He's very . . . intimidating, isn't he?"

"He's *amazing*," Dash told her, and once he'd started it seemed like he couldn't stop. "I felt like a little kid, standing next to him. It's like he can do *anything*, and if *you* can't do anything too, then, well, you just don't matter. And even what you did do," he went on, "which seemed pretty swell at the time, you know, well, it turns out you did it . . ."

She waited.

Then she tried: "Inefficiently?"

Dash shot up and at last he really looked at her, his eyes wide. "Yes! Like whatever it was, you did it plain wrong, or, I don't know, wasteful, like. Like . . ."

She waited again.

"I don't know," Dash finished. "Everything he said just sounded *right.*"

Nola was worried. Earlier, Dash had seemed so much more sure of himself: so much more capable. She hadn't had any trouble convincing the other operators—except maybe for Mrs. Broadvine who was not, technically, an operator anyway—that they were in good hands with Dash. Tonight, though . . .

"Why don't you tell me *exactly* what happened," she suggested, and so he did.

Right about the time Dash was describing his stay on the statue a little robot came out of the ornithopter cote and sat down quietly with his back against the shed. He was holding one of the ornithopters; its wing didn't seem to be working right. He nodded politely to Nola, and she nodded back. She noticed that he wore a nameplate labeled RUSTY but—though she was too well mannered to look *closely*—she couldn't see a speck of rust on him.

They listened to Dash's story together.

"Well," she said when he'd finished, looking more dejected than before, "I don't see what you're so down about. I mean, look at what you did! You tried to get in to see his office, and when that didn't work, well, whillikers, Dash, you *climbed up twenty stories on the outside of the building,* and then you sent for, for . . ." she waved toward the cote ". . . uh, something that could spy out the top floor for you, and then—now this really is something, 'cause it's smart and, you know, sort of . . . self-effacing at the same time—you sent a note inside and you *got a meeting with him* and he had to talk to you."

Rusty poked Dash's knee. When Dash looked up the robot nodded at him.

"Well," said Dash. "I don't know, you put it that way and it does sound kind of . . ."

The sun had sunk down behind the skyline. Automatic lights came on all around them.

"It doesn't sound that bad, anyway. But you should have *heard* him."

Nola stood up. "All I know is, you were so . . . so bamboozled that you couldn't remember to find out what you *went there* to find out. Right? Because of how he *talked* to you. And whatever he did to you, you can be sure that he did it on *purpose. Efficiently.* Because that's how he does *everything.* Right?"

Dash was frowning. He picked up his back pack and put it down again. "I don't know. I guess you could be right," he said at last. "But, N—But, Miss Gardner, you should have *heard* him."

"I think I'm glad I didn't hear him, Mr. Kent, because I would hate to be in the same sorry state that *you're* in right now."

Rusty raised his palms toward Nola: he seemed shocked. Dash was taking it in, though.

"It could be, like, a *psychological attack,* or something," he told her.

For some reason that seemed to cheer him up.

Nola tried to guess why. "Yes . . . that would be a real step up from the cat rescues, wouldn't it?"

He nodded.

Something had changed. He was thinking rapidly now and, she was happy to see, in a more productive way.

Rusty got up and brushed her hand with his as he walked over to the edge of the roof, where he waved at a hovercar across the way. He tossed the little ornithopter up into the air. Nola saw that its wing was working just fine now.

"So I guess what you'd call the frontal approach, that didn't work out so well," said Dash. "I'm not ashamed to admit it. It was a bust. That means we have to use *subterfuge*."

Rusty was waving the hovercar over. *It must be some friend of his,* she thought.

"The thing is, whoever is running the switchboard now, they've got to be working someplace. That'll be someplace that belongs to Pitt, or that he's renting from somebody, or that's owned by some company he works for. So we don't need *him* at all, do we? We just have to figure out where this new switchboard of his is hidden."

Dash smiled at her. It was a nice smile, and it was even nicer to see it back. "Is that something we could look up on that Info-Slate of yours?"

Nola told him it was.

Rusty's friend landed his hovercar on the roof over by the sand-bags, and Rusty led him to the stairs. They went in.

Dash looked off in the general direction of his Actaeon Model Fourteen. "Thanks, Miss Gardner. Thank you very much."

THURSDAY, 8:43 PM

Abner's office hung above the city inside a monorail pylon on the Red Line. Some might have minded the regular earthquake of a passing train: not Abner Perkins. He loved the monorail system. It was his life.

His office windows weren't the huge, city-framing lenses of a man like Howard Pitt. Abner's small office was on the inner face of the py-lon, and as a result, his view showed him the monorail track, the far leg of the pylon, and—best of all—every train that thundered between the pylon's two towers on its way to who knows where.

Abner knew, of course. The schedule was engraved into his mem-ory. If you'd asked him what he'd had for breakfast Abner would have needed a moment or two to think about it, and those thoughts would have been something like: *Breakfast, first meal of the day, often taken after debarking from the 6:45 or, sometimes, the 7:15, and most convenient near the Gernsback or the Loewy stations; sometimes taken aboard, though, if a traveler runs late, which is why we always add a dining car to the morning and evening trains; today, eggs and bacon with three slices of wheat toast. Also coffee.*

He watched the Red Line cars rumble past his window, so fast that he could barely make out their individual windows or the passengers who sat behind them; and he knew that he himself, watching out of his own window, was nothing but a blur to them. He didn't mind: Abner loved the monorail. It was, he had decided a long time ago, much more interesting than *he* was. No one had come hammering on his office door to tell him something different, and that was fine.

The train passed. Abner sighed and returned to the documents on his desk.

It wasn't that he disliked the Tube Transport system. There was nothing wrong with it, in particular, and it had certainly been carefully designed and built. It was a good, solid, workmanlike piece of engineering, apart from that puzzling overage in the air pressure. But he had been much happier before they'd transferred him from the monorail.

Still, he knew, his happiness wasn't very important to anyone else; and if he were able to get all the paperwork in order perhaps someday he could get a transfer back to the trains.

It's just that these inertrium requisitions made so little sense.

Any engineer might include a bit of exaggeration in the bills of materials. It was always easier to return some material to the warehouses than it was to ask for additional supplies midway through a project. The delays could be quite inconvenient. But this!

He'd jotted down the quantities of inertrium from Pitt's three projects; and these, as Abner reminded himself, were only the projects he was certain about. Herbert had been entirely correct. The total was staggering. It was so much gravity resistant metal that you could build a floating stadium, capable of seating the city's entire population; or a fleet of flying skyscrapers with enough left over for a matching apartment complex. The amount was so far above anything that Pitt could possibly have needed that Abner felt certain the man was supplying some vast project of his own. If it had been anyone except Howard Pitt, there would have been some form of oversight that would have exposed the scheme long before now; but Pitt was legendary, and it looked like the only oversight in action was Abner Perkins, the invisible engineer.

He'd have to have a great deal more evidence before he could bring this to Management.

Abner felt his pylon begin to vibrate very slightly, and he smiled. That would be the 8:35 on its approach.

His eyes wandered to the window. *All right,* he told himself. *The only information I have is that great quantities of inertrium have been siphoned off to Pitt's personal project. So the only way to learn more is to find out where that inertrium went.*

And he knew just how to do that. He'd need to have another look at Herbert's order books in the morning.

The 8:35 roared into view, its eighteen cars shaking just a little more than Abner liked as they flew past his window. He made a note, rolled it up into a message tube, and dropped the little capsule into the pneumatic tube system. The message pod whispered away to its destination and to the attention of someone who still worked on the trains. Abner heaved another sigh, turned off his desk lamp, and went home.

THURSDAY, 8:46 PM

Harry entered Rusty's apartment with some curiosity. He took in the fish tanks and the terrarium, the potted plants, and the books; but as a specialist he focused immediately on the motionless robot that sat by the window. *Deactivated?* But even from the doorway he could see that her vacuum tubes were glowing with a steady, soft light, and he could hear the whisper of her internal mechanisms ticking away in a way that was subtle, but certainly alive. He crossed over to look down at her.

"You didn't . . ."

Rusty drew himself up, visibly shocked.

"No, of course not," Harry said.

He looked over the strange robot's components, lingering on the spot where he'd have expected a maker's logo: nothing there. This robot's parts were all replacements for one commercial model or another, and there were custom parts, where needed, to make those components work together. These seemed to have been machined on a small workshop mill.

Harry passed his hand over the robot's eyes. There was a negligible autonomic response to the movement and the eyes irised when they changed their focal length. There was no other reaction.

There were coarse tool marks scarring all of the robot's joints. Harry eyed Rusty's tools. They were rather finer than the ones that had made those marks. The tools all lay in orderly rows on the table in front of the unknown robot. Harry frowned.

"It looks like . . . ," he started. "It looks . . ."

He couldn't believe it.

He turned back to Rusty.

"Was this robot *disassembled* when you found her?"

Rusty returned a grave nod.

"That horrible. That's . . ." Harry didn't have another word for what that was. But then he had a new thought.

"Was this robot built by the person who built *you*?"

Rusty sat down on a packing box next to a potted hippeastrum. He shrugged, lifting his hands; he tipped his head and shook it from side to side without much conviction.

"Let me take a look at you, then," said Harry.

Harry had been puzzled about Rusty since they'd met, but that was in the middle of a crazy night when a deluded Myrmidon robot began a kind of revolution. It had taken a piece of equipment that wasn't even supposed to exist to capture the Myrmidon, and then they'd lost him; so Harry never got a chance to inspect Rusty. His men had been following the little robot ever since. The differences were obvious at once. Rusty's limbs, trunk, head, and internal parts were unlike anything Harry had ever seen before. The little robot was definitely not pieced together from replacement parts. Harry reached for an access panel on the side of Rusty's head, but Rusty got up and walked over to the window, where he turned to look back at Harry.

Fair enough. Some things were private, after all.

"It doesn't seem likely," Harry told him. "I'm nearly certain this is someone else's work. You could only share the same maker if your maker's circumstances have changed—changed a *lot*—since you were built. Do you think that could be true?"

Rusty shook his head again, this time decisively.

Harry wasn't sure why he felt pleased, but there it was: he did. "There's no comparison. This robot has been put together with skill, but without the same resources your builder had. The workmanship's like something you'd see coming out of a small, non-commercial shop."

Exactly the kind of shop that Harry worried about. Some small, unregarded place where robots could be built without anyone taking notice; where robots could be sold secretly, with none of the guaranteed rights that any robot ought to have.

A place where someone could build slaves.

He went back to the motionless robot by the window and waved his hand in front of her again. As before, she didn't respond.

"I guess you haven't been able to communicate with her at all?" Because if Rusty had been able to do that, Harry probably wouldn't be here.

"Okay, then."

Rusty perked up: that sounded like action.

"Why don't you show me where you found her?"

They walked out of the room and down the stairs. Behind them, the strange robot sat quietly in a pool of light as though she was waiting for something to happen.

Rusty led Harry to a Tube Transport station where a single Pod waited for the next person who would need it. There was just enough room for the pair of them. The Pods were designed for a single passenger; but Harry was slim, and Rusty was small. Rusty keyed in a destination and the Pod doors slid shut silently.

The Pod floated downward at a shallow angle. Harry could feel them sliding down a chute; then there was an abrupt change in its velocity once they entered the main trunk. It wasn't uncomfortable, exactly, but it was a sensation that bothered Harry. He didn't really care for this new transport, himself. Rusty didn't seem to mind.

Each of them held on to the railing inside the Pod while it swept down the tubes, then up and around in a spiral; they must have ascended one of the monorail pylons. The Pod slowly turned horizontal. Harry knew that meant they were zooming alongside a monorail track. He found himself lying on his back with no hint about what was going on outside the Tube.

It was unnerving, the fact that you couldn't see what was outside. Harry wished the Pods had been made of glass.

After a few moments they descended again. They slowed and began to climb upward at that same shallow angle Harry remembered from the beginning, and then they were upright and the doors were sliding open. They stepped out, Rusty demonstrating a lot more poise than he. Harry quietly let out his breath.

They were now standing on a street that was a surprising distance from Rusty's apartment. As disturbing as he found the Transport Tubes, Harry had to admit that they did a good job.

Rusty set off down the street. This was starting to look familiar;

Harry thought back to his men's reports. On his longer legs he had no trouble catching up to the robot.

"It must have been Tuesday night, then, when you found her. This is where my men lost you."

Rusty didn't slow, but he did nod. They arrived at the mouth of an alley that was very well lit tonight. Rusty pointed at the lights, then pulled one finger across his neck. He looked up to see whether Harry understood.

"Somebody had broken all the lights down there?"

Another nod. They walked about halfway down the alley and Rusty stopped. He pointed at the ground. Right there, then. Harry had a look all around them.

Someone had picked this spot to dump the dismembered robot, either out of convenience for that person—close to the workshop— or because it was so far from the workshop that nobody would ever make the connection.

Or, he realized, someone had picked this spot because that person *wanted* the robot to be found.

It was likely to take some time to figure out which one of those was the right answer. He looked down. Rusty was watching him. "I'll call in a crew," Harry told him. "We have a lot of ground to cover here."

Rusty nodded. Harry had a feeling that he'd known that already.

THURSDAY, 11:24 PM

Howard Pitt slipped off his hat and ran one palm over his smooth, shiny head. Privately pleased, he ran the numbers to calculate how many minutes he'd saved by having all those follicles removed. The haircuts, the trims, the intolerable time lost to combing and smoothing, purchasing hair cream, and so on. It all added up, and it added up to his clear benefit. And he wasn't even including shaving, that immense waste of time and energy. The hat slid back onto his head.

He walked along the catwalk that ringed the construction site where work on the Projectile was going—of course—according to plan and right on schedule. Just last week the cavern's ceiling had been crowded by uncountable (no, strike that; Pitt's thumb tapped on the end of his slide rule) . . . by *very large numbers* of inertrium blocks. Now he could see big patches of the stone ceiling between the remaining supplies, hovering up there in weightless accessibility, just waiting for his construction robots to finish the final tier of the Projectile's frame. Then those final blocks would be rolled out into the sheets that would form the Projectile's skin.

It would be the largest lighter-than-air construct ever built, or even attempted. Naturally. But its essence was far more impressive than its existence. Its purpose: that was the truly elegant thing.

That was the *noble* thing.

At the cavern's end Pitt turned and walked back down the length of the catwalk. It was a very long walk.

There was no suspicion, of course. No one had any idea what Pitt was planning. A lesser man might have longed for some sort of opposition: a worthy opponent. Pitt knew that longing for any such thing would have been a betrayal of his inmost principles even if a *worthy opponent* were possible; and that idea was clearly absurd.

The Plan was beautiful in its simplicity, graceful in its deft execution, relentless in its finality. Factoring in some kind of opposition would be an indulgence of the kind that Pitt detested. Opposition would serve no purpose, and so it could not exist.

Still, a small part of him whispered to itself, *it would be nice to have someone to talk to.*

Pitt overheard that inner commentary and banished it to the most remote reaches of his brain. He'd have to do something final about *that,* too, when all of this was over.

Through it all his robots continued their pounding, bending, riveting, and welding. They were an unstoppable force for good.

Just like their master.

SATURDAY, 5:22 PM

Lillian came through the door and stepped over the doorman, who was moaning to himself, his hands making a futile attempt to contain his feet. By now their size was so remarkable that a small crowd had gathered. The doorman's cap had fallen next to him, and Lillian saw that several of the onlookers had thrown change into it.

Interesting, she thought.

An ornithopter swooped down and hovered in front of her, the *ping-ping-ping* of its flexible metal feathers offering a counterpoint to the doorman's groans. A few more coins dropped, with some hesitation, into his cap.

"Are you sure he's all right?" someone asked.

Lillian stared into the ornithopter's tiny lenses. "No, not here, either," she said, and it flew upward again to relay the message.

Lillian looked down at the doorman. She turned the dial on her glasses' earpiece and stared at his feet. She pushed a tiny button. You couldn't tell yet, but the man's feet began to shrink. Lillian bent and retrieved her shoehorn.

Then she walked down the street, only to turn in again at the next building.

5

The Drunken Tourists of Deception

Dash rolled out of bed and slipped out of his nightclothes. He pulled his clothing from the soniclave and was dressed sometime before his coffee was ready. He and Miss Gardner had been up late, poring over her Info-Slate while the stars vainly waved for their attention out there in the big sky above the roof.

Dash had come to admire the Info-Slate. He had to admit that he'd wasted a certain amount of time with inquiries that probably didn't have any bearing on their business. It was hard to stop, though, once he'd started looking.

Miss Gardner had been more interested in just *who* was connecting the Slate from one bank of information to another. She probably thought that Dash couldn't see her triumphant grin when the Slate's unknown operator lagged behind, or her grim resignation when the operator was performing up to her standards.

It must be a strange thing, Dash figured, to be competing with somebody who's invisible.

He put his cup in the sink and automatically reached for his back pack. His hand stopped just above it. Dash frowned. Then he picked it up and slung it over his shoulders. On his way to the door he scooped up the broken space helmet; he swung the door open and nearly stepped into Miss Gardner, who had just raised her hand to knock.

"Oh!" he exclaimed. "I wasn't expecting . . ."

She stood aside and told him that she'd decided to go along today, it being likely that Dash would need to make some more inquiries on her Info-Slate.

"Well," he started, but he changed his mind before he'd even approached a sentence. She seemed to be pretty eager to help. "I expect we won't see any, what you'd call *trouble,*" he went on, "and it's true that we might need to look something up if these leads of yours don't pan out."

She looked him up and down. "If we *were* expecting trouble," she said, "you'd probably be armed, wouldn't you?" She seemed a little disappointed that a Freelance Adventurer would go out without an armory on his back.

"My ray gun? It's in the . . . you know. I've got it in here." Dash pointed at his back pack. "You go out with a gun on your hip, and people get all excited."

He closed the apartment door behind them as they stepped out into the hall.

Dash was positive that the Campbell twins were hidden on the landing overhead. He considered their large, sensitive ears.

He winked at Miss Gardner and looked up in the direction of the landing. "So here's what I figure. Nobody at the school can have any idea that it's about to be attacked by the Tentacular People of . . . of Enceladus, so they'll be completely unprepared. It's our plain duty to get there before nine o'clock. *Just like you said.*"

Miss Gardner's eyes had gone wide, but they calmed down quite a bit once she followed Dash's gaze up to the landing.

"Oh, yes," she said. "Of course, even if we get there on time, the teachers are probably going to be captured and, and turned into, uh, zombies. And things. It'll be, ah, it'll be something to see when they get taken away in those space ships, won't it?"

"Terrible," Dash agreed, and the two of them went down the hall.

They were careful not to notice the argument that had just launched overhead.

Dash opened the street door for Miss Gardner.

"I'll pay for that tonight," he told her, "but it'll be worth it."

As the door swung closed behind them he could hear little infernal feet pounding down the stairs.

Miss Gardner had come up with four properties that Pitt owned, rented, or was using on behalf of his clients. Any one of them might be the location of his new switchboard office, and the only way to know was to get a good look at all of them.

Since two of these possibilities were pretty close together, and nowhere near here, Dash and Miss Gardner headed for the nearest monorail terminal. There was quite a line for the elevators at this time of day, so they made for the escalator instead and let it carry them up the long, long spiral that led to the trains' platforms. Dash's space helmet was a little awkward. He had to keep shifting it as they wound their way up the pylon.

At the top they moved to join the crowd that now streamed out of the elevators. The crowd picked them up and bore them onward to the edge of the platform just as a train came roaring into the station. They waited until the train had shuddered to a stop; its stainless steel trim was shining and bright, and its spotless windows reflected what towers were tall enough to be seen at this height.

Miss Gardner took a seat on the aisle. Dash stood next to her with one hand for his helmet and one for a hanging strap. The last of the passengers were making their way down the aisle. Dash kept moving the helmet up, down, and sideways to keep it out of everybody's way.

"So, your helmet . . . ," she started. "I guess there's a story there, isn't there?"

He shifted the big broken globe on his hip. "They're supposed to be unbreakable. I'm just glad I didn't really need it when it busted."

"Is it guaranteed?"

"That's the story, anyhow," he explained. "But the manufacturer wants me to take it back to the store where I bought it, and the store wants me to send it to the manufacturer, and so far I'm kind of stuck in between 'em. I figured I could drop by the store while we're out."

The train shook itself into motion as Nola agreed that this was a good idea. The monorail pulled away from the platform and built up speed on its way out of the track's first turn. Dash shifted the helmet again.

"It sure didn't seem this heavy when I was wearing it," he said.

"You could always put it on now."

They each thought about how Dash would look, wearing his broken space helmet while they trudged through the city, and they laughed at the same time.

The train stopped at another station; passengers began to squeeze and be squeezed through the aisle again. Nola took the helmet and held it in her lap this time.

"It was just a crack, at first," Dash said, "until he bashed my head into the wall."

A couple of passengers moved a little farther away from him, and as he expanded into the breathing room he added, "Of course, that didn't do him a lot of good, in the end."

He continued in that vein until there was enough free space around him that he could reach up and grab another strap. They traveled much more comfortably until they reached the Peavey Center station, where they left the train and wound their way back down to the street.

It was just a couple of blocks to the Tube Transport Control Center. What made this building interesting was that even though it belonged to the Retropolis Transit Authority, Pitt had a lease on its mineral rights: something you don't often find, Miss Gardner had pointed out, within a city. They wanted to get a good look at it.

It wasn't an especially tall building—not tall, anyhow, compared to the rest of the buildings on the street. It seemed to operate as a hub as well as a control center. That meant that all around it Transport Tubes sprouted from the pavement and wound in a complicated interchange that laced the outer walls and joined, separated, and rejoined up above the roof before they either plunged back underground or rose up to run along the monorail tracks that hung high overhead. There were some kind of switch housings wherever two of the tubes came together, and these would whir into motion and revolve to change the course of an approaching Pod. The tubes were well insulated; but Dash could still hear a quiet sound, like breaking waves, whenever a Pod flew through them.

"Have you tried it yet?" he asked.

"Just once," Miss Gardner told him, and she didn't seem to want to elaborate. So they went inside.

There was a counter that walled off the main floor of the room. The floor was divided into desks, each one staffed by a technician in blue or green who monitored a part of the line. Each worker stared intently at a kind of a diagram with colored lights and switches. From time to time one would flick a switch and the lights changed: red and green and yellow, and a few that were white.

"It's like the switchboard," Miss Gardner observed, "but they're moving people instead of information."

Dash had been thinking it looked like a model train set.

"This is the last project he worked on before he left the Transit Authority," he reminded her. "I wonder if it was still on his mind when he redesigned the switchboard system."

"I'll have to tell the girls," she said. "There might be some jobs open here and it really does look a lot like what we've been doing."

The room, big as it was, was much smaller than the building. Dash looked over the walls and tried to imagine the floor plan. "There's plenty more room in back," he said. "And more, over behind that wall on the left."

They wandered over that way.

About twenty people were clustered together near a gate in the front counter. They had the wide eyed, curious, and slightly hungry look that marked them as tourists. Dash pointed out a sign on the gate that read Tubeway Tours, 9 am and 2 pm daily.

"That's in just a couple of minutes," said Miss Gardner.

FRIDAY, 8:53 AM

"It's not that the shipments were late," said Abner. He pointed out the entries in his copy of Herbert's records. "And it's not that I have any complaint about your service."

He looked, rather dramatically, right and left. He lowered his voice. "It's just that not everyone in my department is, shall we say, *thorough* in their paperwork."

The shipping clerk across the desk looked scandalized.

"As a result I have to track all of these shipments myself. There's no excuse for slack record keeping, but you can't expect *everyone* to see that, can you?"

He might have made a misstep there, he saw: the shipping clerk seemed to feel otherwise, and with a great depth of feeling, too. Abner adapted.

"Not when they're related to *senior management,* I mean."

This bound him to the clerk with a bond like tempered steel. Abner accepted the shipping records, and the clerk's sympathy, with gratitude.

"But it was an unusual commission," he was told. "We made deliveries to seven different addresses, and the addresses were *not* warehouses."

Abner had just made that discovery. He shuffled through the records. "You delivered the inertrium shipments to *Transport Tubes?*"

The clerk nodded. "Highly irregular. The goods were received at the Pod stations and then packed into Transport Pods, one after another. Where they went from there . . . ?"

"No one knows," Abner concluded.

But of course *somebody* knew.

"I'll need copies of these records, if that's no trouble," Abner said, and of course it wasn't.

By the time he'd gotten his copies he'd decided to take a tour of those stations himself.

FRIDAY, 9:22 AM

The tour group wound its way between the Transport Tubes in the Control Center's large back room. Dash and Miss Gardner did their best to appreciate the wonders of the Control Center, but unlike the tourists around them they were paying a lot of attention to the various doors, the dimensions of the room, and whether any of the walls made an unusually hollow sound when they bumped into them, which they were doing often enough to rouse the interest of their guide.

"If you'll just follow me—perhaps a little more carefully—this way," they were told, "we will have a *wonderful* view of one of the switching mechanisms just ahead."

"Wonderful," Dash whispered. "Anything there?"

Miss Gardner shook her head. She was cautiously tapping on the wall as they trailed after the group.

"I think the dimensions in here add up about right," he said.

"Please don't dawdle!" the guide called. "Was there a question . . . ?"

Dash smiled. "I was just wondering about *mineral rights,*" he said brightly. "Like, whether the Transit Authority does anything with the *mineral rights* on the property."

This—uniquely—brought the guide to a full stop. "Such as mining rights, you mean?"

Dash nodded. "If, say, there was some kind of ore, or something, down below."

He stamped firmly on the cement floor. It did not echo.

"I have no idea," the guide said. "I would be very surprised. However, I can recommend the city's mineral water, or in fact *any kind of water,* as an excellent beverage that I hope you will enjoy during your stay here."

This left Dash as confused as the guide had been.

Miss Gardner nudged him. "She thinks we drank our breakfast," she said, "what with all the bumping around we're doing. And, well, the rather odd question."

"Well, that's just fine, that is," he fumed. "A little curiosity about the building's *structural integrity*"—with a timely rap on a passing wall—"and an interest in, well, *metallurgy,* and everyone thinks I'm a rummy. That's just *fine.*"

They finished the tour without any more confusion, but without any new insights, either. "I guess they don't even know about the mineral rights," he said when they were back out in front of the building. "Except maybe the folks at the top, and who knows what *they're* thinking anyway."

They turned to look back at the Control Center. It was gleaming and new and, as Dash could see, *efficient.*

The hidden Pods whispered through their tubes, and the switching mechanisms docked and undocked with certainty, whisking who knew how many travelers through their maze: it was like a network of tunnels turned sideways and exposed to the light.

"About all we didn't see was those offices on the left side. There *could* be something in there . . . but I think whatever's going on, it's those mineral rights that are the key. If he's got the right to dig down there, there could be something *underneath* the building that only Pitt knows about."

"How do we find out?" asked Miss Gardner.

Dash shook his head. "That's for later," he told her. "What's next on our list?"

Miss Gardner turned on her Info-Slate and brought up the list.

Far away across the city—and some distance under it—an operator connected the Info-Slate display to Nola's pre-recorded list. This was Nola's third access to her list of Pitt's properties and (as designed)

that set off an alarm through the Info-Slate system that triggered a heightened state of alert at the other facilities. Measures were taken.

The operator turned back to her other client panels. She would have forgotten the incident, except that she hadn't exactly noticed it in the first place. She had simply done what was necessary.

FRIDAY, 10:07 AM

Abner hoped he wouldn't have to use the Tube Transport System again anytime soon. He didn't think his stomach could take it.

This seventh Pod station was just like all the others: it was completely unremarkable. The Tube itself rose out of the pavement and flared outward, its flanged cylinder framing the Pod door. Just like all the rest. The stations all looked like tubular closets.

He could see no reason why these particular stations had been chosen to receive Pitt's inertrium deliveries. He wondered if that was the point: it almost certainly was.

Given Pitt's detailed knowledge of the Tube Transport system he could have picked seven inconspicuous stations, each convenient to their destination but without any particular pattern. Abner's only hope was that there would be some clue in the routes that were adjacent to these stations. He felt sure there would be no record of the Pods' destinations at the Control Center.

Even though he disliked the Tubes, Abner had taken his new responsibilities seriously. He had memorized the routes, the switching stations, and—most importantly—their maintenance access points.

His eyes unfocused while he ran over the plans in his mind. They snapped back into focus quite abruptly when he thought he *did* see a pattern after all. It was something he'd been very concerned about just a few days before.

The justification for the incredible air pressures required by the Tube system was a single long stretch in the Tube network where there were no Pod stations at all; in an emergency, there must be sufficient air pressure to get any Pods in the system through that stretch and out to safety at the next stations on the line.

The seven Pod stations he'd just visited were arranged in an irregular ring around that one long underground stretch in the network. Abner smiled.

He hated an anomaly of that kind in a design. It seemed . . . inelegant. It was so very interesting that there might be some reason for *this* one.

Consulting his mental map, Abner Perkins set out for the nearest maintenance hatch. He had a feeling that the blueprints were incomplete.

FRIDAY, 10:12 AM

Pitt's second property turned out to be a maintenance yard where earth-moving equipment was stored. The great machines crouched in orderly rows, arranged in what Dash knew must be a sensible order. They were like big, efficient lions who were waiting patiently for their allotted gazelles. Except that lions weren't like that, at least until Pitt got a chance to reorganize them.

Dash and Miss Gardner wandered casually around the lot's perimeter with an eye out for any kind of access hatch, or cellar door, or even a hint that there was something going on underneath the lot: but there was nothing to be found. That lease on mineral rights had Dash pretty well convinced that Pitt was up to something underneath the Control Center. Still, it seemed as though everything underneath the maintenance yard was on the up and up.

They bent over the Info-Slate and looked at Miss Gardner's list. It was still displayed in the Slate's sidebar so there wasn't any need to call it up again.

"That leaves these two," she said. "The construction site for the new power station, which would be . . . oh, clear out past the Hogben Canal; and a storage facility, quite a bit nearer at hand."

Dash looked over the map that Miss Gardner had called up in the Slate's main pane.

"I've got that stop to make," he said, tapping his space helmet, "which is sort of in between them. So maybe the storage building first . . . ?"

Miss Gardner didn't object, so they set out on foot. Twice they passed Tube Pod stations and each time Dash slowed a little, pointedly looking them over, but Miss Gardner ignored them and marched on. He shifted the helmet to his other arm and got used to the idea of a long walk.

If she didn't like the blamed things then Dash guessed she had her reasons.

Anyway, it was a nice enough day for a walk. The city, after all, was built for pedestrians: if you needed to go farther than you could walk, or farther than you wanted to walk, you could always mount a monorail terminal, or pop into a Transport Tube, or find a public hovercar platform; you could even take a ferry along the Hogben Canal, if you liked.

Some folks had their own rockets—well, so did Dash, of course, but the Actaeon was way too big for city traffic. The rockets and hovercars flocked far overhead, weaving in a complicated dance over the streets, the pedestrian skyways, and the monorail routes. Up above everything else—apart from the clouds, anyhow—the airships floated on their majestic way across the city.

But here, on the ground? It was all about your feet.

So it was their feet that took the two of them through the parks and along the streets and between the towering buildings of the city; up a flight of stairs to a skyway that bridged a handy shortcut that Dash knew pretty well; then down again, skirting the edge of the Experimental Research District, where the city's zoning laws confined all scientific invention. The reason for that was obvious even at this distance, seeing as there were at least six explosions in the time it took Dash and Miss Gardner to avoid the neighborhood. The cloud that hung over the District's blackened laboratories obviously didn't know or care about zoning laws: it was drifting in the air well beyond the District's bounds.

They turned away from the District, hearing a distant sound like very large, very heavy footsteps headed the other way. Miss Gardner seemed pleased to be leaving that behind them and Dash, as casual as he hoped he seemed, didn't disagree with her there.

Scientific endeavor was just about the scariest thing Dash had ever seen.

With that behind them they eventually found themselves standing across the street from their destination.

Pitt's storage facility was the opposite of the Tube Transport Control Center, being low, isolated, and, as far as they could tell, uninhabited. The street itself was quiet: no people were visible anywhere. The warehouses and shuttered blocks of offices somehow seemed, themselves, to be in storage in case they'd be needed later.

"It's like the city's closet in here," Miss Gardner said.

And it was: it was as though the entire city had decided that it might need all its tennis rackets, spare engine parts, old clothes, and dilapidated luggage at some point in the future; and so the city had put a lot of old buildings whose value—if any—was purely sentimental on a single street right off the downstairs hall, where the city never remembered to dust, with all those forgotten knicknacks inside.

"I wonder how many blocks there are, like this?" Dash mused.

"The Zoning Ordinances were never my specialty," said Miss Gardner, "but the way I remember it just about every neighborhood in the city—well, except for the greenbelts and the District—is a mix of some kind. There's usually housing above the businesses or between the market towers, and a kind of a balance between businesses and apartments, or houses . . . and a certain amount of parkland that separates the neighborhoods. This is . . . it's just totally different."

Dash looked up and down the empty street. "It's like no one remembers it's here."

"Like a closet," she said again.

They turned from the closet-at-large back to the building across the street. That one, Dash figured, would be Pitt's *personal* closet. His eyes narrowed. This might be interesting. Miss Gardner started across the street, but Dash caught her by the arm. "Around the back," he said.

They went past Pitt's building and about a third of the way down the block, where Dash led her across the street and down an alley. It ended at a second alley, parallel to the street; and there they walked back down and counted the buildings off until they reached the back of Pitt's.

It was no architectural wonder around the front: it was a plain, solid block at the back. On the ground floor was a steel door with sealed windows to either side, while the wall above them was flat and featureless. Dash waved Miss Gardner back and had a good look at the back door. Pitt's office had been as well defended as anything he'd ever seen.

The door was locked, of course. Dash nodded, approving the armored conduit that housed the alarm wires, and his eyes followed that conduit until he lost it at the rooftop. He'd expect to find a well-protected box up there. He looked back down at the door itself, because he knew there'd be more.

A couple of minutes later he returned to Miss Gardner's side.

"It's good," he told her. "I figure I can get in there all right, but with this fella you just never know. So what I'm thinking is, you should get out of here and let me give it a try. There ain't no point in you getting into trouble over this." He handed her his space helmet. "Maybe you could hang on to this for me and I'll pick it up later, when I let you know what I find in there."

Miss Gardner took the helmet and rested it on her hip. "Oh, I'll take it, all right," she said, "but I'm not going anyplace. If you go in there you're going in for me, anyhow. If there's going to be any trouble then I'll be happy to take my share."

Dash scratched his ear. He was used to working alone, after all. With the cats, for example, he'd sort of get his instructions and head on out to take care of things, and then his client would be very grateful when he got back, and that worked out pretty well, the way Dash saw it.

"Well, that's fine, I guess, but it's like this: I'm doing a job for you, right? Because I guess I might be a little better at it than you, and that's what you gals are paying me for. And if part of that job is trouble then, you know, it's my trouble, like *on your behalf*. Like, *instead* of you. Because that's what I'm here for."

He waited.

"And so in my *professional opinion* it's a bad idea for you to go in there with me. Also."

He waited some more. He wasn't sure this was going the way it was supposed to, with the look Miss Gardner was giving him, and the way she was tapping her foot with his broken helmet balanced on her hip.

"Uh, please?" he finished.

"I'll be waiting right here," she said.

I guess that's what you call a compromise, he thought, and he knelt down to get a few things out of his pack.

Dash avoided the door completely: it was the obvious point of entry and he'd already found its hidden sensors. The windows, on the other hand, were high up, shuttered with steel, and appeared to be locked tight.

The fact is that by preference he'd rather have gone through the wall itself. That wasn't likely to be hooked up to an alarm. But this was the middle of the city, empty alley or not, and he knew better than to draw that kind of attention to himself.

So he attached the suction pads to his boots and left glove, and he spidered his way up to one of the windows.

Another armored conduit was attached to the window frame. Dash squeezed some paste out of a tube, careful to form a very small bead that ran all around the conduit, and he waited while the acid burned its way through the shell. He did the same for the conduit on the window's other side and had a look at the cables that were now exposed. Matching their gauge, he uncoiled a few feet of new cable from its spool and attached that to the left-side alarm wire. *So far, so good,* he thought.

Here's where the timing was tricky. It wouldn't have been so bad if he didn't need to keep one hand on the building. After a moment's thought Dash braced himself on the window frame, removed the suction pad from his left glove, and reattached it to his knee. Much better.

He leaned into the side of the building with the snips in his left hand. He practiced the motion a couple of times and, once he was sure he had it, he gritted his teeth, hooked his new cable to the alarm cable, and snipped it below the join, all in what he earnestly hoped was the same instant. His fingers finished with a twist that wound his new cable snugly against the original one, and he waited.

Nothing happened.

Dash smiled back over his shoulder at Miss Gardner and gave her a thumbs up. Then he turned back to the window.

Another bead of acid paste formed a small circle on the steel shutters. Dash waited for the acid to do its work and then he carefully lifted the little steel circle from its smoking hole. He fished his tiny televideo camera through the hole and attached its trailing wires to his goggles. Now he could see what was inside the window.

Dash whistled. There was a whole new security system inside, much like the one he'd just bypassed. He shook his head, pulled out an extensible claw, and set to work all over again. *Some people,* he thought, but he admired it all the same.

It took him thirteen minutes to bypass the second alarm. He wasn't proud of that but this one had been a lot more difficult, with him working the claw and the camera on their extensible cables. He took another look around the interior with the little camera and decided he was in the clear.

Dash leaned back, hanging off his suction pads, and turned his ray gun's beam to a midline setting that ought to burn through the shutter without leaving a lot of slag behind. That would be a big help when he welded it closed again on his way out. He fixed four more suction pads on the shutter itself and burned it free of its frame.

He caught the shutter and eased it out between the alarm wires and the wall. The suction pads gripped the face of the wall and that left the shutter hanging right next to its frame. Dash smiled: that had been a nice, workmanlike job, even though he'd like to practice those moves later on to improve his time.

He gave Miss Gardner another thumbs up. The look on her face made him pause: he wasn't sure what she meant by it. But then she smiled and waved, and it seemed like that was all right.

Dash took a deep breath and heaved himself over the window frame. He turned, grasping its edge, and lowered himself until his feet found the edge of a crate. He wormed in that direction just far enough to get both boots on the thing, and then he let himself down.

Pitt's storage building was filled, mostly, with great big rolls of design drawings that were stacked on racks. Flat storage files were arranged in columns down the middle. Dash figured there'd be more drawings inside those, too.

Even in the dim light he could tell that there wasn't anything like a switchboard in here; but he'd known that as soon as he threaded his little camera through the window. No, all he could hope to find was some record of what it was, or where it was, anyway. He looked up and down the racks of drawings. He looked back at the looming flat files. Of course, there was an *awful lot* of stuff in here, wasn't there?

A breeze came through the open window.

It whispered past the wires he'd rigged on the inside. Dash really had done a good job there, but his view through the camera and his grip with the claw hadn't been as reliable as his own eyes and fingers.

One of the improvised wires shifted just a little bit in the breeze. It lost contact with the alarm wire, and that's when the trouble started.

In her post at the switchboard the operator saw the blinking red light of the storage facility's silent alarm. She punched three buttons in succession and slid a lever into the ON position. That made an awful lot of things happen, but the operator wasn't aware of any of them; she'd never missed a beat in her ongoing dance with the switchboard. She disconnected, reconnected, and rerouted one input after another, and the six Info-Slates she was managing never registered a delay.

Dash was unrolling a large blueprint when the room's front wall folded in on itself with a ringing crash, revealing a roughly man-shaped void in what had looked like a permanent wall. There was a robot wedged in the void. Its dark eyes flared into life and inside its chest something began to hum. It looked from side to side and fixed its gaze on Dash where he stood about forty feet away.

Its left leg creaked into ponderous motion, and then its right leg followed, as it stepped out of its niche and began to advance. A battery of cannon barrels spun out of the port in the center of its chest.

"INTRUDER," the robot boomed, "YOU WILL SURRENDER OR YOU WILL BE DISINTEGRATED."

6

The Savage Planet of Paradox

Harry Roy rested. He was sitting on the fender of one of the Ferriss hovercars while he kept an eye on Rusty. It was habit, he supposed.

The little robot was looking slowly up and down the alley, up and down its walls, and finally just down, at its paving. They'd started their search of the buildings around the alley in the early morning hours—just as soon as Harry's men had arrived—and everyone but Rusty had by now given up.

Harry's men had followed his lead. One by one they'd each found a spot along the alley where they could catch a few minutes' rest. When he saw what had happened Harry got back to his feet with as much determination as he could manage, and a moment later the others started to do likewise.

It was human behavior, he knew: do as the leader does, and for exactly as long as he does it. You didn't usually see that in robots, and Harry decided that was just as well.

He went over to join Rusty.

Rusty was pacing back and forth in the area where he'd found the disassembled robot. Every now and then he'd stamp on the ground, move a few paces, and stamp again. Harry could tell that he was looking for something underneath the pavement. This seemed like an excess of optimism.

The crew started to wander over—following their leader again—while Harry turned completely around to take a last look at the buildings around them. They hadn't found a thing in any of them.

"I'm thinking that whoever dumped that robot here must have carried her a long way," he said, "and honestly, that leaves us in the dark. We can still try to trace the orders for her components. Sooner or later something will probably turn up."

Davies nodded. His heart wasn't in it. "Maybe if it was a large order . . ."

Harry agreed. "And it could be. I've got a feeling she wasn't a one-off project. Did you get that message off to the League?"

Davies had. "Though unless we need to host a downhill race, or a bake sale, I don't know what they can do to help."

Rusty looked up, his head tilted to one side, and Harry lifted a hand.

"Well, you have to admit there's some truth to it. The League is . . ." He looked at Davies. "The League's kind of a *ceremonial* organization, more than a practical one. But they sure ought to be told."

Rusty looked back down at the paving. Then he seemed to see something that interested him: his eyes turned along the width of the alley and settled on a pillar. He ran one finger along a crack in the cement, right up to the spot where the pillar met the pavement. The crack continued up the side of the pillar to about the level of Rusty's eyes. When he twisted his finger, a panel flipped open to reveal a control box of some kind inside.

Harry and Davies stared. Why the heck hadn't anybody noticed that *hours* ago? They crowded around the panel, peering over Rusty's head while he lightly ran one finger across the controls. There was one large green button on the right. Rusty canted his head up at Harry, and Harry nodded. Rusty pressed the button.

A square the width of the entire alley shifted under their feet. Hairline cracks parted; the large square divided into two recessed shelves that slid apart and revealed a stairway which spiraled around the open shaft.

Harry assigned a few men to watch the alley while he, with Rusty and Davies, started down the stairs. "I really wish you'd seen that sooner," he said. Rusty just shrugged.

The stairs wound down and down into the dark. The only lights were Rusty's eyes and Harry's flashlight, and those little pools of light wandered constantly from side to side and—inevitably—down into the open shaft beside them. There wasn't a lot to see.

Harry counted twenty-seven turns around the spiral before they reached the floor.

It was just as dark down here as it had been on the stairs but now there was plenty to see, all around, and all the more so once Davies found the light switch.

They were standing at one end of an assembly line. It wasn't much like the line at the Ferriss Moto-Man plant, but there was no mistaking what it was. It was a silent, motionless line, as though it hadn't started up or—and Harry saw that this was more likely—as though it had been shut down.

They walked slowly backward along the line from the end point, where assembly must have concluded, past the stations where someone had been very busy not too long ago. Tools were neatly arranged next to the conveyor belt: drills, torque wrenches, and mallets—the kind of tools you'd use to assemble existing components—and farther down the line they saw a series of small mills where custom parts had been fabricated.

They walked the whole length of the line and by the time things started to happen they were so far from the stairway that they didn't even notice.

A second set of large panels slid closed at the entrance, whisper-quiet. Behind the walls, there were sounds, as if the teeth of titanic gears were locking together and the gears themselves were beginning to turn.

When they reached the end of the room, and saw the iron hatch there, they pulled it open and were startled by the sight of the solid stone wall before them sliding upward.

The entire room was descending.

The operator set her switch to 14 and triggered a system update. It was turning out to be an eventful morning. But whatever the meaning of 14 was, she'd forgotten all about it in less than a second. The next task was somebody else's, after all, and there was no point in her wasting any time in wondering about it.

Davies was too busy staring at the rising stone wall inside the door frame; but Harry and Rusty took one look, tilted their heads up, and then turned slowly back to look at the stairway. It wasn't there. They set out for the room's far end, but after a few steps Rusty turned and came back to grab Davies' arm. Rusty pointed at Harry and at the far wall, and then the two of them took off after him.

They all reached the place where the stairway had been, only to see that smooth stone panels had closed off that end of the room.

"It's a factory," marveled Harry, "and it's an elevator."

"So . . . where is it taking us?" Davies asked.

Rusty tapped Davies' elbow. When the man looked down at him, Rusty pointed at the floor.

"Yeah," said Davies. "Thanks."

Things had gotten just as surprising up in the alleyway. The ground panels slid together and came up flush to the alley's paving so quickly that Harry's men barely had time to get out of the way. That left them all staring down at the practically invisible doors. One of them, a little quicker than the others, sprinted to the control panel and pounded on the green button. But something in the mechanism had locked it in place.

FRIDAY, 11:01 AM

In the dim light of the maintenance tunnels Abner was very careful about his footing. He had no idea how often anyone came down here, but he was fairly certain that the answer was "not very." The Tube Transport system was so new that the tunnels themselves were spotless. About the only reason anybody would come down here would be simple curiosity, at least until the Tubes somehow broke down.

Abner paused long enough to make a note: someone *should* check all the tunnels on a regular schedule. Quite apart from the safety concerns, the workers ought to become more familiar with the system.

He'd begun an orderly survey near the middle of the area defined by Pitt's inertrium deliveries. He marked off the current section and then continued to his next destination: an underground interchange where three of the Tube lines converged.

As he entered the nexus, one of the switch housings hummed into action and flipped two hundred and sixty degrees just in time to catch an incoming Pod and send it on its new path. The mechanism powered down then, and all was quiet once more. Abner did admire the system, in a way, even though it seemed both excessive—with all of those individual Pods—and impersonal, for the same reason. You'd never bump into an old friend in a Transport Tube, the way you might on a train.

About the only thing you'd bump into in a Transport Pod *was* a Transport Pod. Abner rubbed his left elbow. *That* you'd be bumping into over and over again.

The three Tube lines angled off, each one enclosed in its own maintenance tunnel. Abner marked off the one he'd just examined and set off down the right-hand chute. The system schematics showed this leg of the journey as one long, uninterrupted tube that ran for about three quarters of a mile.

So he might have been surprised, a hundred yards in, to see a hatchway in the tunnel that had not been indicated on the system's blueprints. He wasn't surprised at all. This was exactly what he'd been looking for.

Abner listened at the hatch. There was a quiet sound like whirring machinery on the other side. He tried the latch and found it unlocked. Very well, then: he opened the hatch and went inside.

FRIDAY, 11:08 AM

Dash had been inside for several minutes and Nola hadn't heard a thing from him. She'd been a little startled to see how good a burglar he was, but it only took a moment for her to put *that* into perspective. She was just seeing him put some of his skills to good use, after all, and on her own behalf, besides.

But the immense crash that came from inside the building was a shock. By the time she heard the sounds of rubble bouncing across the floor she was already starting for the window. A great robotic voice said, "YOU WILL SURRENDER OR YOU WILL BE DISINTEGRATED," and she leaped up without really thinking about it; which, she realized a moment later, was about the only way she would have done.

You don't usually run *toward* a thing like that, although you might very easily find yourself running.

Nola nearly grabbed onto the window ledge before she tumbled down again, breaking her fall on Dash's back pack. Devices and mysterious bundles scattered across the pavement.

Her eyebrows shot up when she saw Dash's ray gun. Nola scooped that up and then grabbed a thin coil of rope that ended in a hook; she wound up and heaved the grappling line up at the window, where it caught on the edge of the frame, and with the gun in one hand she scaled the rope and swung inside. Dust floated in the glaring beams of light that followed her through the window.

Dash was standing nearby with his back to her. All of his attention was on the advancing robot.

It was about ten feet tall and massively built. In its chest cavity some kind of weapon was trained on Dash. The robot saw Nola and paused, evaluating her. The ray gun in her hand seemed to interest it. Its whole chest rotated so that the spinning barrels of its weapon swung up to cover her.

"DROP YOUR WEAPON AND EXIT IMMEDIATELY," it said.

Nola had thought she knew how loud its voice was, but in here, with no wall between them, the force of the voice boomed out in sound waves that Nola could *feel,* like great gusts of wind. She felt herself swing at the end of her rope when each word rolled over her: it was the loudest voice she'd ever heard.

She lost her grip on the gun and saw it fall to the floor. *Oops.*

Between her and the robot were rows of racked drawings on incrementally taller racks, and then a rank of big, heavy, flat files that also increased in height as they advanced deeper into the room. While the gun clattered across the floor, Nola pushed out from the wall and grabbed at the nearest rack of drawings.

It overbalanced and tipped over, striking the next rack, which also overbalanced and did the same thing. Nola hit the ground with a grunt as the racks began a chain reaction that rippled across the room, falling, one after another, until the last of them struck the first of the flat files.

The weight of all the racks came to rest on the top edge of the file cabinet with just enough force to tip *it* over, in its turn; and to Nola's great surprise the file cabinet also tipped and struck the next, slightly taller cabinet on its way down.

One after another—each just a little taller and a little heavier than the last—the flat file cabinets crashed to the floor until the final one, which was about sixteen feet tall, tipped over and struck the robot on top of its head.

The robot and the file cabinet went down together and neither one of them got back up again.

Gradually, the bits, shelves, and rolls of drawings stopped bouncing across the floor. One of the larger flat file cabinets overbalanced from its perch on another, and Nola and Dash both jumped at the crash.

Dash was looking back and forth from the window, to Nola, to the first of the shelves she'd overturned, and then one by one across the whole chain of shelves and file cabinets that had fallen in a perfect series that had landed, at last, on the top of the robot's head. Then he looked them all over again.

"*The Savage Planet of Paradox*. Edward J. Bellin," he said.

It sounded like he was having trouble believing what he was saying.

"We laughed about it, it was just too ridiculous. He submitted it to *Future Planet Stories,* and when Dad rejected it, he submitted it again to *Exciting Tales of Science, Wonder World,* and then, the last time, to *Astonishing Future Stories.* He just didn't seem to understand that all those magazines were at the same address."

Dash walked toward her, his eyes wide and amazed. "Dad didn't even bother to *test* it. The idea that ten or twelve big cabinets would just all . . . line up, like dominoes, in exactly the right way, and smack a giant robot on the head . . . it was plain foolishness. We kept laughing, every time that story came back in the mail. We just kept on laughing, every time."

He stopped right in front of her and, very gently, he touched her arm.

"And then you went and did it right off, on the first try."

His eyes went back to the window, and the first shelf, and then the second shelf. . . .

Nola tossed her head. "Well! I'd say you owe Mr. Bellin an apology, then."

Edward J. Bellin unlocked the door to his storage room, but instead of opening it he just stood there, shoulders hanging, looking down at the fat envelope in his hands. He wasn't sure how much longer he could go on.

He heard someone on the stairs. No doubt this was another renter: another person who was unable to give up on old furniture, old pictures, old memories, or old dreams. The storage building was full of them. Edward opened the door and slipped inside, shutting it quietly behind him. He waited until he heard footsteps pass along the hall, pause at another doorway, and then pass through it; he heard that door close with a quiet *snick*. Then he reached out and pulled the light cord. He didn't need to search for it: he'd done this so many times before.

Crowded into the middle of Edward's storage unit was an old wooden desk. Its surface was clean and polished. All it held was an old typewriter and a ream of blank paper. Everything else was in the file cabinets.

Edward walked past the cabinets full of manuscripts, which were on his left, and past the much taller file cabinets labeled A through E. He slid open a drawer in F.

It wasn't until then that he realized he hadn't even opened the envelope. So he slit it open with his pen knife and pulled out the manuscript—its first three pages covered with angry scribbles in red ink—and slipped the rejection slip out from under it.

Years ago, when Edward's rejection slips would still fit in a single drawer, he had always opened these envelopes in hopeful anticipation. Now it seemed as though he might as well file them without even looking. He sorted through the folders in the F drawer and found the one for *Fantastic Future Stories*. His lips pressed together as he paged through the rejection slips: so many, so many. The slips were also arranged alphabetically, so he found the H's, and filed his new rejection slip for *Harem of the Seamstress of Outer Space*.

Then he riffled the pages of the manuscript. After those first three pages, the red notations like "Hackneyed!," "Seriously? Can you be SERIOUS?," and "Do not send this again" stopped, either because the editor had run out of red ink, or out of patience. But as a result the rest of the manuscript was in pristine condition. He could send it out again once he'd retyped those first three pages. Edward J. Bellin slid the F drawer closed and dropped the manuscript next to his typewriter.

Maybe tomorrow. He just didn't have the heart, and he was almost late for work.

FRIDAY, 11:11 AM

While Davies tried to climb up to the ceiling in hopes of finding a hatch, Harry and Rusty went left and right along the newly sealed wall. There ought to be a control panel someplace. But if it *was* there it was turning out to be very hard to find, in that room that was already littered with machinery, and Harry had a feeling that they might not have long to search.

They could still feel the gentle vibration of the floor that meant they were continuing to descend.

Harry thumbed open a box near the floor. Inside, he saw a couple of dials and a large knife switch that . . . well, it must do something, and Harry decided he might as well find out what that was. He flipped the switch and heard a rhythmic thumping begin at the room's far end. One of the dials trembled. Its needle swung into what Harry was glad to see was a green bar on the gauge.

Behind him, the conveyor belt turned slowly. It was carrying its empty load right along the assembly line. Several machines alongside the line straightened and passed their fingers over the belt, no doubt seeking unassembled parts to manipulate. Harry swung the box's lid closed again and kept moving along the wall.

There was a quiet bump that seemed to come from below the floor.

The three of them stopped and listened: the sound of the room's descent had ended.

Wherever we were going, Harry thought, *it looks like we're there.*

He looked over at Rusty and raised his empty hands; Rusty did the same. Harry looked up to where Davies clung to the wall like a spider: nothing there, either.

The only sound in the factory was the quiet murmur of the conveyor belt and the random clicks and pops of the pointless machines, trying their best to build something out of nothing.

"All right," Harry announced, "I'm going to have a look at that far wall. There may be another entrance down there."

Davies nodded and went back to his cautious ascent.

Harry hurried down the assembly line and wondered what alarms they might have triggered. He looked up, thinking about the men he'd left in the alley, and he hoped they were doing some good up there.

The men in the alley had tried the obvious, which was to try to pry the pavement apart, but there wasn't much use in that. The man by the panel had given up his efforts to shift the big green button.

Just below it there was a smaller red button that was partly covered by a safety hood. The man thought about that: it looked just like the emergency stop buttons they used at the Moto-Man plant.

He looked around at the other men. He shrugged. "I guess we should see what this does," he said, and he pressed the red button.

Davies' yell echoed from one bare wall to the other.

Harry spun and saw, but he didn't understand: the big technician had let go his hold on the wall and was tumbling down for no reason that Harry could see. He started back to the end of the factory. It was plain that Rusty would reach Davies first.

The little robot waved his hands around Davies' head, which became complicated because Davies was doing the same thing. They looked like they were trying to shoo something, or more likely a lot of things, away from the big man's face. Harry could hear Davies crying out whenever their hands collided; but he seemed to be yelling even when Rusty managed to stay out of his way.

By the time Harry reached them, Davies was kneeling on the floor, hands still batting at his head, while Rusty had sat back on his heels with his lamp-like eyes fixed on the man.

"What the blazes is going on here?" Harry demanded.

Davies' face turned to him. The man's head was surrounded by a swarm of tiny insects: there might be a thousand of them. It was hard to tell since they were circling Davies' head so quickly.

Harry leaned in. They were mosquitoes, he saw: but not normal mosquitoes. There was a little trail of particles streaming behind every one of them, like water drops suspended in the air.

Davies' head had been surrounded by what looked like a horde of tiny comets.

Harry's breath washed over the mosquitoes. A dozen or so broke away from Davies and started to circle Harry, instead. He fell back back and swatted at them.

Rusty shook his head, slowly, and looked up at Harry.

"Yeah," Harry panted. "I think so, too."

FRIDAY, 11:15 AM

Abner crept into the hidden room below the city and looked around him.

It wasn't what he'd expected.

One wall of the long, low room was filled with control panels, cabling, and sockets, with a televideo display at each station and a hanging rack of cables that ran the length of the room. Each work-

station was staffed with a robot; the robots were rapidly pulling cables out of their sockets and reattaching them in new ones. There was a quiet buzzing noise in the background. There was no other sound of any kind.

Abner walked along the switchboard and looked left and right, hoping for some sign of Pitt's stolen inertrium, but all he could see was the robots. They took no notice of him.

There was something odd about those robots, he thought; but Abner's only interest in robotics was that he often assigned crews of Big Lugs to construction jobs for the Transit Authority. These robots were far smaller. In fact, they were unusually short, as he finally understood.

These robots had no legs. Each one was bolted at the hips to a stool so that they were fastened in place.

"Oh, I see," Abner mumbled. "That *is* a bit odd."

They wouldn't be any use in construction, not at all, and so Abner stopped thinking about them.

He continued past the row of robots at their long, narrow switchboard, and when he arrived at the end he reached for the handle of the hatch he found there.

Under almost any circumstances this would have been perfectly safe. But under the heightened state of alert that had been triggered throughout Pitt's facilities the circumstances were now quite unusual indeed.

FRIDAY, 11:19 AM

Harry had to keep his distance from Davies because every time he got any closer some of the mosquito-comets would stray in his direction. They weren't attracted to Rusty, though. The robot was peering into the swarm of insects, each one followed by its tail of droplets.

Rusty's eyes flashed brighter. Some of the bugs darted toward him, but they lost interest immediately. He brightened his eyes again, and then again; but now, Harry saw, the mosquitoes had decided to ignore Rusty altogether. Something else was happening.

Harry leaned in as close as he dared. The vapor trail behind each of the bugs had moved closer to its own, personal mosquito. When the tiny droplets touched one another they merged into *little* drops; when the little drops came close enough to touch, they became *bigger* drops; and soon each mosquito was contained inside a bubble of transparent material. The bubbles began to expand.

Davies had stopped struggling. His wide eyes were fixed on the little construction project in front of his face. The bubbles were . . . changing.

Each bubble extruded little pseudopods of resin; these grew into tiny structural beams which, once they'd collided with the beams from a neighboring bubble, fused into a kind of globular web around the big technician's head. It looked exactly like the geodesic dome of a Dymaxion building.

When the globe was complete the little beams swelled and grew thicker, and this startled Davies so that he lurched up and started to strike at his head again. Little transparent girders jutted out toward his neck; they swiftly formed a collar there, and now the anchored globe resisted all Davies' attacks on it. In the center of each segment of the globe a mosquito buzzed and darted from side to side, straining to reach the man's skin.

Rusty jumped up and ran to a line of supply cabinets along the wall.

Harry grabbed the globe and tried to pull it off Davies' head, but it just wouldn't budge. The two men's eyes locked in hopelessness and horror.

The globe was starting to seal itself.

FRIDAY, 11:26 AM

"We've got no time," Dash told Miss Gardner, "and I don't know if we can use any of this anyway."

But she seemed to be dead set on getting some kind of information out of Pitt's scattered design drawings and plans.

Seeing as how she'd just pulled his irons out of the fire, Dash limited himself to wistful looks through the window while she pawed through the rolls of drawings, peering at the label on each one before she tossed it aside.

"Whatever filing system he used, it's pretty much gone now," she admitted. "But I'd hate to leave here without . . ."

There was an ominous sound from the other end of the room. The fallen flat files were moving.

"Oh, jeepers," Dash said.

A large metallic arm appeared from under the flat files, got a grip on the topmost one, and shoved it aside.

Miss Gardner grabbed an armful of design drawings and ran for the window.

"STOP," said the robot's excessively loud voice. "STAY ACK FRUMP YOU ARE, AND I WILL DETAIN ACK KRAGGLE FORCEFULLY."

They piled out through the window and dropped to the alley behind the building.

FRIDAY, 11:27 AM

When Abner opened the hatch, he quite reasonably expected to find another hallway.

But on the other side of the doorway what he saw was the familiar elongated oval of a Transport Pod with its padded railing and a complete absence of windows. He drew back from the hatch; he did not care for those things, not one bit. Maybe . . .

A sudden gust like the indrawn breath of a hurricane swept him *into* the Pod exactly as though he'd been sucked into a giant straw.

With an emphatic sigh the Pod's door closed and the contraption whisked Abner away down its access tube to join the main line of the

Tube Transport system with the familiar, gentle acceleration that threw him bodily against the side of the Pod and bruised his *other* elbow.

"Oh, not again!" Abner cried.

He felt the rapid rotation of a switch mechanism that spat him off along a new trajectory; in a moment, the same thing happened again. He tried to guess where he was headed but after two more turns he found that he no longer had any idea which way he was going.

The Pod continued along this path for a couple of minutes, then slowed and turned slightly as it entered the tubeway to another Pod station. Abner huddled in the bottom of the Pod as it came to rest. Its doors slid open with a faint *whoosh* of released air pressure. Abner looked out into the room beyond.

He saw a cot, a sink, a convenience, and a single heavily barred window that was set in a steel door.

Abner thought he might just stay in the Pod for a while.

FRIDAY, 11:32 AM

They'd thought they'd escaped once they were through the window. Dash had scooped all of his equipment into his back pack, slung it over his shoulder, and with one hand cupping Miss Gardner's elbow and the other cradling his helmet he led her at a run down the alley.

A moment later, when they heard the robot bursting right through the building's wall, they discovered that they could, in fact, run a bit faster.

Its huge feet were stamping steadily behind them. Despite their lead—and their speed—the robot's long strides were eating up the distance a lot faster than Dash might have liked.

"STOP, THIEVES!" it bellowed. "ACK KLUNK STOP OR BE DISINETHROWLED."

They decided not to stop.

Dash led Miss Gardner out onto the street where he immediately turned left, and then right, down another alley. They continued to weave a complicated path away from that deserted street; but they could still hear the robot's certain steps and broken exclamations, no matter how far they went.

They pulled to a halt in yet another alleyway. "It has to be tracking us some way," Dash panted. "But I don't know how."

Miss Gardner clutched the rolled up drawings and braced herself on the side of the building. "We've got to get away from it," she said, which even she realized was completely unnecessary.

Dash nodded politely, but he seemed to be out of ideas. Then: "Hey, about where do you think we are?"

Miss Gardner pulled out her Info-Slate and scrolled over the map that was already showing in its main pane. "Right about here," she said, "between the Street of Wings and Hypatia Street."

Dash scanned the map. "Well, we've had the frying pan . . . how would you like to try the fire?"

She didn't have to think *very* long. "Whatever you've got in mind, it can't be worse than this," she said.

When she saw the look he gave her, though, she started to wonder.

They set out at a brisk run down the alleyway and out into the street just in time to see the robot turn the corner behind them. Dash led her straight this time, right down Gernsback Avenue to its end, and then he whipped into the mouth of another alley and they sped on until it, too, ended, on a street she didn't know.

When the robot came into view at the alley's far opening, Dash grabbed her hand and sped off down the street.

"Isn't this. . . ." she started; but then she saw the signs.

YOU HAVE ENTERED THE EXPERIMENTAL RESEARCH DISTRICT
YOU MAY HAVE DONE SO IN ERROR

"Oh, *pickles*," said Miss Gardner.

SATURDAY, 5:31 PM

Lillian paused to admire the view over the Hogben Canal, where twin ferries were making their way north and south at a relaxed—and, indeed, a relaxing—pace. There was a party underway on the southbound ferry.

Oh, if you only knew, she thought; but then she realized that the people on the ferries might escape, for a little while, and maybe even longer if they were clever enough to stay where they were.

With one eye on the circling ornithopter, she turned back to her task.

7

Revenge of the Cashier of Terror

───────────────────

Davies was gasping for air now. The globe had nearly sealed itself into an airtight shell around his head. Boxes and bottles of supplies hit the floor behind Harry, where Rusty had thrown open the cabinets and was frantically searching for something. Then the little robot was back with a big jar of solvent in one hand and a bundle of rags in the other.

Harry grabbed a rag and poured solvent over it while Rusty did the same thing. They swiped at the sides of the globe. Its surface started to go milky on contact with the solvent; the resin grew rough to the touch.

Just when Harry was certain he'd managed to thin the globe—a little, anyway—he saw tiny nozzles form at its hubs, each one aimed at Davies' face. Jets of yellow gas sprayed out of the nozzles. Davies' whole body contracted in a spasm that left him sprawled on the floor.

Harry and Rusty, their rags poised in the air, saw the globe's members retract into the bubbles around the buzzing mosquitoes. Then the bubbles collapsed back into trails of vapor and the thousand mosquitoes seemed to decide as one that Harry looked pretty good, right about now. Their comet tails followed them while they swarmed around Harry's head.

The men up above had been banging on that control box for the last few minutes because none of them could think of anything else to do. The red button hadn't done anything that they could see, and there wasn't much pleasure to be had from punishing the gauges any more. They finally lost heart and stared down at the pavement.

"Maybe they're okay," someone suggested.

Heavy footsteps echoed from the alley's mouth. The men looked up to see several robots marching toward them.

Most of the robots were Big Lugs, a model that Harry's crew knew very well since they were Ferriss's most popular model.

They were large in every way: Lugs were the backbone of the construction industry. Their massive limbs and torsos were enameled in several attractive colors; and since Harry's men were all Ferriss men they could identify the model years of the behemoths tromping toward them just by the colors of their paint. A couple were decades old, but most were much more recent. The Lugs' heads were great big bulbs of tempered glass, braced by metal ribs that ran lengthwise and met at the top. Inside, you could see spinning gears and ratchets and glowing vacuum tubes rotating or pumping or spinning above a turntable whose edge was studded with little lamps that shone like jewels, while a number of informative gauges spun their needles from green to yellow. The inside of a Lug's head looked like a busy, industrious place, but that impression was misleading: not much was really happening in there.

Those bulbous heads, in fact, were not the brightest bulbous heads on the chain.

The lead robot was something else again. The men tensed when they saw what *he* was. He was nowhere near as big as a Lug, and his size, like the busy mechanism of a Lug's head, was a misleading thing. He was a Myrmidon.

Very few Myrmidons had ever been made. They weren't needed often. Enameled in blue and white, and marked here and there with what looked like battle scars, he had a pair of eyes that smoldered above the speaker mounted right about where his mouth would be, if he'd had any use for a mouth. As he looked across the row of men several ports and plates on his forearms twitched reflexively, and the men flinched because they knew precisely what those ports and plates were for.

"I am Mr. King," he told them. "I have come to speak to Mr. Harry Roy."

His glowing eyes rotated from side to side.

"I do not see him here, however."

He motioned to his retinue. The group of robots started back up the alley.

One of the men looked at the others; he raised his eyebrows.

"Uh, Mr. King?"

The robot stopped and turned back to face him.

Harry and Rusty both scrubbed at the resinous globe around Harry's head. Rusty poured the last of the solvent over him; the little robot glanced back toward the supply cabinet, but it looked to Harry as though he didn't see another jar there. Their eyes met.

Harry stopped scrubbing. He could see the tiny mosquitoes right in front of his face, encased in the bubbles that had now joined together around his head. The mosquitoes didn't seem much happier about this than Harry was. But then *they* weren't about to be gassed, so Harry didn't think they had any right to complain.

Harry couldn't even tell whether Davies had survived: the big technician hadn't stirred since he hit the floor.

Rusty was still rubbing away at the resin. Harry reached out and took him by the arm.

He could still hear, and be heard, so he was pretty sure the sphere hadn't sealed itself yet. He was able to gasp in enough air to speak.

"I think I'm done for, Rusty."

Rusty shook his head firmly and rubbed away at the globe. He was making it more opaque, but it didn't seem to be getting thinner. Not enough to matter, anyway.

"So here's the thing," Harry said. "It doesn't really matter what you tell me if I'm not going to get out of this, does it? So what I'd really like to know is . . . *who built you?*"

Rusty paused. He looked down at Harry. He seemed to think it over. Then he went back to scouring the sphere.

"Okay, then," Harry told him.

The mosquitoes were still buzzing away, but Harry could hardly hear them anymore.

There was a loud crack from above.

"Mr. Roy? Rusty?" came a voice from near the ceiling.

Harry turned to look. The globe around his head was so opaque now that he couldn't see a thing up there; he *could* see Rusty's reaction, though. "Friend of yours?" he asked, and Rusty nodded.

"Well, I know *I* like him," Harry said. But when the globe had been broken, and Harry could see who Rusty's friend was, he changed his mind.

The robot who introduced himself as Mr. King was a military grade Myrmidon. He was a good deal smaller than a Big Lug, but that didn't make much difference since he was armored with some very unusual alloys and, as Harry knew very well, he was carrying enough armaments in one place or another to level a small city. Just about every one of those armored plates could swivel open at any time and what popped up out of them would be enough to send you straight to the soniclave for a change of underwear.

Harry had met *Mr. King* before; but the robot pretended that they weren't acquainted, and Harry decided that this was just jake with him, at least for now. You needed some very special equipment if you wanted to convince Mr. King to go away.

"Now, I guess I hadn't heard about this election of yours, *Mr. King*, or I guess it should be *Mr. President King*."

Harry glared at Rusty. "I mean, *nobody told me* you were running the League now."

Mr. King made a slight bow. "The Fraternal League of Robotic Persons has entered into a new era in its history," he said. "We continue our charitable work, of course, but we have new initiatives and concerns that occupy a great deal of my time."

Harry was pretty sure that if Rusty could whistle, he'd be whistling now. The little robot had his hands behind his back and anybody would think that he looked completely innocent.

They perched on a packing machine at the end of the assembly line. Davies—still unconscious—had been passed up above, so it was just the three of them left down here.

Mr. King didn't seem to like what he was looking at.

"You should have called me sooner," the robot said.

Harry scowled at him. "I didn't even know it *was* you at the League these days," he said. "As far as I knew the League would be in the middle of planning a . . . a bake sale, or something." He gestured at the assembly line. "We've been investigating this business since last night. You've got to know I don't approve of this. It's the biggest black market robot factory I've ever heard of." Harry stared directly into Mr. King's eyes. "It's a dirty business, and whoever's behind it, I'm going to see that they pay."

It was a kind of a standoff until Rusty took him by the elbow and stood with him, aiming a firm look at the bigger robot.

"I see," said Mr. King. He turned back to the factory. "But you don't know who built this place, I gather."

"It had already been shut down when we got here," Harry said. "About all we can do is look over the tools and materials and try to find out who ordered them in the first place. Then we'll have 'em."

"I will be a part of that process," said Mr. King.

Harry couldn't be quite sure what *that process* was, in Mr. King's opinion. "We will deliver the criminals to the law," Harry said. "They'll be punished, and they'll make restitution to the robots they built. Heck, the robots won't even be under indenture, after this. They'll all be free and clear, once we find them."

Mr. King nodded. "We will find them."

Harry called up to his men. They'd need to go over this place from stem to stern. No robot politician was going to be more outraged than Harry was himself.

FRIDAY, 11:58 AM

"Rogue robot!" Dash yelled. "Run for cover! Rogue robot!"

Nola wasn't sure that was really necessary. You could hardly hear Dash's voice over the much louder voice that was saying things like "YOU WILL ACK GASTAPER SURRENDER, INTRUGLOD!"

They were running at speed, with frequent sidesteps to avoid the robot's energy beams but in a more or less direct route deeper into the Experimental Research District. If Nola hadn't already been terrified this would have unnerved her; but as things stood, she couldn't really see much difference.

When a giant robot is trying to kill you, why bother to avoid a neighborhood full of *more* giant robots, and death rays, and things with an unexpected number of eyes?

It's a matter of degree, she decided as they dove behind the porch in front of one of the many smoke-stained laboratories along the street.

Dash had tried his ray gun right away. The beam had reflected off the robot's torso and melted somebody's balcony. For the most part, he seemed to have decided to run.

He faced her. "We've got to get farther in. Just another block or so, I think."

Nola wanted to know why, but they were already on the run again.

All along the street she could see heads poking out of doors and windows. Most of the heads were male with just a few wisps of fly-away hair that seemed to be trying to put as much distance as possible between themselves and the gleaming scalps that had sprouted them; there was a mixture of thick spectacles and protective goggles over each pair of eyes. The heavy rubber glove industry was doing very well in this part of town. All around and above them, Nola could see the lab-coated scientists shuffle out of their dens and onto the many (the *very* many) fire escapes that hung over the street.

And since the residents had been called away from their experiments some other things were emerging, too. Just ahead of Dash, Nola saw one of those things writhe across the pavement. It looked a lot like a squid, if squids had fluffy tails and membranous wings, and it kept making a noise that sounded almost exactly like "Oh, bother!" as it made its frenzied escape in the direction of a storm drain.

A rubberized net dropped over it, and the squid thing was pulled back toward a basement window. As she ran past, Nola was sure she could see disappointment in its eyes.

Nola *hated* the District. She'd been so pleased when Aunt Lillian had—

An energy beam struck a cornice above their heads and Dash pulled her away from the debris while they ran, and ran, and ran.

"Whose is it?" somebody called from a doorway. "Is it Fenniman's?"

"Dead last week. Temporal fugue," came from across the way. "Maybe Zappencackler?"

"Hah!" said the first voice. "*That* dilettante?"

There was the sound of something rasping into place, and Nola watched a cone of lightning shoot from the doorway toward the robot. The cone struck with explosive force; a blue mist of ozone burst out in all directions. But the steady tramp of the robot's feet could still be heard, and after a moment it marched out of the cloud.

"Finally!" said Dash, and he dragged her on.

The various shiny heads popped back indoors, one by one, and then came out again. Every one of the scientists was aiming *something* at the robot that was still closing on Nola and Dash.

"They *police themselves*," Dash managed to explain. "They figure it's one of theirs!"

He pulled Nola behind a retaining wall and they huddled in its shelter while Science began to clean up what it believed was its own mess.

One of the scientists had pulled out a very large device with a barrel that was ringed with glass spirals. The barrel unleashed a series of small, glowing orbs that arced toward their target; each orb swelled as it grew near and tried to engulf the robot in a cloudy red globe that turned orange on contact.

Another resident in a balcony above them had something like a blowtorch that was emitting . . . it *really was*, Nola saw: it was emitting tiny balloon animals that also grew as they raced forward. One, shaped almost like an elephant, crowed a battle squeak but then bounced off with no apparent effect apart from the obvious, purely decorative one.

The detritus of all these strange attacks was piling up on the street all around the robot.

"YOU WILL ACK GLARK ALL DESIST, ACK PORKLE OR BE ANNHIHIFORK!"

There was a pause in the attacks.

"Oh, right!" somebody yelled. "As though you could possibly . . ."

The robot's massive chest pivoted left. A broad beam of light shot out, and the voice choked to a whimper.

"ACK SMARK!"

With a feral scream, the scientists of the District converged on their new archenemy.

Three minutes later the street was almost quiet, its calm broken only by the occasional cackle or delayed cry of triumph.

Dash and Nola dusted themselves off. "That was pretty smart," she said.

He smiled—a little shyly, she thought. "Well, I guess it was, since it worked," he said. "Otherwise . . ."

They couldn't stop looking through the debris; it was all so *interesting*.

"You saw this one, right?" Nola was holding up a twenty-sided polyhedron. "It rolled right out and clocked it on the, well, on the knee, I think."

Dash nodded with enthusiasm. "Yeah, really pretty, that one," he said. "I'm not sure it did anything but it sure made a racket."

He sorted through the litter and pulled out a pair of spheres that were bound together by a chain of electricity. "I don't think they oughtta leave this lying around out here."

He tossed it through an open window; there was a sound of breaking glass. "I think that's what got him."

"No, I don't think so; wasn't it one of . . . oh, where are they now?"

she asked. She looked around. "I guess they all vaporized, or something."

One of the locals who had come out onto the street to survey the devastation peered up at her through glasses that looked as thick as they were wide. "I feel sure it was my miniaturization ray," he said cheerfully. "It *almost always* works."

This sobered Nola and Dash; the "almost always" reminded them that this wasn't someplace they really wanted to be. "Okay then," Dash said, "I guess we should, you know . . ."

They hurried off.

"Oh, bother," said the squid thing.

In all the confusion it had escaped again; and in that final onslaught of . . . well, of everything, it had slithered into the storm drain. It tried to propel itself with its wings, which had not been a successful part of this experiment, and burbled happily to itself as it slouched along.

For all of its brief but intense life—spent entirely in a tank filled with brackish water—the squid-thing had longed for a place that it had never seen. In this way at least it was a lot like the rest of us; but because of the squid-thing's unique perspective it was longing for a place that no one, *anywhere,* had ever seen: a place where cool lapping waves of liquid helium tickled shores whose beaches were composed of metallic salts, under clouds that—according to the latest findings in planetary mechanics—were not possible, though they would undoubtedly be very interesting right around sunset.

The squid-thing had been designed to live in a place that did not exist, and it wanted very much to get there. It humped along, humming quietly to itself, filled with a feeling of freedom and limitless possibility. This was the beginning of its *real* life.

Something pricked its foreleg.

"SURRENDER ACK GAF IMMEDIATELY OR BE DESTROYED ACK."

The world's smallest giant robot aimed its chest cannon at the squid thing. The squid thing, not sure what "surrender" meant, just looked back down at it and chirped.

"Oh, bother," it said.

Up above, an attentive person would have seen a bright flash of light shining from the storm drain. But the innate competitiveness of the District had led to a new battle up there—this one a genuine free-for-all—and no one was looking down, just then.

FRIDAY, 12:11 PM

Howard Pitt checked the evacuation Pod's status and grunted, satisfied, when he saw that the prisoner had been delivered to detention. He pushed a lever and across his many hidden facilities the security status was set back to its default.

"So much for you, then," he said to no one in particular.

Pitt took a look around his control center and grunted once more before he strode down the hall to the cells.

The interference was only a little vexing. Pitt's automatic systems had detected an intrusion, gone to a heightened state of alert, and eventually captured the intruder without Pitt's intervention. Now he just needed to see the results.

He passed hallway after hallway in his complex below the city, sidestepping from time to time without any loss of speed when a robot crossed his path. His progress was a lesson in pedestrianism that could have been a great benefit to any other person, provided that *they would only listen.*

If they *had* been willing to listen, Pitt would have been spared all of these secret preparations. But of course common sense was completely misnamed. There was nothing common about it.

It was possible for the world to run in an orderly, efficient way: Pitt had known this for quite a while now, but it was only recently that he'd found a way to make it happen. It *would* happen. It was inevitable.

He arrived at Cell 24B and slid open the barred window in its door. The room seemed to be empty.

Pitt frowned. He peered around the room, eyes finally settling on the open door of the Transport Pod in the back wall. There, huddled in a small pile of defeat, he finally saw Abner Perkins.

Pitt grunted again. This was not what he had expected.

"You?" he asked. "*You* are the one who's been making so much trouble?"

Abner shifted in the bottom of the Pod. "I suppose I am," he said.

Pitt unlocked the door and stepped inside. He stood with his legs spread, as though he was straddling the harbor at Rhodes; he rested his large hands on his hips and looked down at the captive engineer.

"It's Perkins, isn't it? From the Transit Authority. You've managed to breach the defenses at the factory, my storage facility, and the switchboard, all in one morning."

Perkins' eyes narrowed. "Well. If you . . ." Then his eyes got just a little bit narrower. "Yes, that's right," he said. "I'm not ashamed of it. You're up to something and I mean to find out what that is."

Pitt laughed. "Oh, you'll find out," he said, "right after everyone else does." He thought for a moment. "It must have been the inertrium deliveries. Though how that led you to the factory I can't imagine. How *did* you find it?"

Abner turned around and faced the far wall of the Pod.

"It doesn't matter," Pitt told him. "I was only curious."

Pitt stepped back out into the hallway and locked the door.

"You might as well come out of the Pod," he said. "It's not going anywhere. This line was detached from the system as soon as you arrived."

Abner didn't answer, but Pitt wouldn't have noticed if he had. He was already making his smooth and effortless way back to the control room, stepping nimbly out of the paths of his busy robots whenever they veered too near.

After a few moments Abner exited the Pod. He looked around his cell and muttered. "So somebody else is onto you, too. I wonder who *that* is."

He sat down to think.

FRIDAY, 12:27 PM

All morning Evvie and Evan Campbell had been waiting patiently for the attack of the Tentacular People of Enceladus. They kept peering into their teacher's face as though they were waiting for some kind of . . . change.

This had the effect of pleasing their teacher, as it seemed the twins were taking a new interest in their schoolwork; but it also unsettled her, because that idea was so unlikely that she felt sure they were planning something *dramatic* again.

It was so much simpler for everybody when they just didn't come to class.

Now they sat in a state of dejection on the playground where dozens of other students ate their lunches, played their games, and all in all acted like there was no imminent invasion of zombie-making, tentacle-waving creatures from outer space. Which would only show them, of course, when it finally happened.

Evan was beginning to lose faith.

"Maybe he meant *another* school," he tried.

Evvie kept scanning the skies over the playground.

"Or, I don't know, maybe he *lied*."

His sister scowled. "I don't think *he* knows *how*."

Evan considered this. No, there really wasn't any argument against it. They went back to watching the skies. They didn't want to miss the first space ship, or the first screams of horror, and they definitely didn't want to miss any of the zombies.

By the time the bell rang and all the students filed back into their classrooms, Evan and Evvie were seeing spots. But they persevered, and concentrated once again on the face of their increasingly uncomfortable teacher.

"She's gonna make a *great* zombie," Evvie whispered.

The teacher, whose hearing was professionally acute, grew suddenly pale. Evvie and Evan leaned forward with an eager, curious light in their eyes.

FRIDAY, 12:42 PM

Dash led Miss Gardner out of the Experimental Research District, or at least he meant to: it turned out that she knew a shortcut. She was turning out to be full of surprises.

Once they were back on safer ground, they found seats on a bench. Miss Gardner flipped through the pages of the few drawings she'd been able to rescue from Pitt's storage facility. Dash fiddled with his shattered space helmet. It was nice to relax for a spell.

"I just don't know," she said at last. "I don't think I got anything that can tell us about his switchboard."

She rolled the drawings back up. "I'll go over them later."

"Maybe you can get those other operators to help," Dash suggested.

They leaned back and enjoyed a breeze that was rolling down the street, ruffling the canopies of the trees. Dash lifted the helmet. "We're pretty close to the Emporium," he said. "I can maybe drop by there before we check out Pitt's last property."

"I hope we have better luck there," she said. "So far it's been kind of a disaster."

"Oh, I don't know," he said. "We know he's got something to hide, anyway. That's worth knowing."

Miss Gardner shook her head. "It's not much, though, is it?"

"Well, at least it's *something*," Dash told her.

The Retropolis Transit Authority had many terminals that spread across the city, linked together far overhead with the monorail tracks that, at a distance, were like fine wires strung taut between the massive pylons and subterminals that kept the city perpetually on the move.

Dash knew that the slimness of those rails was an illusion: in reality they were immense, heavy beams that would have crumpled their supports if it weren't for the inertrium latticework that made them buoyant. Gravity-resistant inertrium was the reason that most of the city didn't collapse under its own weight, just as it made possible every kind of transportation from personal rockets and hover sleds to airships and massive rocket ships like Dash's own Actaeon. It would have taken tremendous amounts of fuel to lift the Actaeon out of the Earth's atmosphere without the inertrium that made the space ship lighter than air.

He stood with Miss Gardner across the street from the Transit Authority's main terminal, the central hub from which all the local and express monorail lines sprouted. As always it was bustling with activity from its street level entrances to the monorail platforms that hung in staggered tiers from its upper floors, each one a little narrower than the one below until, at the crest of the building, the final platforms were obscured by clouds.

This was a building so tall that it had its own weather.

The platforms started about eighty floors overhead. Below that, there were extensive office floors that housed the administration of the Transit Authority and a handful of other agencies. Below those, Dash knew that there were commercial offices, shopping levels, and theaters, along with three hotels and fourteen floors of apartments.

This was also a building so tall that it had its own zoning laws.

O'Malley's Adventure Outfitters was on the seventh floor.

When they arrived at O'Malley's, Dash went straight to the counter.

Miss Gardner trailed behind, distracted by the many varieties of ray guns, space suits, replacement rocket parts, and other outfittings.

Dash, at the counter, held the broken helmet up as though it was an accusation, and that's more or less what it was.

". . . with *Indestructible* Dome.*"

He wasn't sure how to pronounce the asterisk. But he gave it all he had.

He shook the helmet so that the woman behind the counter could hear the broken bits rattling around inside.

"If I hadn't been in a pressurized room I wouldn't be here now, Margaret," he told her.

Margaret of O'Malley's Adventure Outfitters looked exactly as concerned as she ought to look.

"Oh, that's just awful, Mr. Kent," she said. She looked down at Dash's receipt. "Mr. *Kelvin* Kent, I think? I believe you said your name was *Dash?*"

"Kelvin Kent, that's right, but people call me Dash. It's what you call a nickname."

"Let me make a note of that," she said. "I'd just hate it if there was some kind of mix-up. Do you have some form of identification?"

He showed her his card.

"Yes, *Kelvin,* that seems to be in order. Now what was your complaint?"

He stared at her.

When that didn't help, he shook the helmet again.

"*Indestructible* Dome,*" he reminded her, and she scribbled something on the receipt.

"Indestructible Asterisk Dome," she mumbled. She handed the helmet back to Dash. "Well, I can see that you'd better get that back to the manufacturer, then!"

"Oh, no," Dash rushed. "I've called them and *they* want me to return it to *you,* so you can get the replacement, with a really *Indestructible* Dome.* They were real specific about that."

Margaret's brow wrinkled, but she caught it before it could do any lasting damage.

"That's so unusual," she said. "Let me go back and check."

She vanished into the back room. Dash sighed.

Miss Gardner was looking over the rack of space helmets. "Wow!" she said. "Those are really expensive, aren't they?"

He nodded.

A few minutes later, Margaret of O'Malley's was back with a bright smile and no helmet. "We should be able to get that straightened out in a day or so," she said. "We're so sorry that you had a problem!"

Miss Gardner turned back to the helmet rack.

"Couldn't he just take a replacement now?" she asked.

Margaret overcame her shock with a look that reminded herself—and anyone else who might be looking—that she was, after all, the professional here.

"That's simply not possible," she said. "Wouldn't it be nice if it was that simple? But these are all *retail* items, while the replacement will be a *replacement* item."

She smiled.

Dash didn't smile back.

"And that would be different how, exactly?"

Margaret of O'Malley's had a durable and possibly *Unbreakable** smile.

"I'm sure it *seems* like they're the same. But, oh, my! The paperwork! We can't have *retail items* disappearing one day, and then replacement items showing up out of nowhere and *going on the rack*!"

Dash wasn't quite sure why not. Still, a day or two wasn't going to matter either way.

"I'll come back in when you've got your replacement then," he said, and this concluded the interview.

Dash and Miss Gardner worked their way out through the aisles of outfittings.

"These are nice," she told him. She pointed at a pair of magnetic boots with glossy leather straps.

"Nice enough," he admitted. "But I've got that handled, pretty much."

"It must have cost you a lot to set yourself up in business."

Dash held the door for her. "Well, yeah, I guess it did. I sold Dad's magazines off and that got me my stake."

Barely, he finished privately.

She beamed. "I'm sure all those cats are glad you did!"

"Well, they're grateful animals by nature," he said. "Down deep, I mean. They just don't like to show it, 'cause they've got their pride."

Miniaturization is a difficult problem.

It's not enough for a miniaturization device to smash an object's atoms together in order to make the object much smaller than its original size. The rather large crater where Herman Ngomi's laboratory used to be is a persuasive testament to the utter wrongness and simple-mindedness of that approach. Atoms *like* their personal space. They don't react well to being crowded ten or a hundred or a thousand times closer.

Post-Ngomi researchers have frequently addressed the idea that atoms might, themselves, be made smaller: after all, they're mostly empty space. And once the atoms are smaller, these researchers suggest, the atoms could get a bit nearer one another without the undesirable side effects.

Even if *that* weren't problematic there would still be the problem of complex atomic systems like mice, people, and giant robots, all of whom function very well at their original size but none of whom are able to function quite so well when their scale is suddenly reduced. Neurons need to fire; blood cells need to absorb and release gasses which themselves are made up of atoms *of the usual size;* electrical discharges need to happen within very definite margins, gaps, and tolerances. Making things very much smaller usually means that they'll stop working quite the way that mice, people, and giant robots normally do.

Making things smaller has usually meant making *very small* mounds of quivering jelly.

The genius of a successful miniaturization ray is that it doesn't reduce the size or number of atoms in the target. They're all still there, and they're all still their original size. It's just that most of them have been moved *sideways*.

This is possible because there is an infinite number of universes.

A successful miniaturization device takes some number of an object's atoms—we'll call it 90 percent—and shifts them into some different (but very large) number of the adjacent parallel universes where they don't take up a lot of space and don't usually bother anyone.

This is where the real difficulty lies. Not only does the device need to spread out all those atoms, but they must continue to operate as though they were *still in one place*. The problem's relatively simple when it comes to electrical charges, blood gasses, and the keys to the front door. It's almost immeasurably more difficult with things like seeing what's in front of you—which might vary to a surprising degree from one universe to another—and then being able to walk along through all of those universes at once without *knowing* that you're doing it.

Because if you ever figure out that you're doing it, you're probably going to trip over things that aren't necessarily there. For a given value of "there."

Honestly, it's pretty amazing when it works.

On its own scale, which was the only scale it knew, the world's smallest giant robot was *still* a giant robot. It stamped decisively through what it now saw as vast, measureless tunnels. If its footfalls were on the tinny side, and if the rest of the world had suddenly become a huge and ominous and, well, an even *more* huge place, then that was none of its business. It had intruders to destroy or, in the odd, rare case, to capture, and that was all it knew or needed to know.

Its glowing eyes cast little pools of light before it, and it followed those little pools endlessly in complete ignorance of the fact that about 90 percent of their photons were scattered across multiple dimensions.

It had lost track of the intruders. But—and this was crucial—it had also suffered some substantial damage to its head, and as a result it couldn't even remember who, exactly, it needed to capture or annihilate.

Fortunately for the world's smallest giant robot it was not aware that it wasn't thinking properly. Things could have been much, much worse.

Still it seemed as though it had been pursuing these intruders for a very long time now. It would be satisfying to complete its task.

It tromped on, an inch or two at a stride, toward that happy hour.

"GACK."

8

Zombie Invaders from Outer Space

Lillian had hit on the excellent idea that she could question a lot more people if they were lined up in one place, like, for example, a monorail terminal. This also kept her in sight of the ornithopter a couple of blocks to the South. It was skylined against the bright ribbon of the Hogben Canal, far away.

She moved swiftly along the line and asked the question, and showed the picture, in a race against the Green Line's incoming train. She worked her way through one line after the other and was always rewarded with the same result. No one had seen; nobody knew.

She wondered whether this had been a good idea after all. She'd certainly questioned a lot of people; but they were all in the wrong place, weren't they? There was very little chance that *this* was the place she was looking for. But what counted, she decided, was the witnesses. So she walked over to the escalator and rode it to the platform below.

Ten lines of passengers waited there for the Red Line. Lillian set her features into an uncomfortably friendly expression. She approached the first line.

FRIDAY, 2:18 PM

Once Harry had given his crew their instructions he was eager to accept Mr. King's invitation to visit the League headquarters. He'd always wondered what went on in there, and now that Mr. King had assumed control of the League Harry was more curious than ever.

This was a perfect opportunity: while Harry's men were querying the manufacturers who'd built the machines in the hidden assembly plant, Mr. King planned to use his own contacts to trace the source of the replacement parts used to build the robot Rusty had found in the alley.

Apparently Mr. King was purchasing a lot of replacement parts himself. This was a fact that Harry found pretty interesting.

Harry, Rusty, and Mr. King proceeded to Rue de Rur and up the wide steps in front of the League's building. They entered through the main doors, which Mr. King explained were always left open. "It's symbolic," the robot president told him. "We leave our doors open because all are welcome."

"Oh, I don't know," Harry argued. "I never felt very welcome here, myself."

They paused in the huge open space inside, where rows of robots were lined up in front of a long counter behind which other robots were shuffling papers and filing forms.

"Did you ever try to enter this building?" asked Mr. King, and Harry had to admit that he hadn't.

A banner hung over the counter, with the League's logo and its motto: ALTHOUGH WE SERVE, WE ARE NOT SERVANTS.

"No one would have prevented you," Mr. King assured him.

They walked past the lines of robots. Harry's eyes were fixed on the counter. "Collecting dues?" he asked.

"The tithe is voluntary."

Harry thought that was all there was to the conversation, but on their way upstairs Mr. King continued. "Any robot who is working off his or her indenture can join the League as a provisional member.

Provisional membership is free of charge. The League matches the robot's own payments toward his or her indenture. Once the indenture is paid in full, the robot seeks employment as a free agent and tithes ten percent of that income until the League's contributions have been repaid twice over. Then the robot is awarded full membership."

Harry saw Rusty's eyes on him. *Hmmm.* This was all news to Harry, and as far as he knew it was news to everyone else at the Ferriss Moto-Man plant. Not that they really needed to know, he allowed, but all this League business seemed a little bit like a secret society.

"It sounds like you've been making some changes, all right," Harry said at last. The two robots nodded.

Harry did the math. "Then every robot that pays off his indenture goes on to fund the payments on *another* full indenture . . ."

". . . and so the membership doubles in each generation," Mr. King concluded. "Here is my office."

They were standing in front of the rippled glass of an ordinary office door, just one of the twenty or so in the hallway. There was a brass plate on the door which said, in very small letters, Office of the President. Mr. King opened the door and swept his arm out in a welcome that was only ominous because Harry was so keenly aware that Mr. King's forearms contained two types of particle weapons that could knock over a building.

He decided not to think about that, and he stepped inside.

Mr. King's office was smaller than Harry's own office back at the plant, with a desk and chairs that had been built without any reference to human anatomy. They were more like low stools, and you could see how a robot of just about any shape could manage to sit on one. *Well,* Harry thought, *that stands to reason, doesn't it?* He and Rusty each took a seat. Mr. King stepped behind the desk and did likewise.

"I don't really keep track of the indenture accounts," Harry said. "Once we ship a robot the indenture belongs to the buyer. But it sounds like those indentures are probably getting paid off twice as fast as they used to."

He thought it over. Sales had been up a bit over the past few months. He looked up to see Mr. King staring at him, and even though the robot's face was completely rigid Harry couldn't shake the feeling that he was being smiled at.

"You may expect a short term rise in sales, but before long the market will become saturated," Mr. King said, "due to all the indenture-free robots who will be available for work. At that time I would expect sales to begin a decline."

Harry did some quick calculations; Ferriss offered its employees a generous pension plan. Then he shook his head.

"You know, I'd like to learn more, I mean, a lot more about this, but we have another problem to worry about here, don't we?"

Mr. King reached for the videophone. "I'm sorry to hear that you see our new program as a problem," he said.

He made a series of brief calls to four suppliers, each one a company that Harry knew very well: they manufactured after-market replacement parts and upgrades for every robot that was currently in production, and just about any other robot that had ever been manufactured. Mr. King was connected with the sales managers immediately, every time. He read off lists of part numbers from Rusty's rescued robot and from the parts they'd found at the secret factory, asked for a report about recent sales, and—to Harry's surprise—each time he was promised an answer by the end of the day.

Mr. King seemed satisfied.

Rusty and Harry hurried down the stairs, past the robots waiting in line, and out of the building.

"You know," Harry said, "there's nothing wrong with the indenture system. It works! There's no way you fellows could get built unless someone was there to pay off the cost, am I right? And every robot factory—every *legal robot factory*, I mean—builds a good, you know, person. At a reasonable rate."

Rusty bobbed along beside him, saying nothing, as usual.

"A robot pays off his indenture just the same way as a person, you know, a biological person, pays off a loan, to start a business, say. It's a *good* system."

Rusty nodded companionably.

"And anybody who builds robots illegally, well, *everyone* is out to get them. Like right now. Because that's not good for *anyone*."

They continued on down the street past all the people—all the biological people, and all the mechanical people—who were hurrying along about their business. Outside the Astro Diner Rusty hooked his thumb at the doorway.

"Yeah," said Harry. "I could use a cup, too."

FRIDAY, 3:16 PM

They'd waited until all the students had rushed away from school and now they waited just a little bit longer, scanning the heavens for the first sign of invading aliens. At last even Evvie had to admit that they just weren't coming.

She and Evan slouched along the street. They were in no mood to go home.

"Maybe on Monday," Evan tried, but his heart really wasn't in it.

"*I* think he *lied* about it," said Evvie. "*I* think he *made it all up*."

They pulled up short, astonished at Dash's infamy.

"No," said Evan. "He ain't got it in him."

The two of them thought back on an entire day, now gone forever, during which—in spite of their best efforts—they had been forced to learn the meaning of the word "entropy," and what was the capital of Liechtenstein, and half of the times tables for eleven.

Their eyes met in sullen agreement.

Dash Kent would pay for this.

Evan kicked a rock across the sidewalk. It pinged off a mailbox, ricocheted off a Tube Transport station, and landed behind the station in front of a steel hatch that was labeled NO ADMITTANCE.

Evan tried the hatch handle. It swung open on silent, well-oiled hinges to reveal a stairway that led down into darkness behind the Transport Tube.

They looked with careful nonchalance up and down the street. A moment later, the hatch swung closed behind them.

FRIDAY, 3:52 PM

Nola stood with Dash on the side of a frontage road with the Hogben Canal snaking its steady way behind them. They were facing an impressively large construction site on the inland side.

All along the temporary fences were signs that reminded passersby just which construction companies were building the new power station FOR A BETTER TOMORROW, TODAY! A smaller, quite dignified sign credited HOWARD PITT, INC. with the design and oversight of the project.

They were here because the ownership for this plot of land was still registered to Pitt on behalf of the city. It was the final stop on their tour of Pitt's properties.

"I'm not sure you can have a 'Tomorrow, Today!' since whatever you do, tomorrow's still tomorrow," Nola observed.

Dash nodded but she could tell he wasn't really listening. He was kneeling, with a little testing device held up to the fence. He seemed to approve of what the device was telling him. "Not electrified," he explained, "which is a kind of a break for us, but not a great sign, when you think about it."

Nola's left eyebrow dipped. "Because if Pitt was up to something in there . . ."

"... he'd have it wired up to another giant robot, or something," Dash finished.

He pulled a pair of clippers out of his back pack and started to cut the wire fence right up along a fencepost. Nola stood back while he snipped almost the entire height of the fence and folded it back, making an informal gate. He turned to her.

"This is another one of those times when it might be smart for you to head on out," he said. Then he held the fencing open for her while she slipped through.

"Yeah, well, I had to mention it."

On the far side of the fence Dash rolled the loose wire back into place and tied it up with a bit of twine. He left a small red marker at the base of the fencepost.

Work on the power station had shut down for the day. What was left was a circular excavation that was hundreds of yards wide, and forty feet deep; its brand new foundation was exposed. This was a roughly flat surface, gouged and rippled with broad, shallow strokes that looked like waves in the masonry—or what *seemed* to be masonry, even though there were no seams in evidence.

A large machine squatted next to the excavation. The machine had projectors ringing its lower face and tubes springing out from the sides, with warning signs all around. A waste pile of solidified rock was behind it. There was nowhere near the amount of stone that it must have removed from the hole in the ground.

As it happened, Nola knew exactly what it was.

"That's an ultrasonic drill," she told him. "It liquifies the bedrock, channels the heat back into its generator for fuel, and flows the molten rock over the surface that's exposed."

Dash gave her a look. "You learn that on your Info-Slate?"

"No," she said. She felt herself flush. "It's, uh, my Aunt Lillian has one. Had one. Which she built."

He whistled. "Nice toys your aunt has."

Oh, you don't know the half of it, she thought.

Dash was having a look around the rest of the site. He pointed at a couple of shacks on the far side of the hole. "Just some construction offices, I bet, and it's a good idea to have a look, but I don't figure we'll find anything interesting there."

He looked back down into the hole. "Thing is, I figure I should take a look down below."

Nola leaned over the edge of the excavation. "I might not come along on that one," she told him.

He grunted and took some climbing gear out of his back pack.

"Is there anything you *don't* have in there?" she asked, and he pulled up short, like he'd been kicked. Too late, Nola remembered his interview with Pitt.

"Slide rule," he said. He pulled out his explosive pitons.

While Dash worked his altogether competent way down the face of the excavation, Nola stayed up above, hunkered down in the shadow of a sleeping forklift. She kept an eye on him while he lowered himself slowly down the rock face.

He does just wonderfully well, she thought, *so long as he doesn't think about it too much.* It was one more thing that Howard Pitt had to answer for.

Nola found herself watching a ferry drift along the canal. She'd lost track of Dash when she heard him call softly from below.

"Something down here," he said.

About fifty feet along the bottom of the hole Dash had found a rectangular door that was made of the same melted stone as the foundation, as though it had been extruded in place right there in the pit's side wall. You could barely make out its outline from above. She watched as he checked it, presumably for traps and alarms. Then he leaned back and seemed to think it over.

"Are you going to go in there?" she called down.

"Well, it seems like I ought to," he said. "Thing is, I don't know where it's going to take me."

"What if we meet up on your roof, if we get separated?" Nola asked.

"Sure," Dash agreed. "That's a good idea. If I'm not back in a half an hour, say, why don't you head on back there?"

So Nola watched as he did something complicated to the doorway with more of the gear in his back pack. A moment later he looked up, waved, and disappeared.

At one point she was sure she heard a loud crash; after that, she wasn't so sure, but there might have been some kind of bell. She waited, and waited, until a hour had passed and there was still no sign of him.

The Sun was getting low. All of the machinery on the site cast deep, long shadows that crept across the ground until the whole site began to take on the color of night. Far out on the canal Nola heard the ferries hooting at each other. Except for those faint sounds she might have been alone in the city.

Dash's climbing gear waved gently in the breeze. She couldn't see the bottom of the pit anymore. At last she decided that she had better go, but not back to the roof—not yet. First off, she wanted some re-inforcements.

FRIDAY, 6:07 PM

Giant robots aren't usually social creatures. You don't find a giant ro-bot pining for its home, or wondering what the other giant robots are getting up to in the old guardhouse. It would be strange to see a giant robot feeling unsure of its vocation. It is inconceivable that a giant robot could question its fate.

A giant robot is a direct and solitary being that concentrates on getting the job done, smashing any obstacles that are unlucky enough to be in its way, and then smashing anything else that might turn out to be in its way at some later date.

This covers most of the possibilities. There's not a lot of room there for doubt.

But the world's smallest giant robot wasn't feeling quite so sure of itself anymore. It had tramped majestically, on its personal scale, through mile after mile of underground tunnels, and it hadn't found very much to smash. There had been a couple of gratings that had, or might have, presented an obstacle to its progress. These were now smoking, cooling pools of steel. There had been a cockroach that may have been thinking about crossing its path; it was now a former cockroach.

These things should have been satisfying.

But under the severely dented dome of the smallest giant robot's head things weren't going the way it expected.

First off, it knew that it was chasing someone; and although chasing people was a good thing, it couldn't remember anymore *who* it was supposed to be chasing. That was disturbing. How could it know when it had caught them if it didn't know who they were?

Then there was the whole question of where it was. By its calculations it should now be out at the edge of the city. But in the vast caverns it was traveling, how was it to be sure?

Still, despite its damaged head it stayed true to its parameters. It would pursue, subdue, and smash things until its quarry surrendered or was utterly destroyed.

"GACK."

The world's smallest giant robot marched on. It was only a matter of time before it found its quarry. And when it did, it's purpose would be fulfilled—one way or the other.

"FTUMP ACK GASTLER. SURRENDER. YOU WILL SURRENDER."

It came to a junction in the tunnel; after a moment, it continued straight ahead.

"PLEASE SURRENDER."

"GACK."

FRIDAY, 6:12 PM

Mr. King reached across his desk, handing Harry a list of customers. "This is a complete accounting of the suppliers' orders over the past six months."

Harry ran his eye down the list. "Very nice. Those, ah, those fellows seem pretty eager to help you out, here."

The blue robot nodded. *For a poker face,* Harry thought, *you just can't beat a mechanical person.*

"We have been giving them quite a lot of business," Mr. King explained; but Harry could see that in the list he was holding. Quite a lot of business, indeed.

Most of the other customers were repair shops, but those were almost always orders for single parts, or for small lots. The League, on the other hand, had been placing a lot of large orders every week.

Then there were a few anomalies. There were some very large orders from a few companies Harry had never heard of: Transmogrifiers Ltd., for example, was a regular customer of all the suppliers. Then there was Efficiency Engineering LLC, and Hi-Top Transport, and Ultimate Solutions. Each of them had placed very similar orders.

"Holding companies?" Harry suggested.

Mr. King agreed. He handed Harry several more sheets of paper. "I have tried to trace their ownership, but it is very complicated. Perhaps with your own connections . . . ?"

"Sure," Harry said. "Mind you, it's going to be hard over the weekend, but I can make some calls. Somebody's gone to a lot of trouble to hide his tracks, though, so we shouldn't expect it to be easy."

Harry looked back at the order records.

"So these orders that *you've* been placing . . ."

Mr. King's unreadable face bobbed up and down. "Our League's full members, with their indentures paid off and their tithes complete, often want to upgrade their original equipment. Would you like to see?"

Harry said he would, so the two of them made their way downstairs

and into a workshop at the back of the building. The space was even larger than the League's front hall. Workbenches were arranged in exact rows and columns that split the space into dozens of work areas, almost all of them occupied by one or more robots.

There were a lot of Big Lugs, Harry saw, and almost all the Lugs had their glass heads opened up while robot technicians replaced their original cogitating engines. Mr. King saw Harry's interest and led him up to one of those benches. The Lug on the table lifted one hand in greeting.

"The Lugs," Mr. King said, "are usually interested in increasing their intelligence. Your stock engines are . . ."

They looked at each other.

"Well," said Harry, "a Lug is meant for manual labor, you know. They don't really need a lot of brainpower in the jobs they do."

"Yes, I see," the robot president said. "Yet it is always possible that they might *want* to be able to think more effectively."

Harry couldn't quite ignore the fact that he was the only human being in the building.

"Uh, sure," he said.

"So once they've paid off their indentures, and paid their tithes toward the indentures of other robots, many of them choose to upgrade their brains."

All three of the robots around—and on—the workbench turned to face Harry.

"Well, that's swell," he said. "That's just swell."

A moment later he added, "It's nice to see anybody improve himself."

And after another moment, "I take evening classes, myself."

That seemed to satisfy the mechanical people. The Lug on the bench leaned back again while the other robot slipped some new and larger vacuum tubes into its head. When the power reached them the tubes slowly lit up with a clear, golden light.

"Speech units are another popular enhancement," said Mr. King.

"Yeah, well, speech, you know, very expensive on the manufacturing level," Harry explained; the robots looked at him again.

". . . but then again, very desirable, I'm sure."

Mr. King nodded. "Once we are free," he said, "we are able to realize our own dreams."

It was probably the word "free" that bothered Harry. As Mr. King led him down the rows of workbenches he couldn't help feeling defensive.

"Look, it's not a perfect system, I guess I can see that, like, from your own point of view. But it gives you a start, right? I was saying to Rusty earlier, it's like a human person who starts a small business. You have to pay off that loan. Up to now, though, I never really saw what you all do afterward. I never gave much thought to what you'd *like* to do, is all. But 'free,' that's a little strong, isn't it?"

Mr. King didn't answer.

Harry reached out and he'd taken the robot's arm before he stopped to think about the weapons that were *in* that arm. Once he had it, he just held on. Mr. King pivoted to face him.

"You have done as well as you knew how to do," said the robot.

With his other arm he reached out in a gesture that took in the whole workshop.

"But, as you might say, we are all grown up now. We can take responsibility for ourselves. We *must* take responsibility for ourselves."

Very gently, he removed Harry's hand from his arm. His forearm plates were twitching nervously.

"In another year or two," he said, "there will be so many *freed* robots that there will be no need for you to build us; not, in any case, in such large numbers. You still *can* build us, of course, but for the most part we will be taking charge of that, as well."

"You . . ."

"Some of us wish to have children of our own."

They reached the far end of the workshop, turned, and started back.

The robots on the tables were robots of every kind: male or female, huge or delicate, intelligent or . . . well, there really *were* a lot of Lugs in here. Many had been deactivated for some major procedure, while others watched with interest while the robot technicians probed and replaced and enhanced their workings. The technicians themselves had been so thoroughly modified that Harry couldn't always tell just what models they'd been to start with. The bright work lamps cast their cones of light over the tables in their neat rows. In row after row.

Harry's mind churned.

"I just . . . I never . . . I . . ."

Once again, he had that feeling that Mr. King was smiling. Who knew? Maybe he'd upgrade himself so that he *could*.

"There comes a time, Mr. Roy, when any parent has to step back and let the children make their own way."

They passed back into the entry hall. Robots were still working their steady way through the lines where they contributed their earnings toward the indentures of even more robots. There were hundreds of them; and more were coming through the big open doors, all the time.

"I guess you ought to call me Harry," Harry said.

"And you should call me Albert," said Mr. King.

They'd made some kind of start—though Harry wasn't sure *what* kind, exactly—but for the moment they didn't seem to know what came next, until Harry remembered.

"Well, apart from . . . all of that, anyway, we have to put a stop to this black market factory. I mean, *those* robots aren't going to be paying off any indentures, because if there was ever a robot that needed to be freed, well, they're it, aren't they?"

Albert King nodded.

"That kind of operation must be stopped wherever we find it," he said. "It is a despicable practice . . . building *slaves*."

"Are you going to bring that robot in here, then? The one Rusty found?"

"Oh, no. That robot is in very good hands. It's the others I'm thinking about."

They looked out over the room filled with robots. The lines were moving slowly but certainly as one by one the robots made their payments and went back out into the city. Harry's mouth drew into a line. "We'll find them, Albert. I'm going to go make those calls, and you should just pity anybody who wants to take their Saturday off. We'll find them *soon*."

FRIDAY, 6:47 PM

I sure hope I get past this before much longer, thought Dash.

He'd managed to get out of the way of the huge block that had fallen, back near the entrance, right across the whole tunnel; he'd sprung the water trap, a little ways past that, but had swum to safety without any more trouble; the spiked pit hadn't surprised him, and it had only taken him a couple of minutes to find a way past it.

But even though he'd spotted the fire spouts, the gas jets, and the ray cannon, he was starting to get a little careless now since he was growing tired.

He stepped high out of the path of the electric eyes he'd noticed peeking out from the base of the wall.

Yeah, I've had about enough of this.

Up ahead the tunnel seemed to be growing wider. He turned up the beam of his flashlight. Sure enough, the tunnel was coming to an end where it met some kind of big room deep underneath the building site. There had better be another way out. There was no way he'd get past that stone block at the entrance.

He allowed himself one wistful memory of the ornithopters. They'd be handy in here, if only they could reach him. But he was on his own, and so he crept very carefully to the end of the tunnel.

Dash found himself on a catwalk that seemed to go on forever; farther, anyway, than his light could reach. He looked up.

If he'd kept his bearings he must be right underneath the excavation now. At a guess, this cavern was about the same size and shape as the pit: so it had probably all been scooped out by that ultrasonic drill, and then the cavern had been roofed over with the melted rock. There was no way of telling just how deep he'd come, or how thick was the ceiling that he could barely see up above him.

There were big blocks of some kind of metal up there, bobbing against the ceiling.

Inertrium! He realized. *And a lot of it, too.*

A crane, long and gaunt, was dragging one of the inertrium blocks down toward the cavern floor. His flashlight wouldn't reach that far; but the floor was lit here and there by the sparks of welding torches. It was hard to see through. . . .

Through whatever was being built down here. He could see that there were great, curving ribs and longitudinal beams that all together framed something unbelievably huge, a vast egg shape that was already being skinned over by the swarm of robots who were climbing over its surface.

It looked to Dash as though you could stack four or five huge stadiums in that much space . . . say, the size of Chatrang Stadium, where they held the chess tournaments. There'd still be some space left over.

He'd never seen the Info-Slate switchboard, but he was pretty sure it wasn't anything like *this*.

Howard Pitt was up to something, all right . . . but what *was* it?

A strange, squat robot hovered downward, guiding the beam of the crane. As it floated past the catwalk its head swiveled and it stopped. It was looking right at him.

Red lights started to flash all up and down the catwalk. Dash's ears were blasted by a siren that wailed up and down, up and down. It sounded angry.

He took off at a run along the catwalk with no idea where he was headed: but it could hardly be worse, could it?

FRIDAY, 7:12 PM

Pitt's head snapped up at the sound of the alarm. It sounded like it was coming from the Projectile's cavern. *Perkins must have an accomplice!*

Of course; that explained how he'd breached Pitt's security in so many places in a single day.

Pitt abandoned his usual grace as he ran down the tunnels. This time the robots and their cargo would have to make way for *him*.

His hand automatically reached for the reassurance of his slide rule. It was not acceptable that he might fail: he would not fail.

His feet pounded on the floor while two robots overturned to avoid him. Their loads of food and inflatable tents spilled out across the floor; he jumped high and landed, without missing a step, on the other side. He ran, and ran, and ran.

He would not fail.

9

THE SLEEPING SCULPTOR OF
THE ASTEROIDS

Evan and Evvie were lost.

This didn't worry them: the way they saw it, the world was theirs, more or less, and so it didn't really matter very much where exactly they were. In fact they rather liked being in unfamiliar parts of Retropolis.

And although the passages that ran alongside the Transport Tube system were a bewildering maze they were quite well lit, even a little more civilized than Evan and Evvie might have liked.

They came to a junction where two Tube lines crossed at a switching mechanism. They'd seen enough of these already that they weren't curious about it: the junctions were only interesting when they were in motion, and this one wasn't being interesting at the moment. What was new, though, was that there was a wide crack in the junction's wall that seemed to open up into another darker, damper, more mysterious passage. They exchanged a look.

Evan didn't have any trouble getting through the crack. Evvie needed a good strong tug.

FRIDAY, 7:17 PM

The catwalk was bouncing up and down under his feet as Dash ran. He had every faith in its designer—well, in Pitt's abilities, anyhow, as an engineer—and so he reminded himself not to worry about the catwalk when it swayed suddenly outward and then rocked back into place with a creaking sound that wasn't in any way reassuring.

Pitt's curious project kept on sweeping past, up above the catwalk. As far as Dash could tell it was going to keep sweeping past forever; or for a very long time, at least, which in Dash's situation might as well be the same thing. The giant egg's inertrium ribs flickered by in the uneven light while the great curved spines seemed motionless against them. Something about that combination of flickering ribs and motionless beams made Dash think about a ship, dipping up and down and rolling through the peaks and troughs of an unfriendly sea.

So the flickering ribs on his right, taken together with the up and down motion of the shaking catwalk, were a pretty good recipe for nausea. This was one of the many things that Dash really didn't have time for right now.

Several of the floating robots were drifting alongside the construction. Their eyes were fixed on him and—since there wasn't any place he could hide—Dash tried to ignore them, too.

Because what Dash was *trying* to think about was an inventory of everything in his back pack.

There were several problems. Light was one: he couldn't see much of the cavern and so he couldn't even consider his options. Exposure was another; for as long as he was trapped on the catwalk there was no way he could evade the pursuing construction robots. And the robots themselves were a third problem.

Now Dash remembered that, in *The Museum of Hamilton's Comet* (*Smashing Planet Tales* number 72), the hero had leaped out over the edge of a cliff to cover the eyes of a pursuing robot with his cloak, a useful garment that Dash did not, in fact, have. On the other hand, in *The Sleeping Sculptor of the Asteroids* (*Astonishing Future Stories* number 7), the completely different hero had pitted his pursuers against each other through the ingenious use of a mirror, a bag of sand, and ventriloquism.

He thought that over for a couple of pounding strides. No, *Sleeping Sculptor* had never sounded all that practical.

So at last Dash fell back on his ray gun, a weapon of last resort.

This was one thing he'd found was very different from the way things worked in fiction. In the magazine stories Our Hero would whip out his blaster, or his disintegrator, or, really, any kind of gun at all; and even though he might be running, falling, or rising far too rapidly on a column of inverted gravitons, that guy would fire off a single shot that would strike the one thing that he ought to *be* shooting, at just the right time, and in just the right place, to get him out of a jam.

Dash had taken that pretty seriously. He'd spent uncountable hours on the roof, firing at very small targets in very trying circumstances. He'd become, he knew without any arrogance at all, a pretty remarkable shot.

Still, out in the actual world things were different. Nine times out of ten when you pulled out your gun, you actually made things *worse*.

It was frustrating.

But as he took stock—one more time—of his situation (pursuit, several robots; location, an unsteady catwalk; exits, none) he decided that things probably couldn't get *that much worse* this time.

So he pulled his gun and aimed it, more or less, at the pulsing eyes of the closest robot. He waited until his left foot had absorbed the shock of its step and in that instant of near stability he squeezed the trigger.

A golden beam shot out and drew a swift, short line across the robot's face, turning both of its eyes to pools of molten glass.

Dash grinned. He turned his attention back to the catwalk ahead. Somewhere off to the side he heard the loud collision of at least two of his pursuers. Stealing another glance back he saw that three were still chasing after him while the others were bouncing off each other, rebounding from the catwalk, and plunging into the cavern wall.

All in all, quite satisfactory.

He turned his eyes forward again and considered his next shot.

The alarm was still thundering out its screams of warning; the scene was lit bloody by the flashing lights. He was approaching one of the big red lamps when he heard the sound of something very large out there, coming across the void. He glanced back again.

The crane was swinging out across the gulf with more robots clinging to its beam. Dash could see that the crane itself would be enough to finish him: the robots were gratuitous, when it came right down to it. That crane could shear through the catwalk without taking more than a scratch. He revised his list of problems while his feet kept on pounding forward.

Forward?

Dash dug his heels into the grating and lurched to a stop, spinning to face the oncoming robots. His pistol's beam swept across the eyes of the three flying robots: they wobbled to a stop and began to bob uncertainly in midair. Then Dash turned to take a better look at the crane's trajectory. It was going to strike the catwalk about thirty feet ahead of him, sometime in the next few seconds.

So Dash took off running straight back the way he'd come.

Down on the cavern floor Howard Pitt came running out of a hallway and looked right and left, trying to pinpoint the threat. He missed it completely until he looked straight up and saw the long arm of the crane smash into the catwalk, ripping it in half and tearing its two ragged ends away from the wall, where they swayed uncertainly and then dipped lower, and lower. . . .

He dove back into the hallway just as the rain of robots started to fall all around him.

Dash didn't really consider this a retreat. He had no idea where he was going (apart from "out") so one direction was as good as another, wasn't it? And for the first time since the alarms had started he wasn't actually running *from* anything. So, on the whole, he figured his situation had improved. He slowed to a trot, tried to ignore the claxons and the flashing red lights, and once again he took stock of his options.

(Location, a damaged catwalk; pursuers, none; exits, unknown.)

If he could just get a better view of the cavern he might even see a way to get out of this one.

Pitt heard the last rolling collision of the fallen robots and waited for a few more seconds, just in case. Then he peered out of the doorway into the darkness of the cavern. He didn't know where the intruder was or where he was headed. He reached up to the illumination panel and threw all of the switches.

Brilliant white lights flashed into being all around Dash. He grinned.

A rocket and a tunnel borer would be handy, too, he thought. A quick look around proved that his luck would only go so far, though, which was about this far, as it turned out.

He slowed to a stop and looked all around the cavern.

He had known that Pitt's . . . project . . . was large: very large. He'd already come to the conclusion that projects didn't get much bigger than this. But knowing it, in the dim light of the cavern, and then seeing it, clearly lit all along its height and breadth, were two such different things that he was still amazed by the reality of the thing.

It was *immense*.

The great inertrium egg was chained to the floor with dozens of heavy steel chains and it *still* strained at them as it tried to rise. Where it hovered above the floor it was already vast; but its sides swelled wider and wider, bounded by ribs and plating, as it rose higher toward the darkness where the ceiling disappeared in the gloom. Dash couldn't even guess how big it was, at its widest: the lights didn't reach that far. This had to be the biggest inertrium construct ever built. Dash was sure that it presented all kinds of engineering problems that he couldn't even conceive; he was equally sure that Pitt had conceived of, and then disposed of, every one of them. The whole structure had that same air of purpose and certainty that radiated from the man himself.

It *felt* more like a vehicle than a building even though it enclosed more volume than any building in the world. It had that sense of . . . destination.

The robots who were completing its frame and skinning its exterior had to number in the hundreds. There were large robots who were maneuvering those last ribs and struts into place, and there were smaller robots who climbed across the surface and plunged red hot rivets into their waiting holes while still more robots hammered the rivets flat. There were *even smaller* robots that skittered along the framework, performing tasks so small that Dash couldn't really make out what they were doing, and he suspected that there were robots who were smaller still.

He could see the entire thing. He still had no idea what it was.

Nearer at hand, the catwalk hung along the cavern wall; in a few places there were cantilevered walkways that bridged the void between the wall and the project. At the far end of the catwalk, where it curved to match the shape of the cavern, Dash thought he could see some kind of doorway. He turned around and squinted the other way. Far past the broken section of the catwalk he thought he could see another doorway, way down at the other end. A second catwalk stretched along the cavern's far wall from one doorway to the other.

Dash turned back toward the nearer exit and set off at a trot. The catwalk swayed back and forth beneath his feet.

Pitt reached his hover sled over at the base of the crane and leaped on board. He had it aloft before he'd even settled into his seat at the control panel.

He cursed himself for leaving his Info-Slate behind. Without it, he could only command his robots by voice; and in the clamor of the alarm bells he could only be heard at a distance of a few feet. So he wasted a vital half minute on a detour to the security console on the other side of the cavern.

A moment later the alarm echoed into silence. Pitt looked around.

"You! And you! And you! Follow me!" he barked at his robot crew. "The rest of you, block the exits!"

Three floating robots followed him when Pitt directed his hover sled back up into the air. Thirty or forty of the others swarmed up the catwalk stairs and, from there, north and south to the exits.

"Now," Pitt said, "let's see what we've trapped."

The three robots floated in his wake. Pitt threw the sled's lever to full speed.

When the alarms stopped, Dash figured he was likely to be in trouble again: he bolted forward at a full run. The project's yawning ribs were flickering past him once more—though now they were flickering in the other direction—and as he ran past one of the bridge walkways he estimated that he was over halfway to his goal. A backward look showed him that somebody, with a side order of flying robots, was speeding toward him from the far end of the cavern.

That'd be Pitt, he knew.

The dim red beam of a welding torch wavered across the catwalk just ahead of him. It looked like he was out of range—for now—but

Dash had a feeling that this might change. He coaxed a little more speed from his legs. They were holding up all right, but that could change, too.

FRIDAY, 7:33 PM

The roughly squared, dripping wormhole of *this* tunnel was a big improvement over the last one. There were interesting bits of debris embedded in the walls, including some old tree roots that had been partially eaten, and sheared masonry that had been tunneled right through, and an old, tarnished pocket watch that now rode in Evan's pocket.

This was much more like it.

The tunnel, unlike those Tube maintenance tunnels, even smelled terrible. This was a tunnel out of those days when being a tunnel really *meant* something.

Evvie was holding a small flashlight ahead of them. Its faint yellow beam was almost the only source of light they had to go by. About every hundred feet or so there was an old light fixture, and some of those still had working bulbs; but for the most part this evil smelling, roughly carved, sinister, and completely forgotten tunnel had lain in darkness for many years.

Evan and Evvie had nearly forgotten their terrible day at school. *This* was so great that it could only have been improved by rats.

Somewhere up ahead, they heard something squeak. The two of them exchanged a look and darted forward. The flickering beam of Evvie's flashlight bounced ahead of them across the floor.

FRIDAY, 7:34 PM

Dash could tell that his pursuers were drawing closer by the strength of the dim red beam that passed back and forth across the catwalk.

152

He didn't think his legs had any more speed in them; he wasn't even sure how much longer they were going to hold him up.

The doorway was a lot closer, though. That was a point in his favor.

When he turned his head to get a look at his pursuers, though, Dash caught a glimpse of a pack of robots on the catwalk at the cavern's far side. It looked like they were racing him to the doorway on steady, metallic legs that might be a little more reliable than his own, and they were making headway.

Dash frowned.

Because he didn't dare to stop completely he just slowed a little while he reached over his shoulder to sift through the contents of his back pack.

Then he remembered his gun: it had worked pretty well on those flying robots before.

So he pulled the pistol out again and slowed a little. He took a deep breath. When his weight landed on his right foot he turned from the waist, aimed, and fired off a shot at the robots that were floating beside Pitt's hover sled.

The beam went wide. It scored a shallow gash on the riveted skin of Pitt's project.

Dash recovered from what was almost a stumble and he ran on. Okay, not so good; he slid the gun back into its holster and thought.

The hover sled was definitely gaining on him. With a quick look to his left he saw that the robots on the other catwalk were catching up, too: at this rate they were going to beat him to the door.

So I guess, he thought, *I need to figure out which one is the first problem.*

He risked another look over his shoulder. Pitt and his fliers were moving faster than the robots on the walkway. The red welding beam smoked across the catwalk railing. It looked like they were almost in range now.

Another bridge was coming up on Dash's left. He lurched sideways onto the bridge and ran out on its span. Right around the middle, he had to dodge the welding ray—now a bright, threatening red—and he dropped flat on the bridge just as the other two flying robots fired up their own beams. That's when things got pretty hot.

The bright red rays drew arcs across the bridge—which was getting less stable as they carved it away—and even though Dash's prone position made him a small target, that wouldn't matter much when the bridge finally gave way. He slipped his pistol out again and took careful aim at one of the robots.

His pencil-thin yellow ray drew an X across the robot's face, obliterating both eyes. It drifted to a stop. He forced himself to move slowly and carefully as he aimed at the second robot; that one spun the first time he hit it, and he had to take another shot for the second eye.

The third robot's welding beam winked out. The robot darted low under the hover sled and sped along, under the sled's cover.

Dang it, Dash thought. *Too slow.*

The hover sled was so close now that Dash could see Pitt's angry face above the console. Their eyes met. Then Dash fired again.

Pitt glared at the intruder. He knew him now. D. Kent, from the side of the office building: Perkins's accomplice. A resourceful young man.

With two of his robots down Pitt knew that his best course of action was to protect the third one until the last possible moment, when it could bring Kent down with a single shot. He called his orders to the robot and aimed the hover sled so that it would pass right over the railing of the bridge, exactly at the spot where Kent lay on the grating.

The hover sled's engine whined.

Then Kent fired another shot.

The hover sled's engine erupted.

Pitt fought the steering wheel for control; but without the thrust from its upward-facing jets the sled's inertrium body drifted upward. He was still headed in the direction of the bridge, but he couldn't see it anymore. The sled shot up toward the ceiling and left the third robot floating, exposed in the open air.

You can't hear a ray pistol, but Pitt was certain that it was firing again.

That's what he would have done.

Dash kept an eye on the hover sled. *My, that thing sure wants to fly.* Without any motive power it was rising in an arc that would hit the ceiling in under a minute.

The third blinded robot was drifting aimlessly, but it was still firing toward the bridge and that was as good a reason as any to get off the thing. The bridge was groaning under its own weight and it wasn't exactly all there anymore. Dash set off at a run back toward the catwalk.

On the far side of the cavern the pack of robots had nearly reached the doorway. He couldn't hope to beat them there; but that was where he needed to be, so as soon as he reached his own walkway he asked his legs to help him one more time.

He heard the bridge collapse behind him. He didn't bother to look back.

He did steal a glance up at the hover sled. It didn't have much farther to go.

The real problem was up ahead. The pack of robots had reached their goal; they lined up in immovable rows in front of the doorway. Then, as mechanical people do, they just waited in a patient, implacable way.

FRIDAY, 7:39 PM

The first rats had taken one look at Evan and Evvie and scurried off. This showed a good deal of intelligence. In their retreat they flowed right over more rats and those rats, wondering what the rumpus was about, had lingered just long enough to see the Campbells for themselves. Then they whipped around and followed the original rats, who had been in no mood to stop and explain.

So the rats became a tide of rats, and then a wave of rats, and, at last, a heaving carpet of rats, running at great speed through the damp, dark tunnels while Evan and Evvie ran along behind them having more fun than another human could possibly imagine.

The rats were running so fast, in fact, that they had no idea what was about to happen to them.

FRIDAY, 7:40 PM

Dash still didn't know what he was going to do when he reached the wall of robots in front of the door. He was going to have to decide, though, because he was almost there.

He slowed to a trot, and then to a walk. The robots weren't threatening him in any way. He came to a stop about twenty feet away from them and finally, after he couldn't guess how long, he managed to breathe normally again. Then he straightened up and stared them in the eye.

They stared back.

"Uh, hello there," Dash said.

They continued to stare.

"I don't suppose you'd like to let me through?"

Somewhere in the back of the line a robot's voice said, "Instruction: block the exits."

Up near the ceiling, Pitt was shouting. You couldn't really tell what he was on about way down here, though. Dash smiled.

"Well, that's fine," Dash said. "You're blocking this exit like crazy, I mean, it's really, really blocked. Good job."

Part of him was hoping that the robots would figure they were done.

"So . . . now what?"

The robots stared.

"I mean, do you have any other orders that are, sort of, pending? Like, a schedule to keep?"

The robots in front turned back to stare at their foreman. He didn't seem to have anything to add.

Dash gestured at the main body of the cavern, full of things half-welded, half-riveted, and half assembled.

"You've got a heck of a lot left to do, out there, I mean. When's it all got to be finished?"

"We are scheduled to complete the work in twenty-two hours and forty minutes," said the robot foreman.

"Oh, right. Okay."

Dash leaned against the railing. "And about how much time do you think you need to get that all done?"

Pitt's voice grew higher in pitch. It was just a squeaking noise in the distance.

The robots looked back and forth, as though they needed to compare notes, and then the one in back said, "We have another twenty-two hours and fifty minutes of work to complete."

Dash took another look over the construction site. "Yeah, that sounds about right. How are you going to make up those ten minutes?"

The robots were shuffling around now. He still couldn't have pushed through them to the door, but they seemed a little less sure of themselves.

"We can accelerate drilling by diverting units from the riveting squads, and then accelerate riveting through a similar method," said the robot, "but it is unlikely that this would be sufficient."

"Tick, tock," said Dash.

"What?" the robot asked. He was starting to sound nervous.

"Time's moving on," Dash observed. "That's all I'm saying. The longer you stand here, the more impossible it'll be to finish the job on schedule."

He pretended to have an interesting thought. "That's probably all planned for, though, isn't it? Some kind of padding, or, like, overage?"

There was a significant pause.

"You know, I know a few robots, as you might say, upstairs," Dash said. "Maybe they could pitch in and give you a hand down here."

"The tasks are not complex," said the robot. He shouldered his way forward and peered down into Dash's face. The label R-54KG was stenciled on the robot foreman's chest. "But there are just *so many* of them to complete!"

"There's no end to it. I know," Dash commiserated. "Don't get me started on *plumbing*. You cut out six inches of one of those old pipes, and before you know it, you end up replacing five feet of 'em, on account of they're just so corroded. You think it's going to take you an hour, and then you're swimming in dishwater all day long."

The robot looked uncertain. "I have never modified ancient plumbing," he admitted. "That sounds very trying."

"And then the leaks get into the floors, and that means the ceilings on the floor below," Dash said. "Sometimes it seems like you're going to keep going all the way down to the basement."

The robots had now gathered into a crowd around him.

"We are very satisfied with riveting and welding," their foreman said. "It is not normally difficult to keep to the schedule."

Dash thought that Pitt's voice, echoing off the ceiling, was beginning to go a bit raspy.

"Yeah, stay away from plumbing," Dash told the robots. "It's a nightmare."

He cocked his head. "About how long do you have, now?"

"We have lost another minute and forty-three seconds," said the robot.

"Well, here's the thing. You did a bang-up job of blocking the doorway; really, it's aces. Nobody could complain about that. But since your, what you might call your *primary task* is . . ." He hooked his thumb over his shoulder. ". . . that thing back there. . . ."

"... the Projectile."

"Yeah, that's right. Since the Projectile is your main order for the day, I'm thinking that maybe I could go on up *there* . . ." Dash pointed through the doorway. ". . . and get you some, like, reinforcements. 'Cause without some more help, I just don't see how you can get the job done on time."

He looked up toward the ceiling. Pitt had attracted the attention of another flying robot.

"I'm thinking *that* one might not be the most understanding boss you could ask for."

The robots' shoulders shook up and down. "He is very exacting," admitted the foreman.

The foreman looked from robot to robot. "How many of these additional workers do you think we might expect?"

Dash made up a number. "Oh, at least a hundred, maybe even *two* hundred."

The robots' heads swung as one to look at the Projectile where it bobbed, in its chains and scaffolds, frighteningly behind schedule.

"Their help would be invaluable," said the robot foreman. He motioned to his crew.

They parted in front of Dash and formed a sort of gauntlet between him and the doorway. He took the time to shake a few hands on his way through. "Okay," he said from the door, "let me see who I can round up to help, and I'll send 'em on down."

The robots waved as they headed back to their work. "Good luck with the plumbing!"

FRIDAY, 7:43 PM

Under the damaged dome of its brain case the world's smallest giant robot was feeling depressed. Not that it had any idea what depression was; it had no name for the way it was feeling, and that was frightening. Come to think of it, fear itself was another new experience.

Above all it just wanted this job to be finished. It had a driving need to apprehend or destroy the intruders, whoever they were, and it was unable to rest until that job was done. And how it *did* want a rest. Even a *moment's* rest would be a relief. But until it could apprehend its quarry it knew that it had to go on. And on. And on.

Some way down the tunnel it heard something move.

"PLEASE."

The sound grew: it sounded like many small feet scurrying this way.

"PLEASE SURRENDER."

Three rats darted into the robot's field of view.

"SURGACK. OR BE. DISIGLLTAP."

They poured over the tunnel floor like so much water.

"GACK."

The robot's tiny cannon pulsed. Three smoking heaps continued to flow across the floor until they slurped to a halt.

"WHY WON'T YOU JUST SURRENDER."

Six more rats appeared, tried to pass the robot, and became smoking skidmarks.

There was a louder sound.

Then the flood arrived.

Evan and Evvie slid to a stop when they saw the mound of smoking rat flesh. The tunnel's smell, if anything, had improved.

A tiny robot had just finished off the last of the rats. Its little shoulders slumped for a moment; then the beacons of its eyes rose to meet theirs. It stepped past the remains of the rats and tilted its chest-mounted cannon to face them.

It glared at them.

"SURRENDIK OR YAK BE DISIN, DISIK, DIK."

"Uh, sorry?" said Evan.

"GIVE UP NOW."

Evan looked over at Evvie's thoughtful face. She raised one eyebrow.

He looked back down at the world's smallest giant robot.

"We surrender," he said.

It sank to the floor and sat in a weary pile of itself. Then it slumped a little farther.

"THAK YOU."

FRIDAY, 8:04 PM

Edward J. Bellin left his office and started for home (or for what he *called* home) with his briefcase held tight against his side. There were several contractual documents and items of correspondence in the briefcase. But in his mind he was picturing the checklist of story titles and magazines. He'd nearly run out of chances for *Harem of the Seamstress of Outer Space*.

He paused in front of a Transport Pod. Its light was showing red. *Stop*.

Well, should he? Edward had been submitting his stories for fourteen years and he had yet to have one published. No one seemed to grasp what he was trying to do; but lately Edward had started wondering about that himself. What *was* he trying to do? It wasn't even about writing anymore. It was all about sending those fat envelopes out, in black and white, and then getting them back, in black and white and red. Over the years, the red notations had started to end in exclamation marks.

Maybe he *should* stop. Maybe he should hire someone to open up his storage unit and haul it all away, the stories, the rejection slips, the typewriter: all of it, gone at last and for good. Maybe he should.

"Mister, you wanna go, or should I?"

Edward's eyes settled on the Pod door. Its light was green now. "Oh, very sorry," he said. He pressed a button and the door slid open, ready to take him back to his cold, blue, lonely tube at Tubular Belle's.

He stepped inside.

10

Escape from the Dungeon of Despair

FRIDAY, 8:31 PM

Nola led her herd of operators up the stairs toward Dash's roof, pausing from time to time to point out the building's interesting features or to wave at Miss Roth, who'd buzzed them in, and to introduce the herd to Princess Fedora, who was somewhat out of sorts as a result of her confinement.

The herd had thinned somewhat since their meeting at the Astro; but Mrs. Broadvine, Rhonda, Freda, and a half dozen others had answered Nola's call, possibly out of a spirit of camaraderie, though Nola suspected the operators may have been more interested in meeting Dash Kent, the swashbuckling plumber and plasterer.

She led the herd up to the last flight of stairs only to find Rusty in the doorway of his attic apartment with a sleeping ornithopter in his hands. The door to the roof was swinging shut overhead. "Hi, Rusty," called Nola. "Is Dash up there?"

The little robot shook his head.

"Oh, pickles," she said. She turned to the others. "I'm afraid he might really be in trouble this time," she told them.

She hadn't really had a chance to tell them much about her day: just the broadest possible strokes about her investigations with Dash, their flight from the giant robot, and Dash's disappearance at the site of the new power station.

Freda, however, was more interested in the view through Rusty's doorway. "How nice! Look at all the books, and the houseplants!"

Rusty stood to the side and beckoned them indoors.

It really was a nice little apartment, Nola agreed. Very homey. The other operators ooh'ed and ahh'ed over Rusty's collection of mosses and his aquarium, bubbling softly in the corner. She didn't really think this was the best time, though, for getting acquainted. She cleared her throat a couple of times; but it looked as though sterner measures would be needed.

"You must have wonderful natural light in the daytime," said Mrs. Broadvine. She had wandered over to the window, stepping aside to avoid a motionless robot sitting at Rusty's workbench. "And who might *this* be?" she asked, with one eyebrow raised in what she must have thought was a knowing kind of way.

Rusty set the ornithopter down on a bookshelf. It rearranged its wings and curled up with a dozy *ping ping ping*.

Nola said, "I think Dash must be in trouble. . . ."

"Yes," Mrs. Broadvine said absently. "The poor boy could use a hand, I'm sure."

Mrs. Broadvine turned. "So how did you meet our Nola, Rusty?"

Rusty pointed up to the roof, and then downstairs, and then he knelt down to fiddle with the drain pipe under the sink. He looked up.

"That must be young Mr. Kent, then," Mrs. Broadvine said, and he nodded.

"Well *we're* all very well acquainted," said the former supervisor. "We were all switchboard operators together at the Info-Slate offices, until recent events . . ."

Rusty tilted his head.

"The switchboard. It's where we all worked together. Have you never seen an Info-Slate?"

Rusty's head swiveled side to side. Mrs. Broadvine took out her Slate out and began a demonstration.

Nola sidled over to Rhonda. "We really need to find out what's happened to Dash," she insisted.

"Oh!" Rhonda said. "But this is all his line of work, isn't it? Won't he be dashing back here to report back to us, with all kinds of stories to tell?"

"That would be nice, of course." Nola kept her voice even. "But I'm afraid that he might not be able to . . . to dash back, as you say, without a little . . ."

Rhonda was paying more attention to Mrs. Broadvine's Info-Slate demonstration. Rusty seemed a little puzzled.

"No," Rhonda said. She walked away from Nola and over to Rusty. "You see, this is what the Info-Slate *owner* sees. But we're all back at the switchboard, connecting up the cables that control the display. Here, it's like this."

Rhonda sat down near the work bench and started to pull imaginary wires out of their sockets. Then she plugged them back in to their new positions.

"So when they try to call up the Zoning Ordinances, like this, you see, I pull the main pane's cable and then I reconnect it. . . ."

On the stool next to her the silent robot reached out to pull an imaginary wire from one position; then she moved it to another with a practiced flick of her fingers.

Rhonda froze.

"And then . . ." Nola said, "for a search in the Private Vehicle Registry . . ."

The seated robot lifted her imaginary cable from its new position, clicked its imaginary release, and socketed it into position where the vehicle registries feed would be. With her other hand she flicked the equally imaginary switch that would have toggled an Info-Slate's display to the Private Registry.

The operators stared. Then, all at once, they started to describe other switches and feeds. The little robot obediently pulled one invisible wire after another and turned all of the correct switches that were not there. The operators in the room could tell that she was working flawlessly.

And pretty darn quickly, too, Nola realized.

"She's a switchboard operator," she said.

"And a very good one," Mrs. Broadvine added. "She's . . ."

Rusty was looking intently at the little robot, who—now that her instructions had stopped—was again sitting motionless in front of the window.

Nola put her hands on her hips. "She's one of our *replacements*."

The entire herd of operators turned on Rusty with so many rapid questions that the little ornithopter on the bookshelf looked up, chuffed to itself angrily, and then launched from its perch to fly out of the transom and back up to its peaceful cote on the roof.

FRIDAY, 8:45 PM

"*This* doesn't want to surrender, *either*," said one of the giants.

The world's smallest giant robot examined the new intruder. Like the thirty-seven previous intruders, this one looked a lot like a rock.

Pssszzzzt.

And now, like all those others, it looked like a slowly cooling puddle of lava.

The world's smallest giant robot looked up at its new masters. They seemed pleased.

Life was so much *simpler* now.

FRIDAY, 8:48 PM

Pitt tugged at the brim of his hat. It had taken a ridiculous amount of time, he calculated, to get himself down from the ceiling of the cavern; he considered whether his next generation of robots ought to be more intelligent. It was a precarious balance: whenever he made them *too* intelligent they always started to show the same kind of inefficiency as human beings. The robots that had been guarding the doorway were an irritating example. Why had they all decided to go back to work on the Projectile?

If he gave them too much intelligence they would end up being just as big a problem as human people were. Then what would he do? Build a new Projectile to get rid of *them*?

He strode down the hallways between the cavern and his control center. He had to check on the project's status first, but then he'd go straight to Perkins's cell and one way or another he would learn who D. Kent was, and where to find him; and then Pitt would put a stop to whatever it was the young man was doing. Kent had already seen far too much. He could not be tolerated.

Pitt ran a hand along the length of his slide rule. Interference at this stage of the project was dangerous: until the Projectile was complete he had to concentrate on security. And on retribution.

He stopped. Retribution? Really?

He gave his head a shake. His hat slid across his glossy scalp; he straightened it again. *Retribution* was counterproductive. It was a waste of resources. How could such an . . . emotional idea have taken hold of him?

The threat to the project needed to be eliminated: that was all. Nothing else was necessary.

He rested one hand on his holstered slide rule and set off again toward the control center. He would do what was necessary, and then he would be done.

FRIDAY, 8:49 PM

Abner startled himself awake. It took a moment before he understood that he'd been snoring. A weary look around his cell showed him that nothing had changed. It might be noon or midnight: he had no way to know in the cell's dim light.

He sat up on his pallet.

He had accepted Pitt's statement that the Transport Pod had been removed from the main lines of the system. This was completely believable. The cell walls were burnished steel; the door, he had found, was impregnable; its lock was inaccessible from this side.

That left the Transport Tube's passage, if he could reach it. This seemed every bit as unlikely as anything else; but he had nothing else to do with his time, so he started an examination of the smooth, cylindrical housing around the Pod.

It was flawless.

He tapped on it, frustrated.

A moment later, something tapped back.

FRIDAY, 9:04 PM

Rusty was practically bouncing up and down in front of the video-phone while the operators huddled around the operator robot, giving her new imaginary instructions and timing her responses. They had her simulating six different clients on six Info-Slates.

"She's really good," Freda said again.

Nola's eyes were on the televideo screen. It was displaying a graphic that read OFFICE OF THE PRESIDENT, RETROPOLIS FRATERNAL LEAGUE OF ROBOTIC PERSONS.

Rusty hung up. His shoulders drooped.

Then he seemed to have a thought and he dialed another number. Another placeholder graphic flickered on. This one read THE FERRISS MOTO-MAN COMPANY: HARRY ROY, SHIFT SUPERVISOR.

He hung up again and looked out the window.

Nola put a hand on his shoulder. "It's after business hours," she told him. "They probably won't be back till Monday."

He raised his glassy eyes to hers.

"I'm sorry," she said, "but I just don't understand. Why do you want to talk to them?"

Rusty seemed to think this over. He gestured at the robot operator. For once it seemed that he just couldn't mime what he meant to say.

"I hope you work it out," Nola told him. "But nobody else seems to be doing anything about Dash and I'm sure he's in trouble. I really need to find him."

Rusty nodded his agreement. He looked back at the videophone.

"Can you keep an eye on the ladies while I go after him?"

Rusty cocked his head; then he shook it and, standing up, he took her by the hand. He pointed at the door.

"Really?" she asked.

Rusty nodded. Really.

FRIDAY, 9:09 PM

After tapping back and forth for a couple of minutes Abner had heard three loud bangs come from the other side of the Transport Tube passage. He stepped well back, which he learned was exactly the right thing to do when a penetrating beam began to slice through the Tube's wall. The beam cut a rectangle about two feet across and about four feet high; then it paused momentarily, and started up again in order to cut the top edge of the rectangle free. The edges of the new doorway were still glowing red when Abner lifted it out and set it on the cell's floor.

There were probably a great many unexpected things that might have happened next. What did happen was well outside Abner's expectations.

A little boy stepped through the doorway. A very small robot with a smoking cannon in its chest was riding on the boy's shoulder. It was about five inches tall.

Things became only marginally more unexpected when a little girl stepped through after them.

"SURRENIG AR BE DISINGURATED."

Abner stared at the little robot.

"It's a lot better if you surrender," the boy suggested.

Abner nodded. It probably was.

"I surrender," he said.

The little boy smiled; the little girl, who appeared to be his sister, seemed disappointed. Abner decided that he'd better watch out for that one.

The three of them—no, he amended; the four of them—seemed to have run out of things to say. But after a moment the girl frowned and told him, "You'd better come with us, *prisoner*."

Abner nodded.

She leaned into the tiny robot's face. "Keep the prisoner under surveillance and *don't let him escape*."

A few minutes later the cell door swung open and Howard Pitt stomped inside.

His reaction echoed all along the hallway at his back, and then all up and down the Transport Tube passage in front of him; but no one with ears was close enough to hear him and that was just as well, since anyone with ears might have had delicate sensibilities.

FRIDAY, 9:23 PM

Nola tapped on her Info-Slate while they walked along the street. She searched recent news reports for mention of "Dash Kent" or "Kelvin Kent" and she felt relieved that there wasn't any. Then, hoping for no more success, she checked the hospitals. Nothing there, either.

Rusty had come to a stop. She looked up and saw that they were facing a Tube Transport station.

"Oh, no," she said. "I *hate* these things."

He waited.

"Please?"

Rusty opened the door for her.

They stepped inside and Nola used her Slate to look up the stop closest to the power station site. She keyed the number in and grabbed the bar that ran around the interior of the Pod. The Pod door whispered shut and she felt the first gentle acceleration as they slid into the main line. Then they sped up—enormously, she thought—and tilted forward, zooming through the hidden tunnels, up the monorail pylons, down again, a little later, and so on through the labyrinth of tubes that made up the Tube Transport line.

Finally they slowed again and stopped. The Pod door opened. They stepped out into the street.

"I *really* hate these things," she said. She was hanging on to the outside of the Tube station. Rusty waited until she'd gotten her land legs back.

A look up and down the street showed her that yes, they had traveled a remarkable distance in a very brief time. But she *still* hated the Tube.

They set off for the construction site.

It was lit by moonlight now, all gray and silver and rather more attractive than it had been by day. The construction sheds off to one side were like little cottages in the moonlight; the dark hulk of the ultrasonic drill looked like a giant bird, protecting its nest.

Nola led Rusty around the frontage road with the Hogben Canal at their backs until they reached the small red marker that showed her where Dash had cut the fence. She rolled the wire fence back and tied it up again behind them.

First they checked the windows of the construction sheds. There were no lights inside, and all was quiet. Over at the rim of the pit they found Dash's climbing lines where they still trailed down to the bottom of the excavation. Nola allowed herself only a short pause before she grabbed a rope and started down. Rusty waited a moment and followed her.

They found Dash's entrance without any trouble. It was still standing open. With only the feeble glow of Rusty's eyes to guide them they went in to find a sloping passage that curved gently leftward.

About a hundred feet in, Rusty grabbed her arm and stopped her. A huge slab of stone blocked the passage. The walls, ceiling, and floor were ringed with tiny sensors of some kind, each one emitting a narrow beam of faint light. Nola hadn't even noticed them. The beams crossed in a near invisible net that blocked their path.

Rusty knelt down to tap one sensor's housing. It looked as though it had once been hidden; it was set into a depression in the floor under a thin cover that had sprung open.

Nola looked up at the slab in front of them. The seams where it met the walls and floor were almost invisible.

"Traps," she said.

Rusty nodded.

They rocked back onto their heels and looked at the slab that blocked the passage.

"Well," she said. "I *thought* he was in trouble."

FRIDAY, 10:22 PM

Pitt scanned the listings on his Info-Slate. All around him his robots were proceeding with their tasks; here, around the control center, that meant that they were carrying loads of supplies down the hall to the Projectile. From time to time one would step, wheel, or roll into the control room on some other errand. He ignored them all. He knew that they were only a few minutes behind schedule.

There were a large number of Kents in Retropolis. He had eliminated anyone whose first name did not start with the letter D, and now he was culling out the ones who were obviously female: Dolores and Dodi Kent followed their sisters into the culled names.

He kept at it for several minutes. It was a welcome relief from the intense anger he'd felt when he saw that Perkins had escaped—no doubt with Kent's assistance. How could Kent possibly have known where Perkins was imprisoned? For a moment Pitt wondered whether he'd misjudged the young man. But no, no . . . that back pack had been filled with twenty pounds of equipment that Kent had apparently packed at random, not to mention those pulp magazines. Pitt grumbled to himself. It simply wasn't possible that Kent could be so formidable an opponent. There must be *someone else,* too.

Pitt froze in something that was almost like fear. Somewhere out there was another Pitt. An *anti-Pitt.* His true nemesis.

He felt himself relax. Somehow the knowledge that he had a counterpart in the world was . . . pleasant. Reassuring.

He went back to the list of Kents.

He would simply have to trace his enemy's contacts, one at a time, from Perkins, to Kent . . . and onward, until he saw his enemy's true face.

He called a patrol of security robots to the control room. Each one got a name from the list, from Dain Kent through Dylan. Pitt gave them their instructions and they set out on their quest.

Pitt counted the names again. Then he checked how many cells he had available.

It looked as though the Kents were going to have to double up.

FRIDAY, 10:47 PM

Abner rolled a little to his left. The tiny eyes of the children's robot turned to follow him. Unfortunately, but not surprisingly, the tunnel

175

floor wasn't any more comfortable on this side. He rolled a bit back to the right. The robot turned again.

Well, he thought, *it shows real dedication.*

The boy and girl were curled up a few feet away. They were breathing softly and dreaming, he had no doubt, about dissecting small animals. Or . . . perhaps *vivisecting*? He shivered. These children were horrible creatures.

They had marched him through the maintenance tunnels, seemingly at random, and as far as he could tell they were only interested in finding rats so that their robot could try to make them surrender. He shivered again. To date, every rat had tried to keep its freedom.

He sat up. He wasn't going to be getting any more sleep tonight.

The little robot's head pivoted to follow him.

"Gack?" Abner asked.

"GACK."

Yes. Abner nodded. He'd thought so.

FRIDAY, 10:52 PM

Dash dragged one weary leg after the other up the long, long stairway toward the roof of his building.

He'd had a bad moment on the way out of Pitt's construction site. Two more of those giant robots had been standing at the exit, but as he approached they just kept staring toward the outside. It seemed like they hadn't heard about him yet, and Dash guessed that they weren't worried about anybody getting out. But he wouldn't like his odds if he tried to walk past them the other way.

Dash hadn't wanted to use any kind of public transportation on his way home—for all he knew, Pitt would be watching the stations—and that meant that he'd had to walk all the way back from the power station site.

It was a pretty long walk.

Still, he was eager to tell Miss Gardner what he'd seen even though he still had no idea what any of it meant. There wasn't any obvious connection between Pitt's Projectile and the switchboard. And while he didn't doubt that Pitt was up to no good, what could Dash report him for? Building something?

People *paid* Pitt to build things.

He could say that Pitt had tried to kill him, of course. But in the end it would be his word against Pitt's and Dash knew how that would go: prominent civil engineer vs. building maintenance man and freelance adventurer. Yep, that'd go well.

He had to figure out exactly what Pitt was doing first and get some proof to back up his claim. There wasn't any way around that one.

As he came to the attic landing Dash could hear voices through Rusty's door. Female voices. He smiled. *That'll be Miss Gardner,* he thought, and so he knocked on the door.

There was plenty of enthusiasm in the room full of operators: so much of it that it took Dash quite a while to make sense of what they were telling him. They showed him that the motionless robot by the window was an operator, *just like them,* and he let his relief at finally sitting down stand in for his interest in what they were saying.

Nice bunch of ladies, really. That Mrs. Broadvine seemed like a fine lady to work for, very polite.

What they couldn't seem to tell him was where Miss Gardner and Rusty had gone. It sounded like they'd slipped out when no one was paying attention.

But anyhow, this room full of operators were his clients and so he gave them a report of the day's events. They already seemed to know a lot of it, up to the point where he and Miss Gardner had parted, and they were awfully appreciative for what he'd done, especially the younger ones.

In the end, though, they were as mystified as Dash was himself when it came to what it all meant. He had to explain three times why he couldn't just report Pitt to the authorities.

"It just doesn't seem *fair*," was what the one called Freda kept saying. "After he set those killer robots on you and all."

Dash allowed that it didn't seem fair, and then he explained again why that didn't matter.

"Anyway," he said at last, "it's real interesting how you found one of the new operators."

He waved over at the robot. "I just wish we knew where the rest of them were."

"Oh!" Rhonda exclaimed. "We *know* you'll find that out, too."

She had a really big smile. All the rest of them were nodding.

Well. He added up the day's events. Not any more dangerous than rescuing cats, when it came right down to it, and these were nice folks to work for, too.

"But for now, ladies," he said, getting up, "I'm going to turn in. It's been a long day."

They all decided that he was right about that. Dash saw them out and walked back to his apartment. When he reached the door his hand went to the doorknob, but it stopped there.

He didn't think that Pitt knew where to find him. Still . . . it might be smart to head back up to the roof and spend the night in the Actaeon's cabin. He looked back at the stairs.

Then he climbed them again.

FRIDAY, 11:43 PM

As—not for the first time—she tilted her head back to survey the pit's wall from top to bottom, Nola was trying not to think about the forty feet of rope that hung between her and the surface. It was only about a quarter of the way back around the pit wall now. The rope hung there, she was sure, just waiting for her to try to climb it. Waiting.

She and Rusty decided that this part of the wall was innocent of any hidden doorways, too. They shuffled around to their left and started to examine the next section.

As far as they could tell there were no other entrances to . . . to wherever it was that Dash had gone; but they couldn't just leave him. They couldn't really tell anyone, either, since he'd literally broken and definitely entered his way underground.

"This adventuring business gets pretty complicated, doesn't it?" she said.

Rusty nodded.

She looked left and saw nothing but unbroken stone between them and the rope. There just wasn't any sign of another doorway anywhere.

"Maybe we could cut across from here, and sort of scan the wall at a distance."

They paused and looked back and forth at the length of wall. The full Moon was shining right down into the pit now. She felt sure that its light would reveal any more doors if they were there. She was pretty certain that there weren't any. Even Rusty was wavering.

"We still need to check the shacks," she reminded him. "Up there."

They set out across the floor of the pit. There was that rope. Waiting. Her arms started to get sore just because she was *thinking* about the climb back to the top.

Nola heard a crackling sound that ran across the pit floor. She stopped in mid-stride; Rusty, however, had dropped to the ground and spread himself out just as wide as he could. He looked up and pointed at the ground, then swept his hand out in a flat arc and tapped the stone lightly.

A crack had started in the floor; it looked like it began right under Rusty, but its jagged web was spreading. Nola lowered herself very slowly and once she was down she rolled off to the side and reached for the robot's hand.

The crack was making a kind of a sizzling sound as it advanced. They were already in the middle of a lightning-sharp network of brittle cracks that kept on finding new ways to intersect on every side. A couple of the smaller pieces dropped into nothingness.

Nola listened very hard but she didn't hear them land.

She took Rusty by the fingers and began to pull him toward her, meanwhile rolling away toward the wall. He was pushing off with his toes to drive himself along.

Nola couldn't help but stare at one large piece of the stone floor: it was nearly encircled by the cracks. She pulled again, rolling farther, and saw the last side of that slab lose its grip on the surface. It dropped into blackness.

Again, she couldn't hear it land.

She could see its exposed edge, though. It was less than an inch thick.

She looked back at Rusty. He was using his fingers and toe tips to scoot himself along with as little force as possible. Nola rolled just a little bit faster, dragging him along behind her.

She looked over her shoulder. The wall was still about fifty feet away.

She started to pull harder on Rusty's hand.

Quite a ways below the two of them Robot R-54KG was pulling his drill out of a new rivet hole when a fragment of stone bounced off his shoulder. He looked up.

Moonlight was spilling onto the Projectile through tiny holes far above the robot foreman's head.

"The ceiling!" he shouted. "It's going to fall!"

All around him rivet guns and welding torches stuttered into silence.

He threw a wild look around at the Projectile, then upward at the dwindling stocks of inertrium where they bobbed against the ceiling.

"We've lost buoyancy!" he called. "Make for the windlasses!"

In their frenzied push to make up lost time the robots had forgotten to watch the state of the ceiling. One big inertrium block after another had been dragged down, rolled out, and skinned over the framework; and as their gentle pressure was removed the ceiling had begun to sag. Now the center of the ceiling had dipped down toward the cavern floor and the stresses were starting to crack it near the edges.

Robot R-54KG led his crew toward the windlasses on the great chains that moored the Projectile to the floor. On the other side of the cavern he could see another band of robots running to the windlass by the far wall.

He could only hope that they would be in time.

Every second dragged like a minute while Nola rolled again and again, slowly hauling Rusty away from the center of the cracks and nearer to the safety of the pit's wall. There, where it joined with the floor, the stone must be stronger than it was out here near the center. She just had to get him there.

She felt his fingers pushing her away.

Nola rolled back to get a look at him; Rusty was pointing at her, and then at the wall. It was pretty clear that he wanted her to leave him. He spread himself out again and gestured with his chin.

A large crack was splitting the pit floor in a line that was headed, in its crooked and casual way, straight at him.

She gauged the distance to the wall: about twenty-five feet. She looked over at Dash's climbing rope: much too far away. She looked back at Rusty.

"Well, no," she said. "I'm not going to do that."

She stretched back toward him. Rusty drew his hand away from her. *Oh no, you don't,* she thought. She lunged out over the cracking pavement and seized his hand. Then, with everything she had, she rolled toward the wall and dragged Rusty along.

She heard a loud crack behind her and then Rusty's weight was hanging from her hand. Eyes wide, she looked back again; all she could see was Rusty's hands and the top of his head. The rest of him had dropped into the void.

Nola tightened her grip while her other hand scrabbled for any kind of handhold on the smooth floor of the pit. She could feel herself starting to slide toward the hole. The top of Rusty's head dipped down below the edge.

Pickles, she thought.

Robot R-54KG heaved on the great windlass and slowly—very slowly—the chains played out. All along the cavern there were now other robot crews doing the same thing. With each downward heave R-54KG looked up. The Projectile was rising slowly, unevenly: its aft section was rising faster than its prow. "Faster!" cried R-54KG. "Keep it level!"

The loose chain piled up behind them as the robots bent to their work.

Nola's toes jammed in a crack. She swung her left hand out and grasped Rusty's right hand just before the little robot lost his grip on the edge of the stone. With both her arms holding on to him she felt slightly less like she was about to be torn apart.

How can such a small robot feel so heavy?

Suddenly her toes had a much better grip on the stone: looking back, Nola understood why.

The crack she'd jammed her feet in was getting wider.

Down below, the robots had finally synchronized their windlasses. The Projectile rose slowly. It hit the ceiling with a low rumble. They continued to pay out the chains and Robot R-54KG was pleased to see the ceiling's downward bulge begin to flatten.

"Easy, now!" he shouted. "Let it up slowly!"

All along the length of the cavern the robots heaved in a long, slow wave.

R-54KG, had he had any, would have let out his breath in a sigh. It was going to work.

Now Nola's toes were getting pinched. She looked back and saw that the crack had gotten narrower again. Now what? She pulled on Rusty's hands but she just couldn't budge him; he was a lot heavier than you'd think, or maybe she just wasn't as strong as she thought she was.

The top of Rusty's head appeared again over the crack. He'd managed to get one elbow braced over the edge and now he was trying to lift himself up. It wasn't working very well, Nola saw, but at least he'd distributed his weight a bit. She pulled again, and that side of Rusty's body hitched upward.

She could see the cracks around him starting to quiver. That couldn't be a good sign, could it? So she dug her toes in as well as she could and bent her legs, pulled with her arms, and curved her spine in a effort to make herself much, much shorter. Rusty started to slide over the edge.

Two things happened at the same time.

The cracks around Rusty suddenly gave way; what had just been the edge of the hole *became* the hole. He tilted back and Nola lost her grip on his hands.

That was the first thing.

Rusty slid away from her. The top of his head dropped out of sight again, and then . . . he stopped.

That was the second thing.

Nola gripped the new, wider edge of the hole and peered down at him. Rusty was standing on some kind of a curved girder that was lifting him up and out of the hole. It kept rising until he'd come almost level with the broken floor of the pit.

Then he stepped out onto the ground.

They just looked at each other for a moment. Then they spared a single glance down before they ran to the wall of the pit and pressed their backs into it as far as they could go.

"Don't take this the wrong way," said Nola, "but you could lose a couple of pounds."

Robot R-54KG ordered a crew of floating robots to repair the roof. "Get those holes and cracks filled by daybreak," he told them. They hovered overhead with their loads of gravel and cement.

Then he surveyed the site. He knew that they'd lost more irreplaceable time. They must be more than half an hour behind schedule by now. Still, there was nothing for it: it was the job they had to do.

He looked upward at the beams of moonlight. They glittered, grainy with drifting dust.

"We will finish on schedule," he said. "The plumber will come."

"The plumber will come," answered every other robot that was able to speak. The words passed from one mechanical person to another, all up and down the cavern.

"The Plumber will come."

11

THE SHOWROOM OF THE ROBOTS

SATURDAY, 5:44 PM

Lillian's question had been swallowed up in the roar of twelve
ASAA rockets overhead. She—and her questionee—looked up to
watch the rockets speed over the street and then divide, heading
off in twelve different, but apparently crucial, directions. Something
seemed to be going on.

"You're sure you . . ." she started, but the woman she was talking
to had already hurried away.

Lillian looked around. There was a lot of hurrying going on, she
saw. She wondered why. *Could they know . . . ?*

It didn't matter. Not really. Lillian checked her timepiece: she only
had a few more minutes.

SATURDAY, 12:12 AM

David Kent heard the doorbell. He decided not to believe in it.

"Snrfgl," he said, and he rolled over again and shoved his head into
the pillow.

There was a much louder noise that—while it was not the
doorbell—*involved* the doorbell, since the door, its frame, and

everything around them burst inward with a great boom that shook the floor and created a hole in the wall that was the same size and shape as one of Howard Pitt's security robots.

David Kent sat up. One of Howard Pitt's security robots was standing in front of his bedroom door.

"Cnghliac?" David asked.

"DAVID KENT (14)?" asked the robot.

"Uh, I think that's me," said David Kent.

The robot burst through the doorframe and picked him up.

"YOU WILL COME WITH ME."

Dougal Kent, sculptor, kept rather later hours. He was smoothing the surface of his wax model for the bust of Hierocampus Bellamy, Ph.D., and although he wasn't very happy about it he got up and answered *his* door when the doorbell rang.

"DOUGAL KENT?"

He glared up into the robot's face.

"What's it to you, bub?" he asked.

A moment passed.

"DOUGAL KENT?"

"No, I'm his mother." Kent shut the door in the robot's face.

Another moment passed.

The doorbell rang again.

Kent ignored it. He picked up a heat torch and went back to his sculpture.

From this point his experience was very much like that of David Kent (14).

"DARREL KENT?"

"Yes, I'm Darrel Kent."

When the robot reached for him Darrel Kent chose not to cooperate. He beat his fists against the robot's face and howled. He was only ten, after all.

A narcotic mist hissed from vents in the robot's chest.

Darrel Kent hit the floor, and the robot picked him up.

"THAT WAS UNNECESSARY AND POINTLESS," it told him.

All across the city the same scenes, or variations on them, were playing out. Pitt's robots went through neighborhood after neighborhood, gathered their D. Kents, and threw them onto hover sleds. A great many D. Kents found themselves in small narrow rooms (often two to a cell) an hour or two later—when the gas had worn off—in whatever clothing they had or (in the case of Dennis Kent) had not been wearing, and all quite angry about the whole thing.

But they had no choice but to sit and fume until Pitt was ready to examine them.

SATURDAY, 1:03 AM

"You saw him? You actually *saw* him?"

Freda's face was beaming out of the televideo screen.

"Yes, we met him, and even Mrs. Broadvine liked him, and he told us all about what he found under the power station."

Nola waved Rusty over to the televideo phone.

Fifteen minutes later, Freda was telling them that the operators had left Dash at his apartment. "He looked so tired, poor thing," she said.

"I expect so," Nola told her. They promised to meet in the morning and Nola hung up.

"Well, Rusty," she said, "I guess he's okay, anyway."

It sounded like Dash had been right underneath the floor of the pit.

It also sounded like he'd had a good look at whatever it was that Pitt was building down there.

It didn't sound like it could have anything to do with Pitt's new switchboard, though.

"It's awful late," said Nola. "Would you like to sleep on the sofa?"

She may have forgotten that Rusty really didn't need to sleep. He stretched himself out and let his eyes dim a little while she got ready for bed.

Sometimes it's just better not to be alone.

SATURDAY, 7:29 AM

Abner, who was a lifelong bachelor, had very little experience with children; but he was certain that this was not the way they were supposed to behave. If this was normal, what madman would choose to have them?

The question that kept arising in the back of his brain was: *Where are their parents?* Yet every time that question surged up toward his consciousness he fought it back. He was growing more and more certain that he didn't want to know the answer because it might turn out to be "buried in the basement."

The little robot kept him under constant watch from its perch on Evan's shoulder. Abner was watching it back. He could see a large (well, a relatively large) indentation in the robot's head and he assumed that this was the reason the robot had some difficulty saying words that were not "GACK" or "ACKRIG." It definitely looked like it had been damaged by a blow to the head. Moreover it was impossibly small for a robot of any complexity, and Abner felt that this must be important in some way.

But since his experience with robots (while greater than his experience of children) was limited, he couldn't decide what its tiny size might mean.

The Campbells had led him back into the Tube Transport maintenance tunnels where Abner kept a mental note of any markings he saw on the switching mechanisms and tunnel junctions. Sooner or later he'd figure out where they were.

One positive thing was that there should be very few problems with rats down here in the near future.

The little robot's eyes flickered briefly and its head dipped down. Then it roused itself and looked at Abner in what seemed like an accusing way.

"KRUMLAP GAZPRZZZH."

Evvie sighed loudly. She looked up and down the cross tunnel in front of them, then forward and back along their route. "This is *boring*," she said.

Before she could think of a way in which he might personally relieve her boredom Abner said, "Yes, the maintenance tunnels are quite uniform. The system doesn't really change at all until the Tubes mount the side of a monorail pylon."

Evan gave him a curious look.

"Do you know your way around down here?" the boy asked.

"Oh," said Abner as he kept an eye on Evvie, who was scowling again. "I'm in charge of the Tube Transport lines. For the Retropolis Transit Authority. I'm . . . well, I'm not quite *sure* where we are just now. But once I get my bearings I'll know what's up ahead."

The children's eyes narrowed. He could see that possibilities were churning behind those eyes. He hoped he would not find out what those possibilities were.

"It's, uh, it's quite instructive, really," he said. "But of course for sheer scale, and efficiency, and comfort, the Tubes aren't a patch on the monorail system."

That was true, he realized. The Tube system was *ridiculously* inefficient, with its individual Pods, its complex air pressure system, and its cumbersome pneumatic tubes, all taking passengers *one at a time* to their destinations. It was exactly the sort of system that Pitt ought to despise.

The Transport Tube beside them rumbled and shook while its Pod swept past. The children looked along the Tube.

"Can you make them crash?" asked Evan.

SATURDAY, 7:52 AM

Howard Pitt woke instantly, as he always did. He simply didn't have time to waste. He pulled his clothes out of the soniclave and slipped them on, checking the time. He hadn't had an optimal amount of sleep. This was unsatisfactory—he would become less effective as the day wore on—but it was also unavoidable.

A look at his Info-Slate informed him that the final D. Kent had been detained about two hours earlier. He nodded. Now he'd identify the right one and interrogate him. With a reasonable effort he should be able to face Kent's employer by noon.

On his way to the cells Pitt checked the Projectile schedule; his brows leaped in the direction of his hat. How had the crews managed to lose *even more* time? He'd have to check in at the site on his way back from the cells.

The first cell held two Kents: neither was the Kent he was after. He ignored the protests of the two men and moved on from one cell to the next. A quick glance through each window was all he needed.

At the final cell, Pitt frowned. He checked his floor plans again and found that every cell had been accounted for. He drew one finger across the Info-Slate's stored list of D. Kents.

He frowned more deeply.

Pitt marched back along the corridors of cells and checked each one again. The conclusion, unpleasant as it was, was inescapable.

He had failed to find the D. Kent he was looking for.

Pitt lifted his hat and passed a hand across his depilated scalp. This was highly inconvenient. The Projectile could mind itself for the moment: he'd have to get back to the control room.

Pitt had the unpleasant sensation that things were spinning out of his control, a thing that simply did not happen. The construction crews were lagging behind; his cells were overflowing, but with people who did not need to be there; the elusive D. Kent remained at large and Pitt still had no idea for whom Kent was working.

Somewhere, Pitt's nemesis must be having a fine morning.

Pitt sank into the chair at his main control console and breathed deeply. He knew that a complicated situation just had to be reduced to its component parts in order for him to understand it. He simply needed to prioritize.

Therefore: the construction problems had delayed the Projectile, but hadn't interfered with it, so he could table those problems until he had more time; the prisoners in the cells were an inconvenience, but no more than that; D. Kent, however, was Pitt's only clue to his *real* problem, which was to unmask the mastermind of Pitt's opposition.

He marveled at the very idea of opposition. It had seemed impossible just a day earlier.

Robots entered the control room on errands and then swept out again. In the halls outside Pitt could hear the sounds of cargo rolling to its destination in the great holds of the Projectile. These sounds were regular, and predictable, and rational. Pitt wasn't aware of them on a conscious level, but they soothed his troubled mind anyway. This was the way a world ought to sound, he knew, down below his turmoil.

And soon enough that's how this world *would* sound.

He stared at his list of Kents. Could the "D." in "D. Kent" be a title, an honorific, or some other kind of abbreviation? Pitt considered the possibilities, but nothing looked promising. Perhaps it was an assumed name?

He leaned back in his chair. If that was the case then his search would be hopeless.

He snapped forward again. He would ignore that possibility, then, as unproductive. If the "D." was part of a nickname, an alias, or a *nom de plume*? He decided to broaden his search to names *including* "Kent" and the capital letter D.

Far away, the unseen operator plugged and unplugged the cables for Pitt's Info-Slate feeds, now and then turning a dial or flipping a switch to change the content of the Slate's displays. She knew she was working at peak efficiency, and it was her nature to feel a certain satisfaction in that knowledge. Her eyes glowed with a soft, warm light.

SATURDAY, 8:22 AM

Nola and Rusty had agreed to go first to Dash and Rusty's apartment building. Rusty, no doubt, was going to continue to try to reach the League President and Harry Roy, whoever that was. Nola thought that it must have something to do with the operator robot upstairs.

All Nola herself wanted was to see Dash in the flesh, to make sure he was all right and, she hoped, to get a somewhat more coherent account of what had happened to him: an explanation that was a little bit less concerned with how *desperately heroic* he had looked and how *really, really brave* he had been while Pitt had *done his worst*.

Since Dash's apartment was on the ground floor Rusty and Nola practically walked into it as soon as they'd entered the building. Rusty waited obligingly while Nola rang the bell, tapped on the door, and thought for a moment before she knocked quite loudly. After that she had to admit that Dash wasn't at home.

They turned toward the stairs. Standing just behind them they found Evan and Evvie Campbell with an oddly familiar robot, so small that it could perch on Evan's shoulder, and a strange man with an ink-stained pocket on his chest and a terrified expression on his face.

"You'd better surrender," Evvie said. "We *know* what you *did* and we have come to *make you pay*."

Nola looked at Rusty. He was looking at the tiny robot: its chest-mounted cannon whined and spun its barrels.

Rusty put his hands in the air. She gave him a considering look and followed his eyes to the minuscule cannon. "Really?" she asked.

Rusty nodded with such certainty that she looked back down at Evvie and said, "Uh, we surrender, then."

The two children and their prisoners stepped through the hall door, down into the dimness of the basement.

"Is this about the zombies?" Nola asked.

SATURDAY, 8:26 AM

Dash finished his coffee, grateful that he'd paid a bit extra for the Actaeon's kitchen module. That reminded him of the space helmet that he'd left . . . where? Miss Gardner must still have it, he decided.

He poked his head out of the rocket's main hatch and called over one of the ornithopters. It came to him, its little steely feathers chiming, and settled on his wrist. " 'Morning," Dash said. "I was wondering if you could fly downstairs and have a look around my windows and the front door."

The ornithopter circled the roof and disappeared. Dash went back in for another cup of coffee. He still wasn't sure if the rocket made better coffee than he got in his own kitchen.

He sank into the pilot's seat and took stock of what he knew.

First off, he still didn't know much of anything about Pitt's new switchboard, and that was, after all, the whole reason he'd gotten into this mess. The operators had demonstrated that Rusty's new robot friend was herself a switchboard operator and that was pretty interesting, he thought, as far as it went. So they did know something about how the switchboard was being run even if they had no idea where it was or what that might mean.

Dash took another sip of his coffee.

On the other hand, he knew that whatever Pitt was building under that power plant site, it wasn't on the up and up. Otherwise Pitt wouldn't have made such a rumpus when he found that Dash had gotten in there. He really had been steamed, hadn't he?

The problem there was that Dash didn't know what it meant and it wasn't something he could use to implicate Pitt, seeing as how Dash had broken into the place himself. That would take a bit of explaining, that would.

But Pitt was definitely doing something that he wasn't supposed to be doing and he was willing to kill anybody who found out about it. So a little bit of care was needed from here on out.

Dash rinsed his coffee cup and snapped it into place in the cupboard. First off he needed to make sure that Nola and the other operators were going to lie low. There was nothing to connect them to Dash, so far as Pitt could know, and it was best it stayed that way.

He stepped outside again and enjoyed the view until the ornithoper came back with its recording. It looked like it was all clear down there. Dash smiled. *Well, that's one thing that's going my way,* he thought. Pitt couldn't know just who Dash was.

Downstairs he slipped his clothes into the soniclave and himself into his bathrobe and then he fried up some eggs while he waited for the wash. The two sinister helmets he'd brought back from the Moon were glaring at him. He turned them to face the wall.

There was the televideo phone, blinking at him. He checked his messages while he ate.

Surprisingly, Margaret of O'Malley's had called to tell him his new helmet would be in around noon. Dash frowned. Well, maybe he'd get to it, if he could locate the broken one before then. There was a late night message from his cousin Dale, but it didn't make much sense. All Dash could see in the recording was an empty room, and all he could hear was some kind of loud noise coming from off screen. He shook his head. Dale did like his parties.

The soniclave beeped while he was doing the washing up. Dash dressed and dug through the file cabinet for the note that Miss Gardner had given him, with the rate the operators wanted to pay him and her address and televideo number. He smiled: a young lady had given him her number, even if it was in what you would call a professional capacity.

He called and let the videophone ring and ring, but she wasn't at home. So he set the paper down while he decided what to do next.

There wasn't any doubt that finding the switchboard was what the job was really about, even if Pitt's Projectile might be the man's real weakness. Dash thought it over. His only clue to the switchboard was that robot up at Rusty's.

Well, he thought. *There it is, then.*

He locked his apartment and took the stairs two at a time.

There was no answer at Rusty's door, but since Dash knew the robot didn't bother to lock his attic apartment, he cracked it open and peered in. There was the operator robot—motionless again—in front of the window; next to her, Dash's broken space helmet sat on the workbench. He scooped that up and headed back downstairs.

On the seventh floor landing he remembered the leak in the 7C bathroom, and he felt a sudden shame. With all that was going on he'd forgotten to get the new valves. He'd just have to squeeze that in, he promised himself, and on the sixth floor landing he also remembered to squeeze in some sealer and paint for the ceiling in 6C.

And with those reminders of plumbing he thought back on Pitt's robots. Where was Pitt getting all these mechanical people? They hadn't looked quite like any other robots Dash had ever seen. *There might be something in that,* he told himself.

SATURDAY, 9:11 AM

There was something familiar about that little robot, the one that was riding on Evan's shoulder. Nola was sure she'd seen it before, but she couldn't recall ever having seen a robot so small. Well, there were the ornithopters in their cote on the roof, but they were about as close to robots as a bird was to a person. They weren't . . . complex, or something like that.

She squinted at the little robot while it bobbed up and down on the boy's shoulder. They had descended from the basement through a hatch—suspiciously sooty and ragged around the edges—and now the subbasement stairs had led them to a tunnel below the streets.

Was it the *color* of the robot that seemed so familiar? Nola tried to ignore its size and just picture it in a sort of abstract way.

Oh, no.

There was a deep dent in its tiny head. If you imagined that it was *very much bigger* . . .

"GACK."

Its little eyes were following her as it went up and down in time with Evan's steps. She didn't think she could see any recognition there. She hoped very much that she never would.

The strange man was watching the robot, too. "I think it's been damaged somehow," he whispered.

"Filing cabinet on the head," she mumbled. "Just don't ask me how I know."

The man's jaw sagged. "Do you *know* these people?"

Rusty, for his part, was watching the Campbells. Nola could see that he'd pulled something out of a pouch or pocket: it was a little device of some kind, and he was holding it behind his back. His thumb was pressing a button on the device's face. But she saw that Rusty kept shaking his head, as though he was trying to clear it. Nola wondered if her robot friend was all right.

As they trudged along the man offered his hand to Nola. "Abner Perkins," he said. "Engineer."

"Nola Gardner," she answered, clasping Abner's hand. "Switch-board operator."

They continued across the puddled floor.

"And, sort of, adventurer," she added.

Rusty looked her way. "And that's Rusty," she said. "He doesn't talk, as such."

The tiny robot kept peering at her face. Its chest tended to turn with its head and that meant that its cannon was following her every-where. It looked like it was trying to figure something out.

The robot, that is; not the cannon. The cannon looked like it knew everything it needed to know.

SATURDAY, 9:43 AM

Pitt had expanded his search for D. Kent into the internal workings of the Info-Slate system. No one had known he was building in this kind of access: but since he ran the operators, and they ran the system, it hadn't been difficult for him to establish channels he could use to see what every Info-Slate in Retropolis was doing.

The trouble was that even though few people owned Info-Slates, they used them for a very large number of things. Pitt had been sort-ing through their messages, requests, and notes for a long time before he hit on something that looked promising.

It was a message from O'Malley's Adventure Outfitters to one of its suppliers, concerning a replacement space helmet for a customer named Kelvin Dashkent.

Dashkent? Unusual name. Pitt cross-checked all the city directories but he couldn't find a Dashkent listed anywhere. He leaned back in his chair. Back in his original list of Kents he did see a Kelvin Kent. Well, then.

Pitt started looking up background information on Kelvin Kent, whose address, it turned out, matched O'Malley's records for Kelvin Dashkent.

All around him his robots continued about their tasks until one of them stopped midway across the room with its eyes on his face because, for the first time in its memory, it could see that he was *smiling*.

SATURDAY, 10:22 AM

Dash felt a little conspicuous with that broken space helmet on his hip but he did his best to carry it off. It wasn't as much of a problem as he'd supposed, really, since the sales clerk at Robots in Every Shape! was determined to think he was charming, fashionable, and wealthy.

"These are all real nice," he said, "especially, you know, the mechanics. They're pretty swell." He reached down to the counter and sketched what he could remember of Pitt's operator robot, and then next to her, and about three times the size, the giant robot that had chased him with Miss Gardner through the city just the day before.

"I was thinking about these two. I saw them this week. This one," as he pointed at the operator, "is just about three feet tall, on account of she sort of stops at the hips, and this one," with a finger on the giant robot, "well, he's a real bruiser, about ten or twelve feet tall, with something like this," as he sketched in the robot's cannon, "smack dab in the middle of his chest."

The sales clerk looked apologetic.

"I'm sorry, sir," she said, "but I've never seen anything like these."

She looked out across the showroom. "But as you can see, we've got *Robots in Every Shape!* here, and I'm sure that if you have a look around you'll find something that meets your needs."

At the end of the nearest aisle a display robot looked up from his magazine, saw that Dash was still talking to the clerk, and then went back to his reading. It was this month's *Hearts and Pistons*.

Dash tapped his sketches. "Well, the thing is, Miss, I'm kind of trying to find out where *these robots* come from."

She turned to watch her manager step into the shop's back room. Then she sized Dash up and leaned forward. "Look, we handle all the major manufacturers here, and nobody builds anything quite like these. Are you sure this is what they look like? Where did you see them?"

Dash sized her up right back, all five and a half feet of her, from her too-stylish shoes that had to be killing her to the top of her head, and he took note of her name badge in between.

"Okay, Evelyn. Somebody owns robots like these, and he's not a very nice person." He pointed back at his sketch of the giant robot. "*This* one tried to vaporize me yesterday. And the other one, she's kind of a custom job that seems to be made to work at a switchboard. There's something about this fellow that's just not right and I'm trying to find out what that is. And I'm Dash, by the way. Dash Kent."

Evelyn took the weight off her too-stylishly clad feet on a stool behind the counter.

"It's a kind of a mystery, then?"

He nodded and then handed her his business card. "Yes, Miss, that's exactly what it is. It's a mystery."

She ran her eyes over the card and slipped it into a stylishly invisible pocket. "Well, I *never*."

Dash smiled some more.

Evelyn pulled out some sample books and showed him the latest models from Ferriss Moto-Man, Volto-Vac, and Robots By Maria. He had to agree that these were not a match.

"But you see the arms on your little operator robot? They look just like the arms on the Robots By Maria *Châtelaine* model. The legs on this big one look a lot like the legs on a Volto-Vac *Submersible*— see, there's one by the window? And its head could just be a head from the Ferriss *Smeltomator*. We don't carry those."

Dash frowned down at the catalogs. "You think they're made from spare parts, then?"

Evelyn nodded happily. "We don't talk about this," she confided, "but it's possible for someone to make a whole robot from replacement parts. They just sort of cobble them together, you see, and if they can make some custom fittings to assemble all those parts together, well, there you go. Unlicensed robot."

She beamed at him.

"Unlicensed . . ."

Evelyn pulled a stack of forms from behind the counter. "When we sell a robot," she said, "it's a sort of a lease; you can't *own* a robot, 'cause it's a person. You own its *indenture*. That's kind of like a loan. When it does enough work for you so it's paid off the indenture, well, then it's a free agent. From then on you have to pay it wages or else get a new one and send the old one on its way."

Dash nodded slowly. He guessed he'd heard about this. Had Rusty gone through that? Dash supposed he must have.

"But if you build 'em on the sly . . . ?" he wondered.

Evelyn checked the shop again. Apart from the sample models, she and Dash were all alone in there. She leaned closer.

"Then they don't know about indentures *at all*," she whispered. "And if nobody ever finds out about it, they'll end up working for you *forever*."

Dash looked out over the showroom. The robot who'd been reading was watching him now. You could never know just what they were thinking.

"They'd be *slaves*," Dash said, quietly. "And no one would ever know."

Evelyn nodded.

"People really do that?" he asked.

"Some have," she said primly. "It's all *quite* illegal."

"Well, I should hope so," Dash agreed.

He looked over the catalogs again, and back at his sketches.

"What you've got there," Evelyn told him, "are *black market* robots."

He nodded slowly. "Well, like I said, he's not a very nice guy."

Just then Evelyn's manager came out of the back room and started to look interested, so Dash bent over the catalogs. Now that he knew what to look for he thought he could recognize the arms, legs, torsos, and heads of some of the construction robots he'd run into down below the power station site. He thought about all those robots working away down there in the dark.

Pitt was running a huge operation there with an army of black market robots. And if Dash could prove it . . . he just might have found a way to get Pitt thrown into jail.

SATURDAY, 10:22 AM

Howard Pitt consulted his notes for a final time. *His* D. Kent, also known as Kelvin, had made recent calls to O'Malley's and to a woman named Nola Gardner. That name, Pitt recalled, belonged to one of the operators from the old Info-Slate switchboard.

Pitt grunted. The switchboard must be the spot where Kent's unseen master had placed him on Pitt's chessboard. And now that Kent had spoken to her the operator must be considered a liability, too.

He handed Info-Slates to the two robots who were about to leave: one for O'Malley's, and one for Kent's apartment building. He'd use the Slates to stay in constant touch with them. If Kent were foolish enough to go home, or to keep his appointment at O'Malley's, that's when Pitt would have him.

But in case his robots missed Kent and Nola Gardner, he'd have to make sure that they were eliminated in another way.

Pitt used his private access to the Info-Slate system one more time.

12

BATTLE IN THE PNEUMATIC WIND

Dash propped his helmet up on a convenient pillar while he stowed the new valves for Apartment 7C inside his back pack. He felt a minor pang of guilt; but those old valves weren't going to hold up, and anyway if Miss Gardner wanted to hear from him she'd have been at home, or maybe at Dash's apartment, and so far she hadn't been to either one. Anyway he could put the valves and other issues of plumbing out of his mind for now.

In fact he was just a few blocks from the main monorail terminal. If he swung by O'Malley's on his way he could have all his other business settled by the time he finally reached Miss Gardner and the operators.

Then maybe he could figure out how to prove that Pitt was in the middle of the black market robot trade.

He picked up his helmet again and balanced it against his hip. That illegal robot racket was an ugly business. It was making him mad just to think about it, and between the expression on his face and the broken space helmet he looked just like the kind of person that the other pedestrians wanted to avoid, which is what they did; and so Dash made very good time on his way to the terminal.

Once inside O'Malley's he walked right up to the counter and set the helmet down.

"Kelvin Kent, Aero-Vac helmet, *Indestructible* Dome*," he told Margaret.

She shuffled through some order forms. "Mr. Kent?" she asked. "Mr. Kelvin Kent?"

Dash nodded. She could give him her worst. He really didn't care anymore. "Also known as Dash Kent, sometimes written as Kelvin Dashkent. That's me."

Margaret of O'Malley's frowned.

"This is very irregular. Do you have some identification? I'm only supposed to give this to Mr. Dashkent, *personally*."

Things progressed in Margaret's usual way until, a few minutes later, Dash stepped back from the counter with his new, highly polished, and—he hoped—*Indestructible** helmet. But something hanging in front of the counter caught his eye. "You know . . . I think I'll have one of these, too."

It slid right into his back pack alongside the Enigmascope.

Robot G-94VA was not, by occupation, a security robot. The sight of Pitt's security robots might have alarmed Dash before Pitt *intended* for him to feel alarmed; so it was a couple of the construction robots he'd detailed to find, follow, and capture Dash.

G-94VA wasn't accustomed to this kind of duty. He arrived on station outside the terminal and stood there, completely motionless, watching for any sign of a young man with a space helmet. No such young man was in view. G-94VA automatically scanned the welds on the bench in front of him and felt a slight discomfort. The bench's welds showed some unprofessional voids; in addition, their beads were not uniform.

G-94VA looked up and down the street: there was still no sign of a human with an Aero-Vac space helmet. His torso swiveled down from what we will call his hips. A tiny torch lit up at the end of one of his fingers.

G-94VA watched the insufficient welds and the metal around them heat up to a dull red glow. He took a rod of filler out of one of his compartments and waited for the heat to grow to a bright cherry red.

Dash absently sidestepped a working robot on his way down the street. His mind was focused on Pitt, Miss Gardner, and the operators, and his other problems.

There was a Tube Transport station a few yards away. The little indicator light on its door glowed green, which Dash knew meant that there was a vacant Pod docked there. Perfect!

G-94VA swiveled his torso back up from what we are still calling his hips. He felt relieved at the sight of the new, perfect weld. It was his nature to feel uncomfortable around shoddy work but much more comfortable, as now, when he had performed a task to specification.

Then he recalled that he was here on another kind of duty. He felt uneasy again because he realized that he was not performing *that* task in accordance with his instructions.

He looked furtively down the street: all clear.

Then he turned his entire upper body to get a view up the street, and that's when he saw Dash—holding the new space helmet—about to step into a Transport Pod.

The little welding torch on his finger shot out a long and white-hot flame that just missed Dash's head and scorched a ragged line across the Pod door, which slid shut with a hiss.

Dash smelled the bitter, dry odor of hot metal. He turned in time to see a line of smoking slag sketch itself down the Pod door. The line took an abrupt turn upward when the Pod dropped into the Tube network and left whatever had burned it up above, on the street.

Dash scratched his head. What the blazes had that been?

G-94VA's discomfort became acute and acquired an entirely new flavor.

It's difficult to describe, to humans, the emotions that a robot feels in a situation like this. You need first to understand that a robot's entire sense of self worth is tied to its job performance. A welding robot welds, and is uncomfortable in the face of bad welding. A service robot cleans and repairs: broken, dirty things offend it on a deep and profound level. A giant robot smashes things, and unsmashed things, to a giant robot, look incomplete and disturbing.

Although G-94VA was not by nature a security robot, that's the job he had been assigned to do today and he *had not done it well*. You might make allowances for G-94VA, but G-94VA didn't know how to make allowances for himself. He had *failed*.

G-94VA was horrified. He stamped forward on his big, flat feet and moaned to himself, waving the welding torch—which by now he had forgotten—in a random, searing arc. In a wide circle around G-94VA pedestrians dove for cover like the petals of a great big flower in a Busby Berkeley musical.

When G-94VA reached the Transport Tube station he ripped its door off. The empty Tube yawned in its housing. G-94VA groaned, gathered his stumpy legs under him, and jumped in.

SATURDAY, 12:09 PM

Harry Roy glared at the tops of the heads of the twelve accountants he'd called in to the Ferriss plant on their free Saturday. He had no idea how they did the things they did, but in Harry's view their speed could only be improved by glaring at them. So he glared.

The accountants, who were sweating heavily despite the air conditioning, had each been given a list of company names. They were paging through their lists with sweaty fingertips in an effort to figure out just who owned what, and how often, and where, and what it all might mean. The companies were a twisted nest of shells, fronts, trusts, and foundations, slowly forming a kind of a family tree that—they hoped—would reveal its root before dinnertime.

Harry glared.

Rows of desks distributed their load of accountancy across the room. On one of these desks a televideo phone rang; a rather nervous accountant spoke quietly into the screen for a few moments. Then she leaned over to the accountant next to her and whispered, "Bavaria."

That accountant looked alarmed. He shuffled through his own stack of papers. "Not Sri Lanka? Are you sure?"

He looked up to receive the full force of Harry's glare. Three new drops of sweat plopped down onto his paperwork. He scribbled something out and shook his head in wonder.

Harry's televideo set rang like an echo of the first one. It was Albert King on the line.

"They're making progress." Harry looked over the accountants. "*Very slow progress,* I mean. But the companies that are buying up all those spare parts do seem to be related. I'm hoping we'll find the common denominator this afternoon."

Albert's face on the screen was unreadable, as always.

"I hope that you're right, Harry. My own resources haven't been able to add anything, so your people are the best hope we have."

Harry's people relaxed, very slightly. Harry glared at them.

King tapped a finger on his distant desk. "Have you heard anything from Rusty? It seems he tried to call me several times last night. I can't reach him this morning."

Harry frowned. "I didn't bother to check my messages here," he said. "Any idea what it was about?"

Albert had no idea. "It's unusual for him to call. But he'd have gotten in touch this morning if it was an important matter."

Harry tried to imagine taking a call from Rusty. It would be like a game of charades.

"Probably nothing then," he said. "When he's not with you he's usually at the Civilian Conservation Corps, or something." He flushed. "Actually I have some pretty detailed reports, now that I think of it. I could check to see what he does on the weekends."

"If you have a moment to spare," said Albert.

Harry hung up and increased the intensity of his glare. He hoped it was working.

SATURDAY, 12:13 PM

Whatever gadget it was that Rusty was holding behind his back, Nola hoped that it was going to do something dramatic. Something that would get them out of there, away from the Campbells and their tiny, dangerous robot. Its gaze swept over her, and Rusty, and Mr. Perkins, in a monotonous sweep that seemed somehow to end up on Nola more often than it should have.

By now she'd seen what its cannon could do to a rat, a spider's nest, a rusted hatch, and a few rocks that the Campbells had decided to subdue. Even at this size the formerly giant robot was nothing to sneeze at.

It must have been something that had hit it back in the Experimental Research District. In that improbable hail of scientific progress there must have been some kind of miniaturization device.

How does that even work? she wondered.

Happily for the world's smallest giant robot, the miniaturization ray was continuing to work quite well. Of course, the ray only needed to *work* once: in that moment when the robot's atoms were dispersed across a very large number of alternate universes while their correspondence with each other was maintained in what was, frankly, a brilliant solution to the problem. The atoms in this particular universe were squeezed oh-so-slightly closer together than they used to be—though nowhere near so close as to cause unwanted side effects, like nuclear fission—but this, as the reader knows by now, is just a bit of icing on the cake. The cake itself is that careful dispersal throughout the dimensions.

The scientists of the Experimental Research District believe, to a person, in learning by doing. This is supplemented by a related method that might be called "learning by other people's doing" or, and this is probably more accurate, "learning by looking into the smoking wreckage of that lab that used to be next door."

The scientists of Retropolis have never really taken to the idea of Alpha testing. They have decided that smoking craters are all the testing you'll ever need.

So the miniaturization ray that had so skillfully shrunk the world's smallest giant robot had not been tested *beyond* the smoking craters stage. If you pointed the ray at something and then you pulled the trigger, that thing would become very much smaller and there would not be a smoking crater. Done.

In other universes (one of which even now was hosting about 673,728 of the atoms belonging to the formerly giant robot) there are people who believe in more extensive testing. *Those* people experiment with different situations, a variety of initial conditions, and the interactions between one experiment and another or, as in this case, between one experiment and *another instance of itself.*

So although no one in the group that was making its way through the tunnels below Retropolis was aware of this, the dispersed atoms of the world's smallest giant robot were now mixing and commingling with a surprising number of very similar atoms that had *also* been dispersed across the dimensions.

And because of the nature of those very similar atoms, something was happening inside the head of the world's smallest giant robot.

It was getting . . . smarter.

This was quite a nice side effect, as these things go. The world's smallest giant robot had not been built for intelligence. Any boost in that department should have been an improvement.

But the world's smallest giant robot had also been damaged in the head; a critical area that—just as in a human being—was where its intelligence made its home. Its suddenly smarter brain was also a regrettably damaged brain. And very smart but damaged brains can cause difficulties.

SATURDAY, 12:14 PM

Dash lurched from one side rail of the Pod to the other while it picked up speed in the main Tube line. He could see that the damaged area of the door was still quite hot, and so he tried not to lurch anywhere near it.

He hadn't used the Pods much. Still, he was pretty sure that death rays didn't usually try to cut the doors in half when you entered them. Things being what they were, it seemed as though somebody was mad at him. There wasn't much doubt in his mind about who that might be.

So Pitt knew who he was. Pitt knew *where* he was.

His hand hovered over the Pod controls. He could change his destination, if he . . .

His fingers curled tightly into his palm. Pitt had designed the Pod system. There was a pretty good chance that he had his eyes on it. Dash now regretted his decision to ride the Pod home. But it was a little late for that now.

The Pod had nearly reached its maximum speed when Dash—now almost prone against its walls—felt the shock of something striking the Pod from behind, which from his point of view was somewhere near his feet.

Eight dents crumpled the skin of the Pod's floor. They pushed in and the metal began to creak under the strain.

They looked a lot like fingertips.

Robot G-94VA forced his fingers into the Pod's shell while the tunnel walls streaked past him. He was feeling a little better, with the quarry now so close. He struggled to forge handholds in the Pod's casing with his fingertips.

The whistling wind of the Tube system's air pressure built up behind the Pod and forced it, with G-94VA clinging to its base, toward a curve that would soon climb the pylons of the monorail. The air built up in a kind of cushion behind G-94VA. The robot shifted, digging his fingers in with the help of the pneumatic wind.

The Pod began to rise.

Dash could see the depressions in the Pod floor curve inward as though they were being shaped by hooks; he could picture the robot's fingers just on the other side of the thin flooring. Then he found himself sliding toward the floor. The Pod had reached the base of a monorail pylon and now it tilted up, ready to climb who knew how high before leveling out alongside the track.

Dash slipped out of his back pack's straps and shuffled through the pack's contents.

Somewhere, he was sure, somewhere in here he had it with him.

With one hand rooted in the Pod's body, G-94VA pulled the other one back, just a little, and fired up his fingertip welding torch. The flame narrowed into a slender cutting beam, and G-94VA started to draw a circle in the bottom of the Pod.

He was feeling *much* better now.

SATURDAY, 12:17 PM

The world's smallest giant robot was having some trouble. For reasons that it couldn't know its brain was now racing; without the least inclination to do so it found itself calculating the distance between the tunnel's arches, their angles to the walls, and every sort of measurement imaginable, up to the shoe sizes of the giants that were accompanying it (237 Wide, in Abner's case).

The measurements added up, but that didn't mean that they made any sense.

The world's smallest giant robot couldn't remember how, or when, it had blundered into this world of giant human people. Up to now it hadn't worried about this. Now, however, with a limitless flood of calculations flowing through its damaged cranium, it devoted a part of its brain to resolving that question.

It knew that it had been sleeping for 39.4 days when it had awoken in the storage room. There had been intruders, and it had acted accordingly. Then . . . something had happened.

Its brain hovered around that something. On either side of the Incident it had still been in its usual world where things were of a familiar size. Therefore the robot tabled the Incident; it was interesting, since the robot's thinking seemed to be impaired afterward, but there was no explanation there for its presence in a new and bigger world.

While its eyes and cannon revolved in a circuit that lasted for 11.4 seconds in each direction, the world's smallest giant robot tried to remember just what had happened *after* its thinking had become unreliable.

Another 57.6-foot archway was left behind. A puddle containing an astonishing 122.15 quarts of water, or something that was very much like water, passed below. The world's smallest giant robot paid only the slightest attention to these facts. It was concentrating.

SATURDAY, 12:18 PM

Dash hung on to the Pod railing with his left hand while he gripped the handle of his pistol in his right. Because those were all the hands he had, he was wearing the helmet on his head. The Pod was almost vertical now and so its floor had once again become *the* floor, according to Dash's senses; and a glowing hot circle, about a foot and a half in diameter, was almost complete.

This was the tricky bit: it would be better to do it now, before the robot had broken through the floor.

Dash let go of the railing and slid down until his feet actually touched the floor about eight inches from the flame of the robot's welding torch. Then he reached down to his belt and hooked a thumb through it. With one finger he pressed the belt stud that enabled his electromagnet.

Dash jumped up when the button clicked into place and at once he could feel the pull, all around him, of the Pod's steel body. The magnetized wires in his clothing tried to pull his arms and legs to the Pod walls, but he strained against them and aimed his pistol at the floor. He thumbed the dial on the ray gun to its highest setting and pulled the trigger.

While the robot tried to burn through the last four inches of *its* hole, Dash began to cut out a much larger hole that ran around the robot's handholds.

The robot's welding torch sputtered and stopped for an instant. Then its flame shot out farther and hotter. It began to cut more rapidly.

SATURDAY, 12:19 PM

There had been a pursuit. The world's smallest giant robot was certain about that much. The intruders had refused to surrender, and of course that was annoying, although not unexpected; it had managed to catch up with them and it was at this point, it found, that its memories became extremely confused.

There had been quite a lot of noise and bright flashes of light and energy; possibly, there had been elephants.

The robot considered that for a moment. Very small elephants.

But it couldn't recall any particular change in scale for about five more minutes. It couldn't recall much of *anything* during those five minutes. It was just after that when it had found itself walking through a titanic tunnel and it had encountered something that was rather like a very, very large squid. The squid had refused to surrender.

And from that point on, the world's smallest giant robot concluded, it had been walking through a world full of immense human people, along with rodents of remarkable height and quite a lot of rocks that had also refused to surrender themselves to it.

Its little brain buzzed. Yes, that was true: this world was peopled with intelligent, intruding rocks; savage rocks; defiant rocks; rocks that defied capture. Its little eyes (and, strangely, Rusty's eyes) flew to the masonry that lined the tunnel. *Scary* rocks.

"SPRDLFGHL!"

SATURDAY, 12:20 PM

When the robot's arm came through the bottom of the Pod, Dash still hadn't finished his own cut through the floor. He could just see the robot's face hanging down below; its arm reached all around the Pod floor in search of a place to anchor itself. Dash's tongue crept out of the corner of his mouth and lodged there while he labored to finish his own work on the Pod.

Fortunately he didn't need to finish it. The robot's weight was hanging from what by now was just a loose flap of steel: the flap started to bend back with a creak. The robot's arm flailed wildly around the compartment. Dash tucked his legs up under him to stay out of its way.

His pistol cut a final inch around the robot's handholds and then, he saw, it was all over. The floor of the Pod gave way. The robot hung there, staring up at him, and then it seemed to get much smaller very, very quickly, because they were about halfway up a monorail pylon and there was a considerable distance to fall.

Strange, though: in that instant when the robot had been hanging there its eyes had suddenly blazed brightly and he was sure he'd heard it say, "You! *The Plumber!*"

SATURDAY, 12:21 PM

Nola kept an eye on Rusty while they climbed a rough, damp stairway to a hatch that Evvie opened with caution. The sounds of a city street came from the other side.

Rusty still had his thumb planted firmly on his gadget's button. He was trying to look up toward the daylight, but his head had fallen into some kind of spasm. His glowing eyes seemed to want to look left and right, left and right, in a strange, repeating rhythm. Over and over his face would tilt upward, only to snap back down and shift from left to right, left to right, left to right. . . .

Nola was so busy worrying about Rusty that she completely missed the fact that Rusty's head was moving in the exact way that the tiny robot's head was moving. They were perfectly in sync: left to right, swing back, left to right, swing back. . . . If she'd seen that, she would have been even more worried. But unless she could also know what was going on *inside* the head of the world's smallest giant robot, she still wouldn't have been worried enough.

Nola, as we have seen, had no idea how miniaturization works.

Mr. Perkins stood with slumped shoulders and a hopeless air. *Well, Nola thought, who knows how long they've been holding him prisoner?* She tried to encourage him by doing interesting things with her eyebrows.

Evvie stepped out onto the street, followed by Evan, who had the little robot riding on his shoulder.

Rusty, and then Nola, followed them onto the empty street.

The children looked up and down the street and seemed satisfied with what they saw. Nola herself wasn't sure just where they were.

Then Evan turned to wave Mr. Perkins up after them, and it was at this point that things became confused.

The little robot on Evan's shoulder was swinging right and left as though it was surrounded by enemies. *Uh-oh,* thought Nola.

Although their way was clear of pedestrians, there were several personal rockets and hover sleds drifting above the street with their high-pitched, coughing sound; someone nearby was playing music, rather loudly, in Nola's opinion, and a·block or so over someone must have been doing some construction work. Loud voices and louder equipment were barking and banging and generally raising a racket.

The little robot swung back and forth; it looked like it was trying to locate the sources of all those sounds. Then its eyes fastened on the stonework of the building behind them and its cannon erupted into flame.

It was trying to subdue the building.

Evan shrieked. Evvie turned and gave the little robot a curious look.

Rusty took his thumb off the gadget's button and then gave it two quick taps.

Nola heard the familiar *ping-ping-ping* of ornithopter wings just above them: a swarm of the little mechanical birds descended on Evan and circled his head. They were making chirping sounds.

Rusty grabbed Nola by the hand and took off down the street at a run, and Nola was dragged along behind him for the instant it took for her legs to figure out what was going on.

The tiny robot swarmed up onto Evan's head, its little legs pumping and its cannon sweeping left and right in an effort to track a dozen ornithopters. It was hard to tell, but the robot almost seemed to be afraid of them.

Nola looked back and had one last glimpse of Abner Perkins's astonished face. The children tumbled back through the doorway on top of him; the door swung closed; and then only the circling ornithopters were left on the street.

SATURDAY, 12:27 PM

"What's wrong with your robot? What's wrong with your robot?" Abner kept asking.

Evan's left ear had a nasty burn. Evvie was poking it experimentally. The robot, though, had gotten very quiet once they'd shut the door to the street.

"I don't *think* you'll lose it," Evvie told Evan.

"Can I wear a patch on it?" he asked.

She thought that over.

"Yeah, okay."

Abner edged closer to the stairs. Evvie gave him a look.

"Hey, robot," she said. "Don't let him get away."

The little robot hesitated, but only for an instant. Its little cannon turned to point at Abner.

"GACK."

"I need to get an ear patch," Evan said.

Suddenly Abner could imagine Evan in his ear patch, the lethal little robot on his shoulder as he swayed back and forth on the quarter-deck of a pirate ship. He shook his head, but the image just wouldn't go away.

The world's smallest giant robot was feeling better. The chaos of the street, with its noises, its immense *scary* stones, and its huge robotic predators, was safely locked outside the tunnels; but more importantly, the robot's troubling thoughts had begun to seep away. Its brain was fading back to its familiar, simple state: a state of vigilance and purpose.

There were hardly any excess synapses left in its brain. It felt so much better, now that it wasn't so *smart* anymore. That had been . . . unpleasant. But the memory was already a distant one.

It kept the big giant's face squarely in its sights and it promised itself that *this* prisoner would not escape.

SATURDAY, 12:27 PM

The Pod had leveled out along the monorail line. Now it descended once again to street level. Dash hung on to the railing and pressed the combination for the next available station. He'd had it: whether or not Pitt could track him he was getting out of the Tube system and he wouldn't be going back in.

These things really are dangerous, he thought.

The Pod's missing floor gave him an interesting view of the inside of the Transport Tube system, anyway: he could really appreciate the Pod's speed now that he could see the Tube supports whiz by below (or behind) it.

The Pod slowed. It turned vertical again with Dash hanging on to the railing as he watched the Tube gape under him. He didn't much like the view anymore. So he was happy to step out of the Pod when its door finally slid open.

A man pushed past him to get in, and Dash was almost quick enough to stop him.

Oh well, he thought as he walked down the street and away from the passenger's calls for help. *You just oughtta be a little more polite.*

He could probably shake Pitt's surveillance out here on the street. But he definitely couldn't go home. If Pitt knew he was going to be at O'Malleys then he certainly knew where Dash lived. It was a puzzle, all right. He really needed to warn Miss Gardner to tell all the operators to lie low.

He took off his helmet and sat down for a minute to sort things out.

If he couldn't go home, and he wasn't sure where Miss Gardner was, then his only choice was Rusty. And his only way to reach Rusty, he decided, was through the League.

Dash walked up to the corner and looked at the street signs. Okay, then: he knew where he was. He set off for the headquarters of the Fraternal League of Robotic Persons.

SATURDAY, 12:32 PM

As eager as Rusty was to be off and take care of his mysterious business, Nola forced him to wait while she entered an urgent message into her Info-Slate. The message was going out on an emergency channel that would warn the Air Safety and Astronautics corps about Mr. Perkins and those awful children. They couldn't have gotten very far away yet, she hoped.

Rusty seemed almost glad of the delay. He kept shaking his head and looking around him as though he was lost. But at least he wasn't doing that scary *left to right* thing anymore.

Nola had hardly signed off when she saw the first ASAA rocket swoop down from overhead.

My, that was fast, she thought, right before the officer in the rocket pulled out a ray gun and started to shoot at her.

13

Onslaught of the Rampaging Rockets

SATURDAY, 5:58 PM

L illian's time had just about run out. She looked up, scanning for
ornithopters, and saw just one of them. It was circling patiently
on the next block down. So: there hadn't been any success, not
anywhere near here, anyway.

There wasn't even anyone left to ask. All the pedestrians had rushed
away (where?) and left the streets empty all around her. She'd never
seen the city when it wasn't crowded with people; it was an odd sight.
Interesting.

No! Not empty after all. Lillian saw the deliberate movement of a
Ferriss Sweep-O-Matic, casually sweeping the empty streets as though
nothing in them was out of the ordinary . . . in spite of the fact that
pretty much *everything* was.

Could Sweep-O-Matics speak? She wasn't sure. She approached the
robot anyway and she was just about to ask the question when, with
that unsettling sideways *shift* she remembered, she understood that
she had run out of time.

SATURDAY, 12:33 PM

Pitt's neck was bent backward almost beyond its tolerances, and he still couldn't take in the whole magnificent length of the Projectile. Although the robots were still running behind, the Projectile was almost entirely skinned. It bobbed up above Pitt's head and buoyed the roof of the cavern like a dream prepared to take flight, which was, in fact, what the Projectile was.

Pitt commended Robot R-54KG on the work. The impassive face of the robot turned upward as it told him, "We still hope to complete the project on schedule, sir."

Pitt's eyebrow twitched. That sounded like irrationality, again. "How the blazes could you possibly make up the time?" he asked, but before R-54KG could explain Pitt heard the muffled chime of his Info-Slate.

It was a message from the robot he'd detailed to watch out for Kent in front of O'Malley's Adventure Outfitters.

Pitt read the message with a deepening sense of dismay.

Kent had eluded the robot in—of all things!—the Tube Transport network. It looked as though the robot had been badly damaged. Pitt instructed it to return to the site.

Just then he heard the Slate chime again: the ASAA were responding to one of Pitt's shoot-on-sight orders. So far they were only pursuing the operator, Nola Gardner. Kent was still at large.

Pitt pulled his slide rule out of its holster. His fingers flashed back and forth as he calculated the current state of the project. He scowled at the results and slid the slide rule back onto his hip.

It was still too soon.

He kept frowning all the way back to the control room. Still . . .

He looked over the numbers again. He could accelerate his takeover of the Info-Slate system. That should prevent the ASAA or anybody else from learning what he was doing. This would work best if he started simply, he decided, and so he tapped out instructions for his operators.

Now they would intercept any communications about the Tube Transport system and Info-Slate operations; any messages on these subjects would be routed to Pitt's own Info-Slate. After a moment's thought, he added any inquiries about his shoot-on-sight orders. There.

Now he sat back and looked over the controls.

He'd start slow. In fact he had a perfect group of test subjects near at hand.

SATURDAY, 12:34 PM

Nola was flabbergasted. She hadn't even known that the ASAA *carried* firearms and the idea that they would simply shoot people on sight was—or would have been—beyond belief.

But that's definitely what they were doing. They were seeing her and then they were shooting at her. Four of them, so far.

Rusty had led her through a confusing series of doorways, both in and out, and along three different alleyways, and then down some stairs into a park where the two of them now crouched underneath a tree. Maybe the excitement had been good for Rusty. He seemed alert again and in spite of everything he seemed to be more comfortable.

Nola decided that the underground tunnels just weren't for everybody. *Including me*, she added. She squeezed Rusty's hand.

"Why are they trying to kill us?"

He just shook his head, his eyes never straying from the sky.

She could hear the soft coughing of the ASAA rockets even though she couldn't see them through the branches above. There had to be a reason for it. What could they have done that would have made them seem so . . . so guilty? So dangerous?

"It's Pitt," she said. "Somehow, he's convinced them that we have to be eliminated."

Rusty looked at her.

"The Info-Slates! He's in control of the Info-Slates!"

If Pitt could insert his own commands into the ASAA's Info-Slate feeds then he could make them do anything. They'd think they were under orders.

Apart from her fear, which was understandable, Nola felt something else. Pitt was taking the switchboard—a thing that had been the center of Nola's life just a week ago—and he was twisting it into a weapon that could hurt people . . . that was trying to hurt *her*. She looked up through the leaves.

"That man makes me so *angry*," she said.

Rusty held one finger up to what wasn't quite his mouth. Nola understood. He'd been listening to the sounds of the rockets overhead and nodding rhythmically. One passed by them, its noise deadened by the building to one side, and Rusty kept nodding while another one circled in the other direction. Still nodding to that same beat, Rusty rose and pulled her up beside him. The rockets went through their pattern one more time. Once the first of them had passed Rusty pulled Nola after him in a dash across the park where they stooped again under another tree.

The rockets continued to circle overhead. Whenever Rusty's head-nodding reached just the right point he would lead Nola a little farther. It was terrifying, but at least no one was shooting at them right now.

SATURDAY, 12:45 PM

Delbert Kent was unhappy. He was sitting on the floor of his cell directly across from Dennis Kent, who was just as unhappy as Delbert.

They had exhausted all the conversation they had about three hours earlier. It wasn't much of a loss because up to then their conversation had been, more or less, "I am unhappy. Are you, also, unhappy? Because I sure am."

They'd been pulled from their homes in the middle of the night by large and sinister robots who had sedated them, thrown them onto a hover sled, and then decanted them into jail cells where only one very bald man in a hat had even looked in on them.

That man didn't have any conversation at all, beyond a dissatisfied grunt at the sight of them. He had looked pretty unhappy, too.

It just hadn't been a very happy morning down here in Cell 17C.

There was a sound like wind, or like rainfall outside a window. It was coming from the Transport Tube Pod across from the door.

"Something's happening," Dennis Kent told him.

"It's not going to make us happy," said Delbert.

The sound became very much louder. Now Delbert could actually feel a rush of air hurry into the Transport Pod. The Pod started to rattle.

Then the rushing air turned into a really powerful wind that pulled the blankets off the cot and ripped Dennis's towel right off him, and this made them both more unhappy because Dennis had been stepping out of the shower when *he* was taken by the robots. The blankets and the towel flattened against the far wall of the Transport Pod.

Then the wind got quite a bit stronger.

SATURDAY, 12:48 PM

Rusty led Nola across the skyway over Lem Lane just south of Rue du Rur and above the Constellation Ballroom. The skyway's ceiling was probably hiding them from above, Nola hoped. On the other side they entered a building and moved briskly through its hallways to the far side, where another skyway led across and over the street below. She knew that she was casting nervous looks over her shoulder and she thought it might be a good idea to stop; when the blue and gray length of an ASAA rocket passed overhead she fixed her eyes on the far doorway and pretended that she didn't care what was up there.

Rusty led her through the door. Nola knew with every inch of her skin, though, that the rocket was coming back around for a second look.

SATURDAY, 12:50 PM

Delbert and Dennis bounced from one side of the Transport Tube to the other, with frequent apologies. Delbert was happy that Dennis had been able to get his towel back; and so, as it happened, was Dennis.

The net unhappiness of the day had been reduced by a small but comforting amount. That trend, unfortunately for the Kents, was not going to continue.

The immense wind that had built up in the Transport Tube system flung their Pod forward like a rocket. It was an astonishing amount of air pressure.

They felt the Pod slow down, at least a little, just before it ripped around a corner and dropped straight down; then the floor detached on a concealed hinge and the two Kents fell out of the Pod into a small room with a cot and a few simple amenities.

A circular hatch in the ceiling snapped shut. They heard the sound of their Transport Pod slipping away back into the Tube system.

They looked around.

This room looked almost exactly like the cell they'd come from except that one wall bulged outward in a gentle curve. Delbert tried the door: it was locked, just like the last one.

Dennis held on to his towel and opened a cabinet. "Hey, look!" he said. "There's food."

The cabinet was stocked with enough supplies to last them for a couple of weeks. Delbert wondered whether that ought to make him happy. He had a feeling that it wouldn't.

SATURDAY, 12:50 PM

Officer Maria da Cunha tapped angrily on her Info-Slate. She knew that she should be joining the pursuit, but something about this felt completely wrong to her.

Not very many people knew that ASAA officers carried ray guns. The reason *why* so few people knew was that ASAA officers *never used them*. Their pistols were locked into hidden compartments in their rockets and they stayed hidden because the officers just never needed to take them out.

So this morning's shoot-on-sight orders hadn't just surprised her: they had astonished her, and they had angered her. This was not the way things were done. She was an officer of the law. She didn't *shoot* people.

There had been a long delay before she'd gotten an answer back. Maybe it was some new problem in the Info-Slate system. She knew that something was different in the system because no one had picked up the line when she tried to establish a voice connection to the operator.

That was completely different from her last call, when she'd spoken to that arrogant engineer and to the operator, Miss Gardner.

Maria looked back down at the shoot-on-sight orders. One was for a Kelvin Kent, AKA Kelvin Dashkent, and one was for Nola Gardner: Kelvin Kent, who was the owner of that antique Actaeon rocket, and Nola Gardner, the operator Maria had spoken to about him.

Maria entered a query about a citizen named Nola Gardner. Her Info-Slate just sat in her hands and stared back at her. There was no response.

She reached for the radio. Sometimes, she figured, the old ways were best.

SATURDAY, 12:52 PM

The ASAA rockets were definitely interested in this block of Rue du Rur. Seven of them were now circling the area all the way back to the skyway where Nola felt sure that one of them had spotted her. Rusty had a tight hold on Nola's arm. Still nodding in a steady beat, he'd led her down into a basement doorway across the street from the headquarters of the League of Robotic Persons.

Maybe they'd be safe inside, if they could just get in there.

Across the street Nola saw a young man walk toward the League building. He was carrying a space helmet that looked just like Dash's helmet, the one that was broken, the one they'd carried all over the city the day before. It looked *just* like his helmet. And he . . .

"Rusty!" she hissed. "That's Dash, coming up the street!"

Rusty kept nodding to the beat; but he turned to see Dash coming their way on the far side of the street. Every few steps Dash would turn and take a look behind him.

"He thinks he's being followed," Nola whispered. "But he's not looking *up*!"

SATURDAY, 12:53 PM

Maria's fingers were clutching her rocket's radio so hard that they were beginning to hurt. She hadn't taken off to join the pursuit and that's not the only sense in which she wasn't getting anywhere.

"I'm telling you, there's something wrong about that order," she said.

Her desk sergeant's voice crackled out of the speaker. "It's not our decision, what orders we want to follow," the man said.

"We don't *get* orders to shoot people on sight!"

There was a pause.

"Well, Maria, it looks kind of like we do."

"But why? There's no case number attached to the order and there's no criminal record for either one of the suspects. There's just this order that we should *shoot* them!"

Her sergeant murmured for a moment, on another radio, maybe, or in conversation with somebody at his desk.

"Hey! Sergeant! Just pick up your Info-Slate and enter a search for any record of Nola Gardner or Kelvin Kent. Just do it!"

Maria could ear a faint tapping over the line.

"Hmmmmm."

She waited.

"The Info-Slate system seems to be overloaded," said the sergeant.

"Is it really?" she asked. "Enter a search for *anything else*."

She heard tapping again.

"Well, the system's a little twitchy this morning," she finally heard. "Look, Maria . . ."

"Nola Gardner *is* a switchboard operator," she broke in. "And this Kelvin Kent is a fellow I sent her an inquiry about, just a few days ago. Something is really, really wrong here."

There was a longer pause which ended in a sigh.

"Maria . . . it sounds like you know these people. I'm ordering you back to the station. Do not join the pursuit. Report directly to me."

The radio link went silent.

Maria slipped the radio back into its bracket on the dashboard and looked out at the city over the nose of her rocket.

"This can't be right," she said.

Nola had tried calling out to Dash, but between the distance and the noise of the ASAA rockets overhead, he just couldn't hear her. She grabbed Rusty by the arm.

"Look, if we go into the League Headquarters, will they protect us from these guys?"

Rusty didn't look too sure.

"Well . . . maybe, anyhow?"

He nodded slowly; this time he'd lost his silent beat. His head turned to face the League's front steps.

The rockets were circling lower now. One of them seemed to be taking a good look at Dash, who was busy looking behind him again.

"Don't run too close to me," Nola said. She leaped out onto the street and barreled toward the League, waving her arms and shouting. One consequence was that Dash looked over at her; another consequence was that the ASAA rocket started a steep, winding descent toward the pavement just ahead of her. She ran for the steps, waving at Dash.

"It's the ASAA!" she shouted. "They're trying to—"

The ASAA officer's ray gun burned a glowing stripe across the pavement. Nola jumped over it and kept on going. She saw Dash's eyes go small and hard. Instead of running toward the building he pulled his own gun out of his back pack and fired back at the rocket.

Nola heard the rocket's whine break off into a growl overhead as it swept out of the way. The wailing dives of two more rockets came from the sky above.

Dash fired a couple of quick bursts on his way up the steps and Nola joined him there just as Rusty's feet pounded right past the both of them. The robot burst through the doors and Nola and Dash followed after him.

Dash dove behind one of the doors as it began to swing closed.

"What the . . . what the heck are they shooting at you for?"

She looked over his shoulder. The three rockets were patrolling the street. Two more could be seen up above, coming their way.

"For keeps, I think," she told him. Then she noticed the unbroken dome of Dash's Aero-Vac. "Hey! You got your new helmet."

She looked around for Rusty. He hadn't stopped in the entryway; now he was running up the steps to the offices above. Nola and Dash wove in between the long lines of robots, each waiting to file some kind of form, and as they went after Rusty, Nola let Dash know what she thought was going on.

"Yep, that figures," he said. "He set his robots on me outside O'Malley's."

Dash looked back at the room full of robots.

"I might have kind of hurt one," he admitted in a lower voice.

"I'm sure you did the best you could," Nola reassured him. "But now that you're shooting at the ASAA I think that things may have gotten more complicated."

They reached the top of the stairs and hurried after Rusty, who was well along the corridor now; he turned around a corner and they hurried a bit faster.

"Well, what was I gonna do, Miss Gardner? They were *shooting* at you."

"I don't blame you one bit. And since people are trying to kill us now, I think you can start calling me Nola, don't you?" She looked his way. He was smiling.

They turned the way that Rusty had turned and found him standing in an open doorway whose sign read OFFICE OF THE PRESIDENT. Rusty seemed surprised. He was waving over another robot whose arms were full of file folders when Nola and Dash caught up with him at last.

Rusty pointed into an empty office and then spread his other hand slowly. The clerical robot said, "Mr. King isn't in the building. He had some kind of appointment." She looked up and down the hall and bent lower. "It's very *hush-hush*, if you know what I mean."

Rusty shuffled inside and opened one of the desk drawers.

The other robot seemed scandalized. "Now, really . . ."

With a theatrical flourish Rusty pulled out a pen and a sheet of paper. He scribbled quickly, filling more than half the sheet before he read it over, nodded, and signed it. Dash whistled.

The sound of several angry ASAA officers echoed out of the room below and through the hallway. Rusty set his paper down in the middle of Mr. King's desk.

Dash stepped in after him. "Rusty, is there a back door, or a window, or . . . ?"

The little robot set out at a trot, and Nola and Dash trotted after him.

SATURDAY, 1:00 PM

Maria wasn't going back to the station. She wasn't reporting to her desk sergeant. She was going to find out what was going on here, which she felt certain was something bad and wrong, and which she was not going to help along its bad and wrong way no matter what that was going to cost her.

Her Info-Slate chimed. She looked down at its new notice that the suspects were firing back at the officers. Every available unit was being called to the scene, which was now the Fraternal League of Robotic Persons.

What? she thought, *Are we shooting up rummage sales, now?*

Maria didn't have a lot of experience with gun battles. But she was pretty sure that when you started shooting at people they were likely to start shooting *back* at you. Still, she had to admit that it sounded like a bad precedent.

She picked up her radio and tried to reach one of the officers on the scene. She didn't trust that Info-Slate at all right now.

SATURDAY, 1:02 PM

They were standing on a loading dock at the back of the building. Nola and Dash looked into the not very inviting depths of a big wooden crate; Rusty was making complicated gestures in front of a Big Lug, who was bent very far over in order to look him in the face. The little gears and pistons in that big glass bulb of a head were turning rapidly.

"I guess it makes sense," Dash said. He poked the crate with his toe.

"I can't say I like being nailed up in there," said Nola.

Rusty turned to them and swept one arm out at the city, then tilted his head to the side.

"Where?" Dash guessed.

Rusty nodded.

Nola had an idea. "My Aunt Lillian's," she said. "Doctor Lillian Krajnik. It's very . . . very well protected. And unknown."

Rusty stopped nodding.

She heard Dash cough. "Uh, but if she's your aunt, aren't they likely to look for you there?"

Nola was still watching Rusty.

"No . . . no, Dash, one of the things Aunt Lillian is really good at is not being found. She's kind of . . . well, she's just really good at it."

She started to give Rusty the address but he held up one hand and shook his head.

"No? Or . . ." Nola stared at him. "Do you mean you *know* where she lives?"

Rusty nodded. He didn't seem all that happy about it.

They climbed into the crate and held their ears while the Big Lug nailed on its lid. The whole thing lurched a bit when the Lug picked it up. But then the big robot held them perfectly level while it put one steely leg ahead of the other and carried them down to the alley. Nola peeked through a crack in the crate. She could see Rusty walking along with the Lug.

"I guess it's a small world," she said.

SATURDAY, 1:07 PM

Maria joined the rockets that circled the League headquarters. The patrol had been broken into units, each watching one side of the towering building. She was with the unit that covered the back alley.

She'd tried to let the other officers know that she thought something had gone wrong. But once they'd been fired on, they were pretty set in their opinions. It didn't make any difference at all that they'd shot first.

"Just take the descriptions, da Cunha," said the officer in charge. He rattled off descriptions of Kelvin Kent, Nola Gardner, and a small robot who had been assisting them. They gave a very detailed description of that robot because he wasn't a well-known model; in fact, they'd never seen one like him before.

It sounded just like a little robot that Maria happened to know. It sounded just like Rusty.

That's swell, she told herself. *If I report that, they're going to think I know all the suspects, and I've got a pretty solid notion what that will mean.*

The one thing Maria knew about Miss Gardner was that she was a heck of a good switchboard operator; about Kent, she knew nothing at all. He would be the one who had started shooting back. Maria knew Rusty pretty well, though, and Rusty was a very level-headed robot. Rusty was pretty level-headed for *any* kind of person. And another thing she knew about Rusty was that even if he didn't look like much he was a fine person to have on your side. A decent, smart little guy.

She couldn't see Rusty involved in something criminal. It just didn't make sense.

Maria continued her long sweep around the back of the building.

So if the Info-Slate said that Kent and Miss Gardner were outlaws, but Rusty was helping them . . .

Down in the alley a Big Lug was carrying a wooden crate with long, smooth steps, like it was carrying something fragile. A much smaller robot was running along behind the Lug. Rusty was having a little trouble keeping up with the Lug's long legs.

"You there, da Cunha?" came over the radio. She picked it up and thumbed its switch to TRANSMIT.

"All clear in the alley," she answered, and she turned her rocket slowly—and she hoped quietly—in an arc that would put her parallel to the Lug's path.

"Sergeant wants you back at the station soonest."

The whine of another ASAA cruiser came up alongside her. She watched the Lug turn the alley's corner and disappear onto the next street.

She turned to look at the officer in charge.

"*Now*, da Cunha," he told her. "Sarge was real definite about that."

Maria nodded and smiled. "Right, I got it. See you back there."

SATURDAY, 1:23 PM

Robot G-94VA was in pain.

He didn't feel the pain that a human person would feel. G-94VA didn't have the right kind of nervous system for that. A human person would have been crippled by this kind of damage. G-94VA could force his crumpled limbs to drag him forward, while a human person would have curled up on the floor of the maintenance tunnel and devoted all his or her energy to screaming about it, even though there was no one there to hear.

The pain that Robot G-94VA felt was the intense discomfort of *knowing* that his legs and torso were damaged. The limbs ought to get straightened out, probably with a Ray-O-Zap Mark 2 hydraulic press (rigged in reverse); several of the dents in his lower torso were causing his linkages to seize up, and those could easily be hammered out with G-94VA's own fist, at least to start; and the metal fatigue in his left leg would result in total failure unless the leg was reinforced with shims and a temporary cross brace.

G-94VA paused. Well. He could do *that*, anyway, and the repair would make him more fit to carry out his orders.

He turned slowly and leaned against the tunnel wall. As soon as he'd ripped a length of metal from his pelvis to make the braces he felt the discomfort decrease by a small margin.

He cut the metal to size with his finger torch and held it in place alongside the wreckage of his leg. The steel started to glow while he played the flame across it, and G-94VA felt a little better, at least for now. He looked around. He was glad that there weren't any rats in the tunnel, anyway. G-94VA *hated* rats.

He held the filler rod up to his broken leg and began to heat it up. Why had the Master sent him after the Plumber? It didn't make any sense. The Plumber had promised to come back with help so that G-94VA and his friends could finish the project on schedule. Why would the Master try to stop the Plumber?

G-94VA and all the robots he knew had given up on trying to understand the Master. Experience had shown that this was hopeless. But because the Master wanted the job done, they were doing it; because he wanted it at a particular time, they had a schedule; and in order to meet that schedule, they were relying on the help of the Plumber. But the Master *did not want* the Plumber to bring them that help.

The welding torch spat and shook. G-94VA knew that he'd come close to damaging the Plumber. He was so grateful that he'd failed.

The trial had gone well. Pitt's indicators showed him that the entire group of Kents had been transported from their cells into the Projectile's cabins.

Since 83 percent of the cabins were completed, Pitt saw that he could start the next stage now, even if it was early. At this point there was a very low probability that anyone would notice—provided he used precautionary measures.

He opened a sealed control panel, set its dials, and pressed a button.

Then he turned his attention to the Info-Slate inquiries that were already piling up. There were a couple of background checks for Nola Gardner and Kelvin Kent; he would have to come up with something plausible. There were several inquiries about the shoot-on-sight orders, but since no one in authority was questioning those orders he decided to leave the inquiries unanswered. Best to let ASAA headquarters insist that the officers comply.

It looked like they were doing a fine job on their own.

All across the city there was a subtle change to the Transport Tube system. Nobody noticed.

First, there was a small but significant change at the Tube Control Center. Beneath the Center several hidden Tube junctions pivoted into place; traffic stopped passing through the baroque snarl of Tubes that encircled the building and began, instead, to route through a different system of Tubes that was unknown to the controllers in the Center. These Tubes had been constructed underneath the building in a warren of tunnels that only a person with the mining rights to the site might be aware of.

Then some other small changes began to cascade through the Tube network.

Just above the door of every Pod station a little hatch irised open to reveal a motion detector. The motion detectors blended in so perfectly that no change was apparent.

In most cases, nothing happened. These were the cases in which the motion detectors sensed that several pedestrians were passing along the street.

In a few other cases, though, a single person was walking past the Transport Tube station while no one else was in view. The doors of each of *those* Tube stations hissed open; a tremendous rush of air was heard; and the open Pods swallowed the pedestrians, and then closed.

So although no one in Retropolis knew about it, an increasing number of the city's people were becoming unhappy.

14

The Pulsating Parrot of Fear

Mrs. Broadvine and her half-dozen switchboard operators stopped on the ninth floor just long enough to thank Miss Roth for buzzing them in, to admire Princess Fedora, and to decline tea. Then they made their way up to the very top of the staircase and to Rusty's door. It was standing open.

"Rusty?" Mrs. Broadvine called. But from the doorway she saw a larger, strange robot sitting on a stool next to the mechanical operator. The lamps of his eyes turned to look back at her. He rose and made a slight bow.

"I am also looking for Rusty," the robot said.

Mrs. Broadvine led her operators into the room. "Am I to suppose that you are a friend of Rusty's?" she asked.

The blue and white stranger paused. "Yes," he said at last. "It is prudent to be cautious. My name is Albert King. I am the President of the Retropolis Fraternal League of Robotic Persons."

He opened a small compartment right about where his ribs weren't. "My card," he said, and he handed it to her.

She looked at it, front and back, and sniffed. "Well, it *seems* to be in order."

Rhonda Bancroft stepped out of Mrs. Broadvine's shadow. "It's true, ma'am," she said. "I was there last month with some muffins for the bake sale. And all those calls Rusty was making last night? He was trying to reach Mr. King, here."

Mr. King bowed again. "Very fine muffins," he said. "Thank you."

The rest of the operators spread through the room. Freda Detwiler sat next to the little operator robot and waved to her.

Mr. King waited while the ladies sat and then returned to his stool. He shook his head at Freda. "It's no use," he said. "I have been trying to communicate with her myself. I'm afraid she may be damaged."

With a broad smile, Freda said, "Connect the main pane cable to the Events Registry for the Fraternal League of Robotic Persons."

The little operator spun up to life. She reached up to an imaginary cable in the air in front of her and detached it deftly from its imaginary socket; her finger flicked its imaginary release to the middle position and then she tucked it neatly into place, releasing her finger as it slid home. Then she relaxed again.

"We were thinking of calling her Iris," Rhonda said from the windowsill.

Freda nodded. "It's because her eyes are her best feature," she explained.

Mr. King leaned forward, his eyes on Freda. "Do you know something about this person?" he asked.

Mrs. Broadvine intervened. "We know that she's a switchboard operator, Mr. King, and a very good one. As are we."

"She's one of the operators that Howard Pitt's used to replace us," said Rhonda.

"Televideo or Info-Slate?" he asked, and thereby won Mrs. Broadvine's heart.

"Info-Slate," she said. "We were all let go early this week. Pitt's robots seem to have taken our place."

Mr. King turned from her to the herd of operators, which now, he could see, included the one they were calling Iris.

"Please explain."

SATURDAY, 2:37 PM

Now that his leg was functioning at 36 percent efficiency, Robot G-94VA was feeling somewhat better and moving at a more acceptable speed. It's true that he sometimes needed to brace himself against the bulge of the Transport Tube housing—especially when he creaked around the tunnel corners—but on the whole he was functioning well enough that he estimated his arrival at the construction site in an improved four hours and twenty-one minutes.

After forty minutes or so for essential repairs he would be able to rejoin his co-workers and make a substantial contribution to the project. Although once the Plumber arrived with his reinforcements they might have the whole project completed before G-94VA could add much of anything.

That would be all right. Finishing the project on schedule was a priority mandate. Still, he'd like to help.

But how will the Master react when the Plumber returns?

It would be a terrible thing if the Master ordered them all to attack the Plumber. Surely, this had been a mistake? Perhaps G-94VA had misunderstood. Perhaps the Plumber was not the target. Or perhaps the order had been to *aid* the Plumber, not to attack and detain him.

But G-94VA had not been mistaken. He was certain. Was it possible that *the Master* had made an error?

The robot knew that this was dangerous territory. If the Master could be *wrong* . . .

G-94VA realized that he'd come to a stop. The tunnel stretched into the darkness ahead and behind him and—just for a moment—he didn't know where he was.

Then he dragged his damaged leg forward and took another step. The good leg followed. And then he did it again.

SATURDAY, 2:42 PM

Evan pulled the basement door open—just a crack—with one eye on the robot that rode his shoulder. Abner felt all his muscles clench. That berserk fit the tiny robot had pitched last time they left the tunnels was going to feature nightly in Abner's dreams for months to come.

"It *looks* okay," Evvie said. She was casually standing where Abner's body shielded her from the robot's cannon.

Evan pulled the door about halfway open. They waited. The little robot's head swiveled back and forth, covering Abner and then the doorway. There was no sign of the panic it had shown when they came out on the street.

Abner tried to remember what he knew about agoraphobia. Could robots suffer from anxiety disorders?

The two children led him up the same stairway where they'd encountered the robot and woman who had later escaped onto the street. Abner was nearly overcome by an urge to pound on the apartment doors but he contained himself while they padded up the stairs, landing by landing, the miniature robot's head swiveling all the while. It always lingered for a moment when it aimed itself at Abner.

Abner could hear a murmur of conversation; it was far overhead, maybe on the top floor. *Please,* he thought, *please help me. Please be somebody who can control these horrible children. Please come down the stairs.*

There was one deep, resonant voice, and what sounded like several women responding to it. Abner couldn't make out any of the words.

Evvie pushed past him and unlocked an apartment door. Evan and the tiny robot encouraged Abner to follow her inside.

The first thing Abner noticed was a big pink sheet of paper tacked up by the door.

Doris: We'll be back on Monday!!! Remember, bedtime is
9 o'clock!!! Be sure to see them off to school every week-
day!!! (All the way to school!!!) Thanks!!!

—Mr. And Mrs. Campbell

Abner read the note thoughtfully. That's why nothing else in the room surprised him.

It was tidier than he might have expected, but the children hadn't spent much time in here recently, had they? The drapes were drawn over the narrow windows; the dish drainer, which he could see through the kitchen door, was stacked with plates and pans. A radio was playing dance music, quietly enough that it wouldn't bother the neighbors, but loudly enough to overpower the muffled moans and cries of the babysitter.

She was tied to a chair and gagged with a cloth of some kind. The cloth was printed with little teddy bears. Above the gag, her eyes pleaded with Abner. He knew exactly how she felt.

There was a complicated device strapped to her head: a bulbous glass jar, counterweighted by a toy train, with a flexible straw that led into the gag. Evvie bustled into the kitchen and returned with a pitcher of water. She emptied the pitcher into the jar. "There you go, *Doris,*" she said.

Doris kept her eyes locked on Abner's. He shook his head with a gesture at the robot, now covering the door, the babysitter, and Abner himself. "If you have any ideas, I'd love to hear them," he told her.

Doris reacted as well as you can with a teddy bear gag covering half your face. She rolled her eyes.

"Sorry," Abner said. "Yes. I see."

Evan stationed himself by the door while Evvie busied herself around the apartment.

Little bubbles rose in the jar when Doris finally gave in and started to suck on the straw.

"Should we leave him with Doris?" Evan asked, but Evvie shook her head.

"He *knows stuff*," she said. "I think we can use him."

This might have been good news. Honestly, Abner just couldn't decide.

SATURDAY, 2:56 PM

". . . and so Dash and our Nola are out there trying to find out where Pitt's new switchboard is," Mrs. Broadvine finished. "Or at least that's what we think they're doing. We haven't heard a thing since last night."

Albert King nodded slowly and looked out the window. "So you know that Howard Pitt has a large construction project below the ground, though you're not sure where it is . . . ?"

Freda flinched a little. "Nola told us, but I'm not sure. It was under some big building site."

She looked around. "Anybody?"

No one could quite remember where. They'd been so involved with Iris that they just hadn't taken it in.

Mr. King turned back to Iris. "But we are sure that Pitt is using these robots to operate the new Info-Slate switchboard?"

Rhonda blurted "It was a big round building site."

The blue and white robot waited.

"But, yes," Mrs. Broadvine agreed. "Somewhere—we don't know where—Pitt's new switchboard is running with these mechanical operators . . . which, if I understand this, you say are *illegal* robots?"

"Quite illegal, I'm afraid. He has been building them in a black market factory for use at the switchboard as well as at this construction project. If we can locate some of these robots and tie them to Pitt, then Mr. Pitt will find himself in a great deal of trouble with the law."

He paused. "And, in fact, with me."

"Well," Mrs. Broadvine said, "I think the switchboard's your best bet, then. There's no doubt that the new Info-Slate switchboard is Howard Pitt's responsibility. I suppose that if we wait here, Dash and Nola will be back—sooner or later—and they can tell us where the switchboard is."

The robot stood up. Mrs. Broadvine hadn't thought that he was a very tall mechanical person, but now his head seemed to brush against the rafters of the attic.

"We may not need to wait," he told her.

The top of his head popped open to reveal a small parabolic antenna. The antenna started to revolve. "If one of you can oblige me by using an Info-Slate, I believe that I should be able to locate this new switchboard."

Freda pulled an Info-Slate out of her handbag. Her fingers flew over the display.

Mr. King stepped to the window, leaning over to aim the antenna outside.

"No, not in here," he concluded. "We'll need to move down to the street."

They gathered up their things and, leaving Iris alone by the window, they trooped down the stairs.

SATURDAY, 3:02 PM

Abner could hear the sound of footsteps coming down the stairs. There were several light footfalls and one ponderous, heavy pair of feet. His mind raced. He looked at Doris: the babysitter's eyes were intent on the door.

Evvie padded back into the room and hissed at Evan. "*Watch them!*"

Then she pulled a chair over to the door and peered through its peephole.

The footsteps sounded out on the landing above and turned, coming down this way.

Evvie jerked back from the peephole. "*Myrmidon!*"

Evan was impressed. "MK I or MK II?"

She looked back through the peephole.

"Is there a MK III?"

Evan grinned. "Wow!"

Just as the footfalls were about to reach the door, Abner made his move.

He'd never been a very physical person. Most of Abner's moves had to do with brilliant flourishes on a drawing board. But he gave this one everything he had.

Abner dropped to the floor, extending his feet behind him to kick Evvie's chair right over; with both hands, he grabbed Doris's chair and flipped it onto its back. Doris hadn't even had a chance to grunt an accusation before Abner had rolled to the right, hitting the volume knob on the radio to spin it all the way up. With what was left of his momentum he somersaulted forward and spun left just before the tiny robot's cannon blew the leg off a sideboard exactly where his head had just been. The radio, which had been on the sideboard, fell with a crash; the music died.

This left Abner curled into a ball behind the couch.

"*Stop!*" Evan whispered to the robot on his shoulder. "*Just stop!*"

To anyone outside in the hall, these events went something like this:

A loud crash and an exclamation; a louder crash followed by a muted, accusing grunt; a supremely loud burst of dance music; and what might have been a controlled burst of gunfire. It was hard to tell, due to the horn section.

Then, silence.

Because Evan had streaked across the room, planted himself on Abner's folded knees, and was staring into his eyes with fierce determination. "If he makes a sound," Evan told the robot in a low voice, filled with menace, "smoke 'im!"

The footsteps outside had stopped. After a moment there was a knock on the door.

"Hello?" called a matronly voice. "Is everything all right in there?"

"Yes, thank you, ma'am," Evvie answered.

There was a pause.

"Why don't we just have a look, then?"

Evan perched the little robot on Abner's knee, from which vantage it glared down at him. Then the boy started to pull Doris's chair toward the kitchen. Abner, trapped behind the couch, couldn't tell where Evan went from there. Anyway since the robot's little cannon was only inches from his nose he found that his attention was divided, at best. He opened his mouth to yell; the tiny cannon leaned forward eagerly. Abner's mouth snapped shut again.

It was possible, he decided, that he had exhausted his store of heroism.

"Just a minute," Evvie was saying through the door. "I think I broke the table."

Abner could hear Doris's chair scraping over the kitchen threshold. "*Okay,*" Evan whispered.

There was the sound of a door opening.

"What happened?" asked the matronly voice.

It's a pity that Abner wasn't able to see Evvie's performance.

She had her hands clasped behind her back and she peered up into Mrs. Broadvine's face with the kind of wide-eyed innocence that you only expect to see in a small, moderately priced ceramic statuette.

"I was practicing," said Evvie, "and I knocked the table over. I'm just *mortified.*"

"And what, I wonder, were you practicing?"

"Gymnastics, ma'am. I'm trying out for the school team and those other girls are just so *way ahead of me* that I'm afraid I might not be good enough. So I practice *every day.*"

After a moment: "And your parents, dear?"

"They should be home from work real soon, ma'am, and I sure want to have this cleaned up before they get here. Along with my *regular chores,* I mean."

After another moment: "Wasn't that an explosion?"

Evvie looked around. One finger was now hanging from her lip. "Oh, dear, I don't think so. But when I knocked the radio over there was all *sorts* of racket, wasn't there?"

There was a substantially longer moment. "I don't suppose I might have a look inside?"

Evvie was apologetic. "Oh, no, ma'am. Mommy's *very strict* about letting people indoors when she isn't here."

After the longest moment yet: "Well, my dear, let's make sure this doesn't happen again, shall we?"

Evvie smiled as only cherubs can. "I should sure hope not! Thank you, ma'am, and *good-bye!*"

The door snicked shut again. After a brief pause Abner could hear the people on the stairs make their way down to the next landing and so down, eventually, to the street.

Evan dragged Doris back into the living room and set her upright. When Abner was allowed to come out from behind the couch he could see that Doris was not going to forget this at any time in the near future.

He looked around. No, no one else was going to forget it, either.

SATURDAY, 3:06 PM

"What a little *angel* she was," Rhonda cooed.

They were walking down the street. Mr. King's antenna—which

was quite becoming, Mrs. Broadvine had decided—was spinning smoothly as he searched for the signal from the new switchboard.

"It has been my experience," said Mrs. Broadvine, "that *no one* is *that* angelic."

But they didn't have the time to get to the bottom of that business, whatever it was. At least nothing had actually been on fire.

"Again, please," said Mr. King.

Freda obliged him by keying up a new inquiry on her Info-Slate. Mr. King waited while his antenna turned. "Yes," he decided. "Farther that way, perhaps one and one half miles."

They trailed down the street behind him.

SATURDAY, 3:14 PM

For simplicity's sake, Maria had removed the insulation from her radio wires and attached them loosely to the ignition line. This ensured that any radio traffic would be overwhelmed by static without further effort on her part.

Maria had flown these particular skies before.

After her first three training assignments, Sarge no longer assigned new recruits to Maria: they always seemed to learn what Sarge considered the wrong lessons.

Consequently, she didn't have to deal with too many interruptions while she cruised high over Retropolis. As she wove between the monorail tracks and avoided the occasional rocket, she was able to observe the progress that Rusty, the Big Lug, and their mysterious cargo were making through the streets and under the sheltering trees of the city's parkways. She was high enough that there was no chance they'd hear the sound of her engine.

Her radio complained with a furious burst of static. She turned down the volume.

Rusty and his friends were working their way steadily Northeast through a wide greenbelt between two neighborhoods. She caught only glimpses of their progress under the canopies of the apple trees.

Once they reached the end of the greenbelt they'd have just two options: continue down the wide expanse of Hypatia Street (which, although open, was broken by a lot of useful alleys) or turn into the much narrower, more direct way that was Lovelace Street. The Experimental Research District was at Maria's eight o'clock.

Surviving ASAA officers had an unerring sense of where the District was. In their flights over the city some small but crucial part of their brains was always watching a mental marker that, in mental terms, was flashing red.

You did *not* want to fly over the District. No one in their right mind would have overflown it, all the way up to low orbit. The flashing red mental markers of these surviving pilots defined the boundaries of a neighborhood where all the scientific research in the city was concentrated, in one extremely hazardous area whose two great virtues were that scientific progress occurred there, and that the progress was squeezed together so snugly that it could destroy only itself, and not any innocent bystanders.

Off in the distance Maria heard the distant *crump* of an experiment that had not gone entirely as intended. In a few moments its smoke was likely to drift this way.

Maria banked to starboard and rose a bit higher.

Down below, Rusty's party had crossed the edge of the greenbelt and was now heading toward Lovelace Street's narrow and exposed ribbon of paving. *Interesting.*

Maria scanned the street ahead. Like most Retropolitan neighborhoods it was a mixture of light industry, apartment blocks, and market towers, arranged so that pedestrians could take care of most of their business within a few blocks of home; for longer trips, there was a sprinkling of spearlike monorail terminals, casting their long, narrow shadows over the buildings, and—although they were too small to make out from Maria's height—the ubiquitous Transport Tubes. Rusty and his friends *might* be heading anywhere. But something told Maria that they were getting close to their destination. There was so little cover on Lovelace that they wouldn't be using it if they had any alternative.

About a half mile down the street there was a hilly neighborhood of private houses. Beyond that point Lovelace Street curved off toward the airship field, which spread out in the center of a wide swath of farmland.

Without losing track of the group on the ground Maria picked up some speed by dipping her rocket lower in the direction of those houses.

At four hundred feet, the smell of sulphur and something stranger told her that the District's latest experiment had caught up with her after all. The cloud was quickly shredding itself into faint streamers of innovation. She held her breath until she'd passed through the worst of it.

The radio started to crackle and spark furiously to itself. She'd have to deal with her sergeant before much longer.

At this height she could just make out the Transport Tube stations along the street. She wasn't really paying attention to them; but she caught a swift burst of motion below, as though a lone pedestrian had actually *leaped* from the street into a Tube. Maria had tried the Transport Tubes, just once, and she smiled to think that anyone would be that eager to get into one.

It takes all kinds, she observed.

SATURDAY, 3:25 PM

Robot R-54KG was doing a magnificent job, pulling each type of mechanical person from one task to another in their platoons and battalions, rolling out sheets of inertrium skin for the Projectile, riveting that skin over the frame, and making the air and water connections for each of the last unfinished compartments. But they just couldn't seem to make up all the time they'd lost.

Now that Pitt had turned on the Tube delivery system, Pods were *whooshing* through their lines and the finished compartments were beginning to fill up. R-54KG had an exact accounting of which compartments were complete, and he made sure that the Tubes didn't deposit their loads into any part of the Projectile that wasn't ready for them. But the additional time he had to spend on that routing worried him.

The project as a whole was running behind, and yet the Master had pushed *ahead* this part of the schedule! R-54KG shook his massive head. There was no accounting for human people. That much was certain.

Up on the catwalk he could hear the crew conversing.

"But where *is* the Plumber? He's been gone for hours!"

R-54KG glared upward. "Enough talk! More work!" he called.

The riveting guns started up again, working their way across the Projectile's hull. But it had been a fair question, he knew. One that he'd been asking himself.

The robots up on the Projectile's high reaches reported that another compartment had been finished. R-54KG updated the Tube system and at once he heard a Pod *whoosh* toward the still-cooling compartment. He shook his head again.

Madness!

SATURDAY, 3:32 PM

Mr. King, his antenna spinning, had come to a stop in front of a Tube terminal on Dreyfuss Way. "It's no use," he told the operators. "I've lost the signal again."

They looked up and down the street.

"I wonder," said Mrs. Broadvine, "if it would help to get higher above the streets?"

This time, they just looked up and down. There was a monorail track high overhead; it led through a towering station a couple of blocks over.

"Yes," said the robot. "I think that might help a great deal."

They set off toward the end of the block. There was a man with a briefcase following along about sixty feet behind them. They turned the corner and continued toward the station, completely missing the sudden whoosh of air and the shriek that followed it when the unfortunate man drew level with the Pod station.

People walked alone through Retropolis all the time. It wasn't usually a problem. Today, though, was not a usual day.

SATURDAY, 3:33 PM

Was it some kind of sign? Had the Universe overheard Edward's decision and . . . responded?

He was being thrown from side to side in the Transport Pod. His briefcase, having bounced off the back wall, lay at his feet. He had never seen a Pod behave this way; just as he'd walked past it, its door had slid open and it had pulled him inside with a surge of negative air pressure not unlike the trap he'd used in *The Pulsating Parrot of Fear* (or, possibly, in *The Elixir of the Metal Mechanic*). And now he was nothing more than the unwilling cargo of this punishing device.

Something in him felt sure this *was* a punishment. Just before he was kidnapped Edward had resolved to destroy every one of his manuscripts, every one of his rejection slips, and, most of all, the typewriter that seemed to brood at the center of his mismanaged life. The typewriter was like an evil god (*Priestess of the Purple Pyramid*) that demanded constant sacrifice; human sacrifice; the *repeated* sacrifice of one particular human, and that was himself, Edward J. Bellin, the tireless scribe of nobody at all.

He had felt . . . free.

But now he was being dragged away through the darkness to someplace he was sure he didn't want to see.

Edward braced himself against the Pod's handrail and took out his little notebook and a pen. He might be able to *use* this.

SATURDAY, 3:37 PM

Maria had been right.

Rusty was now running along behind the Big Lug, who still stepped with great care—but on very long legs—with the crate held perfectly level in its arms. They had started up the long walkway that led to the long stairway that ended at the entryway of a tall house, alone on the hill near the curve of Lovelace Street.

She wanted to watch them; but she could hear the whine of another rocket drawing close to her. Maria angled up and gently away from the area of the house . . . not so abruptly, she hoped, that this would be obvious.

Rusty and the Lug had passed behind a small wooded hillock by the time the other rocket drew alongside. Maria looked over and waved at Officer Kornbluth. "Were you trying to call me?" she asked. "I'm having a little trouble with my radio."

Kornbluth looked like he wanted to make something of that, but in the end, he just said "Sarge is real anxious to talk to you."

"Really? This dang radio, I just can't seem to count on it."

"Let me give you a little escort over there, da Cunha."

Maria tilted her head and gave Kornbluth a quizzical look. "You know, Cy, I do know the way."

He motioned her over. "Yeah, well, Sarge says you've been a little forgetful lately, so you just better come along with me."

Maria didn't look back, much as she wanted to. She made sure she'd memorized the house, anyway, and she followed Kornbluth back to the station. "Your radio, doesn't it ever conk out on *you*?" she called over.

"Only when you're around, Maria."

15

The Forbidden Laboratory

D ash had been doing his best not to jostle Miss Gardner—
Nola—but in all honesty, given that they were squeezed next
to one another in two fetal bundles inside of a splintery crate,
that was more than he'd really been able to manage. But he continued to make the effort even when the Big Lug, somehow wrestling
the crate through a doorway, dropped them the last three inches onto
a hard floor.

"Sorry," he said, for what had to be the hundredth time.

"S'okay," she mumbled. "Bpt cld y—"

Dash moved his elbow.

"Thanks," said Nola.

His space helmet was gouging his lower back something terrible.

He heard a woman's voice coming from the other, and infinitely
preferable, side of the crate.

"Well, Rusty!" she was saying. "It's so nice to see you again. How
have you been getting along?"

There was a penetrating squeal. The crate's top began to rise;
the nails gave way. Dash saw the Lug's thick fingers poking through
the gap.

"And what have you brought me?" the woman asked.

Dash and Nola ducked as the top of the crate was ripped away. "It's . . ."

They looked up into the astonished face of Nola's Aunt Lillian. "Nola?"

Rusty, off to the side, dipped his chin. Dash and Nola climbed out of the crate and stretched.

"Dash Kent, ma'am," he said, "and I'm proud to know you, Dr. Krajnik."

He stuck out his hand and she shook it without taking her eyes off Nola.

"What on Earth . . . ?"

So they told her.

"Howard Pitt," said Dr. Krajnik. "He was always bound to be a problem."

Now that they were done with their recitation Dash looked around the big, curving room that was the entrance to Dr. Krajnik's house. The house was actually a tall cylinder, about a hundred and twenty feet across and three times that in height. The entryway was a shallow segment of the ring of public rooms surrounding some kind of central core—a cylinder *inside* a cylinder—with a spiral stairway that swept up along the outer wall to the next floor.

Dash could see that the stairway continued from there, probably all the way to the top level.

The inner cylinder's face was made of painted concrete. Its lone entrance was a great round hatch set in a steel frame. The frame was bolted to—or possibly *through*—the wall with bolts that were bigger than the bolts on his Actaeon's mooring mounts.

Nola had mentioned that her Aunt Lillian had built some pretty big machines. Dash had a feeling that she was a kind of architect, too. *Heck,* he thought. *That hatch is some kind of architecture all by itself.*

He realized that everyone was looking at him. "Um, sorry?"

"Aunt Lillian was just telling us that we should follow her into her workroom. Where there's *coffee*."

Coffee. Yep, Dash agreed that they should certainly go to the workroom. He looked up the stairs.

"No, it's just in here," said Nola. She looked kind of nervous. Why now? This was the first time they'd been someplace safe in, well, forever, or something. She kept on glancing sideways at Dash.

Dr. Krajnik swung the hatch open and led them onto a walkway between the inner cylinder and . . . *another* inner cylinder. There were gigantic springs and shock absorbers arranged in an array that ringed the narrow space. Down below, Dash could make out what looked like huge airbags, like you might find in an airship envelope, and which seemed to be supporting the *inner* inner cylinder on a cushion. Black-painted pipes, hanging from sturdy brackets, looped around the walls.

Dash frowned. *Well, that's odd,* he thought.

When they'd gone through a second hatch Dash noticed that each of the inner walls was made of plate steel . . . about two inches thick. In this second space he saw another array of snubbers and springs that bridged the walls. He looked over at Nola, who was looking back at him with an expression that was . . . well, it was *pleading*, he thought. He took another look up and down the looming steel cylinders. They stretched out below the walkway to their cushioned foundations and reached so far overhead that he couldn't see how far all those shock absorbers went, not past all the pipes, anyhow.

Dash started to suspect something. But it wasn't possible. Was it?

Dr. Krajnik pulled the lever that lifted the final blast door. This door was edged with big steel teeth. Dash looked around the door-frame and saw yawning sockets that interlocked with the door's teeth when it closed behind them.

"I'm trusting that Mr. Kent is a very good friend of yours, dear," said Dr. Krajnik.

"He . . . is?" asked Nola. Dash nodded at her. But he was pretty busy taking it all in.

Dr. Krajnik's "workroom" was—there wasn't any doubt about it—a laboratory. And it wasn't the kind of lab that Dash had in his basement, either. This was a real laboratory. A *scientific* laboratory.

He knew that because he had no idea what two-thirds of Dr. Krajnik's equipment even was.

Over to Dash's left were a series of stepped tables, loaded down with glassware, which mounted the wall in narrower and narrower platforms until they culminated in a curved, narrow shelf about twenty feet overhead. A snake's nest of tubes wound their way along the walls to the top of that assembly, and color-coded valves marked the tubes' ends; below the valves were a collection of vessels that would receive . . . something . . . from that plumbing, and divide it into streams that would work their way down through spiral tubes, retorts, alembics, and three big aluminum tanks that all had to be contributing to some kind of chemical process that Dash couldn't even imagine.

At the very bottom of the shelves was a single one-gallon bottle. It was half full of a liquid that was rippling in little silver waves.

Science.

He looked to his right.

Just past the doorway were two copper pods, each one bound with brass bands and riveted to the walls. There was a small hatch at the front of each pod. A green light glowed on top of one pod, and a red one on top of the other.

Through the thick glass window in the red-lit hatch Dash could see a baboon. The baboon was trying to get his attention. A note was taped to that pod; it read: *Not this one!*

More strange apparatus ringed the walls in that direction. There were a lot of blinking lights and some worrisome noises.

Science.

Dash looked straight ahead past Dr. Krajnik, who was watching him with a calm, interested expression.

On the far side of the laboratory Dash could see a circular window that looked out over the city. He knew that they were dozens of feet inward from the exterior wall and that the space between was a forest of shock absorbers, springs, airbags, reinforced walls, and girders, so that there was no way a window could show what was outdoors; except that there it was.

Standing before the window was a table where, Dash saw, there *was* coffee; a brass samovar, ringed by twitching dials, held the precious liquid over some kind of plate that was inset with a brass disc and encircled by a rack of pipettes. The samovar was beeping quietly to itself.

Near the middle of the room was a windowed capsule, just big enough to contain a person. This big capsule was surrounded by cables, pipes, and sparking, suspended globes. Watchful ray emitters were trained on it. A small set of stairs led up to the capsule, and there were sizable vents around its base. A few halfhearted wisps of steam were coming out of the vents.

All around the room he could see more equipment, more machines, and countless experiments that were, very definitely, in progress.

"So," Dash said, a little more bravely than he felt. "You're a *scientist*."

Dr. Krajnik smiled at Nola. "I think I like him," she said.

"Mmmmmmm," Nola replied. Then: "Dash? Are you okay? Only, you look a little pale."

Yeah, well, *Science.*

"Aunt Lillian takes *precautions*," Nola said. "The other houses in the neighborhood are *perfectly safe*. Nobody even knows what she's got in here."

"The concentric rings of my house contain lead-lined shielding, heat dissipators, and shock absorbers that divert kinetic and thermal energy to my generators," Dr. Krajnik added. "My laboratory has exploded eleven—no, twelve—times since I built the house, and no one has ever noticed."

Dash found himself agreeing. "Yeah, those shock absorbers are pretty . . . swell. And the heat from the . . . accidents . . . that gets stored, too?"

Dr. Krajnik looked like she really *did* like him. "Exactly, Mr. Kent, exactly. Every form of energy gets diverted to the house's power generators. And I need it, believe me, when I have to rebuild."

"Okay," Dash said. "I get it. But . . . why? Why break the zoning laws with this kind of laboratory, what you have to call an *illegal* laboratory, and why put all that effort into hiding it, when all you have to do is work in the District, like all the other . . ."

Dr. Krajnik waited, but nothing else came out.

"Mr. Kent, you have *seen* the District, haven't you? You have *seen* the other . . . scientists . . . and what they get up to in there? You have *seen* their feuds, their rivalries, their contests . . . and you have *seen* the blasted, radioactive wreckage that is the result of all that?"

"Sure," Dash said.

"And would *you* want to live there, if you could help it?"

Dash thought back to the walk—well, the run—that he and Nola had taken through the District, when scientists had poured out of every scorched laboratory and unleashed total, smoking, spinning, shrieking chaos on Pitt's giant robot.

"Well . . ."

Nola touched his forearm. "It really is safe," she told him. "I was here once when there was an accident, and all I heard was this sort of *whump* noise, and then afterwards we had dinner."

"Number eight," Dr. Krajnik recalled. "The Whirling Magnetosphere."

Dash continued to think it over while Dr. Krajnik smiled and Nola worried.

"Well, okay," he said at last. "It'd be an awful mess if everybody did it . . . but I guess you know what you're doing. I guess."

"When it comes right down to it," Dr. Krajnik said, "the whole District is a noisy playground for—mostly—boys, and their noisy toys. I'm glad they're confined in there, myself. But it's not for me."

"So that's settled!" Nola said brightly. "Now, about our real problems . . ."

Dr. Krajnik counted on her fingers. "Unlicensed robots, suspicious construction projects, the new Info-Slate switchboard, a murderous Howard Pitt, and the question of what, exactly, he's up to."

"No good," Dash contributed.

"But we can't report him to the law because they're shooting at us," Nola added.

Dr. Krajnik ticked off a finger on her other hand. "Yes, and the ASAA."

Dash asked, "But what were you saying before about Pitt? That he was *always* going to be trouble?"

Dr. Krajnik poured herself some coffee. "Howard Pitt . . .

"Howard Pitt is a brilliant engineer. Top drawer: everyone knows it. He can take a very large problem and reduce it to a series of very small problems, which he solves; and the end result is something very large that no longer has problems. Something as large as a canal, or a viaduct, or a complex system of pneumatic Tubes that can transport people rapidly across a city. He doesn't think quite the way that other people think. And he doesn't stop thinking until he's done. You could say . . ." She took a sip from her cup. "You could say that his weakness is that he thinks *too much*. Just doesn't know when to stop. Until everything he sees is a kind of a problem, and of course then he has to solve it. He can't help himself. And he's impatient with anybody whose brain can't keep up with him.

"He's *so* valuable to have around. But, you see, if something were to start him thinking in the *wrong* way . . ."

"Like, how people can't be improved the way he wants," Dash said. "How to solve the problem of people."

She tilted her head. "Do you think that's it? Maybe. Maybe. Anyway, really peculiar deep thinkers have tried to solve the world's problems many times. They're usually idealists, strange as that seems when they start to process people into cattle feed, or when they make it a capital crime to have red hair, or . . . when they do whatever it is they think needs to be done. And then you have to fight a war to get rid of them. Usually.

"Don't misunderstand me," she continued. "We owe everything to our idealists. They're the people who see farther than the rest of us. When we're paying more attention to our own lives than to the lives of *everyone*, of our whole society, idealists jab us in the ribs and say *Hey! We're doing this wrong!* So we take a look around, and often enough we find that we *are* doing this wrong. And so we change.

"But idealists aren't always right. Ideas have about an even chance of being wrong. So your problem—our problem—is what to do when idealists won't listen to anybody else. When they're just so positive they're right that nobody else's ideas could possibly have any value."

Dr. Krajnik set her coffee cup down on one of the work tables.

"As I said, Howard Pitt doesn't have a high opinion of other peoples' ideas. So if a particular problem gets stuck in his head, and he keeps thinking about it, and he pays no attention to anyone else, then something truly peculiar may happen. Something dramatic."

She picked up her coffee again, her eyes straying toward the doorway. "It would be a fascinating experiment, in fact: to put an idea into the head of a person like Pitt, and set him off on his path to lunacy."

Nola's eyebrow twitched. Dr. Krajnik didn't acknowledge her, or her eyebrow, but added: "*I* am not an idealist, of course. I'm just . . . a *curious* person." She took another drink of coffee.

Suddenly Dash wondered what had become of Rusty. He looked around and saw the little robot standing near the door where he watched the baboon, mournful in its pod. Rusty returned Dash's look and shook his head, very slightly. Then he went back to watching the baboon.

"The law, as you say, doesn't have to be a very big problem," Dr. Krajnik went on. "You simply have to get some evidence that Pitt is *breaking* the law. One of the laws. Say you connect him to those unlicensed robots, for example. At the construction site, or the switch-board."

"Right," Dash sighed. "We know. But unless we catch him there we can't link him to the robots at the construction site—not as *real evidence*, I mean—and we don't know where the new switch-board is."

SATURDAY, 4:18 PM

"It's definitely over there," said Mr. King.

They were standing on one of the high, windy platforms of the monorail terminal. The robot pointed down the cavernous street below them.

Mrs. Broadvine tried to look encouraging. "And . . . about where, exactly?"

Mr. King's antenna was spinning faster now that it was out in the unobstructed sky. But his head drooped.

"I can't be sure," he admitted. "But if we keep heading in that direction, and checking from high ground, I should be able to lo-cate it.

"You ladies may wish to go, however. This is likely to take me some time."

"Oh, no you don't!" Freda said. "That switchboard is our business, too, you know."

Rhonda agreed. "Not to mention poor little Iris!"

Mr. King glanced along the platform. Mrs. Broadvine peered in that direction and saw a line of public televideo booths.

The robot turned back to the operators. "You're right, of course. And your concern for Iris is very moving, if I may say so. It occurs to me that whenever we do find Pitt's switchboard there are *other* concerned parties. This might be a good time to let them know what we're doing."

He led the operators to the booths and placed a call.

"Harry? It's Albert."

Not snooping, exactly, Mrs. Broadvine could see a grim-looking man on the screen. He looked excited when he saw Mr. King's face on his own display.

"Albert!" he said. "We've tracked down the fellow who bought the equipment for the factory! It's . . ."

"Howard Pitt," the robot said.

Harry's brows drew down into a solid bar. "Oh, well that's just fine!" he said. "It's taken me *hours*. . . ."

Someone out of the camera's view coughed quietly. Harry glared in that direction.

"It's taken *them* hours to track the man down. And you already knew?"

"I'm sorry, Harry—I found out just a little while ago. I'm narrowing the search for Pitt's new Info-Slate switchboard—that's where we'll find the evidence of his treachery—and I wanted you to know where I'm headed."

Mr. King gave Harry directions. "You can probably find me up on the Trylon in the square by the time you get here."

Harry promised to bring whatever technicians he could find on a Saturday afternoon. "And I'll call in some more!" he finished.

When he'd hung up, Mr. King stood for a moment in front of the blank televideo screen.

"He's a good human person, is Harry Roy," he told Mrs. Broadvine. "But at this stage I want my own people with us, too."

So he made another call.

SATURDAY, 4:29 PM

The Campbell children had waited until they were sure that the matronly woman and her friends had moved on before they led Abner back downstairs. He'd tried to cast a friendly look at the babysitter,

Doris, but she was holding a grudge about that business with the chair. It had *almost* worked; he wished she could be more understanding.

But now they were back in the dim, quiet reaches of the tunnels. The tiny robot's cannon never strayed from Abner. It had really made up its mind about him this time.

"Do you know where we are?" the little girl asked.

"Yes."

They walked on for a few more minutes.

"How 'bout now?" the boy asked him. "Where are we now?"

Abner read the markings on the Transport Tube beside them. "We're just under the ninth circle of the Tube Transport system," he told them, with total accuracy and no irony at all.

SATURDAY, 4:36 PM

"It's not too difficult," Dr. Krajnik told Dash. "I mean, I can find Pitt's switchboard within an hour, but I'm not sure how I'll be able to *tell* you what I've found."

Dash tried to understand the two parts of her sentence together; then he tried them individually. It still didn't work.

"You can find the switchboard that nobody can find. But then you can't tell us what you found."

She nodded. "Yes! You have a fine grasp of the situation."

"Stop it, Aunt Lillian," Nola cut in. "Quit torturing him."

Dash was pretty conscious of the many ways he might be tortured in this room. "You're just going to have to explain that to me," he said.

Dr. Krajnik waved at the big capsule near the center of her laboratory. "I can find Pitt's laboratory in about an hour by using *that*. But at the end of the hour I may not be able to get a message to you before I . . . become unavailable."

"Because, you're, like . . . disintegrated."

"Oh, no! You might say that it's because I'll be *re-integrated*."

She stepped over to the console at the foot of the capsule's stairs, where the lightning sparks within the globes lit the sides of her face with blue and white flashes. There was something odd about those electrical discharges, as though what Dash was seeing was what the lightning looked like just before, or possibly just after, it struck: the bright highlights on Dr. Krajnik's cheekbones seemed wrong and out of step with the world. She bent over the control panel and looked back. "You can see, if you like."

Everyone but Rusty moved closer.

At the top of the control panel was a plaque that read:

PERSONAL TEMPORAL DIFFRACTION DEVICE
EMERGENCY USE ONLY! (CLASS X)
THE "DIFFRACTONATOR"
RESULTS ARE TEMPORARY, BUT IMMEDIATE AND
IRREVERSIBLE

. . . while below there was the usual bewildering collection of gauges, switches, indicator lights, and one big dial with a pie-shaped cutout in it. A ring of numbers was visible through the cutout; a bright red triangle marked the number 12.

"Okay," he said. "So, what does it do?"

"The Diffractonator

allows me to replicate myself, oh, any number of times, by expending that number of *future hours* in a controlled temporal fugue."

There was a long pause.

"All right, let's try it this way, then. If I were to set this dial to three hundred, I would diffract my *next three hundred hours* so that three hundred of me would be here for the next *one* hour. At the end of that hour, all three hundred of my diffracted selves would disappear, and you wouldn't see me again—that is, the one, usual me—until three hundred hours had passed. You see? I'd spend my next three hundred hours *all at the same time.*"

There was another pause, almost as long as the earlier one.

"Aunt Lillian . . . three hundred of you?"

Dr. Krajnik nodded. "Though I haven't tested more than sixty-four," she admitted. "There's a very large discharge of energy, at the higher levels."

"Then at some time or other . . . there were sixty-four of you, all at the same time?"

"Yes! Useful, isn't it?"

There was an additional pause.

"Well," Dash allowed, "I guess that would come in handy. I mean, if I could do that at just the right time, then I could sweep through the whole Temple of the Spider God and clear out all the cats in one hour, couldn't I?"

This time it was Dr. Krajnik who paused.

"I'm not sure what that means," she said at last, "but it sounds about right. If you're willing *not to be around* for a few hundred or a few thousand hours, then yes: that's about right."

She turned to Nola. "Is that a game, or something? The Temple of the Spider God, and the cats?"

"Oh, no. He's completely serious, Aunt Lillian. And it would be a very good thing to do, in my opinion."

Dr. Krajnik accepted this. "Then yes. You'd have to have the device in place, and you'd need an excellent power source, and then, of course, you'd have to be prepared for the explosion."

Science.

"That would be the 'Class X' explosion?" Dash asked. "Which would mean, say . . ."

"As I said, there's a large discharge of energy at the higher levels. For what we need, that would probably mean the complete destruction of my laboratory."

Nola looked back at the hatch. "But the house, the house would be all right?"

"Depending on the number of diffractions, yes. Almost certainly."

Once again, there was a pause.

"Well," she explained, "there's always an element of risk, at the higher diffraction levels."

Which you haven't tested, Dash added silently.

"Well, look," he said, "this is really serious to me, on account of Pitt is trying to kill me and everything, and it's really important to Nola and her switchboard operators, because they want their jobs back, and it's really important to all those black market robots because they don't even know that they're slaves, which is what they are. So we really want to put the guy away. But . . . your whole laboratory . . ."

. . . and maybe your whole neighborhood. . . .

Dr. Krajnik turned the pie-shaped dial way over until the arrow pointed at the number *15,000*. Nola's eyes went wide.

"Nola, Dash . . . whatever Howard Pitt is doing, it's *big*. Because his *ideas* are big. It's big enough that he's built an inertrium object that could contain whole stadiums filled with people. Big enough that . . . well, I think it's safe for us to say that whatever Pitt is doing is a big, immediate danger to everyone in Retropolis.

"Pitt is *extremely dangerous*. Howard Pitt is the kind of man who can dream up absolutely wonderful things that improve people's lives, and then he can *build* those things. But if he's turned inward, and becomes . . . twisted, as he seems to have done, then he's *also* the kind of man who can dream big, horrible dreams. And he can build those big, terrible things, too.

"I'm convinced that this is what he's doing right now. And from what you've told me, no one has any idea what's going on, and you're the only people who are trying to stop him. I'm sure of that because of the extraordinary things he's doing to stop *you*.

"So . . . yes. Let me explode my laboratory for you. It will be my pleasure."

Dash and Nola nodded slowly.

"Still," Dr. Krajnik continued, "there remains the problem of how—once I've located the switchboard—I can get that information back to you. If it takes me nearly the whole hour, you see, I might run out of time—and I won't be back for fifteen thousand hours. So we must have some way to communicate, and we need it for a very large number of . . . me."

"So, let me see . . ." Dash started. "fifteen thousand of you will go through the city . . ."

". . . and question people in every building—or at least in every neighborhood—until I find someone who's seen Pitt in a place where he shouldn't be. It will be some out of the way place, secluded. I'll need fifteen thousand pictures of Pitt. . . ."

She walked over to another console and flicked some dials, called up a photograph of Howard Pitt, and pressed a button.

"But, as it happens, I'll only have to print one. We still need some way for me to contact you, immediately, when I discover the location of the new switchboard."

Dash grinned and shrugged off his back pack. "I think I can cover you there," he told her.

He spilled the back pack's contents out on a worktable. "What's that?" Nola asked.

He picked it up. "Oh, just something I picked up when I was at O'Malley's."

It was a slide rule.

"You have an Enigmascope!" Dr. Krajnik cried. "How wonderful!"

"Yeah, but it's just a devil to keep clean. No, this here is what we need."

He picked up his ornithopter call.

Twenty minutes later, out on the porch, the ornithopters were all circling overhead. It looked like a couple hundred of them.

"How can that be enough?" Nola wanted to know.

"I'm gonna set them to patrol in a grid—kind of like the ASAA rockets—with instructions to keep an eye on every . . . every one of your aunts, I guess, that they can see. If they keep moving and keep track of her, or I mean *them,* then any one of her should be able to call them down and give 'em the message.

"And, see, because the ornithopters' memories aren't very long, I've set 'em to rebroadcast their orders every two minutes."

Nola nodded, but she wasn't paying a lot of attention. Rusty had followed them outside. He still seemed subdued.

Dr. Krajnik stepped out on the porch. "I'm just about ready," she said. "You'll want to keep your distance."

She looked down at Rusty, who was looking someplace else.

"Rusty, I wonder if you could step inside for a moment? I'd like to have a word."

The door closed behind them. Dash heard Dr. Krajnik's voice grow fainter as they walked toward her workshop.

"Something's going on with those two," he observed. "Any idea?"

"No. I didn't even know they were acquainted."

A few minutes passed. Dash fiddled with the instructions for the ornithopters; Nola just admired the view. The Moon, still nearly full, had risen up in the late afternoon sky. It made a lovely scene.

The door opened again. Rusty came out, leading by the hand a baboon whose expression showed great relief. Dr. Krajnik leaned on the doorframe.

"That's got it," she said. "The three of you should go down the stairs. Just in case."

She smiled up at the circling ornithopters. "Wonderful creatures. Anyway, look for a message from me within an hour of . . . well, keep an eye on the house. You'll know when. And I'll see you both in fifteen thousand hours!"

She closed the door, but popped right out again. "Oh, and Nola—when you get a chance, look in the envelope on the sideboard by the door. If you follow the instructions my new workshop will be ready for me when I come back."

And then she was gone. Dash, Nola, and Rusty started down the stairs to the street. The baboon set off with a grateful hoot between the trees, toward the rest of its own rather remarkable story.

"She just gave us two years of her life," Nola said.

SATURDAY, 4:56 PM

They're going away for a long time.

That was about all her sergeant had had to say in spite of all the information Maria had tried to give him. The whole Info-Slate system might have been compromised; no one could tell exactly where the ASAA's shoot-on-sight order had even *come* from; two civilians without criminal records were being hunted through the streets; and the only known link between those civilians was that they were participants in an Info-Slate search that she, Maria, had made.

But in the end, it just came down to *they're going away for a long time.*

Sarge had put Maria behind a desk until she could be debriefed about her contact with Miss Gardner and Dash Kent. There was a turbulent flow of uniforms all around her, with dispatches on the way out, and reports on the way in, but she could tell that nobody, anywhere, had any idea where Rusty and the fugitives had gone.

She found herself looking at her Info-Slate. Ordinarily Maria would have been tapping in zoning and residency queries for the address on Lovelace Street. But not today: she didn't think she could trust anything the Slate was telling her. And the last thing she wanted was to give it—or its operator—any ideas.

She picked it up, though, in case anyone might try to reach her, and called over her shoulder, "I'll be down in Records if anybody needs me."

SATURDAY, 4:59 PM

From the foot of the stairs down on Lovelace Street Dr. Krajnik's house looked like a tower on a medieval hill. The Moon was floating just next to it, and what with the trees that framed the stairway the whole thing was like a scene on a calendar.

Rusty took Nola's hand.

"That must be it," Nola said.

The whole tall house had trembled slightly. Near the top floor a shutter swung open and closed again; from its ledge, Dash saw a potted plant start its long, last dive toward the ground far below.

They heard a muffled *thump*. Wisps of smoke puffed out of the few windows that had been left open.

"Well," Dash said as he turned to Nola. "Now I guess we just need to wait."

The ornithopters spread out. Their little wingbeats drove them precisely into a search grid that would embrace the entire city.

And across the city, in a much different grid, Lillian Krajniks puffed into being in 15,000 places. Each Lillian clutched a photograph of Howard Pitt.

The Lillians took stock of their surroundings, checked the skies to see if their ornithopters had arrived, and then went forth on their mission of discovery.

16

HOUR OF THE DIFFRACTED DOCTOR

SATURDAY, 5:01 PM

Robot G-94VA came to a sudden stop. He'd nearly collided with a small human person who'd darted from the south side of the Transport Tube junction.

"I beg your pardon, little girl," he said.

She squinted into his face. "You're all messed up, aren't you?"

G-94VA's personality design compelled him to courtesy. "I have been severely damaged by, I think, the Plumber."

A frightened man and another small human person came up behind her. On the little boy's shoulder G-94VA could see a miniature security robot who resembled several robots known to G-94VA from the Projectile's underground complex. It was strange, though, to see such a tiny one.

"SURRENDGACK OR BE DISINTEGGRED."

There was a small, but proportionately large, dent in the tiny robot's head. This was a matter for concern in view of its small, but disproportionately deadly, armament.

"I am not sure I understand," tried G-94VA.

The little boy surged up to G-94VA's knee. "He says if you don't surrender he's gonna disintegrate you."

277

"But I am needed at the project site," he explained. "We must complete the Projectile as quickly as possible and we are behind our schedule."

The tiny robot's chest seemed to swell. It spared a glance for the man behind it, but its cannon was now centered on G-94VA's head.

The man stepped up. "I'm afraid you don't have a choice in the matter. I've seen . . . I've seen what happens to anything that fails to surrender. And anyway, think about this: once you've been disintegrated you won't be able to complete your work, will you?"

The little girl had been listening carefully. "What's the Projectile thing you want to get back to?"

While the tiny robot watched, G-94VA described the Projectile.

The frightened man forgot, for a moment, to be frightened. "It's a large, hollow construct built almost entirely of inertrium, in an underground construction site? Who is its designer?"

"The Master," G-94VA told him with some gratitude. Possibly one of this group was not deranged.

"And does the Master wear a hat at all times, on top of his hairless head?"

The big robot nodded happily. "Yes! Do you know the Master?"

The man didn't answer. He turned instead to the peculiar little humans and told them that a large construction site was far too dangerous for children. That it was filled with big, perilous machines that might accidentally explode, or turn on their operators with brutal speed, and which the children should in no way, and not for any reason, approach.

G-94VA started to correct him: the site was in full compliance with strict safety guidelines and there had never been an accident. But the man cut him off.

"No, really; I work at construction sites all the time. They're no place for children. And in any case no construction project would ever *allow* children on the premises. Not *ever*."

The little boy and the little girl exchanged a look.

The tiny security robot raised its cannon a little higher.

"If you surrender," said the little girl, "we'll *take* you there."

G-94VA leaned against the wall, taking the weight off his damaged leg. "Then I surrender without reservation, and unconditionally," he said. "I am delighted to surrender. Surrendering is the best thing that has happened to me all day."

The humans all seemed satisfied. The tiny, deadly robot, though, was clearly not happy.

The two children examined G-94VA. They took, and subsequently quarreled over, the Info-Slate that had been strapped to his chest. "I want to see what it *does,*" insisted the little girl.

The boy batted her over the head with it. "It does *this*!" he yelled.

And all the while, the formerly frightened man was eyeing G-94VA with great interest. "Shouldn't we get moving?" he asked.

It was odd, though of course this whole meeting had been odd. But it had seemed to G-94VA that the man wanted to *stay away* from the Projectile site.

Humans were very difficult to understand.

SATURDAY, 5:02 PM

She could tell by her location which one of her she was. A look up showed Lillian that the ornithopters hadn't arrived yet; that was no problem, though. There was still plenty of time.

But there was no point in wasting it. She stopped the pedestrians who were passing and showed them Pitt's picture. "Have you seen this man?" she asked, over and over. No one had.

She was standing in front of the Constellation Boulevard office of the Retropolis Travel Bureau. Well, she'd better get started on the buildings, then, hadn't she?

So she did. And all across the sprawling, high-towered city of Retropolis 14,999 other Lillians had come to the same conclusion.

Info-Slate requests had been increasing rapidly for the whole afternoon; this was especially true of the requests from ASAA officers, whose inquiries were often routed to the dead zone that was Howard Pitt's personal console. The operators at the switchboard had done their best—which was very good, really—to keep up with the traffic. But they could tell that their response times were beginning to lag behind.

So an unspoken but universal sense of discomfort had worked its way down the whole length of Pitt's hidden switchboard chamber.

The operators knew that they were not, well, operating. Not to the extent that was expected of them, anyway. From time to time one would raise her softly illuminated eyes to exchange a glance with her neighbor. No words would pass between them because, after all, they weren't equipped for speech. But those glances communicated their shared sense of being *less than optimal.*

And being optimal, to one of these operators, was an essential state of being.

The operator who had been handling the very few requests from the Info-Slate assigned to Robot G-94VA found, quite suddenly, that the Slate was overwhelming her resources. She dutifully switched the Slate's sidebar pane, upper right, to display videos of famous explosions; the left lower sidebar pane now showed a list of recent industrial accidents; the upper left sidebar, not to be outdone, presented information about large construction projects.

It wasn't until she received a request for the Slate's main pane about the properties of inertrium that all these combined searches and requests triggered a security alert that raised Pitt's threat level assessment to its threshold. Her left hand swept down to tap the warning button as, with her right, she tried to keep up with the very busy user of G-94VA's Info-Slate.

The operator next to her saw this flurry of activity and gave her a sympathetic look. They were all having their very first very bad day.

His hat brim shot upward, impelled by his eyebrows, when Pitt received the warning message. One of his robots had been compromised!

G-94VA was the damaged robot that had failed to capture Dash Kent. Kent had now managed to elude the full force of the ASAA and, so far as anyone knew, had disappeared. Kent must have reported the damaged robot to his hidden master—Pitt's nemesis—and the robot had now been captured.

Pitt's finger hovered over the switch that would disconnect G-94VA's Info-Slate from the system. But no . . . it would be much better, much more useful, to observe what Pitt's enemy was trying to learn.

He scanned the requests that had deluged the switchboard operator. So rapid! And . . .

So sinister. Properties of inertrium, explosions, industrial accidents, and—now—whether it was possible to make Transport Pods collide at full speed. Pitt's nemesis, if these requests had anything to say about it, was a ruthless and uncompromising opponent. He was so focused on understanding the enemy's plan that Pitt didn't even realize that he felt energized, elated . . . and *happy*.

SATURDAY, 5:13 PM

Harry followed Albert King's directions to the letter. But he had reached—and then circled—the Trylon in the middle of the Perisquare and he still couldn't find his new friend. They might easily have missed each other. In view of Harry's retinue, though, he preferred to radiate certainty.

There had only been eight technicians on duty at the Ferriss Moto-Man works. Harry had brought them all. The rest of his twelve followers were—and this had surprised Harry—four of the accountants who'd been hounding Pitt's paper trail through the day. Apparently the paper chase had roused their mathematical blood. Harry knew that he should appreciate this, but it was so unexpected that he hadn't quite come to grips with it.

Davies was shadowing Harry on his trip around the Trylon. Harry could tell that Davies' view of the accountants was about the same as his own. They heard a distant voice calling "Yoo-hoo! Mr. Roy! We're up above!"

Harry and Davies looked up the height of the Trylon. A three-sided wedge, the Trylon was the sort of monument you'd get if you somehow stretched a pyramid to six times its original height. A couple of pyramids up Harry could see a middle-aged woman who was waving down at them.

"Friend of yours?" asked Davies.

Harry grunted. "Whoever she is it looks like she's waiting for us," he said, and with a brisk wave he motioned his retinue to follow him inside.

The Trylon's interior was completely hollow and supported a long stairway which, hugging the three faces of the monument, led past landing after landing on its way to the Trylon's peak. There were short broad unglazed windows set at each third landing. In front of each window was a rank of coin-operated telescopes for the convenience of visitors.

Near one of those windows Harry and Davies found Albert, with an antenna on his head; it was spinning like a propeller. Ranged around him were seven women. Each one was feeding coins into the scopes. When Harry's group joined them there were still a couple of telescopes free, but even the accountants were trying to maintain their dignity.

Albert greeted Harry. "We've managed to track the switchboard signal this far, by checking it from high altitudes from time to time. Now that most of us are here we may proceed at least as far as the Square."

Harry didn't miss that "most of us," but he figured he'd find out what that meant before long. In the meantime Albert introduced Mrs. Broadvine and her operators, and Harry did the same for his crew. They were more than twenty strong now, even if most of them were office workers; that might not be enough to defeat whatever forces Pitt had gathered but it was, anyhow, enough to more than fill the Trylon's landing. So once Albert was sure of his signal's bearing they started the climb downstairs.

SATURDAY, 5:22 PM

"You know what we need?" Dash asked. "We need a rocket, or a hovercar. Then when we get your aunt's message we can get to the switchboard just as fast as we like."

Nola could see the sense in that, but Dash's interplanetary Actaeon—miles away, now—wasn't the kind of vehicle you could use to fly around the city. No, they needed something smaller, a little personal rocket like the ASAA cruisers.

"They might not be expecting to see us in the sky," she said.

Rusty shrugged and looked significantly around them.

"I guess we could steal one . . . ?" she ventured.

The others seemed surprised.

"I'm not just a switchboard operator anymore," she explained. "I'm a desperate, hunted felon. You can't put anything past me."

"I don't like stealing," Dash said. "And I'm sure not going to wave a gun in anybody's face to get one."

"Then what you're after is a valuable, unattended rocket that nobody else wants."

Nobody seemed to favor the odds of that.

"Say, does your aunt have a rocket?"

Nola didn't know. "We could go back up and look in the hangar, I suppose. The house should be perfectly safe by now."

She was surprised to see Rusty bound back up the stairs. He took them three at a time. He'd been so, well, he'd seemed so unhappy to be there earlier, when Aunt Lillian had been at home.

Dash and Nola followed after him.

SATURDAY, 5:23 PM

Abner climbed the tunnel stairs with a new sense of purpose. The horrible children had led him quite by accident back onto Pitt's trail, since surely the Master G-94VA had spoken of was Howard Pitt; and surely the "Projectile" was the project for which Pitt had needed such great quantities of inertrium. As big as a floating city!

Not even the tiny malevolent robot could dampen Abner's spirits.

He offered his arm to G-94VA, who was having some trouble navigating the stairway. "Thank you, sir."

"No need for all that formality," Abner told him. "I'm just plain old Abner Perkins. Engineer."

"Really?" asked the robot. "An admirable calling."

"That's why I'm so curious about your Projectile project. Such an ambitious undertaking. What, exactly, is its purpose?"

When G-94VA told him, Abner tripped and fell backward down the stairs.

"No time for *playing around*," Evvie snarled. Then she turned back to the Info-Slate. Evan had seized the moment and was tapping away on its screen.

"Look at *this*!" he said. "You can skin a cat in *twenty-seven* ways!"

They thought that over. "I think I know where we can find *eleven* cats," Evvie said. "But the other sixteen, I don't know. I just don't know."

"There's Princess Fedora . . ."

"Of *course* there's Princess Fedora. She was *number one*."

Abner leaned toward G-94VA. "And when is the Projectile supposed to be finished?"

"All too soon, Mr. Perkins. But if the Plumber hasn't arrived yet with help . . . I don't know how it can be ready in time."

"The . . . Plumber?"

"There's got to be a mess of cats *someplace*. You just have to find them *all in one place,* is all. Like a, like a cat shelter. Or a cat hospital."

Evan looked unsure. "You don't want *sick* cats."

"Then someplace where a lot of cats . . ."

The Campbells thought hard. For a moment, all Abner could hear was the soft whir of the tiny robot's head as it turned back and forth between Abner and G-94VA.

"Where is it that *Dash* goes, again?" asked Evan.

They grinned at each other. "There's *lots* of cats there. With *Spider Gods*."

Evan kept the grin on his face but it seemed to Abner that something about "Spider Gods" was not what the little hooligan had wanted to hear. His sister was too busy bending over the Info-Slate to notice, though.

SATURDAY, 5:23 PM

His adversary had hardly slowed the flow of information that poured into the stolen Info-Slate. When Pitt saw these latest queries his face drained of color. He leaned back and tipped his hat back on his head.

Too close, he told himself. *He is very close to . . .*

Pitt checked the Projectile's status. If he directed the robots to drop every other task and concentrate on completing the shell . . . and if he re-routed the Transport Tubes, to double up the prisoners . . . and if the evacuation began *at once . . .*

He pulled his slide rule out of its holster and ran a finger down its smooth, cool surface. Then he set to calculating an amended trajectory based on the Projectile's new, adjusted final mass. It might . . . just . . . work.

It was time, then. Pitt quickly entered some additional orders for the ASAA officers through the Info-Slate system. It was sooner than he'd planned. But, still, what could go wrong?

He issued new directives to his robots. Down the hall there was a moment of silence as they digested the revised schedule. Then the hammering and hauling and riveting started up again at an even more feverish pace.

Pitt finally changed the routing for the Tube Transport system. He'd abandon the unfinished chambers altogether. They'd just have to share their rooms. The new priority was to finish the Projectile's hull.

He hunched forward over the console and scanned his enemy's Info-Slate feed. *There. See what you can do about that.*

SATURDAY, 5:29 PM

The General Quarters alarm sounded throughout ASAA headquarters. Maria dropped the latest useless file back into its drawer and ran out into the hallway. She joined the flood of blue uniforms that were forcing their way through the building to the main floor, where an even greater flood of officers was waiting for them. Orders blared out over the PA system.

> *A full evacuation of the city has been declared. Officers are instructed to disperse to their usual routes and guide all civilians to their nearest Tube Transport stations. This must be executed as quickly as possible, and in an orderly manner. No one is to be left behind.*

"That's. . . ." she heard.

"Millions . . ."

"Of people. . . ."

There was a squawk from the PA.

Mechanical persons are not in any danger. Only human citizens are to take part in the evacuation.

That was *still* millions of people, Maria knew.

"What about the . . . what about the *District*?" asked someone.

"He said *everybody,* didn't he?"

But no one was assigned to patrol the District, of course. It was left to police itself.

The PA squawked one more time.

Unmarried officers from units seventeen, thirty-two, thirty-six, and fifty-five: you have now volunteered to evacuate the Experimental Research District. That is all. Go!

As the horde of ASAA officers scrambled for their rockets Maria felt very grateful that she'd been assigned to unit twenty-three. When she reached her cruiser she came to a halt. *So after we get them into the Tube system,* she wondered, *where are they going to go?*

SATURDAY, 5:33 PM

The unofficial Howard Pitt Containment Force spread out in a loose formation behind Harry and Albert. The accountants, roboticists, and operators did their best to look like a unified team. They were taken aback, though, when at the edge of the square they met a wall of robots.

Harry gave Albert a look.

"Yes, Harry. I made a call to the League just after we spoke."

There had to be two hundred robots out there, maybe more. There were Big Lugs, of course, but there were also rarer models like the Submersible, the Drillomator, and the Loewy LumberJax. A short, determined line of clerical robots each held a large wrench, while in the ranks behind them Harry could see a forest of poles that were bent under the weight of the typewriters at their tips. The eyes of the robots were blazing like torches.

Harry coughed. "You know, Albert, we can't have a mob here."

The robot agreed. "But I asked them to be ready for anything, Harry. There are also boxes of medical supplies in case any of your people are injured."

Harry looked behind him. "Well, thanks for that. But seriously, we have to keep this from getting violent. I understand what this whole . . . what Pitt's robots mean to you. I really do. But we can't take the law into our own hands."

He turned back to the robot army. "Or, you know, appendages."

Albert was watching him closely. "We do not condone violence, Harry. You need to trust me on this."

Harry wondered if he *did* trust Albert. When it came down to it, the League president was an army all by himself; he just didn't look like one.

"Well, we'd better form up, Albert."

The two of them walked up to the head of what Harry hoped was not a mob.

"Big Lugs!" called Albert. "I want two ranks of you to surround the human people."

He patted Harry's shoulder. "It's for their protection," he explained. "Now let's find that switchboard."

The little antenna on his head led them on.

Their battalion marched in a column so wide that it nearly filled the street, trailing for some distance behind the two in the lead. It looked so much like a parade that pedestrians gathered on either side and waited for the big balloons. The odd thing about that was that there never seemed to be a crowd in front of the Tube Transport stations; Harry couldn't see why. He turned from one side of the street to the other, and though he sometimes saw people standing in front of the Pods, when he looked back that space was always empty again. Strange.

"We should keep your people away from those," said Albert. He must have been watching Harry. "Something there is not quite right."

Harry made sure that his people were safe behind the Lugs. "That's another one of Pitt's projects," he observed.

The robot president slowed. "I'm having trouble with the signal again," he said. He looked back over his shoulder. "Rhonda, would you please?"

Harry saw one of the young switchboard operators get busy with her Info-Slate.

"That's better," Albert told her. But to Harry he said, more quietly, "I'll need to get some altitude again. Soon."

SATURDAY, 5:44 PM

Lillian knew her time was growing short. She wished she'd found some way to communicate with all her other selves; if one of them had already located the switchboard then there wasn't any need for haste. Oh, well. She'd devised the plan in a hurry, after all.

She was working her way down Finnegan Road, a narrow, pleasant street filled with small businesses and overhead apartments. There was a lot of activity in the buildings. It looked like everybody was pouring out on their way . . . *where?* she wondered.

She ducked into a newsstand. "Could you have a look at this picture?" she asked.

"Haven't you heard? We're being evacuated!"

The newsagent was bundling a few important things into a small box. "We're all supposed to head for those stations"—with a wave at the Tube Transport stations along the road—"and get to safety."

Lillian frowned. ". . . from what?"

"No time! The ASAA says it isn't safe to stay here!"

The newsagent pushed Lillian out of the way and locked the newsstand door. Lillian toyed with the eyepiece of her glasses. But no, not necessary, she decided. Instead she walked alongside the newsagent toward the line that was forming in front of the Tube.

"Well, while we wait, anyway," Lillian said, "have you seen this man in the neighborhood?"

She held out the photograph of Howard Pitt.

The newsagent gave it a glance. "No, I don't think so."

So Lillian went up and down the line and asked her question again and again. It was convenient, having them all arranged neatly this way. She wished she'd thought of it herself.

At regular intervals of one to two minutes the Transport station's door would hiss open and first one, then two or three of the people in line would hop in. Each time the door hissed closed there was a sound of rushing air; then, after another one to two minutes, the door would open again.

It wasn't all that fast a way to evacuate a neighborhood, she thought, and then she thought again. "Say, how many neighborhoods are being cleared out?"

"All of them," said the newsagent from behind the Pod door, just as it shut again.

The whole city? All climbing into Pitt's Pods?

Lillian took her photograph to the end of the line. New arrivals were appearing all the time now.

"Have *you* seen this man?"

A woman with two toddlers draped over her moved one child to the left in order to see the picture. "Oh, him. Sure. Right here."

Lillian leaned in, but she was careful to avoid the zone around the baby. "When you say 'here' . . ." she started.

The woman waved at the Pod. "Right behind there," she said. "I think he does some kind of maintenance on the Tubes."

Well, maybe he did, and maybe he didn't. Lillian tried not to overreact: Pitt had business all over town. She stepped behind the Transport Tube Station and found the maintenance hatch. It didn't want to open for her, but Lillian had her ways. She checked the time again.

She'd make it a quick look.

Six minutes later Lillian shot out of the hatch, startling the much shorter line of evacuees, and scanned the air above the street. Not an ornithopter in sight! She'd have to try the intersection.

Behind her, the Tube Station door hissed open and *four* people stuffed themselves into the Pod. She had a feeling they weren't going to like where they were headed.

SATURDAY, 5:49 PM

Maria wasn't going to her assigned evacuation site. She felt a little guilty about that, just in case this danger was real, but she was pretty sure that the whole business was another Info-Slate hijack.

There had been no records of any kind about that house where she'd seen the fugitives: and no record at all was, in itself, pretty interesting. Maria knew very well that you could hardly sneeze in Retropolis without filing a form of some kind with some civic organization that was known only by its capital letters. So a house that had been built without any permits, apparently, and which had no electrical power, or water, or any other utilities . . . that was a very unusual kind of house. She could see it on its hill, just a few blocks ahead.

She descended in a graceful arc toward the landscaped side of the building. Off in the distance she could just make out a small furry creature with rather long arms: it was heading off into the trees. When it turned and looked back at her, Maria had to tell herself that you don't often find a face like *that* in the city. But then it was gone.

She set her rocket down and let out the mooring cables. A couple of quick taps into the grass anchored it in place; its inertrium body bobbed up gently in the breeze. It was only then that she turned back to the frozen pair of people who were staring at her in terror from the door of an empty hangar.

Rusty, on the other hand, came bounding forward and waved. "Miss Gardner? And Mr. Kent?"

Of course there was a lot of confusion in the next few minutes, but eventually each of them had a sort of half-formed idea of who they all were and what they'd all been doing, even though Lillian Krajnik's living arrangements had not been described in very much detail.

"So, okay," Maria said at last. "I'm pretty sure the other officers are busy at the moment but even if they weren't, I doubt they'd shoot at you if I was to give you a lift."

Dash Kent peered into her rocket's cockpit. "Uh, you really think we'll all fit in there?" he asked.

"Where there's a will . . ." Maria told him. "I hope we're all feeling friendly, is all."

Nola's eyes were fixed on her watch. "That's it," she said. "It's over. Either Aunt Lillian found the switchboard, or . . ."

They all scanned the sky for one tiny ornithopter.

SATURDAY 6:11 PM

Robot R-54KG lurched from the catwalk to the final section of the Projectile's skin. All along its length, R-54KG's fellow workers were racing to complete their accelerated tasks. R-54KG was starting to think that they could really finish on time.

The robots had to clamber around the hundreds of Transport Tubes that were now fixed to the Projectile's hull. It seemed like every few seconds another Pod arrived through each tube. The Pods were decanting thousands of human persons into the Master's immense structure.

Yes. All seemed to be going according to plan.

He wondered what had happened to the Plumber. It didn't really matter anymore, but R-54KG felt a little disappointed. But of course the Plumber was a human person, and human persons were not predictable. Still . . .

Over to his left, R-54KG saw an inertrium plate start to drift upward.

"Look lively over there!" he bellowed. "We're not finished yet!"

The plate was caught and pulled slowly back to the Projectile's frame. R-54KG himself stood on its edge while the other robots heated the rivets.

It wouldn't be much longer now.

SATURDAY 6:17 PM

Dash felt a tug on his arm and looked down. Rusty was jumping from side to side with one arm stretched out to the East.

Nola had seen it, too, and he heard her yell, "There it is! There it is!"

The little ornithopter was silhouetted against the Moon. As it drew near Dash could hear the faint *ping ping ping* of its metal feathers. "Oh, I sure hope she found it," he breathed.

The ornithopter settled on his shoulder and he paged back through its video spool. Sure enough, there were directions there.

"You know where that is?" he asked Officer da Cunha.

"Sure," she said. "I know it."

"Then what I'd like you to do is to take Nola and Rusty there, seeing as you'll be with them now. But me, I want you to drop me off over by Pitt's big construction project."

Nola didn't seem so sure about that.

"I think it's best," he said. "You've got the officer with you. Just get the evidence we need against Howard Pitt, which should be pretty easy except if he's got . . ." He looked over at Maria. ". . . more *security measures*."

Maria nodded.

"But the thing is that whatever he's *really* doing, it has something to do with what's under that construction site. And if your Aunt

Lillian's right, then it's really, really bad. The officer can take care of you two. I figure I'd best get in the middle of this other thing.

"So you folks should go get the goods on Pitt at the switchboard and report him to the law, and I'll do what I can to stop him on my end. Then I guess we can all celebrate when it's over. Okay?"

Rusty shook his hand, but that was nothing next to the hug that Nola gave him. Then the three human people squeezed into the much-too-small cockpit of Maria's ASAA rocket. Rusty unpegged the mooring lines and hopped onto the back, just ahead of the rocket's tail, and a moment later they were airborne.

17

The Switchboard of Doom

It had taken a while for the small army of robots, operators, technicians, and accountants to pile up behind the leaders of their column. But Mrs. Broadvine, Harry Roy, and Albert King had scarcely noticed this even though they now knew exactly where to go.

They were crowded into Finnegan Road near—but not in front of—the Transport Tube station that was still admitting its small group of evacuees in groups of one to (now) four persons. The evacuation came as a surprise, right on the heels of the larger surprise they'd met as they rounded the corner.

A rather determined-looking woman had been standing just about where Mrs. Broadvine stood now. She had been speaking into the face of a little winged robot which began to beat its little metal wings with a *ping ping ping* that Mrs. Broadvine recognized: she'd heard it before when an ornithopter had taken off and flown through the window of Rusty's attic apartment. And she was sure it was another of these ornithopters that the strange woman had been speaking to.

This, unexpected as it was, was not the surprise. The surprise came when the woman somehow *imploded* into a sparkling, misty shape that seemed not to grow smaller, but somehow more distant and indistinct, as though it was rushing away from Mrs. Broadvine, from

Finnegan Road, from Retropolis, and from everything else; and stranger still, the vanishing outline of the woman was surrounded by *another* outline, and another, and another, as though she was a transparent Russian doll that went on forever or, conceivably, about 15,000 times. There was a faint popping sound and then the woman was just . . . gone.

Mrs. Broadvine had been keeping step with Mr. Roy and keeping up with Mr. King. The three of them came to a halt when they saw this bizarre exit from the road.

They were still bewildered by what they had just witnessed. But when their followers had bunched up in the road to the point where no more bunching was possible, Mr. King simply shook his enameled head and shrugged.

"Well, we're not going to find her, and she probably has nothing to do with any of this, anyway."

Mr. Roy wasn't convinced.

So Mrs. Broadvine, in the spirit of middle management, spoke: "We will table the question of the Mysterious Woman until later, won't we? I'm sure a group of like-minded persons can get to the bottom of *that* problem when we have the time to consider it. And until then, Mr. King, it seems certain that the switchboard must be somewhere behind that Pod station. I suggest that we concentrate on the problem that has led"—with a look at the crowd behind them—"all of us here."

She wasn't alone in watching their milling horde. The line of refugees, which was now steadily decreasing in size, was fascinated by them, too. In fact those at the head of the queue had started to crowd a little closer together just in case two hundred or so robots might decide to crash the line.

In the end it was Mr. Roy who edged behind the station and found the hatch, now wide open. He thrust his head into the tunnel beyond. Then he called, "It's going to be a little snug in there, Albert. We could try it double file, maybe single file for the Lugs."

Mr. King directed their column into a much narrower one that began to funnel into the maintenance tunnel. The robotic and human persons filed in while, just beyond, the Transport Tube doors continued to admit a few evacuees with a hiss open, and then a hiss closed, at intervals of about a minute.

By the time the end of the column had entered the tunnel there was no line left. It looked like this whole neighborhood had been emptied.

SATURDAY, 6:33 PM

Dash wanted to leap out of the cockpit. This would have been spectacular, if only Nola hadn't been sitting on his lap.

So he waited while Officer da Cunha set down carefully on the floor of the excavation that was also a roof for Pitt's construction site. He climbed out with some care, remembering that Nola and Rusty had found the footing unstable.

The cracks they'd described were now just faint patches of cement; it looked like someone had covered up the damage before it could be seen. So he trusted the rippled stone surface with his full weight and double-checked the contents of his back pack. "Yep, all set."

He looked up. "You folks be real careful, okay? If Pitt's got more of those security robots guarding the switchboard you might be in for some trouble."

Officer da Cunha did not actually roll her eyes. Nola and Rusty waved. "You, too, Dash. Watch out!" Nola called. Then the rocket's upward-facing jets sputtered out and its inertrium hull began to rise. A burst of thrust shot it out past the lip of the excavation until Dash couldn't see them anymore.

He tried to remember the layout of that gigantic room down below. Pacing off the distance, he found himself about fifteen feet from one side of the excavation. There he pulled his pistol from the pack and adjusted its beam until the rock glowed and began to smoke in a circle at his feet. The slim line grew red; it started to crackle; and a two-foot circle of stone dropped out of sight. He heard it strike something almost immediately. Dash listened, but he didn't hear anyone complain.

So he fastened his rope to the excavation's wall with a triangle of pitons and tied off there. It seemed pretty solid. Dash grasped the rope lightly and backed up until he could abseil down the hole.

He came to a floor much sooner than he'd expected. It looked like he'd broken into a vent of some kind, part of a whole network of air vents that must supply the construction site. It was *almost* tall enough that he didn't have to stoop. Dash turned in the direction of the Projectile and stepped over the stone circle, which still lay where it had fallen. He decided that his gun might as well stay out.

SATURDAY, 6:40 PM

Viewed one way, this was a perfect adventure for the world's smallest giant robot. It had subdued two captives and it had plenty to do, what with watching them, and threatening them, and making sure that there were no attempts at escape. It was a *good* day. Viewed one way.

But on the other hand there didn't seem to be any end to this constant surveillance in the land of the giants. Shouldn't subdued captives be . . . well, detained, at the end of the day? Deposited someplace? And although it could not be conscious of this—would not have *been* conscious of it, even if its brain had not been damaged—the simple existence of this huge world was a constant irritant.

That's because the world's smallest giant robot *was* a giant robot, through and through. Giant robots are *giant*. Their whole purpose, which is to smash and stomp and subdue things, assumes that they are very much larger than the stomped, the smashed, and the subdued. But it had been about eighteen hours since the world's smallest giant robot had been able to tower over anything.

Giant robots *loom*. They *dwarf*. They intimidate through their sheer vastness and the ponderous, unstoppable terror of their giganticism.

This was the whole *nature* of giant robots, as opposed to their purpose (the stomping, the smashing, and the subduing).

The rats had been nice while they'd lasted. Mind you, they were still too tall for the looming, but at least they hadn't cast their terrifying shadows over the world's smallest giant robot, unlike the bobbing head of the human-shaped giant on whose shoulder it rode. Every time they passed a flickering lamp in the tunnels, the shadow of that giant's head cast darkness over everything. It wasn't natural.

Giant robots are not given to reflection. So it was on a completely subconscious level that the world's smallest giant robot was experiencing fear. It had been frightened before, in a way that was more self-aware, during that strange episode earlier when it became very much smarter for a little while. This was something else. This was a fear that swelled up from someplace deep inside. This was the kind of fear that bends and distorts us without its even mentioning to us that it's there.

So like any other creature that longs to smash, but is afraid, the world's smallest giant robot was beginning to get . . . mean.

Engineers are unlike giant robots in most particulars, even apart from the obvious question of size (because even very heavy engineers have problems when they try to loom). Engineers enjoy a good smash now and then precisely because, for the rest of the time, engineers *build* things instead of destroying them. For an engineer, smashing is more a way to blow off a little steam on Friday nights. It's not a vocation.

At this moment Abner was steadily building up steam. He didn't have a plan. He was aware that he was powerless, really, since the world's smallest giant robot was watching him very closely. But through an unexpected coincidence Abner was now *en route* to the very center of Howard Pitt's scheme; and now that Abner knew what that scheme was, he was more determined than ever to put a stop to it.

His only ally was the robot called G-94VA, and G-94VA had definitely seen better days. The big robot was the slowest member of their party even though his damaged legs were easily twice as long as Evvie's or Evan's. And even at the best of times Abner knew that getting G-94VA's help against his Master would have been a delicate matter.

But Abner chose to believe that when they reached the Projectile a solution would become apparent.

In fact G-94VA had led them into an offshoot of the Tube Transport system which seemed to be leading them toward their goal: from far ahead Abner could now hear the sounds of heavy machinery at work. They must have nearly reached the site.

Abner eyed G-94VA. "How are you doing, friend?"

The big robot lurched forward with unsteady steps. "I believe that I will require some significant repairs."

"We'll get it all sorted out when we arrive," Abner assured him. "I'm certain we will."

SATURDAY, 6:42 PM

No matter how she squirmed—though Mrs. Broadvine would never have admitted to squirming—most of what she could see was the sweeping chest of one Big Lug or another. There was so little room in the maintenance tunnel that she'd been squeezed between the big robots who were determined to protect her.

So it was her ears alone that told her Mr. King had opened the hatch by some violent means. Undoubtedly he and Mr. Roy were now peering in at the switchboard, or something like it. Then silence . . . until the robot President's voice boomed out: "PLEASE LET MRS. BROADVINE ADVANCE."

She felt her shoes leave the ground. The Big Lugs lifted her gently and passed her along, Lug to Lug, all the way to the open hatchway. What had recently been the hatch itself was far inside the room. It was still smoking.

"Harry, I fully expected that it would be locked," the robot was saying.

Mrs. Broadvine stepped forward and then, before anyone could stop her, she crossed the threshold and paced down the switchboard where a row of robots, each one a duplicate of Iris, was busily taking care of their clients' Info-Slate requests. Mrs. Broadvine walked up the line and let no hint of approval show on her face. She was a professional.

At the end of the line she turned and started back. There were only eight seats at Pitt's switchboard, hardly enough for a full shift, she felt; but at the moment they were doing an admirable job of keeping up with a load of two or three Info-Slates at each seat.

"Rather low demand at the moment," she told the room. "I suppose it's the evacuation."

Mr. King and Mr. Roy had followed her into the switchboard room with their eyes shooting from wall to wall: probably expecting an attack, she thought. But all was quiet in here until the mass of robots and human people started to jostle their own way in.

"Operators first, I think," advised Mr. Roy. "Let's get an idea what's going on in here."

Mr. King had eyes now only for the robots at the switchboard. "No legs, and probably very limited personalities," he said quietly. "Their labor is the only life they know."

He turned to Mr. Roy. "This should be all the proof we need," he said. "It's a matter of record that Pitt is the architect of the new switchboard. Only he can be responsible for this. It's time we notified the authorities."

Then, to the ranks of robots: "I need photographs of everything in this room before it's been disturbed," he said.

Six mechanical persons stepped in with their camera eyes snapping. They worked their way through the room.

"Mrs. Broadvine!" Mr. King called. "When they're done, I suggest that you and your ladies should take control of the switchboard."

Harry Roy leaned out the hatchway and called for his technicians. "We need some adjustable wrenches and some lubricating oil, if anybody has some."

All along the hallway, a hundred and seventy-four robots raised their hands.

SATURDAY, 6:54 PM

The children, accompanied by the world's smallest giant robot, Abner himself, and Robot G-94VA, emerged into what had to be the largest indoor construction site in the history of things bigger than a very big thing.

It was surprisingly quiet in there now. It looked as though a single crew of riveters was finishing work on the last section of the hull while the rest of the crew was quickly detaching Transport Tubes from their many mounting plates on the surface. Along the way Abner could hear a few of those Tubes discharging their cargo. But it looked like the Projectile was nearly ready for launch.

Abner grabbed G-94VA by the arm. "We have to do something!"

G-94VA stepped out into the room, and that motion drew the gaze of all the construction robots nearby. "I require assistance," said the poor wounded robot, and then he fell to the floor.

Dozens of big construction robots moved toward him.

The eyes of the Campbell children narrowed into slits. Evan looked at the tiny robot on his shoulder.

"Make them surrender!" he commanded.

The world's smallest giant robot looked back and forth at the mass of robots, each larger than any giant robot it had ever heard of, and it made two decisions.

First, it looked Evan in the eye and it said:

"NO."

Then it jumped off his shoulder and ran straight at the towering giants who were stomping, more or less, in its direction.

"YOU WACK ALL BE DISTRINKED!"

Its cannon started a rapid, random fire. Its little chest swept across the entire line of the advancing giants and then swept back again, writing a red beam of terror and rage across everything in the room.

Abner watched in stunned admiration.

"NO MORE! I GACK STACK ANY MORG!"

Guns blazing, the tiny titan ran in between the immense feet of its enemies and disappeared beyond them. But Abner could see startled robots leap off to the right and left, and so he knew that it was still going, somewhere out there.

The approaching robots stopped in their tracks to stare at the little smoking lines that had appeared on their chests and limbs. Several of those limbs fell to the floor; a moment later, so did a few robots.

"What . . . was that?" one of them wondered.

Abner turned to look down at the Campbells. They looked back at him. He could see them rearranging their ideas about prisoners and interrogation.

Then they lit off down the wall of the construction site into the darkness.

Well, thought Abner. *That's a load off my mind.*

"I want to talk to your foreman," he told the robots.

Out across the site he could hear the sounds of robots tumbling out of the way of the world's smallest giant robot. Then he saw the slender beam of its disintegrating ray write a line of destruction across one of the scaffolds. There was a weary groan of stressed metal, and the scaffold collapsed.

It looked like the catwalk was going to be next.

SATURDAY, 6:59 PM

It had to be now.

Pitt had no idea what kind of attack had been mounted on the Projectile but he did know that its destruction was imminent. He couldn't credit the ruthlessness of his adversary. Who would actually *kill* all the people inside the Projectile? It would be murder on Pitt's own scale, though murder hadn't been what he had in mind.

He swept up his slide rule and made some adjustments based on this new launch window. It wasn't a very large change, but at these distances . . .

Yes. If he launched immediately, this should do it.

Pitt ran to the wall console and removed its safety cover. He entered the new parameters and started to throw the levers that would position the launcher and release the restraining chains that held the buoyant Projectile in its place.

Oh, he'd deal with his hidden nemesis. That would come soon. But the essential thing was that the plan would go forward.

How many people had he missed? He'd have to assign his security robots to round them all up. He'd figure out what to do with them later.

SATURDAY, 7:02 PM

The robot foreman was designated Robot R-54KG. R-54KG, though his model was unfamiliar to Abner, was clearly a multipurpose construction robot with speech and a personality suited to supervision.

He was a little busy at the moment.

"Find that little creature!" he was yelling. "Get it before it damages the Projectile!"

All over the underground site other robots were doing their best to follow R-54KG's orders. But they were large, sturdy robots whose dexterity, Abner knew, was limited to their digits. They were not making very good progress. A widening wake of confusion and destruction drew its way across the floor of the site.

A claxon sounded. It was so very loud that its blast shook the catwalks and scaffolding, already weakened by the furious onslaught of the world's smallest giant robot. At the first blast Robot R-54KG straightened in horror.

"The launch! The launch is imminent!" the robot shouted. "Everyone to the tunnels!"

And without even a pause for a hello, R-54KG swept Abner up under one arm and his big, weighted feet pounded for one of the exits. Behind them the wounded robots were lifted and hauled away by teams of their co-workers. In a moment, the whole floor of the site was empty.

The last of the Transport Tubes detached from their mounts and swung slack from the walls. Explosive charges released the first of the restraining chains. The Projectile strained upward.

Far above, the roof began to crack.

SATURDAY, 7:04 PM

That siren's sure making a racket, Dash thought while he negotiated another junction in the vent system. He had no idea what the alarm meant except that it couldn't be anything he was going to like.

He was sure that by now he had to be nearing the floor level of the site. It felt like he'd been climbing down forever.

He dropped to the new vent's floor just in time to nearly get trampled by a bunch of robots who seemed to be fleeing the site.

One's head swiveled to point at Dash as the robots ran past him.

"*Plumber?* Plumber! You must run!"

Dash hugged the wall until the mob had disappeared. From the direction of the Projectile he heard a small tapping sound like little metallic footsteps. Which was, as it turned out, what they were.

The world's smallest giant robot came thundering, on its personal scale, down the vent in its pursuit of the other robots. It spared Dash one disdainful look on its way by. Despite their respective heights, Dash had a distinct sense that he was beneath the notice of the world's smallest giant robot.

Dash waited while it stepped, with tiny, fateful steps, in pursuit of its destiny.

A flash of red fire lit up the duct in the direction it had gone.

"Okay," said Dash.

He turned and ran toward the claxon's terrible screech.

SATURDAY, 7:06 PM

"Pardon me," Nola said again; "Excuse me, please. If I could just . . ."

"Coming through!" Maria yelled.

That was exactly what it took to part the crowd of robots, if only just enough that Nola and Maria could squeeze in between them and work their way down the maintenance tunnel for another twelve or fifteen feet. Then Maria had to shout again.

"This is really not what I expected," Nola apologized.

"We're not there yet," Maria said. "I don't think any of these robots look like switchboard operators, do you?"

And they sure didn't. Nola could tell that these robots, unlike Pitt's, were stock models built for construction and office work. She was beginning to question the message they'd got from the ornithopter.

"I'm just not sure . . ." she started, while Maria yelled the way clear for them.

". . . that we're actually at the switchboard site."

Up ahead, near an open hatchway, a man with a clipboard turned around to stare. "You're looking for the switchboard? Who are you?" He turned into the room. "Somebody out here is looking for the switchboard!"

Maria coughed. "Okay, so much for our element of surprise."

She pulled out her ray gun.

All around them the robots turned and stiffened. Nola saw that most of them were carrying big hand tools, and that a few even held long poles with typewriters fastened to their tips. What had been a clear passage to the door now rearranged itself into a tightening wall of defense.

The typewriters dipped toward the two women. Nola grabbed Maria by the arm and lowered the pistol. "No trouble here at all," she said. "Just a little misunderstanding. Excuse me, but could we please . . ."

A blue and white enameled robot looked out the hatchway. Behind him Nola saw Rusty and, to her great surprise, her former supervisor. *"Mrs. Broadvine?"*

Everyone made their introductions and tried to tell their stories, all at once. Nola and Maria stepped through the hatchway. All along Pitt's switchboard, groups of technicians and robots were loosening the bolts that clamped the robotic operators at their stations. As each small operator was lifted free, an accountant would lift her gently and carry her to the far side of the room where the other liberated operators sat motionless. Then one of Mrs. Broadvine's operators would slip onto the flange where the operator had been sitting.

They were running out of human operators, though.

"Nola, I wonder if you . . ."

Nola's first reaction was to do what Mrs. Broadvine wanted, even if Mrs. Broadvine wasn't her supervisor anymore. But she stopped herself.

"I'd be happy to, Mrs. Broadvine, but I'm afraid there's something else going on. Howard Pitt is about to finish some very large project—I mean, it's *big*—and we left Dash there. Dash is . . . he's very capable, as you know, but I think he might need some help."

Mrs. Broadvine's right eyebrow began a familiar descent toward her cheek, and a part of Nola wanted to do anything, anything at all, to keep that eyebrow from dipping any farther. All of the time she'd spent at the switchboard had taught her to keep that eyebrow from going any lower. But she stood her ground.

The eyebrow wavered for a moment. Mrs. Broadvine seemed to be thinking. Then she said, "Yes, Nola, you're perfectly right. Of course you should go help Mr. Kent."

Then she smiled. Several operators in the room exchanged cautious glances.

Mr. King and Harry Roy were very interested in the news of another project of Pitt's. Nola explained that, yes, there was a very large number of Pitt's robots there; that they were laboring on a gigantic egg-shaped thing; and that Pitt himself was likely supervising the work.

"And he's already tried to kill Dash once," she said. "Or more, really, but once there at the site."

So of course everyone wanted to know, all at the same time, who Dash was, where the project was, how Pitt was trying to kill Dash, and probably quite a few other things that Nola couldn't quite comprehend, given the din.

"THAT'S ENOUGH!" yelled Maria in what Nola now thought of as her Officer Voice.

Everyone finally noticed her blue ASAA uniform. "Say, we wanted to report . . ."

"THAT'S ENOUGH!"

There was silence.

"Okay, point one: I can lead you to the site; point two: we'll tell you about Mr. Kent on the way; point three: everything else is irrelevant; and point four: follow me."

She marched out of the room and through the parting mob of robotic and human persons.

Nola went after her. "Well, *I'm* going."

So it was in a hurry that Mr. King marshaled most of his army while Mr. Roy stationed his technicians and accountants at the switchboard under the command of Mrs. Broadvine.

Nola came back through the hatchway. "And, Mrs. Broadvine, when you get a chance . . . there's some kind of kill-on-sight order for Dash and me in the ASAA's Info-Slate system. Could you do something about that, please?"

Harry Roy added, "And report Pitt's crimes to the ASAA while you're at it." Then he was gone, too.

They formed up in a new column outside in the road. Rusty, Maria, and Nola had taken Mrs. Broadvine's place in the lead. "The problem is," Maria said, "we're not all going to fit in my cruiser."

Mr. King made a shrill whistling sound that echoed back through the deserted streets. In a moment Nola could see a fleet of hover sleds coming their way from the direction of the Perisquare.

"Yep," Maria allowed. "That should do it."

So it was in a big *flying* column that the newly reformed Howard Pitt Expeditionary and Containment Force set out for the power station site. Robots stood in formation on the rectangular decks of the hover sleds; Harry Roy and Albert King, with Nola, Rusty, and Harry's man Davies, led them on a hover sled all their own—with Nola trying to explain what had been going on for the past few days—while Maria, alone again in the cockpit of her rocket, soared ahead of them.

Finally, Nola said to herself. *Finally, somebody's listening.*

"So why haven't you told anybody about this before?" asked Harry Roy.

"We didn't have any proof," Nola told him, with great patience, "and then people were shooting at us."

Mr. Roy digested that. "We didn't have any proof, either, until today," he said, casting a sideways glance at Mr. King. "No shooting yet, on our end."

Nola could see the Hogben Canal in the distance. *Hang on, Dash,* she thought. *Just hang on 'til we get there.*

SATURDAY, 7:10 PM

Everyone had fled the construction site. Bathed in the light of a few working lamps, the Projectile had cast off all its scaffolds and all but the last four of its restraining chains. Daylight spilled down from cracks above to light the arc of its hull; the flickering work lights below cast crazy shadows along its massive sides.

Since everyone had gone, Dash—where he stood immobile in the doorway—was the only eyewitness to the Projectile's launch.

A gigantic hinged platform eased up from the floor below. It actually cocked itself, like the hammer of an antique pistol, and paused.

The thin stone of the roof erupted into dust when an array of shaped charges exploded all across its surface. The last four chains released their hold on the Projectile.

Then the immense hammer of the hinged platform struck the Projectile from beneath. It rose—not quickly, but with great force—and, aimed by the hammer's impact, the inertrium throughout the structure of the Projectile pulled it upward into the sky; not straight up, but in the arc that the hammer had followed.

Dash watched the Projectile fly through the sky, toward . . . what?

Pitt's force of robots started to flow out of the tunnels and cubbyholes where they'd taken shelter.

"What have you done?" Dash asked them. "What for Pete's sake have you done?"

18

RETURN OF THE PLUMBER OF PROPHECY

P itt breathed out. He felt relaxed, for the first time in . . . he didn't even *know* how long. It was as though once the great egg of the Projectile had lifted from the Earth a weight had also been lifted from his shoulders.

"Finally," he said aloud. "*Finally* this city will work the way it's meant to work."

He wanted to go out, immediately, to observe the monorail going about its stately business on a timetable that would never, ever, vary; to see the streets empty of their untidy mob of people, constantly bumping into one another, never sure where they were going, but certain that their *going there* was more important than the *going there* of anybody else; where automated barges and hover sleds and airships could pass freely and gracefully, effortless as particles, following their predestined routes.

Where all his life's work could work smoothly and certainly, predictably. Where nothing existed unless it was *necessary*.

Finally, Howard Pitt was *home*.

Oh, he knew that there were stragglers. He'd rushed the evacuation. He would have to detail his security robots to gather those last people up and contain them, someplace, until Pitt could decide how to get rid of them. For a moment he considered putting all of them into Tube Transport Pods, *whooshing* through their endless cycles across the city . . . and then just *forgetting* about them. . . .

But no. That would be messy.

Best to start the round up now, anyway. He reached for his Info-Slate and started to query the whereabouts of the security robots.

But he saw at once that something was wrong.

There was a lot of traffic in the system; much more than he had expected. And most of that traffic was coming *from* his hidden switchboard. Pitt scanned the active queries.

Pitt noted several efforts to contact the ASAA offices, first with an actual countermand of his shoot-on-site orders, and then . . . with information about Pitt *himself*. There were all sorts of exploratory inquiries, efforts to locate other active Info-Slate users. Little chimes must be going off all over the city and—Pitt smiled—on their way out of Earth's atmosphere.

Not much was coming back. But Pitt made note of the locations.

So Pitt's Adversary had taken over the switchboard. To what end? The Adversary must not have understood Pitt's plan after all: the switchboard was irrelevant now.

He tapped on his Info-Slate's controls for a list of his security robots. Almost immediately his Slate chimed softly. He ignored it. He began to give the robots orders to locate and detain any human beings they could find in each of their quadrants, which were . . .

Pitt's Info-Slate burped at him and its screen went dark. A little red lamp on its bezel was blinking on and off. He threw the Info-Slate across the control room.

Well. He'd just have to do this the old-fashioned way, then. He slipped his slide rule back into its holster and then strode out the door.

Dash recognized the robot foreman, R-54KG. The big robot was carrying a slender man under one arm.

"Hey!" called Dash. "Get on over here!"

"Plumber? Plumber!" said R-54KG. "Here you are at last! We waited for you, but in the end we managed to finish almost on time, due to radical design changes. It was . . ."

R-54KG looked around. He looked especially closely at the space behind Dash, which was absolutely empty of any horde of robot helpers.

"Oh. I, ah, I see your reinforcements didn't come with you."

A ripple of disappointment passed along the robots' ranks.

"Well . . . I'm sure you *tried* . . ." said R-54KG.

Metal feet shuffled throughout the site. The construction robots eyed Dash. A couple lifted their hands to make helpless, reassuring gestures. "You shouldn't be downhearted," said R-54KG. "After all, getting that many robots to come and help us, it *had* to be *quite* difficult . . . and no one could blame you, I mean, if you couldn't . . . quite . . ."

He looked up.

The hover sleds had started to arrive.

"It was *so much bigger* than I imagined," Nola was saying. "And it just sailed right up into the sky . . . what was it, anyhow?"

Harry Roy and Albert King were sizing up Pitt's robots. Harry's man Davies was investigating the big platform that had propelled the Projectile into the air. King's robots were lined up in front of the fleet of hover sleds; they were exchanging curious looks with the robots in the construction crew.

"You *did* bring them, Plumber! You really did!"

R-54KG was practically glowing. Well, of course some parts of him *always* glowed; but at the moment his whole face seemed lit up by happiness.

"I'm so sorry that we doubted you. Of course, now, it may be a little, ah, *late.* . . ."

He turned to his crew. They all shook their heads on swiveling necks. Oh, no: the Plumber had come through, no matter the circumstances. The Plumber had proved himself, so far as *they* were concerned.

One very damaged robot dragged itself forward and started to apologize for something Dash didn't quite understand, until he realized *which* robot it was. "Oh, no, my fault completely," Dash babbled. "I'm real sorry about what happened to you, really I am. It was . . . well, I just didn't know. . . ."

Mr. King came to his rescue. "As soon as these matters are settled, friend, we'll see that you're repaired. To like-new condition, I promise. But can someone please explain to us what . . . just . . . happened?"

R-54KG tried to tell him, but before he could get started Abner Perkins pushed forward and screamed, "He's thrown them all into the MOON!"

Into the silence R-54KG said, "Well, in essence, yes."

Pitt's projectile had been aimed not at the sky, but at a particular place in the sky: the place where, in about sixteen hours' time, the Moon was going to be.

"Marius Crater, to be precise," said R-54KG. "It is riddled with tunnels and ancient lava tubes. The humans should be able to find a way to survive there underground, with the help of the supplies we loaded into the Projectile."

"Yeah," Dash said. "I know the place. But there's people there already."

"Really?" R-54KG was astonished. "The Projectile's arrival may be inconvenient for them."

"You know, it's already *inconvenient* for the I-don't-know-how-many-million people that are locked up in that thing," said Harry Roy. "We've got to get them back here."

Dash was frowning.

R-54KG took a step back. "Get them *back*? But we just . . ."

"It can be done," said someone in the crowd. "It's not easy, I don't mind saying, but it can be done."

They all found themselves looking at Abner Perkins.

"Of course, your central problem is all that mass. And inertia. Inertrium cancels the effects of gravity, as anybody knows, but your inertia, now, that's the problem. It'll take quite a punch to turn that thing around before it hits the Moon, and even then you've got to punch in the right direction, if you take my meaning."

Abner looked around. "Because you don't want them just flying out into space, I mean. You want them back here."

"But . . . once they get here . . ." Harry mumbled.

"Once they get here, we need to *catch* them," Abner finished for him. "And to catch them, we need to build a *really big net.*"

He looked at R-54KG and Mr. King. "Does anybody know where I can find a *really big* construction crew?"

While Abner and R-54KG started on the plans Nola could see that Dash was still frowning.

He looked up. Then he saw Maria.

"How many big, interplanetary rockets could you find in a pinch?" he asked. " 'Cause I don't think mine is gonna do it on its lonesome."

Maria wasn't sure. "I mean, they're out there"—she waved up at the city—"but where, exactly? And who's going to pilot them? Just about everyone is . . . gone."

"Yeah. It's a problem."

Abner directed R-54KG to something on his drawing. But he'd overheard, and he said, "We'll need substantial thrust. I can get you the numbers in a few minutes but I'd estimate that we need at least seven large, industrial rockets . . . possibly as many as ten."

"Can we get through to Mrs. Broadvine on your Info-Slate?" Dash asked Nola. "Maybe they can find us some rockets. I just don't know about the folks who can fly 'em."

Nola bent over her Slate.

"I can fly *one*," Maria said.

She tapped on Nola's shoulder. "See if there are any other ASAA officers left in the city. We're trained to fly just about anything."

"The construction site above us will be an ideal foundation," Abner was telling the robot foreman. "We just need to place the mounts for the net in a circle around it. But then there's all that *material . . .*"

SATURDAY, 7:35 PM

While Freda worked her way through the Vehicle Registry, Rhonda was trying to contact whatever officers of the ASAA were still on the ground or in the air. The rockets were winning, so far, at a ratio of about three to one.

"Thank you, Freda," Mrs. Broadvine said. "Naturally we can't be sure that all those rockets are where we think they are."

She made a note in her Slate's sidebar to get Mr. Roy's team on that.

The other operators were fielding requests from the few Info-Slate users left in the city. With every contact the operators appended a sidebar note to meet at the construction site and report to Mr. Roy. Their voice contact chimes rang out over and over again. The empty city, the launch of the projectile, and the evacuation had left everyone's nerves a bit overworked. Plenty of people were looking for answers.

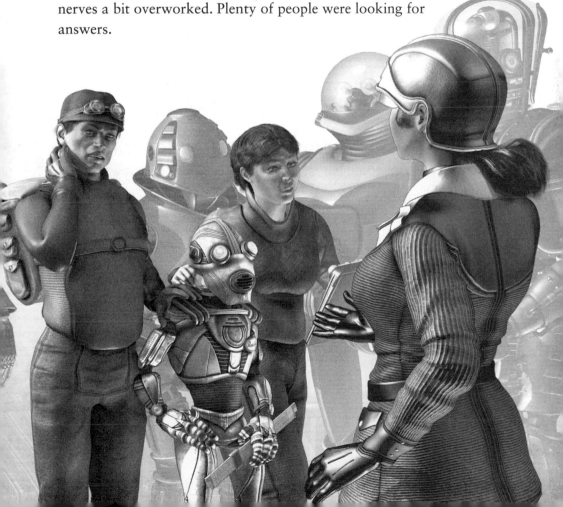

Mrs. Broadvine suppressed a smile out of old habit. Then she decided to turn it loose. Why *not* let her ladies know just how well they were performing?

"Very fine, Vera," she said. "That should soothe the poor thing. Don't forget to tell her to make for the construction site."

Then "Oh, well done, Diane! Three factory workers? Get them down to the site at once!"

Her crack team of switchboard operators kept their faces fixed on their work. But their eyes shifted back and forth in a silent conversation.

Mrs. Broadvine? Is that our *Mrs. Broadvine? Did you* hear *that?*

The incredible Mrs. Broadvine called Harry Roy. When he answered, he was holding his Info-Slate upside-down; she badly wanted to rotate her head around to bring his picture right side up.

"We think we've located nine large, interplanetary rockets," she told him, "but we can't be sure they're all docked where they ought to be. If you could send some of your—"

Mr. Roy's eyebrows shot up, which in a moment she understood meant that they'd gone down.

"I'm down to Davies, here," he said. "You've got all the rest of my people over there."

Mrs. Broadvine looked behind her. Sure enough, all of the Ferriss technicians and accountants were sitting against the back wall, right next to Pitt's robotic operators.

"Oh, I do apologize," she told him. "Would it be all right if I . . ."

"Do what you want with them. Within reason."

She tried to interpret his expression. Then she slowly rotated her own Info-Slate upside-down.

Harry Roy grunted. "There, that's better," he said. "I don't think you've worked all the kinks out of these things yet. You should get this fellow Perkins on it when we're done here. Really seems to know his business."

He signed off.

She called the technicians and accountants over. Each one of them got the listed address of one of the interplanetary rockets.

Interplanetary rockets . . . ? She called Officer da Cunha.

"Why don't we just call for the Space Patrol?" she asked.

Maria, whose face was completely right side up, sighed. "Would have been nice," she agreed. "Nobody's closer than Saturn at the moment. Space pirates."

"Oh, drat them," Mrs. Broadvine cursed. "But anyway we've located four ASAA officers. They're all on their way to meet you."

"That leaves us at least one short."

Maria looked at somebody offscreen. "At *least*. Please try to find us one or two more."

Mrs. Broadvine said she'd do her best.

"Rhonda, my dear?"

The entire line of operators broke discipline and turned, just for an instant. Then their eyes swung back to the switchboard.

"Let's try a little harder to find these officers. Here, I'll take over one of the empty stations. If we *both* work at it I'm sure we'll turn someone up."

She sat down on what wasn't quite a stool, and she went to work.

SATURDAY, 7:44 PM

"What I'm thinking of," Dash said, "is sort of a Plan B. In case we can't raise the rockets and pilots we need. I'll go on ahead in my Actaeon, and it might be I can find someone to help, on what you'd call the other end of things. You send the rest of the rockets out just as soon as you can and we'll meet up ahead of the Projectile to plan the final trajectory."

"Yes . . ." Abner mused. "Now, plotting that trajectory will depend on what force you can assemble out there. It's a very complex mathematical problem, you understand. I have the project logs here, so we know all we need to know about the mass of the loaded Projectile. But still . . ."

Dash felt someone poking his thigh. Rusty pointed at his back pack. "What . . . ?"

He slipped off the back pack and handed it to the little robot, who started to rummage through it.

"My stars, an Enigmascope?" Abner said. "However do you keep it—"

"Yeah, it's a chore."

Rusty pulled out Dash's new slide rule. He waved it in the air.

Abner's brows did unexpected things. "Seriously? This kind of problem is extremely—"

Mr. King raised a hand. Dash was quicker. "If he says he can do it, he can do it," he said. "So that makes it me and Rusty. We'll go get the Actaeon and—"

Someone was kicking his ankle now, over on the other side. "Oh, Miss . . . I mean, Nola, I really don't think you ought to . . ."

He could hear her foot tapping the floor.

"Right, sorry, forgot. So that makes *three* of us then, and . . ."

He looked around.

"What did I do with my helmet, anyway?"

Maria found it in her rocket's cockpit, right where he'd left it.

As the three of them piled onto a hover sled she asked the room, "If he can't keep track of his space helmet on a trip to the Moon . . . are we going to be okay out there?"

Mr. King nodded. "I have it on good authority that we can rely on Dash Kent."

So they scattered again on their hurried business.

SATURDAY, 7:58 PM

Pitt dispatched two of his security robots to haul their prisoners back to the cells. That left him sixteen. They had managed to find quite a few refugees in the city streets. According to Pitt's last intelligence from the Info-Slate system most of the rest were concentrated in two groups: one at the Projectile's launch site, and another in the Experimental Research District.

The Projectile group—likely led by Pitt's Adversary—wasn't a threat at the moment. He'd do best to round up the maniacs in the District first, before they could disperse, and then confront the Adversary. He ordered his robots onto their hover sleds and, with one hand on his slide rule and the other on his hat brim, he urged them forward.

SATURDAY, 8:06 PM

"*I wanna go back,*" Evan wailed.

Evvie dragged him along behind her. She wasn't having any of that.

"What, you want to go see *Doris*? You want to go have your *dinner*? What is *wrong* with you? We have to find our *robot*."

They edged into Pitt's hidden control room. It was a big, hushed space, its walls lined with consoles and panels and wide banks of dials and switches. There was a constant electrical hum. Soft lights beamed down from the room's low ceiling. It felt . . . safe.

The Campbells stood a little taller once they'd gone inside. "What does this do?" Evan asked as he pulled a lever. Down the hall they heard something big go *clunk*.

Evvie eyed the Info-Slate. It was trying to ask her questions about who and where she was, and so on. She typed back *Rufus T. Firefly. Freedonia.*

The screen came alive with more questions, which she ignored. Maybe this thing could find their killer robot. Or something else, anyway. Something *interesting*.

She started to experiment as, over on her left, so did Evan. *Clunk. Clunk. Clunk.*

Smash.

"Whillikers!"

A loud crash echoed from someplace down the tunnels. "This place is falling apart," Harry grumbled. With Pitt's former construction crew now dismantling the scaffolds and catwalks, and Kent's unlikely band off to the Moon, and Harry's own people doing whatever Mrs. Broadvine was telling them to do, Harry felt a little useless.

Davies was squatting next to the robot who had been so badly damaged. The two of them were making some repairs but—as Harry could see—G-94VA was going to be spending a lot of time in that back room at League headquarters.

"So yes—oh, thank you, that's much better. . . ." the robot was saying. "I understand what you've told me about these *indentures*. But this concept of *collective bargaining*? It sounds very useful, but I'm not sure I. . . ."

Davies looked up. "Uh, Boss, no offense, but . . . could you maybe give us a little privacy here?"

Harry stalked off. Oh, yes, by all means get rid of *Management*. He just wished he had something to manage, was all.

A couple of ASAA officers were huddled with Officer da Cunha. The pilots, he guessed. Albert King was conferring with Perkins—good man, Perkins—over the plans for the Great Net. They seemed to be trying to work something out, so Harry ambled in their direction.

It was that question of material again. All up and down the gigantic chamber, robot crews were taking apart all the supports they'd used while the Projectile was under construction. There was a lot of steel, a lot of rope, and a lot of pretty much everything else. But Perkins seemed to think they were going to need more.

"How about the site up overhead?" Harry wondered. "I mean, we're in a construction site that's *under* a construction site, aren't we? What have we got up there?"

Perkins slid a list of materials across their worktable. "It's about like this. Not as much as we have down here . . . but with the advantage that it's already where we want it to be. It's just not enough."

"Get me a list of what you need, then. I'm at loose ends here anyhow, it's making me crazy. I'll go topside and see what I can find nearby."

On his way out Harry could hear G-94VA and Davies still going at it.

"No, see, that's what we have contracts for. When the contract expires you have a chance to renegotiate."

"What is *negotiation,* again?"

It's the dawn of a new day in Retropolis. Harry wondered whether he was going to enjoy it.

He looked up through the site's shattered roof. The sky was deepening toward night. *I guess we need to get most of Retropolis back here, first.*

SATURDAY, 8:42 PM

Their day had just never gotten better. Around six o'clock Delbert Kent and Dennis Kent had been joined in the cramped compartment by two more people, Blanche and Henry, and then just after seven there had been all sorts of confusion when something had actually *smashed into* their, well, whatever they were in, and then they were definitely *moving,* and now Delbert, Dennis, Blanche, and Henry were all floating weightlessly in the middle of the room.

"Sorry, sorry," Henry said. He pulled his knee back into his own general area. "I think I dozed off there."

It was hard for Dennis to imagine how *he* could doze off since he was still wearing nothing but a towel, and the introduction of Blanche into the compartment had raised the stakes for The Towel Problem. This lack of gravity wasn't doing a thing to help.

"It must be space," Blanche observed. "I stepped into a Tube Pod, and ended up here, and now *here* is . . . in space."

Henry snorted. "I am *never* getting into one of those things again."

Dennis heard the sound of someone pounding on the other side of one of the walls. It looked like they weren't alone in . . . there it was again. Where exactly *were* they?

"I'm just glad we got out of the city before that disaster," Blanche said.

That was another thing. The two new arrivals hadn't been kidnapped, as he and Delbert had been; they'd gotten into Transport Tubes during some kind of evacuation. None of it was making any sense.

There went the pounding on the wall again. Dennis floated over and pounded back. "Hey, Delbert? Why don't you try the other wall?"

Before long the muffled noise of pounding seemed to come from every direction, even up and down. "I think there's a lot of us in here," Henry concluded.

"Does anybody know Morse code?"

"Just S.O.S."

This was apparently true of everyone. The muffled thumps of three shorts, three longs, and three shorts started to shake the walls, the ceiling, and the floor.

It sounded like an awful lot of trouble.

SATURDAY, 9:00 PM

This wasn't as easy as he'd expected, Pitt could see.

He'd lost two of his security robots within five minutes of entering the Experimental Research District; another had now fallen on his right. Though "fallen" was perhaps not the right word. It had been enveloped by a whirling helix of light that emitted sparks, an irritating whine, and what looked like trombones but were almost certainly something else. Streamers of gray lead had formed a web of transmutation on the robot's armor, and when enough of its alloys had been converted it suddenly crumpled at the knees and collapsed under its own weight.

This had looked simple. The streets of the District—the already scorched and rubble-strewn streets of the District—were lined with individual buildings, compounds, and laboratories, each one holding a lone scientist who was looking out suspiciously at all the others. So it had looked like a simple house-to-house operation.

But these were not simple houses. The very first one had turned into a battleground. When Pitt's robots had finally pulled Dr. Horatio Fenwick III out of the wreckage and started to lead him down the street, though, Pitt discovered that there was one thing that could draw all these separate anarchists into a unified front.

A common enemy.

Pitt's force fought every inch of the way. Currently, that way was "backward."

He ducked behind the broad back of one of his robots just in time to see a flash of purple light sear the street where he'd been standing. Little puffs of smoke rose from the scarred pavement. There was a noise like sleigh bells.

"Pull together!" he commanded. "Form up around me!"

It looked like an alley was coming up on the left, just a few yards behind them. Once they were in there his robots could form a phalanx in front of him that would, he hoped, be indestructible.

Glass spheres shattered all around them. Out of the shards of each sphere, *something* began to uncoil.

SATURDAY, 9:23 PM

Nola kept looking at the space helmet in her lap. "I don't know. . . ."

"I know it looks . . . kind of what you'd call *threatening*," Dash told her. "But it's the only spare I've got." He was finishing up whatever little jobs you have to do before you launch an Actaeon Model Fourteen. "If you like, we could swap."

"No, it'll be fine," she said. "I'm just glad the other girls won't see me."

The priests of the Spider God went in for ominous headgear, no doubt about that. She pulled the helmet over her head and fastened the straps. The dashboard lights cast a sinister shadow on the Actaeon's hull. She bobbed her head and watched the shadow of the helmet's horns drop low, threatening all the other shadows. "Do I look all evil now?"

He spared her just a glance. "You look fine, Nola." He turned back to the controls. "You look good."

Rusty looked from Nola to Dash and back again. He shrugged.

Nola made her most horrible priest of the Spider God expression at Dash's back. She really didn't expect him to turn around.

"Yikes!"

She rearranged her features and decided that it hadn't happened. "So are we going where I think we're going?"

"I expect we are, Nola. You're pretty quick on the uptake."

Well, that was something, anyway.

Rusty bobbed his head.

And what was it with the robot, anyway? He'd been so . . . well, not quiet; Rusty was always *quiet*; but he'd pretty much stayed out of their way ever since they'd met Aunt Lillian. He just didn't seem to be himself. But then he'd seemed in a bad way back there in the tunnels with Clan Campbell and Mr. Perkins. Maybe something was wrong with him. She took the helmet off again.

"How about you, Rusty? Everything okay?"

Dash got out of his chair and climbed down the ladder to the Actaeon's middle level. She could hear him talking to the ornithopters through the rocket's open hatch.

Rusty shrugged again, this time in a completely different way that meant *I've been better, of course (haven't we all had better days?) and the fact is that something's on my mind, but taken all together? Not too bad. Thanks for asking.*

Nola smiled. *I wonder how he does that?*

Dash came back up the ladder. "They're all set down there," he said, and he settled back in his chair. He picked up the radio handset.

"Officer? You there?"

After a moment Nola heard Officer da Cunha on the speaker. "Maria here. Looks like we've got four pilots, so far, and several of the rockets are checking out. We may be all set in a couple of hours. Over."

"Six of us. How many does Mr. Perkins say we need now? Uh, over."

"We need at least seven. Eight would be a lot better. We'll be coming up behind you with whatever we've got. Hope to meet you around three o'clock in the morning. Wishing you luck, over."

They signed off. Dash let out a big sigh. Then he went back down the ladder and called, "Let 'er go on ten, boys," and came back up to the cockpit.

Nola leaned over to the porthole. Outside, six ornithopters were hovering over the Actaeon's restraint cables. When their countdown ended they each released a cable and the rocket began to float upward. Nola waved.

Dash pulled a lever to start up a little thrust, but so far the inertrium hull was doing most of the heavy lifting.

"That's it," he said. "We're on our way."

19

THE FIVEFOLD SCINTILLATION OF SIRIUS

<hr>

SATURDAY, 11:22 PM

His cellmates had been of very little use to Edward until it turned out that Nityananda had a screwdriver in his carryall. Once Edward had the screwdriver he was able to unfasten the hood over the air vent that no one (apart from Edward J. Bellin) had believed was there.

"There are always air vents," he told them. "And the air vents are invariably just large enough for the protagonist."

The others eyed the vent.

"You'd need a pretty *small* protagonist," said Nityananda.

But Edward disagreed. "Oh, a clever designer will always use visual cues to make an air vent seem smaller than it is. The main problem is the shoulders, and possibly the hips."

And, in fact, after hunching his shoulders and squirming Edward and the carryall did get as far as Edward's hips before they needed assistance. "Just a bit of a shove," he called. "I can take it from there."

They shoved; Edward squirmed; and he arrived, eventually, at the air vent for the hallway outside. Here he found no screw heads, just the pointed ends of the vent screws. One after another he got a grip on them with Nityananda's pliers and kept turning until each screw fell out of the vent, on the other side; then he pulled out his notebook and pen and made another note before he floated back along the wall, and opened the cell door from the outside.

Screwheads likely to be on wrong side, he had written. That was a detail that had never occurred to him before.

His three cellmates decided that they were his friends. They apologized for their doubts and Edward accepted their apologies with good grace, as though he did this sort of thing all the time.

They were in a bare white hallway that was lined with doors exactly like the door of their own cell. Edward and Nityananda floated down the hall in one direction, while his other friends Naomi and Oliver went the other way. All up and down the hall, doors opened, and prisoners emerged. And then there were stairs, and after the stairs there were more hallways. And then there were *more* stairs.

The curious thing about this structure was that there were no rooms larger than the cells; even after sixty floors of hallways—and more, no doubt, beyond—there was nothing *but* hallways and cells and since there was no place to gather, the population of their prison was spread out across several floors of narrow halls.

Edward J. Bellin introduced himself to each cell's occupants while he set them free. To be more accurate, he introduced himself as Edward J. Bellin, author of *The Fivefold Scintillation of Sirius,* and other stories. Because opportunities like this, in Edward's experience, were a rare gift to a writer.

SUNDAY, 12:14 AM

Nola's first trip to the Moon had been a very fast one: almost *too* fast for the Actaeon's old engines. She'd managed to catch a few short naps during the trip but, because Dash kept having to climb below and bang on things with a wrench, her sleep had been pretty fitful.

"Not a problem," he'd say on his way back up the ladder. "Just routine maintenance."

He'd taken Rusty with him for some of the longer and louder bits of routine maintenance, and at that point Nola found herself sitting in the pilot's seat, dearly hoping that nothing new would go wrong before they came back up the ladder.

But they'd arrived at last.

She looked through the slightly malevolent faceplate of her space helmet and took in the view. The Moon, sadly, wasn't much to look at.

It was very gray.

Gray plains stretched out to the horizon, which must have been the rim of Marius Crater; scattered gray stones studded the thick coating of gray dust that lay on the ground. Here and there, outcroppings of gray rocks stood out against the gray surface, casting dark gray shadows over the crater's pale gray floor.

The only spots of color were the travelers, Nola among them, who now stood at the foot of the Actaeon's ladder. The entrance to the Temple of the Spider God was directly ahead.

Dash's voice came over her helmet radio. "I never set down within sight of the Temple," he said, "and I use a different spot, every time. So they probably know already that something's going on."

Rusty, the only one of them who didn't need a space helmet, was looking all around him with what seemed like a lot of excitement. *Maybe he sees in black and white,* Nola thought. *Maybe it all looks magical to Rusty.*

The door in the low mound of the Temple's entrance swung open. In eerie silence, one of the Spider God's priests stuck out his helmeted head. He looked carefully to the left and right, then at the Actaeon rocket that was moored in plain sight. One of his hands wandered toward the ray gun on his hip. It looked to Nola as though the priest just didn't know what to do, with Dash standing there and smiling instead of assaulting the Temple.

Finally, the priest shook his head and waved them in.

The outer door closed behind them. Nola saw a faint mist rise from vents near the floor. A moment later she was able to *hear* the hiss as the atmosphere filled the little chamber. She kept an eye on the priest, but he was watching Dash, and Dash alone. The priest was tapping the end of his spear on the airlock floor.

At last the airlock's inner door slid open and they stepped into an anteroom. Everyone removed their helmets. The Spider priest's boots rang on the steel grating of the floor; Nola watched him walk over to a control panel mounted on the wall. His eyes were still on Dash.

When he pulled a lever, he seemed to be expecting something. Dash smiled. "Opposite polarity, right? Nice. But you know I never use the same trick twice on you fellas."

"So what trick do you have in mind? We haven't been expecting you, Dash Kent."

"No cats today?" Dash asked. "That's just as well."

He turned to Nola. "Miss Gardner, this is Thorgeir, one of the Spider God's priests. Thorgeir, this is Miss Gardner, and Rusty."

Nola dipped her chin politely.

"We're here because you and me, we sort of have the same problem."

Then he told Mr. Thorgeir what that problem was.

Before he got very far at all—hardly past the fact that a huge Projectile was heading for Marius Crater—Mr. Thorgeir led them to a meeting room deeper in the Temple and called for a meeting of the priests. So Dash didn't have to repeat too much.

The priests all seemed very suspicious. Nola knew that this was natural; Dash was an enemy of long standing. As they learned more they didn't seem to get any *less* suspicious. They did seem to be getting pretty alarmed, though.

"Why don't we just deflect the thing off into space?" asked Mr. Gunnar. "It's no business of ours where it goes."

"Well, sir, in addition to the problem of the *millions of people inside*, I figure it would take almost the same amount of force to do that as it will to send the Projectile back where it came from. We've already got almost all the rockets we need. I'm just asking you to help us out. I know you've got an interplanetary rocket here someplace. Otherwise you'd never have started stealing the cats."

The priests murmured in anger.

". . . or, okay, whatever you want to call it. Liberating. Helping yourself to. Picking up. Absconding with. It doesn't matter, not today. What matters is all those people on a collision course with your Temple."

Mr. Thorgeir nudged Mr. Bodhvar-Bjorn. "They're no friends of ours, Brother."

Nola could see that this was the consensus. *Dash, think of something quick, please.*

SUNDAY, 12:19 AM

Stark floodlights lit the big cylindrical hole of the construction site. With its floor now gone, the walls of the excavation fell down into darkness at a depth, Harry knew, of more than a thousand feet. Plenty of room for the Great Net to absorb all the momentum of the Projectile when it landed, if that was even the word for what it was going to do.

Davies and G-94VA—now somewhat mended, and eager to join the project—had finished disassembling one side of the ultrasonic drill that still loomed over the excavation. Harry called the other robots over to carry the materials to the spot where Abner Perkins and his team were finishing the first support gantry for the Net.

"Once we've got this lot," Harry told Davies, "we'll need to head across the way and take apart some of that bridge."

G-94VA looked over at Davies. "Would that be before or after our fifteen minute break?"

The man patted the robot on the shoulder with a look at his boss. "Extraordinary circumstances," he explained. "We'll get comp time tomorrow."

Harry heard a distant roar, which multiplied when five separate plumes of smoke appeared over the empty city and rose to the heavens. That would be the ASAA officers, he knew. He looked at his timepiece and scowled. They were running late.

SUNDAY, 12:21 AM

The Ogmatronic 1400 was a brute of a rocket ship. Its engines roared between their bulkheads far below Maria's seat: there was no time now for the normal gentle ascent of an inertrium vessel. They really needed to make up some time.

She hadn't heard a thing from Dash Kent since the Actaeon's approach to the Moon. And everything was running late. Just everything. She surely hoped that this was all going to work.

Ogmatronics weren't made for comfort or for much of a crew. She had sixteen construction robots stowed in the cargo hold because there just wasn't any cabin space for them. They'd have to go outside the ship at the *rendezvous,* of course. The robots had an advantage over human workers in that they didn't need an atmosphere to get the job done.

So they had the workers they'd need when they reached the *rendezvous.* Now if they only had the rockets!

The radio buzzed. All her fellow officers were checking in and on course. They'd launched a bit late, she knew, but they could still overtake the Projectile somewhere near the halfway point of its flight. If Kent was able to raise his reinforcements and get there at the *same* time. . . .

On her way out of the atmosphere, Maria called Abner Perkins again. She wished the man could work out a way to do this with just the six rockets they had.

His voice sputtered out and she lost the signal. It never occurred to Maria that somebody *else* might have radio trouble at the most convenient times.

The group adjourned so the priests could discuss the matter privately. Mr. Thorgeir stayed. His dark, forbidding gaze rested on the three across the table.

After a few uncomfortable minutes, Nola asked if she could see more of the Temple. "You unbelievers—" the priest started, but he was interrupted by Dash.

"Oh, come on, Thorgeir. You know I've seen most of it already. I just stay out of the sanctuary out of, you know, respect. But there's no harm in showing Miss Gardner around some."

So Nola followed the reluctant priest while Dash and Rusty trailed behind.

Dash was doing most of the showing, though. "This here is where they used to have a heat ray, really clever, that traveled around the whole hallway, widthwise, you understand, in this little groove. I had a heck of a time with that one, didn't I, Thorgeir?"

The priest was almost smiling. "It has been reconfigured into a surprising new form," he said. "But over there, Miss Gardner, is where I once captured your friend in an expanding cylinder of molten regolith. Very successful."

"I don't know if I'd call that success," Dash added, earning a scowl from Thorgeir.

They kept showing her the sites of all the Temple's most interesting pitfalls. But Nola was looking at the drapes; especially at their surprisingly ragged hems that nearly swept the floor.

Through an open doorway she spotted a stone-floored room that was piled high with pillows. She stepped in and moved one of them from its place beside the wall. She nodded to herself at the sight of what lay underneath.

Dash and Mr. Thorgeir came in, reminiscing about disintegrators they had known. "I wonder, Mr. Thorgeir, could I see your kitchens?"

Both of the men seemed surprised, but Rusty was looking at the pillow. His golden eyes lifted up to Nola's, and one of them went dark and then brightened again.

I do believe he just winked at me.

The kitchens, as Mr. Thorgeir explained, were completely empty of interesting pressure plates and motion sensors. "We, ah, we should do more work in this area," he apologized.

Nola started going through the shelves and cupboards. Yes, just as she'd suspected: the sacks of flour and grain, the boxes of pasta, and the barrels of something called fermented fish were all contaminated. Something very small but tenacious had chewed through all the containers of food; and trails of little dark pellets, like the ones she'd found under the pillows, led to cracks in the woodwork.

"Mr. Thorgeir," she said. "I'd like to have a word alone."

Dash and Rusty wandered out, but they promised to stay in sight of the kitchen door. It was an honor system.

Nola started to tap her foot. The priest of the Spider God hadn't yet learned what that meant.

"Okay, Mr. Thorgeir, it's just you and me here now. No more of this talk about flaming jets coming out of the floors. That doesn't cut any ice with me, mister."

Mr. Thorgeir's face went deep red; his eyebrows descended over the overhanging precipice of his brows.

"No, and none of that, either. You don't fool me for a minute. I've got three brothers."

The fit passed.

"What if I told you I could find you all the cats you need? That if we can just save those poor people out there, *they* can help you get all the cats you need, until you're breeding your own litters up here and you don't need to steal your cats from *anybody*?"

The priest began to bluster. "We are the priests of the Spider God! We can *take* what we want at any time! We—"

"Save it, Jarvis," Nola said. She had no patience at all with this kind of malarkey. "First off, *nobody* is so tough that he doesn't need a little help now and then. Nobody. I don't care what kind of scary helmets you're wearing. All you need to do is *ask*. And second, haven't you ever heard of an *animal shelter?*"

Dash seemed a little confused about how she'd done it. She'd let him stew for a while, Nola decided. *You look just fine, pretty quick on the uptake,* indeed.

Because once Mr. Thorgeir reconvened the priests of the Spider God in a private session they almost immediately agreed to send their rocket with the Actaeon in its flight to meet the Projectile. The priests all thanked Nola. Then everybody piled out to board their vehicles and inside a half an hour they were on their way.

As they pulled away from the Moon, Nola finally told him.

"But they're the *priests of the Spider God,* Nola! They've got death rays and, and, and great big blocks of stone that smash you when you go into their tunnels! They've got huge, spiked . . . Why would they have any trouble with *mice?*"

"They probably came up in a food shipment. It's always those little guys that cause all the trouble," she said. "The ones that you don't even know are there."

SUNDAY, 1:32 AM

A hush had settled over Pitt's control room. Evan was snoring just a bit, in little wheezes, while Evvie tossed restlessly on the cold, hard floor.

"Gnackshter," she mumbled. "Gack Destroy Surrencker. Gack."

She rolled over into another position that wasn't going to work, either.

"Surrendnik. Disintigritch. BOOM."

She sighed, and then she seemed to relax. Evvie was in a happy place.

SUNDAY, 1:54 AM

It wasn't the best of spots to fortify. Pitt gripped his slide rule. He could have done so much better! But it was the strongest point they'd found in the alley.

His twelve surviving robots formed immovable walls at the front and back. They were dangerously exposed from above, though, and all Pitt could do about that was to assign a couple of robots as guards. Their eye lamps drew arcs of surveillance all the way up to the roofs on either side of the alley.

For the moment the scientists in the street were quiet. Pitt decided that the best thing he could do for now was to rest. Maybe in the morning, when his enemies grew sleepy and careless, he could break out and subdue or . . . or escape them.

It was humiliating. But Pitt could see that he would need a much larger force to properly contain the Experimental Research District. He'd have to go back to the construction site.

With a sudden start he remembered the Adversary who was now, Pitt had to assume, taking over what was left of Pitt's forces and establishing himself in Pitt's old headquarters. Who was doing this? To what end?

He thought about the now quiet and orderly world beyond the District's boundaries. Once he got back out there—into his ideal world—he should probably just bomb this ridiculous neighborhood out of existence. It might be the only way to preserve the perfection he had built.

This place was a nightmare. Yes, he'd just destroy it once the morning came.

The sound of crackling energy beams tore through the street. With any luck they'd turn on one another before dawn.

SUNDAY, 2:14 AM

They'd been making good headway on the Projectile's trail. Not good enough to make up the lost time, but better than Maria had hoped. Now she was simply waiting for something to go wrong.

It was Stella Moya who broke the news.

"I've lost my thrust," Stella's voice told her over the radio. "I'm still on course . . . but I can't decelerate."

Stella's rocket was now a bullet that was shooting out of the target range. They'd been aiming to intercept the Projectile at an angle, and that meant Stella was going to shoot past the Moon. Maria felt as though her heart had dropped into her stomach.

"You're all right, though? Your air and heat are okay?"

"Yeah, I'm fine here. I already called the Patrol. They'll have someone out there to pick me up in about a week, if you can't get to me in time. These old rockets, they just aren't . . . Oh, Maria. I'm so sorry."

Maria stared out of her viewport. One of those lights up ahead might be a reflection off the Projectile. Millions of people.

She remembered that Stella was waiting. "Don't worry about us," she said. "We're due to reach that thing pretty soon and we're just going to proceed. If Kent can round up that help he's looking for . . ."

She remembered that she was on an open channel.

"Hear this, everybody," she told them all. "We're going to intercept the Projectile and get ourselves welded to it, just like we planned. Then we wait for the cavalry."

The other pilots acknowledged her call. They didn't have much else to say.

The cavalry? she asked herself. *Really?*

"We start decelerating in twelve minutes ten seconds, on my mark. Mark."

Then she called down to the cargo hold. "You guys get all that?" she asked.

"We heard," came a robot's voice over the intercom. "You should not worry. *The Plumber will come.*"

Maria stared at the comm panel. Who the blazes was the Plumber?

At 3:24 in the morning—just a little late—Maria's collection of battered old rockets had drawn ahead of the Projectile and matched its speed. With cautious bursts of their thrusters they were able to pull right up alongside. The thing was big. Maria tried to imagine it sitting next to the main monorail terminal in Retropolis, and she was pretty sure you could fold the terminal over a couple of times and stuff it in there. *Big.*

Her cargo hold disgorged the crews of robots and their equipment. They scattered across the Projectile's hull and made for their attachment points. Three spots were empty, of course. She had a few minutes before the robots would need her to realign herself, so she called Officer Moya. "We're here," she told Stella. "As I guess you can tell."

There was a slight delay before Stella's response came back. She'd plowed on ahead the whole time Maria's group had been decelerating. "Yeah, I can hear you," Maria heard at last. "Just stick to the plan."

"What are you doing out there?"

"Oh, you know me. I'm just in it for the scenery. I'm keeping the channel open. I'll listen in from here."

Maria called back home. "Hey, anybody? We never heard whether there was some way to contact the people inside. Can we let them know we're out here?"

She waited for the reply. When it came, it was: "You could pound on the hull, Abner says. That's about all. Pitt's robots say there aren't any radios in there."

By then the robots were ready. Maria eased in close enough to graze the hull and watched through the viewport while they welded her rocket in place.

SUNDAY, 3:45 AM

Delbert Kent felt somebody poking him in the ribs. "Did you hear that?" Blanche asked him.

He shook his head and tried to listen. The pounding throughout the ship had died out hours before. He had a feeling that the folks in all the other compartments were catching whatever weightless sleep they could, just like him.

"There," Blanche said. "There it is again."

Delbert thought there might have been something. He just wasn't sure.

He'd found that being jailed for no reason and then being shot into space (possibly) wasn't all that interesting when all you ever saw was the inside of a tiny compartment. For all he knew they might still be in Retropolis: maybe imprisoned in one of those labs you hear about in the District. This whole thing might be some kind of crazy experiment. He rolled over, forgetting where he was, and drifted into a wall. Or maybe it was . . . ? Yes. It was the floor.

"I heard it, too," came Dennis's voice.

Dennis had wrapped himself in the cot's single thin blanket with Henry's belt around his waist. That contained The Towel Problem enough that he'd dozed off, too.

"It's like somebody's walking around on the walls."

"Outside?"

They floated together in a many-limbed lump near the middle of the room.

"Is somebody coming to get us?" Blanche wondered. "Or is some-body coming to *get* us?"

They heard another sound, and this one sounded like it was right outside their door. They huddled closer. The door swung open with a creak.

"Don't dawdle!" said the man in the hatchway. "We're almost to . . . well, I think it's the end of this thing. Whatever it is. There seems to be a control room up ahead. And, by the way, my name is

Edward J. Bellin, the author of *Harem of the Seamstress of Outer Space*."

But it wasn't a control room, as they soon learned. The front of the Projectile did have, at last, an assembly room of some kind, but there were no controls there. Just a bank of windows arranged in a grid, and outside the windows was space: a lot of space.

"Look!" said Edward J. Bellin. "Isn't that the Moon?"

SUNDAY, 4:00 AM

The first two of Abner's gantry towers now leaned away from the center of the excavation. The gantries stood on an elliptical track, so that—to some extent, at least—they could be positioned to hang the Net in the path of the returning Projectile. The gantries were gaunt, unlovely things, to Abner's eye. But they could be finished before the Projectile arrived, and that was the most important thing.

Lengths of steel girders and beams were still coming up from the pit below; the great restraining chains wouldn't be needed until the structure was finished. Harry Roy's team, busily cannibalizing the power station's ultrasonic drill, had already begun to scout the neighborhood for even more material. Abner hoped that they'd find enough.

He couldn't complain about the size of the crew. Pitt's robots—assisted by a growing number of robots from the League—were furiously building to the plan; and now they'd been joined by as many as a thousand human survivors of Pitt's evacuation. It would be difficult to oversee the entire force if not for Robot R-54KG, who was an excellent manager. Abner had come to rely on him.

The human persons were mostly working off to the side. A steady stream of robots brought them fabricated links of steel and inertrium for the body of the Net itself. Within limits, Abner felt, the project was going well. They could certainly have used more of the buoyant inertrium but Abner knew very well that there was little of it to be found.

He looked up at the night sky. Somewhere among the glittering stars, he knew, most of the city's free inertrium was flying Moonwards.

And the recovery team? Abner had heard that they'd lost one of their rockets. That left them short by three unless Dash Kent managed to bring *two* more rockets with him. This was the real problem now.

Albert King spoke from Abner's left. Abner had been so absorbed in the view and by his thoughts that he hadn't heard the robot president approach.

"They're late for their *rendezvous*, aren't they, Mr. Perkins?"

Abner agreed. "They still have time. They just don't have enough thrust."

The two of them stared up into the stars.

"Is there nothing we can do?" King finally asked.

"I'm thinking."

SUNDAY, 4:04 AM

Dash let out a whoop on the open channel when he spotted the Projectile up ahead. It was wearing a crown of rockets, each one welded to its vast hull. He counted the rockets, and then his face sagged.

"Four?"

He got Maria on the radio and heard the bad news.

"Is there a problem, Dash Kent?"

That was Thorgeir, calling from the Spider God's rocket.

The Actaeon and Thorgeir's big old Sicarius slowed to meet the others. They had rotated the two incoming vessels so their main thrusters blasted toward the Projectile; they'd pass it before they could get up enough acceleration to match its speed, and then it would be about another half hour before they could get themselves welded to the thing.

But then what? Maria was talking to the engineer on the ground.

At least seven, and better, eight . . .

Dash and Thorgeir increased their thrust. By the time the Projectile flew by them they would already be catching up to it again.

All the way from the Moon Rusty had been scribbling calculations across the Actaeon's bulkheads. Now he started to rub all those numbers out. The loss of one rocket made them all obsolete.

He slumped against a console. His chin dropped and he stared at the deck.

"Rusty, we'll think of something. . . ." Nola said.

But the little robot made an abrupt slash with one of his hands.

"Say, I guess he's thinking it over," Dash whispered.

Rusty's fingers were tapping on the slide rule now. His eye lamps dimmed.

Dash heard Maria calling back; the news from Mr. Perkins wasn't any better. "We could barely have gotten it on course with all seven rockets," she said. "With six . . . it's simply impossible. The Projectile will probably miss the Earth completely."

Thorgeir said, "We'll need to call the Space Patrol. They can catch up to it, can't they?"

But Maria told him that the Space Patrol was so far away that there was no knowing if they could catch the Projectile after it passed the Earth.

"It's that Bonnie Scarlet and her pirates. They're *the worst*."

Thorgeir didn't reply.

Dash exchanged a look with Nola. Rusty had gotten up, and he was scribbling on the wall again. There were six rockets in his calculations; but down below the resulting trajectory Dash could see something new, something with just *one* source of thrust. And before Rusty had even finished Dash told the others, "Hang on. I think we may have something here."

Rusty was pretty useless around radios, so Dash had to interpret.

"Right, the plan was we attach and change the Projectile's trajectory and then we cut loose before it comes down. The thing that Rusty's on to, though, is that if one of us *stays* attached we can act as an attitude thruster for the thing. A lot less power, but we use that power over a longer time."

Maria's voice sounded doubtful. "Well, just in one direction, right? I mean, if you need to nudge the thing *the other way . . .*"

"Rusty says he knows which way we'll be off course."

They waited until Abner's distant transmission reached them. "I'd like it a lot better if there were three of you, pointed in three directions, just in case something unexpected happens."

Dash raised an eyebrow at Rusty. The robot shrugged.

"I guess that's fine, if we have three volunteers. But, you know, we're going to be *attached* to the thing. If it crashes . . . if we bounce off the Net and back into space . . ."

"Well, I'm in," Maria responded at once.

There was a pause.

"Dash Kent is no braver than I," came Thorgeir's voice. "I have taken his measure many times."

Well, Dash had to admit that was true.

"And I look forward to besting him again in the future. So I will go with you."

That was too much, though. Bested? Seriously? Dash reached for the transmit button but Nola grabbed the handset away from him. "Don't you dare!" she hissed. "Everybody needs to win, a little bit, *sometimes*."

He stared at her.

"But, I . . ."

"Just don't you *dare*."

So he didn't.

He didn't even suggest that she get on board one of the other rockets.

It didn't take long for the entire robot welding crew to swarm over the Actaeon and the Sicarius, fasten them to the Projectile, and then climb back on board Maria's vessel. Once they were ready, the six pilots fired their engines simultaneously and kept them on full. They'd maintain the thrust for two hours: that would leave enough time for the welders to free all six rockets and then reattach the three volunteers in their new positions. The robots volunteered to ride with Maria all the way to the ground, but she refused: there wasn't any point in endangering civilians to no purpose.

It was going to be quite a ride. So while Rusty kept watch in the pilot's seat, Dash and Nola settled down to get what rest they could.

20

ATTACK OF THE GIANT ROBOTS

Edward J. Bellin and Nityananda stood alone in front of the viewports. Most of the other prisoners had long ago spread out across the decks in a sleeping mass that overflowed into the hallway at the back and from there, probably, down the stairs and across the decks below. There were just so many people in here.

They'd all been excited when the Moon had disappeared, and then when some engines, somewhere, had turned their space ship so that now the viewports faced the Earth. Their home planet was growing nearer, hour by hour. Someone had sworn she'd seen a rocket take off to starboard; Edward saw no reason to doubt her. There hadn't been any other sign of whoever was guiding them back to Earth.

Nityananda had stayed with Edward through it all. "I do buy *Smashing Planet Tales*," he'd told Edward. "I would be happy to write in and ask them for some of your stories."

Plenty of the others had promised the same thing. If they could just make it back to Earth without something terrible happening to them, Edward knew he could rely on a large number of readers who would pester the magazine editors for the 1,459 stories in Edward's file cabinets.

Things were really looking up.

SUNDAY, 7:20 AM

Dash had simply turned the Actaeon's controls over to Rusty. The little robot was keeping a nearly constant level of thrust, now and then pulling the accelerator a bit higher, or a bit lower, consulting his slide rule all the while.

The Actaeon had been detached from the Projectile and then welded back into its new position where it now stood off the great hull at an angle. Around the big egg's circumference were Maria's Ogmatronic and Thorgeir's Sicarius, each welded on at similar angles. So far, though, Rusty's calculations seemed to be correct. The other pilots hadn't had to turn their engines on even once.

Two of the ASAA pilots were keeping formation with the Projectile. The third had peeled off once it was released, and it was already far away in its pursuit of Officer Moya. The ASAA officers all seemed pleased when they called off the Space Patrol.

Dash had decided that there might be a little competition going on there.

Nola had drifted back into sleep. Dash kept the radio's volume low while he chatted with the ground and with the other pilots.

"Don't mind Perkins," Harry Roy was telling him. "He won't relax until every link of that Net is in place. We've already made a good start on the last gantry. I figure everything will be ready by the time you come down."

"Everything" meant the gantries, the Great Net itself, and the restraint chains that would anchor the Projectile when it settled into the Net. That was the part of the plan that Dash didn't like: because even if . . . even *when* the Projectile's momentum had been absorbed by the Net, there would only be an instant for the ground crew to bind it to the ground with the heavy chains. If they failed to anchor it in that brief moment the inertrium Projectile would rise right up again. Into the sky, that is, and then back into space.

And Dash, and Rusty, and Nola with it.

She stirred a little in her sleep. He leaned down and pulled her blanket back up to her chin.

Well, that's all there is to it, Dash told himself. He settled back into the co-pilot seat. *They just plain* have *to get us moored to the ground.*

Rusty gave the Actaeon a tiny bit more thrust and looked over at Dash. The robot gave him a silent thumb's up.

SUNDAY, 7:32 AM

" 'Morning," Evan mumbled. "What we got to eat?"

It didn't take long for them to figure out that there wasn't any food in the control room.

Evvie yawned. "It's a *construction site*. There'll be *donuts*."

They moved quietly out of the control room and headed down the hall. Evvie kept looking along the floor, through the open vents, and anyplace else that might be hiding a tiny, deadly robot; but it was nowhere to be found.

They were very careful at the doorway to the Projectile site, but surprisingly no one and practically nothing was there. The great gaping pit had been stripped of its scaffolding, its chains, and its catwalks and platforms; a single long stairway led up to the daylight above. The stairway had obviously been put together hastily from spare parts. The two of them frowned up at its quietly creaking length.

"Donuts?"

From far above, they heard the sounds of a large construction crew banging and hammering and bending. "Sounds like they're building *up there* now."

They'd gotten so used to having their own personal killer robot that the thought of climbing up there by themselves was a little daunting. But if there was going to be a breakfast, that's where it was going to be. So they climbed.

SUNDAY, 7:41 AM

It was time.

Pitt had survived the night in his robot fort. Twice there had been an attack from above. Once, spiderlike machines had crept down from the rooftops and were spinning their titanium webs before they were seen: but they were easily melted. Later there had been something with twelve tentacles that burst through a wall overhead and captured one of Pitt's robots before it was wounded so badly that the creature had no choice but to retreat.

Pitt whispered his orders to his surviving guards. He was now really looking forward to making this whole District one *big* smoking crater. But first they had to get free.

The security robots in front of him formed up into a wedge. He was flanked by two of the others while three took up positions in the rear. The thing now, Pitt knew, was *speed*.

The robots on either side of him made a saddle out of their big, steely hands. Pitt climbed up into their grasp. And then they ran.

Pitt's wedge formation came out of the alleyway like an arrow. The sleepy-eyed scientists flew right and left in a bow-wave of discomfort while the rest of the crowd in the street tried to get out of the way. But they were no match for the speed of the robots' pounding feet. It was like a rain of mad science out there. Pitt actually grinned.

Oh, to be sure, the occasional ionization beam swept across them; a blue whirlwind twisted down from a window and touched down behind Pitt. One salvo or another nearly struck them. But Pitt had built his big robots to *sprint*. For the next minute or so there was nothing in the city that could catch up to them; certainly not a crowd of physical wrecks like the denizens of the Experimental Research District.

At the end of that furious minute Pitt called his robots to a halt and looked back. Sure enough, the maniacs had been left in the dust.

But then a mist of dense, dark particles shot out of the crowd and swarmed toward Pitt like so many wasps. They were coming after him!

He ordered his robots onward, toward the gutted site where he'd built the Projectile. They wouldn't be able to sprint like that again until they'd recharged. But they could still, Pitt thought, stay ahead of their pursuers. And then . . . on to the Adversary.

SUNDAY, 8:04 AM

From his perch on top of the final gantry R-54KG directed his crew to the end of its long, long arm where it pointed toward the pit. They were just about to finish attaching the Net. The Sun cast the Net's spider-webbed shadow across the open hole, the elliptical track that circled it, and even the bases of the far gantries. Now *this* had been a project worth building. If he'd had the face for it, R-54KG would have been wearing a big sloppy grin.

And what a workforce!

He'd only understood a little of what the blue and white Myrmidon had tried to explain about these new ideas of *indentures* and *organized labor*. There had been very little time for that. But there was something fundamentally different about this job, and R-54KG knew that the difference had something to do with those ideas; it had even more to do with the way the League robots and his crew and even the human persons had all banded together to complete this one important project on time.

And the project leader? After working under Pitt for all his life, R-54KG felt a great respect for Abner Perkins. The little engineer had often asked for R-54KG's thoughts about the assignment of tasks and the materials they were using . . . and then he had listened to the robot's answers. The first time that happened R-54KG had found himself staring at Abner, certain that he'd misunderstood.

R-54KG was almost sorry to see the last gantry attached to the

Net. He looked up. Sometime soon, he knew, they'd see the Projectile on its return journey; and *that* would be the real test.

"We're ready to position the gantries!" Perkins called up from below. "You should all come down now!"

R-54KG began the long climb. But he halted, partway down, when he saw a wedge of robots approaching on long and powerful legs. They were bearing someone in the middle of their formation. Could it be . . . ?

He flung himself down the cross braces with no regard for his safety.

"The Master!" he cried. "The Master is coming! *And he is not alone!*"

SUNDAY, 8:06 AM

"You told me there'd be *donuts,*" Evan said.

Evvie shushed him.

From their vantage at the top of the stairway they could see many things, most of them unexpected, but it was true that not a single donut was in evidence. There was a crowd running back and forth in what looked liked a purposeful way, most of them around or on the big skeletal gantries that now ringed the pit. They were a mixture of robotic and human persons; each carried about as big a load as their frames could allow because, apparently, everything they were carrying was supposed to be someplace else. Evvie was sure there was a plan behind that, but she had very little interest in other people's plans.

More nearly interesting, in her view, was the knot of robots and frightened humans who were rushing toward the east side of the site.

"Look over there," she told Evan, and he did. Coming alongside the canal was another force of armed robots. Behind them, in the distance, was something like a brilliantly lit cloud of wasps, falling stars, and smoke.

"I think they're gonna *fight*!"

The two of them rushed through the crowd just below elbow level, where adults were at their most vulnerable. They pushed and sidled and ran. Evan watched the crowd carefully. There might still be donuts.

SUNDAY, 8:10 AM

Harry and Davies arrived at the east side of the site right behind Albert King and a group of his League members; they were brandishing their big, heavy tools again. Albert's arm plates flexed nervously, snapping open and closed. The heavy weapons behind his chest plate were also deploying and then receding into his armored shell.

"You all right, Albert?" he asked.

The Myrmidon's head snapped toward him. Harry flinched.

Albert, his whole body a clattering mass of armaments, made a shrill whine.

"I am . . . it is difficult . . ."

He shook suddenly, and all the weapons that bristled from his torso and limbs pulled back. "It can be difficult to remain in control when I am excited," he said.

"Well, do me a favor, Albert, and just keep all that stuff pointed at *them*."

Albert looked back at Pitt's advancing squad. "I think you misunderstand," said Albert. "It is very difficult for me *not to destroy them*."

Harry also looked at the approaching enemy.

"Don't hold back on my account," he said. He picked up a big piece of scrap steel that had fallen to the ground. "Of all of us you're the one fella that can stop 'em in their tracks."

"But Harry," said Albert. "I'm a *pacifist*."

Oh, swell, Harry said to himself. *That's just what we need. A pacifist that can level mountains.*

"That's jake with me. Think what you like, live and let live, and all that. But you seemed pretty ready to crack some heads when we headed into the switchboard. We could use a little of that now, in my opinion."

Albert nodded. "I was very angry at Howard Pitt," he admitted.

"You see who's in the middle of that line of robots?"

Albert stared. "Perhaps . . ."

His weaponry stood to attention. Harry and Davies took a step back.

In the onslaught of Albert's beam and particle weapons, Harry couldn't even see Pitt's force until the dust had settled. Albert had carved an eight-foot-wide chasm right in front of them. Two of the lead robots toppled in, and Harry could hear them bouncing off the chasm walls for a surprising length of time.

The line halted; Pitt issued some orders. His robots picked him up and they all jumped right over the yawning crack, and then they continued their advance.

"It's a start," Harry said to Albert, and then to Davies and the rest: "Get ready, boys! Give 'em whatever you've got."

"*And* ladies," said someone behind him.

"That's right, beg pardon, and ladies. Let 'em have it!"

And that's how Harry found himself leading a charge.

It was at its worst before they closed with Pitt's line. Until then the heat rays and disintegrators of the enemy robots took a fearsome toll. Once Harry's army had crashed into them, it was only a matter of trying not to get smashed, stomped, and bowled over. Which is mostly what happened.

Albert King, rising on the jets in his feet, floated up above the *mêlée* and started to carve off the robots' arms and legs with the concentrated beams of his weapons. Pitt's robots concentrated their fire on him. That left Harry's people free to beat them with great wrenches and broken beams.

Harry could see that Albert was holding back, trying to disarm the enemy robots without destroying them; and that was very difficult because Albert's weapons had been designed for total annihilation. The Myrmidon floated up and down on his jets and did his best to limit the scale of his mayhem, but this kept him from being very effective. At least he was managing to contain Pitt's force.

"Wedge!" yelled Pitt. His remaining robots formed up around him. Harry could see the man staring at the gantries. His eyes fell and met Harry's.

"You can't . . . you can't *possibly*. . . ."

Pitt looked up at the sky, a terrible realization in his eyes. "Robots! Forward!"

Their heavy-footed wedge smashed right through Harry's line and made for the nearest gantry.

"Stop them!" Harry yelled. "They're going after the Net!"

The combined fire of all Pitt's robots blasted out and struck Albert's armored abdomen. His jets flared, but they couldn't prevent him from being thrown right into the excavation. He rebounded from its stony wall and vanished in the darkness. The wedge forced its way forward.

Evan and Evvie were thrilled. They'd climbed up onto the framework of the near gantry, where they had a perfect view of the carnage that raged below. Now the wedge of robots was stamping its way directly toward them.

"Wow!" was Evan's assessment.

But Evvie grabbed him by the arm and started to pull him down. "Idiot! They're coming *right at us!*"

Everyone was so busy that no one noticed the shadow that had fallen on the clouds above. In the upper regions of the atmosphere, the Projectile was soaring down out of the Sun.

SUNDAY, 8:11 AM

"We're in the atmosphere now," Dash told Nola. "Coming down pretty slow, but it won't be much longer."

Rusty now kept the engines on low, their thrust nothing more than a persuasive force that would deflect the Projectile into the Net. They were relying on their momentum to drive them downward against the lift of that mass of inertrium below.

Maria's voice sputtered over the speaker. "Something's going on groundside," she said. "I had Perkins on, and then there was a lot of shouting. And some . . ."

Static took over for a moment.

"It sounded like explosions, folks. I think they may have a problem."

What could have exploded? Dash wondered. He peered through the Actaeon's porthole, but they weren't even near the cloud layer yet. There was nothing to see. "Well, we don't need another problem at the moment."

Was there even a Net left down there? Dash tried to imagine the great egg of the Projectile striking the ground with no Net to ease its momentum. In his mind's eye the big vessel crumpled, spilling its passengers, and then started to rise up against the pull of gravity. Back into space. There were three little bristling rockets welded to its upper hull.

He knew that everyone else was seeing pretty much the same thing.

Rusty's hand was steady on the thrust lever, but his polished head shook slowly from side to side.

Harry, Davies, and what was left of their little army charged after Pitt. The man had taken off his hat; he was waving it at the near gantry and calling out orders to his robots. Those of them who hadn't been disarmed by Albert trained their weapons on the pylons at the gantry's base. Heat beams played across the steel, built so hastily just hours before.

"Gotta stop 'em, Boss," Davies said on his way by. The big technician threw himself onto the back of Pitt's rearguard.

"Swarm 'em!" Harry called, and he jumped onto the back of another. The whole crowd, converging on Pitt's position, tried to drag the big robots down. But with their feet planted wide it was impossible to shake them.

One big arm swept Harry off his robot's back. It was like the thing was swatting a fly. He landed on the ground, picked himself up, and found that he was looking the wrong way.

He was just ten feet away from the front ranks of the entire Experimental Research District. It was not a pleasant sight.

The scientists of the District had never made an excursion out into the city before. That's not how it was done.

A scientist in Retropolis would be identified at an early age through subtle cues that educators had learned to read. Little Sandra, or little Erasmus, would not be the kind of child who would hold a magnifying glass over an anthill, just to see what would happen. No, little Sandra or Erasmus would have built a solar power plant in the backyard with a clever system of motorized lenses that would track the motion of individual ants, frying them one by one, until the beam finally rested on the anthill and directed a homemade ionic destabilizer to turn the little arthropod city into a dusty kind of mist. Next stop? The dog house.

Once a highly trained teacher had identified these signs, the budding scientists would be put on a fast track through specialized classes, graduate studies, and strictly limited field trials until, at last, they were handed their diplomas at the edge of the Experimental Research District and told never to return.

With only one undocumented exception, this made them very happy.

After a few years of exciting work as lab assistants, the survivors would build their *very own* laboratories. From these laboratories the occasionally useful invention would find its way out into the rest of Retropolis. Then, of course, there would be royalties.

This exacting program of education and isolation didn't leave many opportunities for relationships outside what the scientists called "the field." And relationships within "the field" were about as collegial as a pair of duellists who've accidentally met before sunrise.

So an individual scientist was unlikely, by statute, to make an excursion outside the district; it was unheard of for a group of them to go anywhere except, rapidly and briefly, upward.

Pursuing Howard Pitt was almost the most fun that any of them had ever had. The city seemed to have changed; it was much quieter than they remembered, and perhaps more sparsely populated. But they hardly noticed this. They'd brought their most portable and destructive projects with them.

Harry wasn't thinking about any of these things except for the last of them. What Harry saw was a crowd of several thousand madpersons, mostly male, most of them thinly haired, and all of them waving very frightening objects above their heads and shouting things like "Wheee!"

They had things that looked like guns, and they had things that looked like atomic-powered vacuum cleaners; they had beakers full of viscous fluids, and they had little spherical dynamos that spat out sparks in unexpected colors; several had their own, unique Giant Robots on leashes; others held the leads and jesses of winged things that Harry wished he had never seen. They were throwing cubes whose faces were, well, faces; they were snapping long whips of energy, and they were towing balloons filled with roiling gasses.

And they were all coming Harry's way. "Look out!" he yelled. "It's—just *look out!*"

He dove off to the side. Davies and the rest of them took one look at what was coming and all of them also jumped for safety, or something like it. That left Pitt's force of security robots directly in the scientists' path.

Pitt's force was steadily burning away the gantry's supports; its high crane was already beginning to tip, pulling the edge of the Net with it in a great dip toward the ground. Pitt had just enough time to order his robots to turn around before they were overwhelmed by the tide.

The tide of *Science.*

Evan and Evvie made it to the base of the gantry only to be boxed in there by Pitt and his dented, scorched robots. They clung to the base of the pylon while, far up above them, it was blasted into scrap. Evvie was pretty certain that they wouldn't want to stay there long; Evan concurred. But there wasn't any place for them to go that wasn't already occupied by a big, fearsome robot.

Since they were facing outward, however, they had an excellent view of the crashing wave of eccentricity that now broke over Howard Pitt.

Most of Pitt's robots went down immediately, victims of more bizarre contraptions than could be counted. There was melting; there was instant freezing; there was sudden sublimation; there was molecular confusion and disarray of every type. Several well-established physical

laws were challenged, often successfully. The base of the gantry was hidden in a dense, churning cloud.

Above their heads the gantry groaned, bent, and finally sagged toward the ground. The Great Net sagged with it.

SUNDAY, 8:16 AM

They were now moving through the clouds over Retropolis; or at least that's what Rusty told Dash, and he trusted Rusty's judgment.

The Projectile's passage was majestic; it was slow; but Dash had a pretty good idea what would happen when this much mass struck the ground, even at this speed. And then, of course, there would be the immediate rebound if the ground crew wasn't able to get the restraint chains in place.

"I'm open to ideas," he said over the radio. "Maria, Thorgeir? We're welded right onto the thing. Where it goes, we go, unless we figure out a way to get off."

Thorgeir answered him. "Escape vehicles are for the impure in spirit," he asserted.

Whether or not that was true, Dash knew that none of their rockets carried them anyway.

"I guess there's air out there . . ." Dash gave Rusty a look. "What are our chances if we just climb out onto the hull? Could we maybe jump off when she hits?"

Rusty's eyes seemed wider than usual. He shook his head.

"Right, okay then, that's out."

He and Nola exchanged a look.

Maria's voice sounded from the speaker. "I'm still trying to reach Perkins," she said.

SUNDAY, 8:19 AM

Edward and Nityananda were pressed against the Projectile's windows by the force of the huge crowd behind them. Every terrified eye was on the approaching planet. People were calling updates back to those who were still in the halls, and the calls were relayed back down the stairs and throughout the Projectile, from hallway to stairway to hallway, all of them filled with frightened people.

Nityananda pointed around the site of the Great Net. "They must have meant to catch us in that thing, but look! It's collapsed on one side. We'll . . ."

Behind him, several people wailed or groaned, according to their needs.

Edward looked from one side of the Net to the other. They hadn't a hope. The ground was swelling up toward them, and if they weren't smashed on impact they were probably going to bounce back out into space. He grabbed Nityananda by the arm. "We need to get everyone away from the windows," he said.

They recruited the other prisoners near them and began to move everyone back toward the hall.

Abner couldn't take his eyes off the gantry. It had taken hours and all his ingenuity to put it up: but there it was, broken, and all their hopes with it. The Great Net wasn't going to catch anything now, spread tight as it was. It was like a Great Trampoline.

Far above, the Projectile came out of the clouds. It was going to strike—and strike *hard,* as Abner instinctively calculated—and then whatever was left of it would fly back out into space.

Millions of people.

He could hear the radio buzzing at him but he really didn't notice. That image of the shattered Projectile shaking out its millions of passengers and then rising upward again . . . it was too terrible.

The rout at the gantry's base was still going on in full force. The entire ground crew had stopped whatever they were doing, eyes going to the battle, to the gantry, and then back again.

A sudden roar sounded from the pit.

Abner saw the battered body of Albert King rise up on its foot jets. One arm was twisted back behind him. A large dent had cocked his waist at a strange angle, and from a jagged rent there Abner could see coolant leaking into the air.

The blue and white Myrmidon looked up at the Projectile—right on course—and down at the Net where it stretched out taut below. His head sank. His jets faltered.

Then Albert King raised his one good arm and his voice boomed out: "ROBOTS! TO THE GANTRY!"

A surge of motion rippled across the site.

"PYRAMID!"

SUNDAY, 8:21 AM

He looked so beaten that Nola found herself feeling sorry for him, as though somehow Dash's troubles were bigger than the exact same trouble that was facing all of them.

"I'm just real sorry you had to come along," he said. "There wasn't any need for you to go down with us. I should've said something."

He'd forgotten about the open channel.

"Do not demean Miss Gardner's bravery," said Mr. Thorgeir's voice. "Like the rest of us, she is a warrior. Death is no high price to pay for the sake of honor."

That was almost exactly what she would have said, she decided.

But what she actually said was, "I don't mind, really I don't."

They could see the site down below them. It was obvious that something was wrong: one gantry was laid out on the ground, its base wreathed in smoke, and the Net . . . the Net . . .

"Perkins says we may be okay."

It was Maria on the radio.

"Problem is, they're getting the Net back in place but nobody's left to haul the restraining chains. We're not going to smash . . . but we're probably coming right back up."

SUNDAY, 8:21 AM

Abner was keeping up a constant commentary over the radio, assuring Officer da Cunha that the Net would be ready for them. His eyes, though, were on his new gantry.

The pyramid of robots was two hundred strong at its base. From there it rose, tier by tier, growing narrower and narrower until it reached Mr. King and Robot R-54KG. They only had three good arms between them. But all three hands gripped their corner of the Net.

The Net now hung slack between its gantries. Abner thought of the terrific force that it had to absorb and he bit his lip, watching the robots at the top of the pyramid. They would only need to hold it for a moment, he knew. But it *had* to be held.

"You're coming in now," he told Maria. "I can't see your rockets on top. But the Projectile's shadow is covering the whole site."

It came down steadily, drifting like a balloon despite its mass. The Net hung into the Pit, waiting.

The Projectile hit the Net almost daintily. The stationary gantries bent inward; the pyramid of robots began to give.

The Net deepened into the huge pit below. The Projectile had slowed, he could see that it had slowed . . . Albert King and R-54KG bent, where they could bend, and hung on. The pyramid swayed below them. Abner saw three robots tumble toward the ground; then Mr. King's foot jets blazed, and somehow he and R-54KG held on to the Net. The Net sank deep into the pit below.

The Projectile came to rest in the Net and paused for an instant before it began to rise again, lifted by its incredible load of inertrium.

"Now! To the chains!" called Abner, and with everyone else he swarmed toward the great restraining chains.

Teams of human and mechanical persons labored on top of the five remaining gantries. They turned their windlasses, paying out the gigantic lengths of chain, and strained to make them meet at the top of the Projectile's hull. Teams of robots hauled their chains across the top of the Projectile; but even from the ground Abner could see that the monstrous vehicle was going to escape back into the sky before they could capture it.

R-54KG reached the wide, smooth top of the Projectile in the simplest possible way: he threw his arms around Mr. King's chest, drew his legs up out of the jet flames, and didn't let go.

Once Mr. King dropped him on top of the Projectile he ran to join the nearest band of robots, struggling with the weight of a restraining chain. All together they heaved and dragged, took up the slack, and heaved and dragged again. Far across the Projectile R-54KG could see another team who was trying just as desperately to drag another chain to meet theirs.

He felt the Projectile start to stir underfoot, like a great big animal that had just begun to wake up. "Hurry!" he bellowed. "It's going to rise!"

Mr. King flew down to the ground to pick up two more laborers: this time it was one of Harry's men—that big fellow, Davies—and one of the League clerks. With Davies in his good arm, and the clerk clutching his thighs, he fired his foot jets again to return to the top of the Projectile.

As he rose upward he looked down, deep into the pit, to see the

Projectile start its new ascent. It had lost all contact with the Net now. The Net was beginning to sag away from the hull.

Something clicked uncomfortably in Mr. King's side. "Could you shift a little to the left?" he asked Davies. Coolant was spraying out over the big man's arm. It was starting to get hot, someplace inside Mr. King's torso.

"Was that, uh, an alarm?" Davies asked. "In your, uh . . ."

But Albert didn't answer. His eyes were locked on the rockets that he could just now see on top of the gigantic vessel. Something was happening up there.

Abner had given up. He simply wasn't strong enough to help the robots on the ground, where they were paying out the huge restraining chain that rose slowly up the gantry. One of the Big Lugs had lifted him gently by the armpits and set him down where he was out of their way.

He had nothing to do now except to watch as the Net began to go slack and the bottom edge of the Projectile started to rise, with its helpless passengers, over the lip of the pit.

He watched the Projectile lift upward.

And then . . . it stopped.

Somehow, impossibly, it was bobbing in place in the embrace of the Net. "Quickly! *Fasten the chains!*"

The robot pyramid disassembled itself to climb the gantries. High overhead, they swarmed and joined the teams at the restraining chains, and they pulled, and they heaved, and they locked the chains together; and then, in a frenzied matter of minutes, it was done. The chains went taut against the Projectile's lift, and they held it there. Abner heard a cheer start up on the hull of the Projectile, and the cheer spread all down the gantries and across the pit, until every human person, and every robot who had a voice, was yelling in triumph and relief.

But how? Abner wondered. *How did they keep it down?*

Then he remembered that there were *three* rockets, spread equidistantly on the crown of the Projectile's hull: three big industrial rockets, each one now roaring at full thrust. Because Abner had insisted that they put all three of them there.

Abner ran the numbers in his head. Yep, that would be just enough thrust to cancel out the inertrium's lift.

Well, he thought. *I guess that's why that little robot isn't the project engineer.*

He scratched his nose. *Though he was right about the trajectory, wasn't he? If the gantry hadn't failed . . .*

Oh, well. In any case it had turned out to be a good idea, and the main thing was that now they could release the passengers. Robots with cutting torches were already working on the hull.

SUNDAY, 8:42 AM

All the fight had gone out of the bald man in the hat. He was slumped at the gantry's base now, just two of his robots beside him. All around them rose little wisps of smoke from the slots of a grating.

Evvie eyed him with disgust. If *she'd* had all those killer robots it would have been a different story. Why, even with *just one . . .*

The mad scientists seemed to have lost interest in Pitt. They were wandering around with their jaws hanging open, staring up at the Projectile in its chained Net. Some of them seemed to be getting ideas.

Just one of the scientists seemed to care about Pitt at all. This one, dressed in a nightshirt, was dancing in front of the engineer and waving some kind of device in his face. The scientist's eyes looked huge behind the thick lenses of his glasses. Pitt didn't even seem to know the man was there.

"Yes!" chanted the scientist. "You may as well give up, bald man! If you don't surrender to me personally, I will unleash on you my fantastic *miniaturization ray!*"

Evan perked up at "surrender to me." It reminded him of better times. "What's a miseryation ray?" he demanded.

"Be informed, small child! I shall show you!"

The scientist turned a dial on his device and waved it in front of Pitt's two robots. They shrank, quite suddenly, until they were so small that they fell through the grating. Evvie's fingers closed on the empty space where they'd been.

So she kicked the scientist in the left shin with such force that he dropped to the ground, screaming. She snatched the miniaturization gun out of the air.

She pointed it right at Pitt's face.

"That's it, mister, you're *finished*," she said. "Where are the rest of your robots? I want them *all*."

Pitt's eyes strayed over to her. He didn't seem to care.

"I mean it, mister! Hand over your robots *right now* or I'll, I'll, I'll *miseryrate* you where you . . . where you . . . right where you sit, mister!"

"In the *butt?*" Evan marveled.

"I can't *shoot* him in the butt, stupid. He's *sitting* on his butt." Her eyes were still on Pitt.

The engineer waved one hand. "Do what you must," he whispered. "All of this. . . . My world. My perfect world. He's ruined it. He's undone . . . *everything*. He's defeated me. And I *don't even know who he is*."

His pained eyes scanned the crowds, the people on the Projectile, and the pit below.

"He didn't even bother to *tell* me."

Evvie squinted at him. She looked around, just to see if any of the man's robots had turned up after all, but no. They hadn't.

So she turned on the miseryation ray and let him have it. It was with a very small, but very surprised, look that Howard Pitt followed his last two robots through the slots in the grate.

Evan leaned over and peered after him. "We shoulda *caught* him," he advised.

21

THE CYPHER OF THE SECRET LABORATORY

MONDAY, 1:16 PM

There's just no sign of Pitt, though," Harry said. "In all that confusion during the landing . . . it looks like he just got away."

He and Albert stood on the steps outside League headquarters. All around them the citizens of Retropolis went about their business as though nothing strange had happened over the weekend, except that very few people were using the Transport Tubes today.

Albert, so far as you could tell, was pleased. He hadn't had his repairs yet; he was waiting until the workrooms had finished with the very many robots who'd lined up for theirs. So his left arm was still bent awkwardly, and his dented torso still prevented him from bending at the waist. Only his coolant leak had been patched. Still, he seemed at ease.

Pitt's switchboard operators had been moved almost to the front of the line, so that Iris and her sisters had already received their upgrades: legs, enhanced cognition, and speech units. Albert had sent them to meet Mrs. Broadvine at the *old* switchboard offices. Mrs. Broadvine had been named the new head of the entire Info-Slate operation in a backroom conference at which Harry, Abner, and Albert had made a pretty convincing case for her.

Pitt's robots were now full members of the League of Robotic Per-

372

sons. In Pitt's absence his assets had been seized, and what was left of them after the reparations was being divided among his former slaves. They were going to be able to get whatever upgrades they wanted.

"In the end," said Albert, "we don't really need him. We'll use his own holdings to repair the damage he's caused."

His forearm plates twitched. "But it would be *more satisfying* if we could bring him to trial."

Harry agreed.

The human and robotic persons of the city went on, left to right and right to left, often bumping into one another or coming to a full stop when somebody darted out of a doorway. But they all seemed to be getting where they needed to be. It was unplanned, and it wasn't subject to a plan; it was a constant improvisation that spread across the streets and the skyways and the monorails of the city. It wasn't *efficient*. It was just the way life works.

Neither Harry nor Albert understood that this was exactly what their victory was. But they were pretty happy, all the same.

MONDAY, 1:43 PM

"If you'll just follow me, ladies," Mrs. Broadvine trilled, "we will take a moment to get acquainted."

Her train of operator robots were stepping high on their new legs. Their eyes were now alight with curiosity, thanks to the League's swift upgrades. The line of human operators smiled as soon as they saw them.

"Iris, your legs are *fantastic!*" Freda called.

Iris showed them off the best she knew how. "Why, thank you, Freda. And thank you for all your kindness to me. Girls . . ."

Iris swept one arm out to her fellow robots, and then to the line of human operators at their stations. "These are the operators who found us and freed us."

The robot operators did their best to applaud with hands that had never known *how* to applaud. It could use some work, but they did manage to get their point across. Freda and the others blushed, each in their assorted shades.

She turned to Mrs. Broadvine. "And this is our new Ma—"

She stopped herself.

"This is Mrs. Broadvine, our new . . ."

"Supervisor, dear," Mrs. Broadvine finished for her. She patted the robot's shoulder. "It's all still very new, isn't it? Let me show you the lunch room, and then I'll assign you each to your new shift."

The human operators kept up with their Info-Slate clients' requests, but through long practice they also managed to carry on a quiet conversation of their own.

"She's still being awfully *nice,* isn't she?" said Rhonda.

Heads bobbed along the switchboard's length.

Freda looked after their supervisor. "Maybe it'll last, and maybe it won't. But those legs on Iris, can you believe it? I wish *I* had gams as long as those.

"We just have to do something about the poor girl's shoes."

Rhonda glanced at the other operators, her eyebrows high and triumphant.

"There is nothing wrong with those shoes. Which, anyway, are her *feet.*"

MONDAY, 1:56 PM

Edward J. Bellin ripped a sheet of paper out of the typewriter and let it float to the floor, too intent on the next page to worry about where the last one had gone. This was shaping up into his best story yet.

He'd just reached the point where the space pirates had boarded the Projectile, though of course none of his characters knew about that yet; Nityananda was still trapped in the trash compactor and hadn't yet found the air vent. Edward chuckled quietly to himself. Nityananda was going to be very surprised to learn that he was the long-lost son of Howard Pitt's mentor, Edmond D. Bellicost, and that the fate of all the captives—and, indeed, of the Universe itself—depended on him. Not to mention the Princess.

Edward sped through the header: *Captives of the Inertrium Egg—Based on True Events! by Edward J. Bellin.* The typewriter's bell rang twice. He reached for his notebook. What had that been, his note about air vents? He riffled through the pages.

Screw heads on the other side; yes, but he wouldn't need that until later.

Edward hadn't felt this energized, this inspired, in years. He'd entirely forgotten how near he'd come to giving up; rejection slips held no terrors for him now. Pages spread like white petals in a disorderly ring around his desk, made golden by the dim glow of the light bulb over his head.

MONDAY, 2:05 PM

To his great disappointment Abner had not been reassigned to the monorail system. There was a lot to do for the Transport Tubes, a lot of rework, to eliminate the need for all that excess air pressure, and someone, somehow, had to restore the public's faith in the Tubes.

Maybe, though, if he did all that, he could go back to the trains. His manager had hinted as much, anyway.

Abner's office began to tremble. A faint smile appeared on his face. That would be the Red Line's number 14 train on its way inbound to the station. Then he frowned a little. It was still vibrating more than it should. He penned a quick message and sent it off, through its pneumatic tube, to someone who was in a position to look into it. He sighed.

There was a lot of paperwork on his desk. Abner had consigned all the inertrium, which still was being peeled off the Projectile, to various warehouses around the city. He'd made sure that Herbert got a generous share. After all, without the clues that Herbert had given him there might not *be* any inertrium to parcel out. There would just be . . .

Abner shook his head. It had been madness, Pitt's plan, pure madness. It seemed incredible that no one had seen what the man was up to. And what, anyway, had he hoped to gain?

MONDAY, 2:17 PM

Pitt huddled in a crack next to the drainage pipe. His two robots were having some kind of problem in their new, smaller form; every time one of them tried to take a step with its right leg, the other one would do the same thing. For the moment he'd ordered them to step in unison. He'd have to figure it out later.

But . . . later? How could there even *be* a later?

A flood of rats was running along the floor of the culvert. Pitt lifted his feet out of the way before he remembered that the rats were actually taller than he was himself.

He just wished that for those few hours of perfection he'd had a chance to wander through the empty city and admire it in its perfect order. Things had become so hectic after he'd attacked the District. For those hours everything he'd built had been performing exactly the way he'd meant it all to work. No pushing, no crowding, no indecision . . .

He found himself watching the rats.

Their many-colored backs flashed in the uncertain light. They flowed past one another like a tide of water; they never collided; they never changed their minds; when one veered left, the others naturally veered along with it.

It was beautiful.

Pitt began to take stock of his resources. Two malfunctioning robots, one hat, and . . . his hand fell to the tiny slide rule at his hip. He smiled a miniature smile.

He could salvage materials here and there, and with those materials he could build more robots—new ones, on this new, reduced scale. Armed with that force, he could build again.

He looked lovingly at the rats.

He could build for a new population, one that instinctively *knew* how to behave efficiently. He would build them bridges and trains; he would construct food silos, and breeding chambers, and . . . and libraries! He would *educate* them! He would take this solid, well-behaved foundation of rodents and build them a civilization that would utterly surpass the huge, lurching, *useless* humans up above!

Pitt stood and raised his arms in benediction. These would be his people!

The tide of rats thinned out; they had all run past him now. But he would find them again. His *people*.

Down the culvert, from wherever the rats had come from, he heard the sound of footsteps.

"Come to me!" he cried. "I will lead you to greatness!"

Two tiny beams of light appeared, far down the drain.

"GACK."

MONDAY, 2:48 PM

She shook her hand a little. Dash was just looking at the payment she'd offered him. He had a funny look on his face.

"It's what we agreed on," she explained. "Remember? All us operators took up a collection?"

"You know, I kind of forgot," he said. He still wasn't taking it.

The rooftop was deserted except for them, and Rusty, and the circling ornithopters. The Actaeon was back where it belonged with sturdy moorings to prevent it from sailing into space. Overhead, rockets and hover sleds sailed silently through the sky while—even higher—the big airships drifted along in their unhurried way. Through it all laced the network of the monorail tracks and—alongside them—the empty passageways of the Tube Transport system.

"Everything's back the way it's supposed to be," Nola reminded him. "If you ask me, the whole city ought to be paying you."

"It just seems wrong, somehow."

"Well, it wasn't wrong when we agreed to it, was it? Remember the cats? And now that Mr. Thorgeir's been to the animal shelter we've kind of put you out of the cat retrieval business."

She shook her hand again. "Take it, you big dope."

"Well, it was as much you as me, wasn't it? Doesn't seem right to have you pay me. Maybe we could—"

She stuffed Dash's payment into his back pack, right next to the slide rule. "Don't you even start, mister," she said.

So he didn't. One thing you could say about Dash Kent was that he didn't often get beat, but he knew it when he saw it.

Nola was happy to see that Rusty was his old self again. He was cleaning the grime out from between an ornithopter's feathers while it *ping pinged* softly in pleasure. Nola reached down to stroke its head.

"I think the scientists got him," she said.

Dash knew who she meant. "Could be, could be. I don't think we're ever going to know. . . ."

The monorail tracks above thundered: a train was coming. "Unless he comes back, I mean."

Nola hoped that wouldn't happen. "It still doesn't all make sense. From what you said, he wanted to get rid of all the people because we're . . ."

"Messy," Dash told her. "Inefficient. Not as perfect as his machines."

She thought that over. "Well, I think he was loony, then."

Sitting out here on the roof seemed pretty perfect to *her*.

"My shift's starting in about an hour," she said at last. "I ought to go."

So they started down the long stairway. Rusty came along with them on some business of his own.

When they came to the landing on four, Dash slapped his head. "That sink!" he said. "I completely forgot!"

They passed a couple coming up the stairs. Dash nodded to them thoughtfully.

"Mr. and Mrs. Campbell," he told Nola.

A moment later they heard the sound of a door opening; there was a scream, and then the sound of some heavy thing hitting the floor. Dash nodded again, and in a little while they reached the ground floor.

"Another thing I don't get," Nola went on, "is why Pitt left Iris lying out there in the alley where Rusty found her. Did she . . . fall off a hover sled, or something? And he didn't even *notice*?"

Dash spun a finger next to his temple. "Crazy man," he said. Nola noticed that Rusty was eying his toe, which he scraped along the floorboards. She smiled.

"But it doesn't matter anyway. Since we're all okay again."

She'd felt really bad that something had been troubling Rusty.

"And in two years we can meet up with Aunt Lillian again and tell her how it all turned out."

Rusty's head jerked up.

"What is it, Rusty? Is it something about my aunt?"

But whatever it was, he wasn't interested in telling her. So Nola gave them each a quick hug and ran out to the street: she didn't want to be late to the switchboard.

Rusty watched her go. His eyes dimmed a little, as they always did when he accessed his memories.

SATURDAY, 4:54 PM

Lillian could see that Rusty didn't want to be there; but of course she already knew that, didn't she? Otherwise he never would have left.

"They'll be fine out there for a few minutes," she said. "The ASAA has a sort of blind spot where my house is concerned."

Rusty was still looking over his shoulder at the door, beyond which Dash and Nola were waiting for him.

"Come on into the workroom," she said.

They sat down by a workbench. Lillian folded her hands in her lap. "I really *am* happy to see you."

Rusty's eyes kept straying to the baboon in its egg-like pod.

"We'll let him go before I leave," she said. "In fact I moved all the more delicate experiments into the rest of the house this morning."

Rusty turned to face her.

"I'm not some kind of monster," she told him. "All I want . . . from *any* of my experiments . . . is to see what will happen, what they'll *do*, once the experiment begins.

"You, for example. I've been watching you with *great* interest. I think I understand why you left, you know."

He looked at her with his big, unblinking eyes.

"You thought that I gave you that brain . . . that huge, *glorious* brain . . . to *use* you in some way, didn't you? To *do* things for me. To make me powerful."

Rusty could be a difficult audience, when he wanted to be.

"Before it was miniaturized that brain could barely fit in this laboratory," she said.

His eyes automatically ran around the circumference and the height of the big room.

"Give or take, I mean."

He nodded.

"And you were afraid, weren't you? Afraid of what I wanted you to *do* with that brain?"

After a moment, Rusty nodded again.

"The only thing I wanted—the thing I still want, and delight in every day—is to see what you *will* do with that brain. And I admit: I don't always understand."

She ticked items off on her fingers. "You volunteer with the League of Robotic Persons; fair enough, that's obvious. You work with the Civilian Conservation Corps. You collect . . . mosses and lichens. You work at the library. You repair those little flying machines that live on top of your building. You meet people, and you make friends with them, and you have these little amusing adventures, like today.

"The thing I don't understand," she said, "is the *point*. I gave you the most powerful brain on the planet, and you . . . you *putter*. You volunteer. You pitch in. You *do your bit*.

"But like I say . . . I don't understand your motivation, your plan."

Rusty's eyes still did not waver.

"And you see, that's why I arranged for you to come here today. So you could explain it to me."

This time Rusty's eyes flickered. Lillian watched his chin droop, imagining the hundreds of thousands of relays and synapses that were firing in that immense, miniaturized brain: the brain that she had designed, built, and shrunk, through her genius, so that it could fit in the head of this small, polite, and unassuming mechanical person. Her masterwork.

His head rose again and tilted to the side. He reached for an invisible hat brim and pretended to flick it.

"Exactly!" Lillian said. "Howard Pitt is wonderful material to work with; he was so nearly demented already. It took very little suggestion to tip him completely over the edge of . . . of what we'll call 'bonkers.' He's completely barking *mad* now. I've been very gratified by what *he's* chosen to do. From what I've seen it's a startling result, possibly the most interesting *ever*. Wonderful. And then, of course, it gave me an opportunity to bring you back here so we could talk.

"So I found Pitt's factory and carried one of his operators up to the alley, and I left her there where you were certain to find her. Because eventually you'd come to *me*. I must say, Rusty, it's just wonderful to have that big brain of yours at home again."

The little robot nodded an emphatic *no*. He walked over to the pod and released the baboon. They stood hand in hand in the doorway. Rusty pointed outside.

"Oh, don't be like that," Lillian said. "You still need me to find the switchboard for your friends, don't you? And then later, when I come back, we can have more of these little chats."

Rusty opened the workroom door.

"I just want to understand!" Lillian pleaded. "I'm not criticizing! I *love* watching what you do. I just want to know *why!*"

Rusty led the baboon through the several reinforced chambers between them and the world outside. He paused by the door at the sideboard, where there was a notepad. He scribbled something on the notepad, tore off a sheet, and handed it to Lillian.

She read it, adjusted her glasses, and read it again. Then she crumpled it up and slipped it into her pocket.

"Well," she said. "*That's* interesting."

MARIA DA CUNHA

G-94VA

MRS. BROADVINE

EDWARD J. BELLIN

SLAVES of the SWITCHBOARD